D0763785

Magic
Flute

PATRICIA MINGER

swp

SHE WRITES PRESS

Copyright © 2016 by Patricia Minger

All rights reserved. No part of this publication may be reproduced, distributed, or transmitted in any form or by any means, including photocopying, recording, digital scanning, or other electronic or mechanical methods, without the prior written permission of the publisher, except in the case of brief quotations embodied in critical reviews and certain other noncommercial uses permitted by copyright law. For permission requests, please address She Writes Press.

Published 2016
Printed in the United States of America
Print ISBN: 978-1-63152-093-8
E-ISBN: 978-1-63152-094-5
Library of Congress Control Number: 2016945049

For information, address:
She Writes Press
1563 Solano Ave #546
Berkeley, CA 94707

Cover design © Julie Metz, Ltd./metzdesign.com
Interior design by Tabitha Lahr

She Writes Press is a division of SparkPoint Studio, LLC.

La Perichole (Metropolitan Opera Version) by Jacques Offenbach
© Copyright 1956 by Boosey & Hawkes, Inc. Copyright Renewed 1984. Reprinted by Permission.

Epigraph from Donald Soto's article, Flicka in 3/4 Time, Opera News, March 2000 - Vol. 64, No. 9. Reprinted with Permission.

Lyric from "Ar Ben Waun Tredegar" reprinted with permission.

THIS IS A WORK OF FICTION. NAMES, CHARACTERS, PLACES, AND INCIDENTS EITHER ARE THE PRODUCT OF THE AUTHOR'S IMAGINATION OR ARE USED FICTITIOUSLY. ANY RESEMBLANCE TO ACTUAL PERSONS, LIVING OR DEAD, IS ENTIRELY COINCIDENTAL.

This book is for

Orva Hoskinson,
Marcia Hunt,
and
Susan Oliver

Who helped me find my voice

Music isn't about perfection, anyway.
It's about humility and process,
And more than that,
It's about humanity.

—Frederica von Stade

May 1980

LIZ MORGAN SLIPPED INTO the orchestra pit at the last minute. Hands and fingers flickered over passages from *Magic Flute,* and she encouraged a few notes from her own instrument. The random practice stilled, gave way to a single note from the oboist. The strings, followed by the winds, descended into a whirl of tuning. After a few moments, the busy hum coalesced into a second simmering silence. The house lights faded, and the conductor, slim and dapper, came to the podium amid applause. He turned and raised his baton. A third silence, the final phrase of incantation, settled over the hall.

Poised with her flute at her lips, Liz felt the gathering of energy: an indrawn breath, and then, in the charged void, sudden sound. Music. She felt the first isolated chord of the overture under her sternum. Slowly the strings approached the allegro, and then they were off, passing the theme from one section to another, now in the trebles, now in the basses. Her line rose in smooth counter-point to the orchestra. Notes pulsed in measured perfection, binding together voices of reed and shaft and string.

The curtain opened, and the singers commanded the audience's attention. By the end of the second act perspiration stained the soprano's costume, dripped off the tenor's face. In spite of the heat Liz shivered. Anticipation prickled in her solar plexus as the violins meandered toward her big moment. She wiped the sweat from her lower lip and raised her flute, ready with the passage long ago burned into her muscle memory. She placed her solo deliberately on the restrained brass accompaniment. Her instrument's primitive voice wove enchant-ment around the singers.

At the end of the opera, taking her solo bow, it occurred to Liz that per-haps Titus was right about her ego.

The applause over, Liz began her descent to the commonplace. She cleaned her flute and put it to bed in its case. Calling good night to her colleagues, she headed for her car.

The sun had set, but unseasonable heat still shimmered over the city. Liz walked slowly, noting the quivering stars. Stimulating, exhausting, the energy still cycled through her, seeking release. She wouldn't sleep for hours yet.

She unlocked the passenger door of her green Sirocco, tossed in her book bag, and set the flute case on the floor. As she started around to the driver's side someone called to her.

"Hey, Lizzie." Titus ambled up, swinging his trumpet case lightly.

"Hey, Titus. Quit calling me that." She leaned against the car. "Where were you?"

He settled himself next to her. "Talking to people. You were excellent."

"If we had to do opera, at least it was Mozart."

Titus laughed. "You don't mind. You and your big solo."

"Why settle for being some no-name second chair?"

"Ha. In five years you'll be teaching kids in the suburbs."

"You're so wrong." She tugged his white-blond ponytail. "I'm going to play with all the major orchestras, wait and see."

"Man, ever since that master class with Galway you've lost your mind. Didn't anybody tell you? Wind players don't get big solo careers."

"So I'll be different. You know what he said."

"You should be a singer. Sure got the ego for it."

"Have you got a problem with that?" she snapped. He always led her into this trap, his banter gradually penetrating her optimism, even on a satisfying night like this.

"Hey, I'm just keeping your feet on the ground."

"When I want you to do that I'll ask."

He grinned. "Come on, don't get all huffy on me."

She glowered at him.

He set his trumpet case on the ground and leaned closer. "Coming over? You're so sexy, nights like this."

"Not tonight," she said. "History final's tomorrow. Thank God that class is over."

"You know that stuff cold. Come on, you'll be in England all summer."

"Wales," she corrected automatically. "Maybe. I haven't even called my aunt yet. And I have to be back in time for Cazadero in July."

"Thought you weren't going to teach up there anymore."

She shrugged. "They need somebody for second session. It's money. Besides, I like it up there. You can really see the stars." She leaned back and gazed at the sky again. "You know, what we played tonight won't reach the stars for years."

"You're thinking of light."

"Sound moves in waves too."

"Not the same. Doesn't travel where there's no atmosphere."

"I don't care. I think all the great music is up there somewhere; it never really ends."

"You're such a kid."

She stuck her tongue out, annoyed with him all over again.

He laughed and reached for his trumpet case. "How about tomorrow night?"

"I don't know. My roommates will be out, so I'll have a little time to work on the Boccherini."

"You're gonna die alone if you don't get out sometimes."

"Maybe I'll come by later, like around nine?"

He pushed his chin out in assent. "There's my ride. I'm takin' off. Good show, Liz."

"You too. G'night."

They kissed, and she got into her car. From the scrambled cassettes in the backseat she pulled a recent practice tape and poked it into the player. The mercury smoothness of her flute, underlaid with pinpoints of lute music, filled the little car. A favorite passage danced by, faintly punctuated by the squeak of fingers moving along strings, but the tape began to squeal. She punched EJECT, but the metallic ribbon stretched and snapped. Sighing, she tossed it on the seat next to her.

As she merged onto the freeway her mind slipped back over the night's work. Despite her complaint to Titus about opera, she loved every note of the laughing, enigmatic score of *Die Zauberflöte*. Her LP of the 1959 Covent Garden cast now popped and crackled from age and use; Liz knew every passage, every nuance. It kept her mother's voice alive.

How on earth could her mother have given it up to get married? She could never do that for Titus.

Titus. She whistled lightly through her teeth, reconsidering. Maybe she would just show up tonight after all and surprise him. She smiled to herself and changed lanes. She made every green light as she cruised down Army Street. As she approached Dolores something caught her eye and sent a little twinge through her gut: A car a block away, silhouetted against the twilight, headlights dark, its trajectory jerky and erratic as it approached.

"Drunk," Liz muttered. She glanced over her shoulder and signaled, but the car at her right bumper sped up.

The car was almost on her now, lurching into her lane. Panicking, Liz jammed down the accelerator, but as she shot by the car to her right and tried to move into the lane in front of it, her car fishtailed sharply, clipped by the drunk driver weaving past on her left. The Sirocco skidded sideways into the oncoming traffic. The steering wheel snapped out of her hands. Hurled against the door, she couldn't move, couldn't see, couldn't breathe, couldn't scream. Smoky friction burned in her mouth and nose. The infuriated blast of a horn filled her head. A pair of headlights slammed into the passenger door and drove her into a telephone pole, shattering sound and light.

* * *

BREATHING.

Bleeding.

A pulse of red intruded. Slowly, Liz opened her eyes. The hood of a yellow Mustang was jammed into her passenger seat, one headlight burning holes in her retina. The sickly sweet smell of engine oil slicked the air.

She started to sit up, but her stomach roiled and pain assaulted her left side, and she fell back again. The crushed driver's door seemed molded to her body. Her left arm was caught fast in a gash in the steel, from her hand almost to her elbow. She didn't dare try to push herself up. She must be bleeding; there was blood on her sleeve, in her lap, in the shower of safety glass around her. Clutching the dashboard with her right hand, she looked up through the opening where the windshield had been. Two cops, their faces looking like radar blips in the throbbing red lights, raced across the street.

They've got to get my flute out before they tow the car. I'm playing tomorrow.

A fuzzy sensation, like blood returning to a limb that has fallen asleep, pressed against her eyes, her throat—the grayness of unconsciousness.

Chapter 1

ON A MORNING LATE IN AUGUST Liz rose in slow panic from a deep, still sleep. She moved gingerly, testing her body. For weeks, pain had jarred her every move, grinding and tearing from her collarbone through her rib cage, from her shoulder to her elbow to her hand. Today felt like a good day. She opened her eyes, and the first thing she thought of was her neglected flute. Yes, today would be a very good day.

She got out of bed and winced into her clothes. She settled her left arm into its protective sling, pausing to gently flex her fingers as much as she was able. Her Army Street roommates had brought all of her stuff to her parents' house in Pacific Heights. The disorganized pile blocked the fireplace at the far end of her old bedroom. Her flute, which had survived the wreck, waited atop the pile. She had walked warily around it for three months, avoiding even looking at it. Now she picked up the padded case and cradled it a moment before setting it on the dresser, a reminder of work to be done. Then she went downstairs.

Her stepmother, Madly, stood at the island in the kitchen reading *The New York Times* with a cup of coffee. Dressed in a suit of deep lavender, she carried her graceful height like royalty. A still deeper purple scarf at her throat darkened her blue eyes and offset her silver-blond hair. She looked up smiling. "Good morning, kiddo."

"Morning. Can I get a ride to school in a bit? My advisor needs me to sign some stuff about the leave of absence."

Madly's eye flicked toward the clock. "I have a luncheon at noon. I can't be late."

"Just drop me off. I'll get home okay."

"Of course."

"I can hardly wait to get back to work." Liz awkwardly rummaged for a bowl and spoon.

"It won't be easy, you know."

"But they *moved* this time, Madly, my fingers *moved*." She surprised herself by suddenly smiling. "I know I won't be able to play today. But something's finally working!"

Madly opened her mouth, and Liz abruptly headed off the inevitable lecture on patience. "Have you heard from Da?"

"He'll be back when he can. He does have deadlines."

"He manages to show up for your fund-raisers and stuff." She shook shredded wheat into her bowl.

"Liz."

She winced even before her stepmother spoke. "I'm sorry; I didn't mean that the way it sounded. But he didn't even call to find out how the last surgery went."

"The world can't stop for him because of this."

Liz leaned against one of the high stools, her eyes fixed on the ragged remnants of fog blowing past the window. "Yeah. It only stopped for me."

"I know how you must feel."

Liz slapped the counter. "How can you? You never understood why I want music so badly. Do you know what this is like, wondering if the only thing I've ever wanted is going to be taken away by some stupid drunk?"

Her stepmother held her gaze a moment. "Maybe not. But I lost my husband of eight years to cancer." Her quiet remark silenced Liz and brought a flush to her cheeks. "I know about loss; believe me, I do. And I wish I could make your father be different, but . . ." She shrugged.

Liz nodded. They'd long shared this resignation about her father's ways. Disregarded messages from his publisher and agent always cluttered his desk.

Madeline reached over and touched her stepdaughter's shoulder. "Listen, I spoke to my lawyer about suing the guy who hit you. He thinks there's a case."

Liz considered. The irony that it had taken something so dramatic for her stepmother to finally admit that her music was more than self-indulgence was not lost on her.

"No," she answered finally. "Just settle with our insurance company."

"You have a year. We shouldn't settle yet."

Liz shook her head. "Just get the medical bills and the car paid for. I'm really sorry about the car," she added. The green Sirocco had been her parents' gift when she graduated from high school, and she had loved it.

"But we can get more than just damages," Madly said. "He thinks we should try for the biggest settlement we can get, based on loss of livelihood."

"I don't accept that," Liz snapped. She took a breath. "I haven't lost anything," she insisted. "I'll be playing again in no time. We can't sue him for something that won't happen."

Madeline glanced over at her stepdaughter. "Maybe. Just think it over, okay? We don't have to decide this minute."

Liz nodded. She could barely hold back the tears. She was haunted by one panicked moment before the invasion of anesthesia, when the possibility that she would never play again had slipped under her guard.

* * *

THEY SKIMMED ALONG GOLDEN Gate Park and up the hill into the lingering fog. Madeline left her at 19th and Ortega, and Liz watched the sapphire Mercedes drive off before she made herself look up at the stucco building that housed the San Francisco Conservatory of Music. The fifteen stone faces over the entrance contemplated her, and she frowned back at them before slipping in the door and practically tiptoeing toward the staircase that led to her teacher's office.

Classes would start later in the week, but the building seemed empty. Two violinists came toward her in the hall, chatting, and they stopped and shrieked when they saw her, descending on her with a babble of questions. Faintly embarrassed, and yet touched, Liz gave them ambiguous assurances. She was acutely aware of how they looked at her hand—the morbid curiosity in their eyes.

She went on up the stairs and knocked softly. When the door opened she stifled an urge to reintroduce herself to her mentor.

"Liz!" Julia Bradshaw drew her into a cautious hug. "It's so good to see you."

"Thank you, you're very kind." The words came automatically. She'd said them hundreds of times over the years in response to praise.

Her teacher gave her an affectionate shake and drew her into the softly lit room. Liz swallowed hard at the comforting smells of pulpy music paper and sweet valve oil.

"Come have a seat." From the day they'd met, almost nine years earlier, Julia had reminded Liz of a tiny wren with her quick precise movements and alert, intelligent eyes. She pulled a file folder from the stack on her desk and focused on Liz. "First things first: How are you? How is your hand?"

"All new parts. They finally shipped me off to this guy in Oakland who's supposed to be the best in the business. Artificial joints, reconstructed tendons, grafted nerves. I should be good as new."

Julia looked at the splints that held the swollen fingers in position.

"Well, not yet," Liz admitted. "There'll be lots of physical therapy first."

"And what are your plans? They've granted you a medical leave for the entire year."

"I guess I'll have to get a job till I come back. My scholarship's gone, and I don't want to be freeloading off my folks." She made a face.

Her advisor gave her a piercing look. "You seem to be handling this fairly well."

"I just want to get on with it. No sense moping around because I'm losing a year."

Into an awkward little silence rose the sound of a voice singing somewhere in the building.

Julia pulled some forms from the file and paused, as if reading them over carefully. Finally she put down her pen and looked at Liz directly. "Have you thought about what happens if you can't play?"

Liz stared at her. "I have the best surgeon in the world working on me. I just need time."

Her teacher got up and walked behind her, out of sight. "I think this leave of absence might be a good time to reevaluate your plans."

"What do you mean?" Liz tried to turn, but a twinge in her rib cage stopped her.

"We've gone over and over this. It's not realistic for a wind player to expect the kind of solo career you talk about. It isn't like you're a violinist or a cellist."

"But I'm different. I'm going to make it."

Julia sat down again, her head tilted as if she were allowing a concession.

"Performance is everything to me. I'd be nobody without my playing," Liz whispered.

"Of course you wouldn't. There are lots of ways to use your talent."

"What, like teaching?"

Julia frowned. "If it wasn't for people like me there wouldn't be people like you in the orchestra pits and on the concert stages."

In spite of the warning in her teacher's tone, Liz pressed recklessly on. "I'd find a way. I do this because I can't *not* do it."

"Not alone." The bite in Julia's voice was now unmistakable.

Liz held her gaze for a moment longer but then retreated. "I'm sorry," she mumbled, ashamed. "I don't mean that."

"All I want you to do is think about it, hard and realistically, while you're away. You need to make some decisions. I know you have a passion for music. I hear it in your voice every time you speak of it. That will always be with you."

"You're just saying that because you think . . ." Liz swallowed. "You think that my fingers . . ."

"No," Julia said. "Whether or not your hand heals—"

"I'll show you," Liz said. "When I get better I'll work twice as hard as I ever did. I'll be the best you ever taught."

"You're already that," Julia said. "You probably always will be. But what I'm talking about can't be had by any amount of hard work. There are things you can't control."

Liz gestured to her sling with her good hand. "No kidding."

Julia looked at her with a slight frown and a half smile. "Would it be so bad? To play in an orchestra and teach and maybe do some local performance? Why does it have to be all or nothing?"

"It doesn't." Liz examined her left hand and shook her head slowly. "At this point, that actually sounds pretty good." She looked up at her teacher. "I guess I better get going."

Julia nodded. "I do have a meeting in a few minutes. Just sign these for me, and then go home and concentrate on getting better. I shouldn't have brought all this up now. You've already got too much to cope with."

With great effort, Liz withheld the sarcastic reply she would have liked to make and signed her name, committing to a year in purgatory. She put down the pen and stood up.

Julia came around the desk and held the door open. "Don't be a stranger, Liz. I want to know how you're getting along."

Liz left quickly, blinking tears away. She had to prove Julia wrong.

Chapter 2

ON THE DAY AFTER THE THIRD surgery, when Liz saw her fingers move on their own for the first time since the accident, she nearly choked on the rush of adrenaline that seized her throat. Following that, she went religiously to physical therapy. At home she manipulated her joints, worked each finger, squeezed little rubber balls to strengthen her hand. Slowly the pinky and index fingers remembered how to fold into place, but the middle digits refused to cooperate—they moved only a little, even when she strained until the back of her hand ached and trembled with the effort. At first she thought she was having a difficult day, and then that she was tired, and then, after that, that she was overworking herself. Days turned to weeks turned to months. October came before she dared to challenge the surgeon.

Madly was in Atascadero for the wedding of a niece. She had offered to stay and drive Liz to her appointment, but Liz had insisted she go, so she had reluctantly left that morning. Liz was on her own.

It took four different buses to get to Oakland's Pill Hill, where her specialist had his office, and by the time she got there, her left side ached from the cold humidity and her hand felt stiffer than usual. Although she was on time for her appointment, she had to wait. She sat moodily in the waiting room. The fluorescent lights hummed as she shuffled through the magazines. She read all the cartoons in the *New Yorker* without smiling and sighed as she set it aside. Finally she just sat staring at a black-and-white photograph on the opposite wall. It showed a chubby baby's fingers clasped in the loose-skinned, dark-veined hand of a grandparent.

The receptionist's window snapped open. "Miss Morgan? Dr. Rouse is ready for you."

But after she was shown to the exam room she was left alone to wait again, staring absently out the window in the overly bright room. The East Bay hills wore a shroud of gray fog.

When the doctor came in he was focused on her chart. He looked up briefly, then continued reading for another moment. She could see the physical therapist's letterhead on the paper in his hand.

"Well, how is it?" he asked at last, setting aside the folder.

"Stiff."

"Show me." He put her through her paces. On this cold day her elbow tingled, and she fancied that the pins and rods themselves ached. It seemed that he was being gentler today than he had been when he'd manipulated her hand on previous visits.

Finally he stepped back and leaned against the counter with his arms folded. "And you've been doing the exercises?"

"Every day. That's my job right now."

"What has the physical therapist said?"

"She keeps telling me to be patient. But shouldn't it be improving by now?"

"It has improved. You have close to full range with your first and fourth digits, and your thumb is about 75 percent. That's a lot."

"It's not enough."

He didn't answer. Instead he took her hand again and extended the two middle fingers, testing them against his own. He looked at her.

"Miss Morgan, I don't think we can expect much more."

She swallowed, barely able to draw a breath. "More—more surgery?"

He shook his head slightly, letting go of her hand and pushing his own deep in the pockets of his coat. "Your hand was completely crushed. Perhaps if I had seen you right after it happened, I could have done more. As it was, it was an outside chance at best. As it is, you'll be able to use your hand close to normally, since you're right-handed. But for the kind of work you want to do . . ." He shook his head slightly. "We probably can't expect too much more."

Liz felt a heavy heat seize her chest. "So I won't play again. I might as well not have even bothered with the second and third surgeries."

"I've successfully worked on patients who were in a similar position. If you had any chance, this was it."

Liz turned her hand one way and another, looking at the scars that ran up and down her wrist and over her palm, across the back of her hand and in faint lines along the base of her fingers. It looked like a plastic Halloween prop. She looked up at him. "So there's nothing else you can do?"

"The surgery was cutting-edge technology. The nerve grafts just didn't completely take."

She continued to watch him. He looked away, at her chart on the countertop, but his eyes were unfocused, unmoving.

"Medicine isn't magic, Miss Morgan. We fail sometimes."

Only a day ago she had been able to touch hope, stave off this gray desolation.

After a moment he said quietly, "I am sorry."

She stood up. Inside of her head she felt herself sway, though her footing seemed steady enough. She didn't look at the doctor.

"You should continue physical therapy," he said.

Liz turned her wide eyes on him. "I don't see why."

"You'll want to maintain the flexibility you do have."

"Thank you." She left the room, careful to shut the door quietly.

* * *

BY THE TIME SHE GOT HOME, the quiet despair that had propelled her out of the office had modulated to the numbness she had grown accustomed to living with. The house was cold and silent. She went upstairs; she would deal with dinner later. Just now she wanted only to lie down and put the day from her mind. She dropped her coat on a chair, pushed off her shoes, and eased back on the bed.

The brace she wore at night, heavy and hateful, lay on the table next to her, and the sight of it goaded her. "God *damn* it!" She snatched it up and flung it across the room with all her might. It hit the wall near the dresser with a sickening thud, like a live creature, and dropped to the floor. The impact sent her mother's picture toppling over against her flute case.

After a moment Liz got up and righted the picture. As she did, she felt as if she was seeing it anew.

Her father had taken the formal black-and-white portrait, but it was her aunt who had given Liz the picture. Her mother looked back over a shoulder at the camera, her eyes large and luminous, her smooth skin perfect, her mouth soft but serious. At one time Liz fancied that the pose beckoned, as though her mother was saying, "Come, follow me." Her mother, who had dumped this burden of music upon her and then abandoned her.

She stared at her flute case for a long moment before she picked it up and sat down on the cane-backed rocker. She unzipped the cover, flipped up the catches, and opened the case. Her flute's keys had left worn patches in the bed of purple velveteen. The flute itself seemed to catch and magnify light. She could almost hear its overtones, here where she'd practiced for so many years. She put out a finger and gentled it over the shining surface. She remembered precisely the moment when light and sound had first merged and led her, with magpie covetousness, to the flute.

She had been a silent child at the age of seven, still lonely for her mother and her home. And then her stepmother took her to a youth symphony concert. A slim shadow of a girl arrested her wandering attention. Or rather, the girl's flute did. Liz watched the light slide up and down the shaft and itched to touch it, to hold it, to make those lovely sounds and have the light draw to her as it did to that other girl—so much so that she, silent for the two and a half years since her mother's death, felt compelled to tug at her stepmother's sleeve and whisper, "Madly, can I do that? Can I?"

In something of a trance she fitted the instrument together now, her hands awkward. For a moment she supported it in the joint between her thumb and forefinger, feeling its cool familiarity. Steadying it with her whole right hand, she shifted her left thumb to the proper place and felt her index finger nestle in the center of the key.

She took a sudden, deep breath and raised the flute to her lips. She blew a tentative note, low and broad, like a kid with a Coke bottle. Then she tightened her cheeks and pulled it up an octave, producing a sweeter tone. Her embrasure, which had suffered from this hiatus, wobbled and struggled to sustain the note on high. She stopped, breathing hard. Then, with her left pinky, she groped for the funny little G-sharp key, hoping her other fingers would automatically fall into place. Her little finger found its way home, but her two middle fingers slipped right across the instrument, and she could not bring them back to the silver keys. They lay inert across the delicate line of hinges and springs.

A tear dropped. She watched it darken the lining of the flute case. She began to tremble from deep inside, and she clutched her flute, doubled over, shaking with the tears that were now pouring down her face. "No!" she roared, her voice ragged and explosive. Deep, puncturing sobs she hadn't shed before because of broken bones and painkillers now clawed and scratched up from the heat of her chest. She hugged the flute, pressing it to her breast, rocking like a mother grieving her child.

At first the anguish tore at her, as dark in her mind as a storm at sea, brutal on her still-healing body. Then, gradually, she calmed, though her body occasionally tightened with a shudder.

In a pleading whisper, she repeated, "Oh no."

Chapter 3

FOR DAYS, LIZ COULD NOT escape blurred fragments of Vivaldi's flute concerti. They surrounded her soul with a corona of grief. She seemed always to be out of breath and her heart felt constricted. She lay on her bed, sometimes for hours. At other times she drifted around the house, unable to settle to anything. Silence distressed her to an unreasonable degree. She shrank from the sun and stayed up all night, reading incessantly with lights ablaze.

Slowly the grief passed through her, leaving an aching detritus behind, like a flood path of sorrow.

One evening she was in her room, clumsily folding her clean laundry, and she started at the sound of Madly's voice. She hadn't heard her stepmother come up the stairs.

"Hey, kiddo." Madly had not encroached on Liz's retreat, though at times Liz had half-sensed that her stepmother was watching over her. Now she paused in the doorway, almost hesitant.

"Hey." Liz pushed the drawer shut. "How was your day?" she asked shyly.

Madeline relaxed and came into the room. "Nice. I was over at the de Young for the opening of the new exhibit." She seemed to size Liz up. "Hungry? I brought home Chinese."

Liz shrugged. "No. Yeah. I could eat."

"Come downstairs, then, while it's hot."

To Liz's relief, Madly chatted about trivial topics during dinner. Liz gingerly offered the correct responses, conversation feeling strangely heavy on her tongue. She began to relax when she realized that Madly would not ask about the last few weeks and helped herself to seconds of the Szechuan chicken, seeking out the cleansing feel of the hot peppers that made her nose run and her lips burn.

"So have you got some work for me?" she asked through a mouthful of chicken.

"Anytime you're ready," Madly said.

"I guess it's time I surfaced." Suddenly it was all Liz could do to hold back tears, for this was an admission that it was time to move away from her dreams.

"I'll make some calls tomorrow."

Liz studied her plate, but she felt Madly's scrutiny.

"It might take your mind off your troubles."

"I guess."

"Liz, what about some counseling?"

Liz scowled, a bite poised on her fork. "A shrink? I don't need a shrink. I'll be okay."

"But I don't think you are. Okay."

"I know I've been kind of depressed. Fine, a lot depressed. But I'm over that now." Liz stopped when she heard the tremor in her voice and applied herself to her food again.

Madeline sat back, a glass of white wine in her hand. "When was the last time you went to physical therapy?"

Liz put down her fork. "I guess the last time you drove me there."

"Why?"

Liz couldn't answer.

"I see." Madeline touched Liz's right hand lightly, then stood up and began to collect the dishes.

"I'll do that," Liz insisted, shaking the tears out of her eyes.

* * *

AFTER WEEKS OF GETTING USED to the idea, Liz called Titus. She had gone to a couple of concerts at the Conservatory but had somehow missed seeing him each time.

Titus didn't sound surprised to hear from her. Briefly, she wondered why he had not called her, why he didn't ask how she had been. But she knew why.

He agreed to meet her on a Sunday. People lay beneath the trees in Golden Gate Park like overripe fruit, their sweaters and shirts discarded in the hazy Indian summer heat. Liz sprawled on the grass with her unneeded sweatshirt under her head, waiting for him to show. A somnambulant breeze rolled over occasionally.

Telling Titus that her career was over would feel like breaking a vow of silence. As long as she didn't say it out loud, maybe it wasn't true. She struggled to an upright position and sat with her head in her hand. Madly and Julia had both hinted at the unacceptable, and she felt the words chasing each other around in her head like a fugue. She wondered if all of them—her friends, Madly, Julia, even Titus—had known, and had tolerated her inability to accept it only out of pity. She had become what Titus would deride as a "wannabe."

He came finally, leaning his bike against a tree before flopping down on the grass next to her. Just as he reached her she sensed a withdrawal, ever so slight, that warned her not to hug him impulsively

"Hey, Lizzie. Guess what?"

Alert to an unusual energy about him, she bit back the urge to tell him not to call her Lizzie. "What?"

He looked at her out of the corner of his eye, his lips pursed like he was trying not to smile. "They posted the soloists for *Messiah* on Friday."

For a moment she heard the mockery of the gods and couldn't speak. When she did, she hoped he could not detect the effort it required to reply. "And you got it. Congratulations." She leaned up against him, smelling the sun and sweat on his skin as another impulse, less generous, followed. "I'm so happy for you," she told him determinedly.

He lay back on the lawn, squinting, the golden hair on his arms and legs shining in the sun. It was hard to imagine that December was only weeks away. She closed her eyes, feeling the warmth on the back of her head, through her clothes. She flexed her shoulder, which still ached sometimes, wishing she could spread it in the sun to heal.

"So are you gonna be there?"

His hesitation made her open her eyes and look at him before she answered. "You don't want me to come."

He pushed himself up to sit cross-legged and scrubbed a hand through his unkempt hair. She saw where his glance went, saw him flex his own fingers. "You do make people kinda uncomfortable." He hunched his shoulders as if he expected her to argue.

She did not. In the months since her surgeries, especially since it became clear that physical therapy was failing to restore her dexterity, she had seen friends withdraw, felt conversations lag in her presence.

"I know," she said. "I'm having a hard time."

He gave her no opening, no chance to reveal her turmoil. He idly pulled up grass and didn't look at her. He didn't want to hear the truth. Not on this day when he was golden with triumph, on this day when he wanted to be praised and encouraged. Now was not the time to tell him of her misery. But in the vulnerable silence she spoke.

"Maybe you've already guessed. I'm not getting any better. I won't be able to play again. Ever." She could hear the shake in her voice. It was the first time she'd said it out loud. It sounded untrue.

"That's rough." He did not appear surprised.

"It's awful, watching you and knowing I can never be there again."

Suddenly he yanked up a clump of grass by the roots and flung it away. "Know what your trouble is? You can't let anyone else have their moment."

"I'm not trying to take away your moment. It's wonderful that you got it. But I needed to talk to someone."

"It's always about you. You've always got some big drama going on. It used to be how successful you were gonna be, and now it'll be how you'll never play again. And you know what? I'm sick of it. Sick of watching what I say, sick of you feeling sorry for yourself, sick of your envy." He tore up another tuft of grass each time he spit out the word *sick*.

The air and blood in her chest froze, solid and heavy. And then hot anger shot up through her, tearing open her lungs. "Too bad I wasn't killed," she hissed. "It wouldn't have been so hard for you."

Her sarcasm hit the mark. He seemed to be embarrassed by his outburst, and he would not look at her. "I'm sure it's hard and all."

"But?" She prompted him when he hesitated.

He took a deep breath. "I think we should just go our own ways."

She studied his profile for a long moment. Her anger had drained away with her venomous outburst. This did not hurt; it barely registered. "Why didn't you just dump me to begin with, and get it over with?" She asked out of curiosity, nothing more.

He shrugged. "You seemed kinda, you know, fragile, with the accident and everything."

"And you think I can take it now?"

He reddened but did not back down. "At least when you could play you were upbeat."

"What do you expect? All I have to look forward to is hanging around with musicians while I can't play. What kind of a life do you think that'll be?"

"I wish you just wouldn't hang around at all," he snapped.

Her anger still did not return, not even at these words. Instead she looked at him with a cool gaze, letting his words penetrate. "I guess you're right. I'm asking a lot."

He hunched his shoulders, backpedaling. "If you would just—you know—be happier. People wouldn't be so bothered."

Her stomach tightened. "What great advice. I'll try that. Be happier. Great idea."

"Come on, you know what I mean."

"No, you're right. I only bring people down. But I'll tell you something right now. I'm not going to sit around while everybody else succeeds." Her sudden certainty took her by surprise.

He gazed at her and shook his head. "It's gonna kill you to have to be ordinary."

"I'll never be ordinary. Never."

* * *

LATE THAT NIGHT LIZ CREPT downstairs in search of something to occupy her mind. She had read everything in the house, though none of it had made any lasting impression on her. She idly scanned the living room for a new magazine and then up to the shelves that held the leather-bound encyclopedia. Then her eyes fell on the shelf holding her father's books.

David Morgan had published five lavish collections of photography in the last fourteen years, but her favorite was his first, filled with images of her native Wales. She pulled it down, opened it on the glass-topped coffee table, and sat cross-legged on the Persian carpet before it. He had captured the poetry of the dark hills and wild seacoast. Liz paged through the images. The scenes all seemed familiar, though her memory faltered, unable to distinguish between a place she knew and a picture she'd memorized. The silhouette of hills sometimes resonated like the overtones of a chord, felt rather than recognized. Wales almost seemed like a place she had never lived, a place from a fairy tale.

She flipped to the front of the book. "The voice of God called our hills to rise . . ." She read the familiar words of the foreword, trying and failing as usual to hear them in her father's voice. She turned back one more page, to the dedication: "To my wife, Margaret, in loving memory." She swallowed hard and closed the book with a slightly shaking hand.

She sat motionless for a long time. In her undisciplined mind rose unruly scraps of Mozart. Joyful music. For a while she ignored it, but at last she gave in to the spell. She perused the record cabinet, her head cocked, reading titles. Liz knew exactly what she was seeking. *Die Zauberflöte* was her mother's only existing recording, made at the time of her London debut. Her only record, and her only appearance at Covent Garden, as it turned out. The next year Margaret Morgan had handed her career back to the gods who had bestowed it upon her, and Liz had been born.

There it was, between *Die Meistersinger* and *The Merry Widow*. Liz put it on the turntable and retreated to the couch. The first chord, echoing from a lifetime ago, stabbed her. She closed her eyes, bracing herself against the assault. But she waited for her mother's first scene and knew that it was not punishment she sought, but comfort.

At last came her mother's voice—high with flute, sweet with cello. As she listened, Liz relaxed for the first time in months. Her mind felt clear. Alert. She listened and drew in the sound like nourishment. Her mother's voice. Her voice. Her own.

Chapter 4

LIZ SLEPT DEEPLY, AND SHE woke with the odd and immediate sense that a dream had been in the room with her. Sitting up abruptly, she glanced around. Nothing seemed changed. Outside, a flock of geese racketed through the sky. Liz got up to look out the window, and only as she extended her left hand to push aside the curtain did she remember that she would never play again.

She sank down on the window seat, idly watching the cool sun ride the moving clouds, absently massaging her left hand. Small fishing boats crossed back and forth on the bay. Fifteen years ago, when her father had first brought her to San Francisco, the sight of ships leaving the harbor had made her speculate wildly about running away, going back to Wales. She stared, not seeing the vessels so much as remembering the sense they had brought her, at the age of six, that escape was possible.

"Right then," she told herself. "Can't lie about all day." She headed downstairs to the kitchen, where she heard someone moving around. Expecting her stepmother, she stopped in the doorway. Her father was standing by the stove while a teakettle gurgled, preparing for the boil. Dundee, his marmalade cat, sat on the forbidden counter, watching the rising steam as if it were prey. The sweet smell of pipe tobacco hung in the air like humidity. Madly would scold him for smoking in the house.

"Liz!" A smile turned her father's features all round and soft.

"Hi, Da."

"All healed, are you?"

She glanced at her hand. *Hamburger*, someone had unkindly said in her hearing at the hospital. "As healed as I'll ever be, I guess." She noticed with some satisfaction that her father's face sagged at her tone.

"Well," he said. He looked everywhere but at his daughter. He wore his travelling jacket. She knew how that jacket smelled—of pipe smoke and the soft mustiness of the hundreds of places he had been. He'd had the jacket as long as she could remember. She wanted to bury her face in it and be held.

"I'm sorry." He spoke to the kettle. "You're not in school?"

"What would be the point?"

More silence. She rubbed the cat's head and scooped it onto the floor.

"Where have you been? Since last July?" She suddenly noticed that her jaw was clenched and she consciously relaxed it.

"Baja. On a boat a lot. Doing a book on Steinbeck's trip. And then, well . . ."

"So. I guess you couldn't call from a boat," she conceded.

He hesitated but gave in to the fiction she was offering him. "No," he finally agreed. "No, I couldn't."

She turned off the kettle just before it splashed over.

"So what are you doing?" He settled on a captain's chair.

"Right now I'm helping Madly with bulk mailing stuff for her foundation. I'd go nuts with nothing to do."

He received that information in further silence. He picked up his pipe from the table and examined it. She swished hot water in the ceramic teapot, drained it, and added fresh leaves.

"I know you were good."

"I don't want to talk about it." Her voice rose with warning as she filled the pot with the boiling water.

"But I did hope you would succeed."

She met his gray eyes, so clear when they looked through a camera lens, so cloudy when they regarded his own child.

"Really? I thought music was the last thing you wanted for me."

"It was because of your mother."

"Oh, no, it wasn't Madly's fault. She paid for the lessons and drove me all over the place and came to my concerts, even though she thought I took it too seriously."

"Not Madeline. Your mother."

"My—" Liz stopped abruptly.

"Very like her you are. Very like." He did not look at her, spoke with the resignation she'd never understood.

Never before had he volunteered information about her mother. Liz trod carefully. "She was good, wasn't she?"

For the first time she saw her father smile at a memory of her mother. "That she was. Magic. Such a tremendous voice from such a tiny thing. The opera world was eating out of her hand when she gave it up to have you."

"I remember her voice."

"Do you?"

"She used to sing to me all the time. Hymns and lullabies. She sang in Welsh a lot. But other stuff too. Probably opera." Liz fell silent, remembering. Then she looked over at him. "Did she regret it? Giving it up?"

"I was the one who regretted it. She never seemed like the same woman." He shrugged. "But it was a relief to her."

"A relief?"

"She hated the stage. She was nearly ill with fear before a performance."

The idea astonished Liz, so drawn to the spotlight. "I must be a throwback," she remarked, half to herself. A vision filled her, a mixture of daydreams old and new.

Her father gazed at her. "It made her no end of unhappy."

His version did not agree with Liz's experience. "Why? Why do you say she was unhappy?"

He considered. "Everything she did was sacrifice. She had to leave her home when she was sixteen to study in London. When she made it, she was anyone's equal. But then she gave up all of that when you were born."

"But if she hated it, why on earth did she do it?"

"The mines were closing. There was nothing but poverty for her. Her Da wanted her out of that, and she had promise, so he scraped and saved and sent her away to London." He drew on his cold pipe, rubbed his thumb over the bowl, and tucked in into his pocket. "She told me once that she had nothing for her own, not even her voice. Except you," he added after a moment. "You were her pride and joy."

"I want to sing, Da."

His eyes grew round, the pupils dilated. He shook his head, dismissing the notion. "It will break your heart."

"It's too late to worry about that."

* * *

SHE CONSIGNED TITUS TO the dark little room full of things she refused to mourn. But she brooded over his prediction: *ordinary*. All that night and into the quiet early morning she cultivated what she had told her father. *I want to sing, Da. I want to sing.* Of course. Obvious. She'd been coming to that conclusion for days now, ever since she'd listened to the caress of her mother's voice over the specter of the flute.

The dense grief lifted ever so slowly, still in her indelible memory but no longer an active impediment to daily life. She could hardly admit, even to herself, that she had shut that door. But a fearful curiosity began to replace the chaos of mourning inside. She pushed it away at times, feeling a grave disloyalty, as to a dead child. But not completely. As the days passed she stretched the idea like a muscle, a little more each day, until her tolerance allowed her to picture it, a glimpse here and there, dim and unfocused. On the worst days she continued to deny the notion, but on better days, when she walked around the neighborhood and felt health returning to her body, she daydreamed.

One morning, when Madly and her father were out of the house, Liz approached the piano and sat contemplating the familiar keyboard. The only time she had ever opened her mouth to sing was during the technical exercises in the solfège classes at the conservatory. For most of her life she had borne the solemn taboo against reminding her father of her mother in this way. But in Wales, when she returned to visit, song and laughter had always seemed inseparable. This had made her feel isolated from her relatives, who would as soon sing as speak.

Tentatively she played middle C. As it faded, she sang—"*Ah*"—to match the tone. Her voice came out thin and soft. Because she couldn't think of any other song, she fell back on a Christmas carol.

"*Once in royal David's city . . .*" Tonic, fourth, fifth, she played and sang the line.

Well it was in tune, anyway.

She hugged herself, her mind reaching back for the sound of her mother's voice.

"*Fy nghariad a dorrws 'y nghalon i bron . . .*"

The line rose in her throat before she could identify it, and she sang it as her mother had, tender, wistful. In Welsh. She remembered no more, and could not translate the words, but that one line from a long-forgotten song soothed her like a hand pressed against her sternum.

Chapter 5

THE NEXT DAY LIZ TOOK MUNI to campus for the first time in weeks. As usual, Julia was pleased to see her.

"Come in, come in," she said when she opened her office door. "How are you?"

Liz sat down and could not find words to begin. She looked over at the picture on the piano, her teacher's daughter in her blue band uniform, holding her flute with a toothy grin.

"Is everything all right?"

"I've changed my mind," Liz began slowly, pulling her gaze away from the photograph. "No. That's not quite true."

Julia looked at Liz's left hand. "So. He couldn't help you. I thought he was supposed to be the best there is."

Liz was touched by Julia's tone. She cared nearly as much about this as Liz did. She took a breath. "I want to change my major."

"To pedagogy?" Julia seemed to relax.

"I don't want to teach."

"What then?"

"Vocal performance."

Julia blinked. "You've never studied. Have you?"

"No. But I can learn."

"I don't know if the voice faculty would take you."

"But you said I could switch to pedagogy."

"That's different. You can't expect a performance department to take you without an audition."

"Then I'll audition. I have until next May before they kick me out of here. I'll learn."

"This doesn't seem very realistic."

"I'm just moving on, like everyone keeps telling me to do."

"Liz."

She reined herself in, hearing how belligerent she sounded. "I can do this," she said in a more neutral tone.

"People usually come to the voice department with some training." Julia leaned forward and spoke soothingly. "You still have time. Let it rest awhile."

"Are you telling me I can't try?"

"That's not my place. But I wish you would save yourself more disappointment. You don't know that you can sing."

"I don't know that I can't. You know me," Liz said. "I'm too impatient to be a teacher." She gestured helplessly, groping for the right words. Finally she pressed her right hand against her breast. "When I'm onstage I touch greatness. I can't bear to lose that."

Julia sighed. "The choice isn't yours anymore."

"Who would I talk to in the voice department?"

"I don't think—"

"Never mind," Liz said, unwilling to let her finish. "I'll ask downstairs." She got up.

Julia sighed again. "See Derrick Chamberlain. He's the Chair. It would be up to him."

"Will you recommend me?"

Julia said nothing.

"I know you think this is nuts. Maybe it is nuts," Liz conceded. "But I can't live with silence all my life. I just can't."

"Don't rush into this."

"I don't have a future as a flautist."

"I know that and you know that," Julia said. "But as far as I'm concerned, no one else has to know yet. If we say nothing it buys you time to make up your mind what to do."

"My mind is made up." Liz opened the door, but then she paused, hoping for something more from her teacher.

Julia shook her head. "Let me know what happens."

* * *

DR. CHAMBERLAIN HAD THE PORTLY stature and goatee of a smaller version of Pavarotti, though he lacked the world-famous tenor's charm. He responded to Liz's hesitant taps on his door with a curt "Yes, what is it?" When she entered, precisely on time for her appointment, he didn't acknowledge her at all. He was opening his mail with a phone cradled on one shoulder. He kept her waiting while he sliced envelopes. His side of the phone conversation consisted mostly of bored murmurs, just enough to keep his attention occupied.

Liz sat uneasily on a hard metal chair, noting the expanse of the professor's glass-topped desk. Term was over that very day. He was obviously anxious to be gone.

Perhaps Julia was right after all. Sitting there, it no longer felt reasonable or even sane to be basing her life on this ephemeral whim. Just when she made up her mind to leave, however, he hung up and glanced at her as though just noticing her.

"Yes? Miss Morgan, is it? What do you want?" He slit open another envelope and squinted at the contents without removing them.

"You might have heard that I had to stop playing the flute." She raised her left hand, snug in its light splint, as evidence.

"Oh. Yes, I had heard something about that."

"I want to change my major to vocal performance."

"Mrs. Bradshaw mentioned that to me." He looked at her with a slight frown and pursed lips. "How long have you studied voice?"

It was a reasonable question. "I haven't."

His eyebrows rose.

"Listen, I'm still a musician. I may not have the precise techniques of a singer, but I do have an education. I can learn to sing."

"Perhaps." He shrugged and swung his chair back. "But why here? Your failure doesn't compel us to offer you anything more."

"I did not fail." For the first time she felt herself on steady ground.

"Does it matter how it happened?"

"It matters that I didn't fail. I was doing well. I work hard. Ask Julia."

"That's beside the point. You want me to make room for you in a program that is based on proof of potential, yet you offer me none. You can't reasonably expect me to give you a place that by rights belongs to someone else."

"But can't you just give me a chance to try?"

"We require applicants to complete their audition by March 1." He stabbed another envelope. "No one learns to sing in two and a half months."

Her chest felt like it was caving in. "Couldn't you give me a little more time?" she pleaded. "A chance to find out if it's possible? I've been granted a leave of absence until the end of the school year. Can't you give me until May?"

"You ask me to break the rules for you, but you give me no good reason to do so." He was losing interest.

"I'll do whatever it takes if you'll give me a chance."

"But has anyone ever told you that you could sing? Has someone said, 'My God, you're wasted as a flautist?'"

She ignored the sarcasm, sinking for a moment deep into the past and hearing her sparkling mother, then seeing her father's pained face the one time she herself sang after her mother's death. "My mother was an opera singer."

"That is hardly relevant."

"I can do it, I know I can. I was a good flautist. A *great* flautist."

"That still isn't enough. In my experience"—he idly fingered the letter opener—"instrumentalists don't make very impressive singers."

A slim knife blade ripped up Liz's belly, a sharp, cold rage. She sat up straight, forgot to be a suppliant. "What do you mean?"

He smiled faintly. "A player turned singer often lacks a certain emotional depth. I believe it comes from being habitually at something of a remove from passion. Perfect execution does not reliably lead to transcendent expression. That takes an awareness that I find lacking in persons who have limited themselves to external instruments instead of developing the instrument we are all born with."

Stunned, Liz didn't answer for a moment. Then she stood up. "All I wanted was a chance. Not a guarantee."

"I'm sure you're disappointed," he said.

Liz thought he had probably never experienced thwarted ambition. She didn't move.

"But you mustn't expect the world to compensate you for it," he continued. "I can't help you. If you get some training and wish to reapply, of course you'll get due consideration."

* * *

LIZ WENT BACK TO JULIA'S OFFICE immediately. There was no point in drawing things out further.

"So he turned you down?" Julia drummed the eraser end of a pencil on her desk.

"Pretty much." She didn't care to elaborate further.

"What next?"

"I'm withdrawing."

Julia's eyes widened. "But, Liz!"

"I can't even finish last year's juries . . ."

Before Liz could go on, her advisor cut smoothly in. "Finish your leave of absence. Let me deal with the juries. Come back in September, when you're not saying to yourself every day, 'I used to play.'"

"I'll probably be doing that the rest of my life." Liz glanced down at her permanent reminder.

"Perhaps," Julia said gently. "But don't turn your back on your gift."

"My gift has been revoked."

"Not your mind, Liz, and not your heart. There's music in you yet."

Liz flinched. The words beat at her with tiny fists of truth she could hardly bear. Nothing else in the universe moved, no song, no laughter, no cry of despair. Only sterile waiting into which she had once poured magic fire music. "Listen," she said, "I know you're trying to help, but you're only making it worse. There is no point in pretending I could come back."

"You could," Julia insisted. "Not on your current terms, perhaps. But in some capacity. I can't believe you would ever completely give up."

"I haven't," Liz said. "Not really. But whatever happens next won't happen here. I'm done with this place. Or it's done with me."

Julia looked unhappy. "I hate to lose someone of your caliber."

Liz's unreliable mouth attempted a smile that wobbled. "Coming here meant everything to me. I hate to leave."

"Don't disappear, Liz. Think about what I said."

"Oh, I won't disappear," Liz replied, almost managing to sound jaunty. "You'll hear from me. I promise."

As Julia walked her out, Liz self-consciously kept her head down, nervous about running into anyone she knew.

"If you need references, or any kind of help, please call me," Julia said.

"I will," Liz replied, but she said it absently. She was aware only that this was truly the last time she'd be there. The building seemed foreign, as it had years ago when she had first come as a grade-school prodigy. But now the familiar corridors and concert halls no longer resonated with life—not for her.

She and Julia slowed a few feet from the front door. Liz stopped and looked around, impressing everything on her mind. Then, at last, she looked at her former teacher and tried again to smile.

"Thanks for everything. Not just today. But all the time I was here. I'll never forget it."

"I'm going to miss you," Julia said.

Liz gave her a hug and went alone out the door and down the steps without turning back. In her mind she deliberately pictured her Sirocco parked at the curb, remembered the weight of her book bag, her flute case cradled in the crook of her left arm, a whistle of contentment on her lips. And then she reminded herself that these things were all gone, and she would never be back.

Chapter 6

IN FEBRUARY, LIZ LEFT SAN FRANCISCO in what felt like the worst storm of the winter. As the British Airways jet heaved off the runway, the overhead storage compartment twisted against the frame of the aircraft. She quickly closed her eyes, holding tight to the armrests. She could almost feel Valkyries thundering through the sky, snatching and dragging at the plane.

As she poked at her supper, unaware for once if anyone was staring at her awkwardness, she replayed the arguments she'd had with her parents.

"Don't run away," her father had advised. But he hadn't been able to offer her an alternative she could live with.

"How will this help?" Madly had demanded after multiple dead-end conversations, her patience finally growing thin.

"I want to learn to sing. I have to see what happens."

"Oh, Liz, when are you going to give up on this nonsense?"

"Not until someone proves to me that I'm not good enough."

"I just hope you're not heading for another broken heart."

This statement had kept Liz from telling Madly the other reason she felt compelled to return to Wales. She didn't want to hurt her well-meaning step-mother by insisting that only her long-dead mother could offer her the comfort and guidance she needed.

The pins and rods that stabilized her elbow had been removed in January. She would never be quite free of the tingling that ran down to her little finger, or the stiffness that impaired her range of motion. She had a permanent ten-degree crook in her wrist, and two fingers that worked only up to the middle joint. She continued to exercise her hand in an absentminded way, but only because she wanted to seem as normal as possible.

At Heathrow she resisted the urge to quicken her pace as fellow passengers surged around her. She ambled down the chutes and ladders until she reached Immigration and presented her British passport. The officer carefully compared her photo to her face, looking back and forth several times. Liz did not hold this scrutiny against him. The picture, taken only two years ago, probably looked like someone else altogether. Her thick brown hair was now cropped to shoulder length, and her heart-shaped face had lost its roundness. The last time she'd looked in a mirror she'd been startled at how gaunt she looked. But the biggest difference was her expression. In the photograph she looked as though she was about to burst out laughing. Now, she knew, she held her face still and shuttered.

Satisfied at last, the agent licked his thumb and turned a page. "Very good, luv. Been away a while, have you?"

Liz nodded. "A couple of years."

He handed back the passport. "Welcome home, then." He nodded at her and turned his attention to the businessman behind her in the queue.

Home.

Unchallenged at Customs, Liz crossed the terminal and emerged into the sun. Freed from eleven hours of confinement, suddenly bombarded with the brittle racket of construction and traffic, Liz looked up at the broad, winter-cold blue sky, and took a deep breath. Somewhere in the night the balance had shifted. She was no longer running away. She was coming home.

The bus to Cardiff took three long hours. Her eyes grew heavy. Behind her the murmur of conversation made her smile in her half-sleep, comforted. The sound of her grandmothers, her aunt. Her mother. English softened by Welsh—a gentle, open singing of the language. She slept and dreamt of her mother.

* * *

AT CARDIFF LIZ CHANGED BUS for train. Rush hour streamed and surged around her, and the sour-sweet smell of the Brains brewery permeated the air as she crossed Saunders Road to the station. The train passed quickly through the city's slim outskirts, then ducked behind a small ridge and into the countryside. Hedges and diffident stone walls divided the fields. Leaning drowsily against the glass, Liz saw scattered horses and sheep, a few cows and goats, a white goose. On the horizon, trees spread bare branches in lacy alertness against the pale, low sky.

After only a quarter of an hour and a couple of pauses at tiny platforms, the train deposited her at Caerphilly. She rang her aunt and waited to be collected from the station.

Ellen had the same round face as Liz's father, but her expression was openly delighted to see her niece even before she got out of the Fiat. She left the car running and hopped out eagerly. Liz gave herself up to a warm, hard hug, the kind her stepmother never thought to give.

"Not a word, dear," Ellen said when she released her. "Toss your bag in the boot and let's be off home. I want to know everything, but you'll want to rest first."

They wedged Liz's bags on top of two sacks of plant food and one of dog kibble in the back of the car. In only five minutes they arrived at the whitewashed stone house at the end of a lane off St. Martin's Road. All was cool gray and green. Even in their sparse winter foliage the trees loomed larger than Liz remembered, reaching branches over the gray slate roof.

Ellen pulled around to the back of the house. Except for the bare canes of the rose bushes, the garden was thriving. Frivolous red geraniums and some other pink and lavender flowers filled the boxes under the kitchen windows. Green broccoli, purple kale, and white cabbages grew in straight rows.

The familiar kitchen drew Liz in. Soft light gleamed on the buttery yellow enamel of the Aga and the stainless steel kettle. Benjamin, their arthritic half-retriever, shuffled over. Embarrassed by the tears that rose in her throat and stung her tired eyes, Liz got down on one knee to fondle his ears.

"Why don't you go up and have a lie down?" Ellen suggested. "We'll have tea around half six and you can tell me your plans. Your uncle has choir practice tonight, but Kate will be coming."

"I think I'll just wash up. The jet lag gets worse if you sleep at the wrong time."

"I don't mind what hours you keep."

But Liz would not be tempted. "I'd just be up all night." She struggled to her feet, her carry-on feeling twice as heavy as when she packed it.

The staircase seemed narrower, the ceilings lower, the furniture a little more crowded than Liz remembered as she hauled her bag up to her cousin's old bedroom. She rubbed the cat that was carved on the newel post for good luck. The wood under her hand was dark and shiny from years of the whole family doing the same. The floorboards creaked in the same places they always had as she went upstairs.

She knelt on the window seat in the bedroom. Winter was squeezing the daylight short, but she wasn't looking out at the garden; instead, she touched the bottom pane of glass. She never saw it without remembering it broken. She had shattered it by throwing a shoe when she was six years old—the day she was told that she had to go to America to live with her father and his new wife.

* * *

LIZ WOKE FROM HER UNINTENDED nap an hour and a half later, a crick in her neck and grit in her eyes. She splashed her face with water and combed her hair. As she turned at the bottom of the steps to go to the kitchen, she caught sight of her mother's spinet in the darkened parlor. She tiptoed in and ran a finger over the golden wood. Ellen kept it dusted and polished.

Liz opened the keyboard and played the line she remembered hearing her mother sing. She waited hopefully, but the next line stayed stubbornly out of reach.

"Ah, Sleeping Beauty." Her uncle's voice interrupted her. She blinked as he turned on the lamp and came in to give her a kiss. He had lost part of his right leg in an RAF training accident in the fifties, and he walked with a slight limp and the faint snick-snick of an artificial joint. "Look like your mother, you do. How are you, luv?"

"I'm all right. It's so good to see you." She got up and gave him a hug.

Liz had mistaken Ian Taeffe for a policeman when she was small, when he wore the blue uniform of a British Rail guard. Now he managed employment affairs for the entire southwest region of BritRail and wore a suit and tie to work. But she still found him reassuring.

Ian took Liz's hand in his own, inspecting it. "How is it?"

Liz shrugged. "It doesn't hurt anymore."

He pressed the damaged hand firmly. "What will you do?"

She couldn't bear for him to see her as less than courageous. "Start over. What else?"

His elastic face spread into a broad smile. "That you will, my dear. That you will."

He left for choir practice, and Liz joined Ellen in the kitchen. Her cousin, Kate, looked up from where she was laying the table. "Hullo, Liz."

"Feel better?" Ellen said, spooning a savory pie onto plates.

Liz nodded sheepishly. "I guess I did need a nap after all." She sniffed. "Do

I smell apple biters?" Her aunt made a gingery baked apple with a distinct zip that Liz had loved as a child.

"I didn't forget."

Liz glanced over at her cousin and found her staring at her scarred hand. Their eyes flickered up and met. Liz flushed, and her cousin's fair skin colored.

"It's too bad, what happened to you," Kate said, all awkwardness.

Liz took a sharp breath, but she merely nodded.

"What will you do now?"

Liz took a filled plate from her aunt and passed it to Kate. "I want to be a singer."

"You sound like nothing's changed."

"What I want hasn't changed. I'm not giving it up just because of the accident."

Kate's brow wrinkled as she took in Liz's statement. "Could you not teach?"

Liz sighed. "Why does everyone tell me to teach?"

They sat down, and over the steaming steak-and-kidney pie, Ellen steered the conversation away from Liz's dreams. She spoke of family and quizzed Kate on how she was faring in Cardiff.

Liz mostly listened, only half assimilating the content. As tea went on, for the first time in months, she relaxed. She returned to a time before her ambition—a time when comfort was an immediate and sensate experience, when a warm bed and good food and kind people could alleviate the fears and grief she'd accumulated.

It wasn't until they were savoring the warm apples that Ellen brought up Liz's plans again.

"So you're wanting to sing. What about the short term? Did you have some sort of work in mind?"

"I don't know. I've got three-quarters of a music degree and a lot of opinions. Music critic?" She sighed, suddenly feeling the burden of her uncertainty. "Just something to keep me afloat. I'll have the money from the insurance settlement, but I want to save that for emergencies."

They finished eating, and Liz and Kate took care of the dishes, Kate washing and Liz drying as they had always done. Liz kept Kate talking about her love life as long as she could, but finally her cousin came back to their earlier conversation.

"What makes you think you can sing, anyway?"

Liz shot her a startled look before she realized that the answer might not be so obvious to everyone. "My mum."

"But that doesn't mean you'll be any good."

"Oh, I'll be good."

"You can't be good at everything."

Liz shrank from her cousin's relentless reasoning. "But I *will* be good. I *have* to be. I won't settle for a boring little life."

"Maybe you won't have a choice." Kate shrugged. "You've always acted superior because of this destiny that you invented for yourself, haven't you? But you might have to give it up."

Liz glared at her cousin. "I didn't invent it. I have talent. I worked very hard."

"You didn't invent the talent, no. Just the cloak of grandeur."

"What do you want me to do, spend my life apologizing? You must be happy that it's all been taken away!" She twisted the drying rag in her hands.

"Well I am sorry for that. Truly." Kate spoke softly, stubbornly. "But it just doesn't seem so unfair, that you have to live like the rest of us. Since you've been queening it over us so long."

Liz covered her face with her right hand. The wretched anxiety that she would end up doing exactly what Kate suggested filled her with a hollow, ill feeling.

Presently Kate spoke. "I'm sorry. I guess I really don't understand how it is for you."

Liz slowly rubbed her face. "Forget it. I didn't know how patronizing you found me." She could not bring herself to meet Kate's eyes.

They continued cleaning in moody silence until Kate turned to put the cast iron pan on the stovetop. "I might know of work for you in Cardiff," she said. "If you're interested."

Though Kate's offer was made with hesitation, Liz knew better than to reject the underlying apology. In a neutral tone she said, "What kind of work?"

"Some friends of mine have a bookshop, and they need help. I think Bert wants to open another shop this year."

"Should I call you?"

"Why don't you come into town Monday after I finish work? I'll take you over there." Kate gave her a small smile.

"Okay," Liz said. After a moment she added, "Thanks."

Chapter 7

BY SUNDAY LIZ WAS SOMEWHAT reassured about the wisdom of returning to Wales. The terrible dark days that had so bewildered her father and step-mother lay outside the experience of her extended family. Here, she felt able to thrust off the obligation to mourn her past.

Not one to rest for long, Liz headed out for a walk on Sunday afternoon. Ellen and Ian lived close to the center of Caerphilly, not far from the castle and the train station. It had been nearly fourteen years since she'd last lived there, and Mountain Road still seemed like a small village within the city. Stone buildings crowded together, none more than two stories high, and the sidewalks were narrow. Bits of color relieved the gray, white, and black facades— the red and yellow Royal Mail logo, the blue lettering of a Wall's Ice Cream sign, the orange banner in Wimpy's window. It looked like any of hundreds of High Streets in Britain. It was where Liz had spent her early childhood.

The gray skies of Wales made the green of the landscape more vibrant. She took it in like oxygen. On the way back up the hill, she crossed the road to St. Martin's churchyard. Twilight blew in off the ocean like a storm. The cemetery sprawled down the hill next to the church. Here the grass grew wildly, and spots of floral color drew the eye away from the gravestones. The older stones were gray and monotone, but at the top of the path closest to the road, stark gilt and white letters on black stones spoke emphatically of loss.

After a few moments, Liz found what she was looking for. She was strangely unprepared for the shock of it.

IN MEMORY OF
MARGARET MORGAN
1934–1964
BELOVED WIFE AND MOTHER

On the same stone followed the names of Liz's grandparents. Their more recent deaths had occurred only one heartbroken year apart. Beneath that the stone read simply *Peace, Perfect Peace.*

Like a fish breaking the surface of water in a shining arc, a picture flashed through Liz's mind. It startled her, for she firmly believed that she had no memory of that day—but now, with preternatural clarity, she saw it: The interior of St. Martin's, candles pushing through the darkness. Herself, almost four years old, tucked between her father and her aunt. A swell of golden organ music rising out of the confusing burden of the occasion—a hymn that, though she did not know the words, was familiar. Her mother always sang it. Where was her mother, that she was not there to sing it with her? Liz sang alone in the cold dark, making up nonsense to fill the phrases she did not know. Almost at once her father bent and shushed her. She did not understand the pain in his eyes, but after that she fell silent for a long time.

In the present she was silent again. She kept waiting as the skies darkened and became restless, and as she did, her thoughts straightened out of their convoluted helix and she reached back through her life to her mother, whom she missed every day. A whisper of presence seemed to ride the wind.

Mum, I'm so lost. You would have been so proud of me, but now . . . She sighed deeply. *Am I just refusing to face the truth? What did you give me?*

The tenuous sense that she would be heard faded. She tried to picture living in Caerphilly, where she would likely have ended up had her mother lived. A ghost of herself flitted among the pram-pushing, Saturday-marketing, Sunday-chapel-going village dwellers. She hovered there for a moment, close to her mother's death and her own birth. How could she resume that life after fourteen years in pursuit of a comet?

Feeling the chill, she started back toward her aunt's house, but suddenly, on an impulse she didn't even try to understand, she pulled open the heavy door of St. Martin's and went in. Evensong was in progress, and a few heads turned. She sank into a back row. The prayers milled over and around her. She closed her eyes.

So many people had told her, last year, how lucky she was to be alive. The words had made her angry, yet today she knew it was good to be alive in the freezing February evening, rather than passively awaiting eternity. She had more to do. She had music to make.

The assertion of a pipe organ interrupted her pagan meditations. The congregation began to sing. She kept her eyes closed, but her trained ear analyzed and wondered. Deep inside she heard where she fit, was nearly tempted to open her mouth. She did not, a wave of uncertainty dampening her resolve. But neither did she leave the church. She suffered the harmonies to join in her head, resonating with the balance she had sought at her mother's grave.

Chapter 8

ON MONDAY, LIZ TOOK THE TRAIN to Cardiff, and she and Kate walked to a shop on Queen Street, a pedestrian mall in the center of town. The chipped red and gold letters painted on the glass read "Swann's Antiquarian Books." Brass bells on the door rippled a greeting, and Kate led Liz into a warren of tall, deep shelving bays crammed with books and crowded by cartons on the floor. Notices for upcoming events in town cascaded down the front of the sales counter.

The woman behind the counter smiled when she saw them, exposing perfect white teeth all the way to the gums. She was model thin and tall, her dark hair short and chic. Though dressed casually, she obviously knew precisely what shade of red to wear.

"Cheers, Kate. Is this the prodigal returned?"

Liz shot a sideways glance at Kate, who didn't notice.

"Liz Morgan, Caroline Butler," Kate said, tugging off her gloves. "Caro, she needs a job."

"How long will you be here? Kate said you left university to come over."

Liz cringed internally. What else did Caroline already know? "I'm not sure. I was in an accident, and I had to take a year off. But it might be long term."

Caroline raised her eyebrows. "Can you work then, if you're still recovering?"

"I'm all right. My hand and wrist are a little stiff, that's all."

Liz felt Kate draw breath to speak, but before she could say anything Caroline continued, apparently satisfied. "Bert has some grand plans for the new shop, but he's away a lot on commissions and estate sales, and this place needs a bit of straightening up," she said with a sweep of her hand. "We'd have plenty of work for you. Tell me a bit about yourself."

The jangling of the bells on the door spared Liz the painful recital of her recent past. A man flourished into the store in a rumple of wool and tweed. His temples were graying, and his face was florid from the weather.

"How are you, Kate? Perishing cold out," he said in greeting, blowing his nose. He went behind the counter, tossed down a large envelope, and took Caroline by the shoulders. "We're all set, my love! I've signed the papers for the new shop!"

She snatched up the offering, breaking into her broad smile. "Terrific! When do we open?"

"There's some work needs doing first, and I'll have to order in stock. And hire a clerk. Six, eight weeks or more."

"And look what Kate's brought us, just in time." She turned him to face Liz.

Kate introduced them. "Bert Swann, my cousin, Liz Morgan, from California. I told her you might have a job for her."

He eyed Liz. "Going to university, are you?"

"Not right now."

"First visit?"

Liz laughed. "I was born here."

"On holiday, are you? I'd probably need you full time by the summer. You wouldn't be free to come and go," Bert cautioned her.

"I want to work full time. I need the money."

He squinted at her, pursing his lips. "Should I ask if you have a work visa?"

"Better. I kept my citizenship here."

That seemed to decide him. "Clever girl." He nodded to himself and glanced at Caroline, who telegraphed her agreement. "Right then. I'd be obliged. Work it out with my partner here about your wages." He patted his slight potbelly in satisfaction. "Now then, I'm off to see about finding a carpenter. Cheers, Kate. A pleasure, Liz Morgan." And he bustled out again.

"Can you start Monday week?" Caroline asked.

"I can start tomorrow if you want."

Her new employer smiled. "High marks for willingness, but Monday week will be fine. I have to work out the budget yet."

* * *

EARLY MARCH ENTERTAINED A FEW mild days, previewing a hesitant spring. Feeling liberated, Liz left her lovely, light-filled bed-sit at the top of a brick house on Rhymney Terrace and strolled to Swann's Books with her coat open and her scarf loose. Walking upstream of the students milling toward

University College, she squinted in the unexpected sun. New plants rose and stretched amid the palpable smell of decay and growth in the moist earth. *Daffodils soon*, she thought, noticing the plump green blades along the edge of the path.

When she arrived at Swann's a little after ten, white clouds were beginning to tumble across the sunlight, bullied by the rising wind. The morning evaporated as she toiled up and down and around the shop, emptying cartons and filling shelves with stock bought at estate sales and auctions. She barely heard the phone ring or the clang of bells each time the door opened.

The rain returned at noon; Caro came back soaked when she went out to get their lunch at the chip shop. They ate in the office. Steam rose from Caro's sodden coat, and the tiny windows clouded over as rain slapped against them in spiccato bursts.

"Kate tells me you're a flautist." Caro coated her fish with tartar sauce and licked her fingers.

Damn Kate. "Not anymore." Liz concentrated on drowning her lunch with vinegar.

Caroline speared a bite of fish. "I thought you might want to play in the G-Triple-S-G orchestra when we do *Mikado* this spring. Gilbert and Sullivan Society of South Glamorganshire," she added when Liz wrinkled her brow. "I expect I'll be doing Yum-Yum."

"I don't play anymore," Liz repeated, more stridently than she intended.

"Your hand?"

"Yes," she admitted shortly. She'd managed to adapt to her handicap to the point that it was barely noticeable to anyone else, but she still felt the numbness at the end of the day, and the stiffness in her fingers never went away. She did not want to be reminded.

Caro studied Liz. "Why did you come here?" she asked, direct and curious as a child. "Love affair gone off? Or did you not pass your courses at university? I can't figure you out."

Liz reached for her soda. "Why do you have to figure me out?"

"You have some secret you've not told me." She did not withdraw the question.

"I was a performance major at San Francisco Conservatory," Liz said, weighing each word carefully. "The car wreck last May ruined my hand for playing. I had to give it up."

Caroline stared at her. "No, truly? Why didn't you tell me?"

Liz shrugged. "It's hard to talk about it."

"So what are you going to do now?"

Liz took a deep breath. "Well, I'm going to sing."

After a considerable pause, Caroline asked, "Do you study?"

"Not yet. I just called the college and the university last week to get some recommendations for teachers."

"Stick with Welsh College. The teachers at the university are a stuffy lot."

"But I'm such a beginner. Welsh College isn't going to be interested."

Caroline considered her. "Maybe you should try out for *Mikado*. You may as well find out if you're any good."

"Oh, I'll be good." She immediately wished that she had not said that, but Caroline appeared not to have heard.

"Try out for chorus. You can carry a tune?"

"Yes," Liz said warily.

"Then it's easy. All you have to do is go and sing a song."

"I'm not a singer yet. And I can't act," she said firmly.

"You don't need any training for chorus," Caroline said. "As long as you can smile and sing and not trip, you'll be smashing. I'll help you."

Liz hesitated, reluctant to make a fool of herself in front of Caroline.

"You have nothing to lose now, do you?"

"I guess I don't."

Caroline got up and paced in short steps, thinking. "Have you ever seen *Mikado*?"

Liz sat down in the vacated chair behind the desk. "No. I played for *Pirates of Penzance* once in high school."

"Terrific, you can learn something from that. You've heard it a million times, so it'll be familiar."

"But I—"

"Are you busy tonight?"

"Not really."

"Stay to tea then, and I'll help you. It'll be fun," Caroline said, contemplating Liz with calculation in her eyes.

"Singing it's probably really different than playing it."

Caroline was undaunted. "They say that there are musicians, and there are singers. You should be a refreshing change."

Liz flexed her left hand, doing the strengthening exercises that had become second nature to her. She thought about her last meeting with Julia Bradshaw.

There's music in you yet.

* * *

AFTER WORK, CAROLINE HUSTLED Liz upstairs to the flat over the shop where she and Bert lived. The space was tiny: four square rooms split by a narrow hallway. There seemed to be nearly as many books upstairs as in the shop. Caroline shooed her into the parlor and turned on the heat. Liz sat on the ottoman as her friend searched through the stack of music on top of the upright piano. Ornate Victorian furniture crowded the room. If four people sat on the love seat and the two chairs, they would be nearly knee to knee.

"Did the furniture come with the flat?" Liz asked.

Caroline rolled her eyes. "It belonged to Bert's mum. She passed last year, and we got stuck with all of this. I like the carpets, though. And the piano's a dream. Here it is." She pulled *Pirates of Penzance* from the pile and sat down at the piano.

A part of Liz wanted not to be persuaded, but Caroline seduced her. The music was straightforward, but her voice felt odd and exposed. Never before had she paid it so much attention. But working music was a pleasure too long denied. She repeated lines until they became consistent, then wove two together, then added a third, until the entire song flowed smoothly.

"Don't even think about acting," Caroline said as she saw Liz off. "All you have to do on Tuesday is sing. If you can follow instructions and smile, you needn't worry about anything else."

* * *

THROUGH THAT WEEK LIZ SANG in the bath, tasted the words as she walked to work, hummed as she ate her meals. In bed each night she purposely delighted herself with the thought that she was planning to make music again, only to dampen her joy with a blanket of inconsequence: She needn't care. No one who mattered would ever hear about it.

The night before the audition Liz lay awake and listened to the raindrops plop in the garden like fat beetles. She pictured herself onstage as she lay in the dark and massaged her fingers. Caroline was wrong. Auditions were not easy. Not at all. They were the difference between triumph and humiliation.

She pulled her downy up around her ears and curled up with her back to the wall. Why couldn't she have taken up poetry or painting?

Chapter 9

THE UNIVERSITY COLLEGE MUSIC building where auditions were held was a stark brick rectangle. The black and rusty red of the badly lit lobby and corridors oppressed Liz as she followed in the draft of Caroline's self-confidence. So different from the soft, creamy light in the halls of the Conservatory.

A black-clad giant of a man presided over the sign-up list. The dome of his bald head shone in the low light. Caroline greeted him casually, picking up a never-finished conversation.

"So, Simon, you'll be the Mikado again?" She signed her name and handed the pen to Liz.

Simon pursed his lips and flattened one eyebrow. "If they'll have me."

"Nonsense. Who else will they get? Anybody good been here yet?"

"No sopranos," he told her dryly. "We're running on time, for a wonder. You can go straight in."

"This is my friend Liz Morgan. She's never done this before, and she'd like to get it over with." She spoke in a confidential tone, as though Liz were not in the room. Liz struggled with the truth of the statement versus her objection to being categorized as a neophyte.

"Be my guest." He waved toward the doors behind him.

"Have fun!" Caroline said.

Feeling like Alice in pursuit of the White Rabbit, Liz opened the door to the auditorium and tiptoed in, aware of her heartbeat. The hall was unpretentious, all lines and flats, no ornate detail. Fixtures on the sides of the house washed dull light over a bank of seats, not more than fifteen rows. A dusty black curtain filled the proscenium. Below the stage, to one side, stood an upright piano. A young man sat playing softly, pausing to work out each chord as though he was composing on the spot.

"Good evening," a cultured voice said from nearby, and Liz started. A second man sat in the last dark row of seats, watching her. Her mouth went dry as she mumbled a greeting. The speaker rose and took her information sheet, unfolding his long limbs with the grace of a heron. Even his face and his fingers were long, and his eyes seemed to be a soulful purple in that light.

"I'm Huw Parsons, the stage director. Giles Offeryn is our music director." He gestured toward the pianist near the stage.

Liz introduced herself automatically. "Elizabeth Morgan."

"Go down and give your music to Giles." Huw settled back into his seat, his eyes already scanning her bio. She had to go through with this now. She walked to the piano, sure that the director was noticing how she wobbled in her borrowed high heels.

The pianist watched her progress, his left hand fiddling with the bass keys, and smiled at her when she approached. She smiled back reflexively, warmed. His eyes reflected his deep blue shirt.

"What will you sing, then?"

Liz handed him the music she clutched. "Just this."

He propped it up on the piano. "Oh yes, Edith's first act solo."

She stood next to him until he glanced up.

"Go ahead up onstage," he said. "We can hear you better there."

Blushing, Liz did as she was told. She forced herself to walk to the exact center of the stage, missing her flute suddenly and intensely. Without it she didn't know what to do with her hands. She lifted her eyes to position herself in the lights as Caroline had suggested. She took a deep breath, relaxed her clenched fist, and tried to claim whatever composure she could.

When she looked down at him, the pianist was waiting, his hands poised on the keyboard. She nodded to him, a gesture so natural to the old soloist in her that her instincts took over. With her next breath she felt a familiar tingle of excitement and heard the piano begin.

It was a silly verse of a silly song. She sang with a studied smile, careful and stiff through the first page. "Just sing through the chorus response in the middle like it's part of the solo," Caroline had advised her. "It's only two lines."

Liz forged ahead through the response, gazing at nothing over the head of her judge. But suddenly she faltered, the words drying up, startled from her mind. The pianist was singing the chorus part along with her, his baritone forced into falsetto to mimic a women's chorus. A surge of adrenaline shot through Liz, and hysterical laughter threatened to burst into the verse, but she caught herself and picked up the words from him. The second half of her solo demanded all of her concentration; she felt she teetered between disaster and flight.

When she finished, she headed for the exit with nothing but escape on her mind.

"Your music, Elizabeth Morgan," the pianist called.

She stopped and turned back to him.

"Quite nice," he said with too broad a smile as he handed it over. "Sorry if I threw you."

"Thank you," she bit out, feeling the color rise in her cheeks, and she would have sailed right up the aisle and out of the hall if the director had not stopped her.

"Tell me, Miss Morgan," he said, looking down at her bio sheet before him. "You've only ticked chorus. Would you be interested in reading for a role?"

Surprise knocked Liz flat-footed. She managed half a nod and half a shrug. "Sure, why not?"

He selected several sheets from the stacks on the seats in front of him and offered them to her. "We'll have you read for Pitti-Sing and Peep-Bo. Do what you can with these."

She smiled without comment as she accepted them.

"See you Saturday at two," he said, setting her free.

Liz plowed through the door on scattered flurries of elation and despair and nearly fell over Caroline.

"You were quite good!" Caroline said, catching the swinging door.

"How do you know?"

"Well of course I was listening," she admitted shamelessly.

"I'm just glad it's over." Liz made a wry face. "That piano player sang along with me at the chorus part. I nearly lost my place. Felt like a fool."

Caroline laughed. "He was probably trying to put you at ease. Huw and Giles do everything they can not to intimidate people."

"Well, they want me back in spite of that."

Caroline paused and raised her eyebrows. "For what?"

"Pitti-Sing and Peep-Bo."

Caroline relaxed, her vast smile spreading over her face. "I'm kind of surprised, but that's terrific!"

"Thanks. Now go do the same." Liz shooed her toward the door.

When Caroline had gone in, Liz leaned against the wall and relived the two minutes of music she had just made. The uneven tympani of her heart shook her chest. She shut her eyes and felt the moment when she had stopped being careful and suppressed laughter had loosened her voice. When the pianist had broken through the scrim of her concentration she had hurled a mental curse at him. But that lovely flourish at the end of the piece had been a product of her surprised mirth.

She had not dared to hope to fly so freely again. A smug smile stole over her face.

Chapter 10

AFTER TWO DAYS OF CAROLINE'S relentless coaching Liz noticed no discernable improvement in her acting ability. She wished she had stuck to her original plan of taking some lessons.

"No more dialogue," she insisted on Friday night as she followed her friend up the stairs to the flat. "We'll go over the music, but that's all."

"Suit yourself. You are coming along." Caroline shook her cumbersome key ring, searching for the right key.

"Why are you making such a project of me?"

Caroline paused, her hand on the door. "You're good," she said, as if it was obvious.

A pulse of vanity, or fear, burned in Liz's chest.

As they went through Pitti-Sing's short solo, she regained her balance. She tried to sing lightly and cleanly as Caroline did, played with the phrases as she would have on her flute. Caroline patiently played and encouraged until Bert came home from Cygnet.

"I'm back, love," he announced, poking his head into the parlor. "Staying to tea, Liz? I'll run you home after."

"Yes, thanks." She gathered up her much-marked music and followed them to the kitchen. "Do you think I have any chance at all?" she asked.

"It depends on who else shows up," Caroline told her.

"You have a rather nice sort of Mozart voice," Bert offered, filling the kettle at the sink.

Liz swallowed. "Is that good?" she asked, trying to keep her tone casual.

He shrugged. "If you like Mozart."

* * *

WHEN THEY ARRIVED AT SHERMAN Theater on Saturday, Liz knew herself an outsider. Once she'd been able to walk into a room full of musicians and know that she measured up to any of them. Now all she had to offer was instinct—no skills, nothing on which she could depend.

A couple of dozen people clustered in knots of conversation among the first rows of seats. As Liz and Caroline came down the aisle a blond woman detached herself from a group and bore down on Caroline with the sleek grace of an Abyssinian cat. Her skin looked like she spent summers in Cannes rather than winters in Wales. Her mouth had a slight pout, and her eyes were perfectly made up to accentuate their large size and long lashes. Jangling metal bracelets announced her approach. Watching her, Liz experienced a moment of gratitude that she did not have such elite beauty to maintain.

"Well now we'll see who gets the upper hand." The blonde sucked Caroline into her gossip, excluding Liz. "Huw will have to listen to my husband."

The derision in her tone puzzled Liz, but Caroline looked at her shrewdly. "A nice chance for Giles."

"And maybe for some of the rest of us, too," the blonde retorted with the heat of rivalry.

"I'm sure he'll use good judgment."

Caroline's neutral reply seemed to infuriate the other woman, who drew in her breath—to toss back an insult, Liz thought, but all she managed was "Of course he will." She stalked off with only a quick, incurious glance at Liz.

"What a little witch," Liz said when she was out of earshot. "Who is she?"

"Diana Offeryn. Remember the accompanist who sang along with you at the audition? That's his wife. She seems to think she's finally going to get a big role."

"And will she?"

"Giles is the only reason she didn't stay in the chorus where she belongs." Caroline said, scanning the auditorium. "She won't work at it, so she's not very good. Anyway, they seem to be having—"

A tall young man with unruly dark curls bounded up behind Caroline and put his arms around her waist. "Caroline, when are you going to leave Bert and marry me?"

She turned, laughing, and pushed him away. "Christopher. I was just looking for you."

"Of course you were." He smiled at Liz curiously.

"This is a friend of mine from California, Liz Morgan."

"Welcome to Wales," he said. "Here to watch?"

"I'm called back for Peep-Bo and Pitti-Sing."

His glance measured her, his eyes amused. "Some competition for Diana. Good. How much experience do you have?"

"As a matter of fact, not any at all." She said this as though it was a big joke. Perhaps she could act after all.

Christopher laughed. "Then it's high time you got some."

She managed to laugh with him, in spite of the dread the thought of competing with the catty blonde inspired.

Caroline touched Christopher's arm, drawing his attention back to her. "I'm looking forward to working with Giles."

"Oh, he'll be smashing—perfect, as always."

"And Diana?"

His reply was a snort. "Not to worry. He has more integrity than that. But he does have to live with her." He gave Liz a wry smile. "I'm no big fan of the girl, even if I did stand up for Giles at the wedding."

Liz looked across at Giles, who was standing near the piano talking with the director. Christopher laughed when he caught her. "It's highly nepotistic. We're all family—if not actually, then practically. But enough chitchat; they're wanting to start. Sing pretty, ladies!" He sketched a courtly bow and sprang away to inflict himself on another woman who had just arrived.

"Is he always so . . ." Liz groped for a word.

Caroline gave her a sidelong glance. "Oh, he's a big flirt. If you want my advice, I'd stay clear of him. He goes through women like a hot knife through butter."

Caroline hustled her to a seat, rolling off a litany of names that Liz didn't even try to remember as they went. Banter knotted the group tight; she had nothing to contribute. Caroline soon grew preoccupied with old friends and preparation for her own performance, and Liz, left to her own devices, glanced around the auditorium. Simon, again dressed all in black, sat motionless behind the others, watching. He raised an eyebrow in recognition, and she smiled shyly. In front of her, Diana busied herself with a compact, meticulously reapplying lipstick that exactly matched the pink knitted shell she wore. Christopher was off to one side, spinning a web of words around an unsuspecting female. Liz watched him thoughtfully, mesmerized, until he turned and caught her eye on him. He grinned. She returned his smile tentatively.

At last Huw called them together. After reintroducing himself and Giles, and giving a quick rundown of the plan for the afternoon, he got things underway.

Liz had planned to let as many people as possible read the scenes first so that she could assess the competition, and especially, learn from it, so a shock of stage fright seized her when she heard her name called for the very first scene. So much for that plan.

"Good luck," Caroline whispered, and with a tight nod Liz clambered over several people, hurried down the aisle, and joined the small group on the stage, clutching her pages with their useless notes. Christopher bounded up the steps after her, scanned his script briefly, and tucked it into his belt behind him. He rubbed his hands together eagerly and sauntered over to Liz.

"Smile," he said. "This is comedy."

She relaxed a little. "You've done this before?"

"I thrive on the attention," he said, shameless.

She laughed in complete understanding. Her smile lingered as she contemplated the absurdity of her situation. Watching the dynamic of the group, she understood that she wouldn't be cast today. She suspected that Christopher's assessment was correct: she was just there as a foil for the regulars who were certain to get the roles. She couldn't imagine a good reason to continue the charade, except that she needed to see it through. Her stiffest competition had only ever been herself.

As they began to read, unexpected help came from Christopher, who engaged her particularly as they exchanged lines, drawing her into the scenes with his energy and the amused challenge in his eye. She forgot about her competitors' scrutiny, about the production staff's scribbled notes, and about Caroline, who must not be disappointed. She delivered the ludicrous dialogue in surges, losing and then finding her place again, and carried herself with the dignity of a duchess at a ball who knows that her gown is split down the back.

In a single moment, as she reveled in some particularly ridiculous line about "Katisha's left elbow," Liz happened into a spot on the stage where the lively acoustics exploded every consonant. She suddenly heard her own voice spring back at her, and her heart dropped at the acute realization that every eye in the hall, in that second, was focused on her. And then a miracle: a snicker rippled among the watchers. Warm stimulation shook her, just as it had during the solo recitals she would never relive.

Caroline smiled her brilliant smile when Liz got back to her seat after the scene. "Terrific," she whispered. "You lit up like a beacon!"

After reading dialogue, singing Pitti-Sing's solo was almost easy. She performed with unleashed enthusiasm, beyond caring that she had to go first. She finished the song staring triumphantly into Giles's eyes. After a second he gave her a slight nod, looked away, and wrote something on his pad.

After an hour and a half, Huw dismissed everyone but those called back for the four major roles.

"You want me to stay, right?" Diana asked, all confidence.

Huw blinked at her. "No, I think we're finished with you for today, Diana. Thank you."

Liz cringed inside, embarrassed for her.

Diana looked from Huw to her husband.

Giles shook his head. "I'll see you at home, Diana."

Finally she exited, her bracelets clashing as she shouldered a bag big enough to contain a small dog. Liz deliberately allowed her a few moments' head start before making her own way toward the exit, but Huw stopped her before she could escape.

"Miss Morgan, before you go, could you fill in the back of your sheet?" he asked. "'Previous Experience'?"

She shrugged. "I don't have any."

He gazed at her over the top of his spectacles. "I see. Thank you for coming."

Well, she had never pretended to be an actress. With a word to Caroline and a wave to Christopher, she left the hall behind.

* * *

AFTER A QUICK STOP AT HER flat to change her clothes, Liz went for a walk in Bute Park, the emerald lodestone of Cardiff. Dog owners accompanied their tumult of canines along the river path, and Liz shyly greeted the people as she patted and played with their dogs. She meandered along the river and past the cricket grounds almost to the green edge of Pontcanna Fields before finally sitting. As she collapsed on the bench, she felt her bones sag. She savored the familiar post-concert weariness: gray ashes of fatigue shot through with the embers of a lightning strike.

Mockingbirds celebrated the greening trees and the well of sunlight between the banks of the river. All around Liz, spring moved, the powerful river sauntering silently past, the wind tickling the rise of new grass; and there were more stirrings she couldn't see but vaguely sensed—germination, photosynthesis, cell division, fragments from an education largely displaced by her passion for things musical.

She sat for a long while, resisting what was creeping up on her. Her mind turned over kaleidoscope images from the afternoon as she stared into the water. Some singers with letter-perfect memorization had undermined themselves with an edge of uneasiness, while others had come across as comically confident, if oblivious to the incorrect pitches they sang. There were those, like Caroline and Christopher, who appeared intimidatingly relaxed and prepared. At least she'd sung in tune. And Christopher, bless him, and her adrenaline, had lifted some of her anxiety.

Caroline had warned her that anyone who tried out for the more glamorous roles and wasn't cast might well be offered Pitti or Peep. Liz must not let herself want it. But that flicker of laughter, the focus of lights, eroded her objectivity. She absently rubbed the fingers of her left hand to relieve the ache from the cold.

Desire wound her into tight desperation.

Chapter 11

CAROLINE GREETED LIZ GAILY WHEN she arrived at the bookshop on Monday morning. "I'm doing Yum-Yum! Did Huw ring you?"

"Big surprise," Liz said, smiling. "Congratulations. I haven't heard. No phone."

Liz did not speculate out loud. Her unreasonable hope disintegrated thread by thread as the morning wore on. Every call distracted her, but Caroline never beckoned her to the phone. Liz felt her friend watching her, saying nothing.

When Bert appeared at noon Caroline pounced on him.

"Can you look after the store for half an hour? We need to go check the cast list."

"Huw rang you already."

"Yes, but Liz isn't on the phone."

Bert looked at Liz with what she hoped was not sympathy. "Off you go, then. But be quick. I'm running a business, remember?"

"When did that ever trouble you?" Caroline asked, pecking him on the cheek. Then she grabbed Liz's hand and led her in a dash to the theater.

Caroline took Liz directly to the bulletin board in the lobby of the music building, where they scanned the list in silence. Liz's eye went immediately to the two roles she'd read for. *Pitti-Sing: Gillian Bryce. Peep-Bo: Diana Offeryn.* She turned away.

Caroline grabbed her arm. "You're in!"

"No I'm not."

She pointed to the chorus list. "Yes you are. That's you. 'Elizabeth Morgan.'"

Liz read her name. "I guess I am. Let's go back. Bert will be waiting."

She began to walk quickly, and in a moment Caroline caught up with her. "Aren't you pleased?"

"Sure." Liz kept her head down.

"You didn't honestly think you would get a role?"

"I shouldn't have."

"You have to pay your dues. Diana was bound to be cast. And Gillian's a regular."

"You don't need to defend their decision."

"It was your first try. If you get some chorus experience they may cast you next time."

"I'll probably be back in San Francisco by then."

"So you won't do chorus?"

Liz opened her mouth to reply and paused. She knew exactly what Caroline was thinking, and to her shame, she knew it was true. She thrust up her chin. "Of course I will."

* * *

UNABLE TO FACE CAROLINE WITH an excuse, Liz went to the first chorus rehearsal. Steady rain spread a sheen of a black and white through the streets. When she arrived, she shook the rain from her clothes and checked her watch. Early, for a change. She pulled open the heavy doors and peeked inside.

A circle of yellow light encompassed the piano. Low light filled the stage above, visible through an opening in the curtain, but did not spill out into the house. Giles sat alone at the instrument in the orchestra pit, and music drifted up like penetrating incense, vaguely familiar. Each chord pulled away from the keyboard reluctantly, as separate as smoke rings. He seemed completely focused on what he was playing as Liz walked slowly down the aisle, but when she paused four rows from the front, listening, he turned his head.

"*Croeso*, welcome," he said, continuing to play.

She came closer. "Thanks. I'm Liz Morgan," she reminded him. "In the chorus?"

"Yes, of course. You made a rather nice job at callbacks. I'm glad you're here."

"It's all new to me," she confessed.

He laughed, bringing two short chords out of the piano and resolving the contemplation of the music. "Between you and me, this is a debut of sorts for me too. I've never conducted Gilbert and Sullivan before." He swung around on the piano bench to face her. "Canadian?" he asked, tipping his head as if to listen to her accent.

"Welsh."

He looked puzzled.

"Mostly raised in California. I'm back on an extended visit."

"Ah." He nodded in comprehension. "I thought I heard something not quite American."

"What were you playing just now?" she asked, taking off her coat.

"That? Just a folk song. I'm working on an arrangement."

"How does it go? That part you just played."

He looked at her, shrugged, and played a few bars, singing in a warm baritone. "*Fy nghariad a dorrws 'y nghalon i bron.* My love nearly broke my heart," he translated.

It was the song she remembered her mother singing. She didn't tell him that. Instead she said, "Nice. I like your voice."

He dipped his head in acknowledgement. "Yours is quite lovely. Do you study?"

"Voice? Not at the moment. I'm looking for a teacher. Do you know anyone?"

His eyebrows rose at what he must see as her presumption. "How serious are you?"

"Very."

His face remained impassive. "Let me jot down a few names. You'll have to audition for them, you understand."

"Of course." She watched as he wrote names and phone numbers on the back of a rehearsal schedule.

"Where else do you conduct?" she asked when he handed her the short list.

"Here and there. I'm on—well, something of a sabbatical. I coach singers and play for voice studios. One day a week I still teach piano at the grammar school."

"That must be rewarding." Even as she said it she wondered why she did. From the look in his eyes, she thought that he, too, found the remark fatuous.

"Not particularly."

She wanted to take it back, to apologize for saying something so false, but the lights in the sconces came on and the sound of voices preceded a trio of choristers entering from backstage. As the women gathered, chattering like sparrows on a wire after a rainstorm, Liz retreated into silence. Again her usual bravado felt out of place. She wanted Caroline's familiar presence, or even Christopher's flirtation, but they were scheduled for separate rehearsals.

"Liz, come down here next to Eileen," Giles said, beckoning her out of the fourth row where she'd sat down as the rest of the chorus assembled. "She'll keep you out of trouble."

Liz relocated and exchanged names with those nearby, divulging no more as conversations continued over and around her.

At exactly seven o'clock Giles glanced around the hall once more, then welcomed them.

"Most of you probably know this score better than I do," he admitted easily, immediately winning the allegiance of the veterans. "I'm just here to remind you of a few things. This is Gillian, who is our Pitti-Sing." The chorus offered a scatter of applause to the slim girl who bobbed up. "Diana was supposed to be here too, but she must have been held up. She'll be our Peep-Bo." They greeted this news with silence, and he went right on. "Let's begin with some warm-up exercises, shall we?"

In spite of what he had confided to Liz about inexperience, Giles appeared more than competent. They ha-ha-ha-ed and ho-ho-ho-ed through some scales, the lightness he asked for immediately delivered simply because everyone was smiling. When they began to learn the music it was the same. When they failed to come in on his cue, he usually shook his head, cutting them off. "My fault," he would admit. "I'm afraid I'm not quite clear." "We've some snakes in the hall," he teased them when they slurred a final S sound through two beats. And when they mastered a tricky bit of harmony, he stopped to congratulate them. "That's it exactly! Let's do it again so we don't forget."

It was always *we*, Liz noticed.

As they lurched through the first reading, Liz deliberately sang quietly, making notes in her well-thumbed score. But the voices around her were loud with contagious enthusiasm, and eventually she forgot to be hesitant. She had never felt quite like this as a flautist. In those days the music had broken away to join with other strains somewhere beyond her. A strange sensation of being supported by the voices pressed pleasantly against her back and chest, alive and warm.

After an hour of hard work he gave them a break. The chorus dispersed to find water and the loo.

Eileen smiled as they stood and stretched. "You were at the callbacks too."

"I remember you." Liz was grateful to be remembered herself.

"You were quite good. You're from America?"

"California. I'm kind of on an extended visit. I have family in Caerphilly."

"I'd like to go to California," Eileen said, predictably.

The doors behind the stage banged as though a breeze had suddenly kicked up. In sauntered Diana from the wings, leaning with the weight of her bag. Everyone watched her entrance.

"I hope I haven't held you up." She languidly made her way down the steps to the orchestra pit.

Giles revealed neither concern nor annoyance at her tardiness. "You'll have some catching up to do. We've quite a strong group."

Married to the conductor. Why bother to be on time? Liz made a silent meow at her own cattiness. But some of the respect she had formed for Giles evaporated.

Diana nodded to Gillian, a fellow principal, and then briefly scanned the milling chorus. When her glance flicked over Liz and Eileen she paused to direct a superior smile their way. Liz recognized it from her Conservatory days, the glacial graciousness directed at a presumptuous, and currently unsuccessful, rival. She was amazed to realize that she had inadvertently made herself an enemy by daring to vie for the same role—one that consisted of perhaps six spoken lines and fewer sung. She shook her head, almost amused.

"She can do as she pleases, can't she, married to him." Liz felt her heart jump as Eileen echoed her train of thought.

Diana turned to her husband. "Why do you need me then, if they're so good? Am I a principal or not?"

"I won't be teaching this music at the principal rehearsals, and you're in a good bit of it."

"But I've done *Mikado* before. Why do I have to sit through all the chorus rehearsals?"

"I need you here," he said. "You can be a bit of help with the new choristers, can't you?"

"I thought that was your job," she said.

Giles either did not hear her or chose to ignore the remark. "Sopranos are sitting up here," he said. "Let's get back to it, shall we, ladies?"

Diana sat in the front row with a little flounce. The chorister whose chair she had appropriated did not bother to argue with her; she wisely shifted to another row. When they began, a slight constraint lay over the previously jovial chorus. When they began to take apart the first act finale, Liz noticed that Diana did not bother to open her score and that she sang with an obvious burden of boredom. As the others scribbled Giles's indications in their music, she surveyed them with an impatience that made Liz squirm.

But even Diana's presence failed to supersede the music. Near the end of rehearsal Giles brought them to their feet. "Let's just go straight through the whole first act finale," he challenged them. "Do the best you can."

"*With aspect stern and gloomy stride*," sang the women as Giles's hands marched up the keyboard and back. At first he sang the major roles, shifting from falsetto to his own smooth baritone as he cued the chorus around the lines. Eventually the choristers piped up spontaneously, and soon Liz joined in this sport as well. Giles alternated between piano and conducting, listening with intense concentration to the tuning when he stopped playing. They flashed through varying tempi, keys, and moods with surprising cohesiveness. Even Diana seemed to put her heart into the effort as their collective sound warmed the room and brightened the lights.

"*For joy reigns everywhere around!*" they finished, cutting off cleanly where he indicated.

"*Go dda,* ladies!" Giles said, standing up from the piano and smiling at them. "We'll meet again on Thursday. Thank you," he concluded, pressing his hands together and giving them all a little bow.

The catchy chorus music followed Liz home and jigged through her head even after she'd gone to bed. She lay in the dark, smiling. *With laughing song and merry dance . . .*

* * *

THE BELLS ON THE DOOR CLANKED, and Liz glanced up automatically. Though the man's back was turned as he took in the shop, she knew him. She came out from behind the counter.

"Da?"

He turned abruptly, his smile an afterthought. "Well. Ellen said I would find you here."

She hugged him. "Why didn't you say you were coming?"

"Didn't know myself. Madly suggested it."

"Where are you going now?"

"Nepal. Katmandu. But I had to meet with my publisher in London first. Will I take you to supper tonight?"

"Sure." Instantly she winced. "Oh no, I can't. I've got rehearsal."

"Rehearsal?" He stared, and she hurried to explain.

"I'm in the chorus for *Mikado* with the Gilbert and Sullivan Society."

He scrutinized her as if gauging her degree of delusion. "Can you not miss once?"

"I guess so." She looked down at her scarred fingers. "I don't want to, though. Listen, I'll ring Caroline and see if she'll come back early to close up. Then we can have some tea and I'll still be there by seven."

She took him to Barnaby's. They collected their food, cafeteria style, and unloaded their trays at a table near the back of the low-slung room. Nearby, a dark-haired child danced around a table, aiming blows and Kung Fu kicks at his father, complete with sound effects.

"Rhys, not in here," his mother said, not even bothering to look his way. He continued his assault, unfazed, as Liz and her father began to eat.

Liz wondered if Madly had sent him to convince her to come home. There seemed little to say, she realized, after she described how she was adapting to life in Wales. He eyed her every now and again as if unsure what insane behavior she might display next. But it was he who finally broke the ice of the failing conversation.

"You surprise me."

"How?"

He gestured vaguely with a knife in one hand and a roll in the other. "You seem happier than I expected." She waited for him to elaborate. "Madly thinks you've crawled into a hole and pulled it in after you."

She turned his words over carefully, trying to picture life in San Francisco. She would find a job, find an apartment. She would call her old friends, who would remind her acutely that she no longer lived in their world. She would be as ill-suited there as the ghost of herself she had pictured in Caerphilly.

"What's wrong with what I'm doing now? Bert and Caroline need my help. And I've committed to this show." She stopped, feeling how tight her throat was becoming as she defended herself. The child at the next table fired an Uzi at the top of his voice. His parents ignored him. She frowned at her father, feeling her heart pounding between her lungs.

"See, Da, I'm making music without feeling like my life depends on it."

The light did not change, the boy exploded a grenade with his vocal chords, and her father stared at her. She heard the words repeated, *making music.*

Her father shook his head sharply. "Madeline's concerned."

"I know. Tell her that I'm sort of okay." She glanced down at her impaired hand. "I just need to . . . well . . . be quiet and content, and then listen. And then I'll know what I'm supposed to do next."

He looked at her again in his uncertain way, but without the wariness of a moment ago. "How much you are like your mother," he said softly. "She always told me that if she was quiet the Lord would put wisdom in her heart."

A warm wave of emotion rose through Liz's chest and stopped up her throat. After a moment she said, "You do get why I'm here."

"I suppose I do."

* * *

CAROLINE STUCK HER HEAD OUT of the office at Swann's late the next morning. "Liz, phone. It's Huw."

Liz stopped shelving musty volumes of Victorian rhetoric and sat back on her heels. "Huw? What does he want?"

"I don't know, do I?"

Liz climbed to her feet and took the phone from Caroline. He was going to tell her he didn't need her in the chorus after all.

"Liz Morgan? Huw Parsons here. I wondered if you would do me a small favor."

"What is it?" Liz tugged at the phone cord and frowned at Caroline, who was blatantly eavesdropping.

"Gillian Bryce has been offered Perichole over in Newport. She won't be doing Pitti-Sing for us after all. I wonder if you might consider undertaking the role."

"Undertake—" An image of brilliant spotlights filled Liz's mind and stopped her thoughts. "Uh, can I call you back?"

"Of course." He sounded mildly surprised.

"Sorry, there's a customer up front," she fibbed. "I'll call you right back, I promise. What's your number?" She hung up and froze, facing Caroline.

"Well?"

"He wants to know if I'll do Pitti-Sing."

Caroline jumped up and grabbed her by the shoulders in glee. "You little goose! Why didn't you say yes?"

"I'm not an actress!"

"He must think he can teach you. Ring him back, tell him yes!"

"But I—"

"I told you, I'll help you. Just tell him you will. Isn't this what you wanted, anyway?" She picked up the receiver and handed it to Liz, who took it reluctantly and dialed the number she had hastily written down. Butterflies buffeted one another, trying to get out of her belly.

"Mr. Parsons? It's Liz Morgan. Sorry. I'd be happy to give it a try, if you're sure."

"I'm confident we can bring you along. Thank you. We were in rather a spot."

Caroline grinned as Liz put down the phone.

"What have I done?" Liz said, her hand on the receiver. But after a stunned moment she mirrored Caroline's expression.

Chapter 12

"WELL LOOK WHO IT IS," Christopher greeted her that night when she arrived at the principals' rehearsal. "Our new Pitti-Sing."

"Singing and dancing my way into your heart."

He raised his eyebrows thoughtfully as she joined the little group gathered around the piano. In addition to Caroline and Chris and Diana, she recognized Simon from the auditions. His basset jowls and imposing size, along with a tremendous voice, made him a perfect Mikado. His wife, Jane, had the role of Katisha, the brazen and devious "daughter-in-law elect." They looked alike as fruit from the same tree, in that way long-married couples do. Simon greeted her politely, and Jane offered her a warm welcome, as if she was delighted with Huw's choice.

Curtis, the patter baritone who played Koko, gave Liz barely a glance and proceeded to ignore her the rest of the night. He seemed like a wizened old man, but gradually Liz realized that he was so high-strung that he was practically coiled into himself. The tall, golden-haired man standing next to Curtis was exactly what he looked like: a tenor, and the hero of the piece. He introduced himself as David and gave Liz a broad smile, which she couldn't help but return.

Giles did not lead them through their music as he did with the chorus. Liz foresaw a lot of work in the next few days learning the small ensembles in the second act. Although her breath rode shallow in her chest, she delivered her solos with conviction. "If you're going to make a mistake, make a loud one," a teacher had once told her. "Then we'll know what to fix." So she laid it before them all, vulnerable in the knowledge that she was likely making mistakes left and right.

Giles stopped her frequently, in his polite, understated way, with corrections and suggestions, and as he did Liz's frustration mounted and she began to sing off pitch. At the break she sat down at the piano to pick through a phrase that had eluded her. Christopher sauntered over and leaned on the instrument.

"Having trouble?"

"I think I'm in over my head."

"You'll get it. Pitti-Sing is a gem of a *comprimario* role. Much better than Peep-Bo. She's into everything—championing the lovers, harassing Katisha, abetting Koko at his most devious. You should have a grand time."

"Can I help?" Giles came back to the piano.

"I'll get it."

"Don't be a bully, boyo," Christopher said. "Give her some time to learn it."

Giles looked at him, but he only grinned.

"I'll be fine." Liz got up and went back to her seat.

After the break the cast reassembled around the piano and spent another hour on the ensemble music. Liz managed to hold her own, but only just. She headed home that night still wondering if she had made a mistake.

* * *

GILES HAD SCRIBBLED THE NAME and phone numbers of three local voice teachers on a torn scrap of the *Mikado* schedule. Liz kept it tucked away in her wallet. She mentioned it to no one. But after a couple of weeks she could stand her self-imposed suspense no longer. She called the first name on his list.

Genevieve Ponnelle lived in Llandaff, a suburb of Cardiff, easily within a half an hour's walk. The voice on the phone sounded smooth and urbane—very English, very cosmopolitan. And devoid of enthusiasm.

Liz developed all the typical stage fright symptoms as she crossed Llandaff Fields: the pounding heart, the sweaty palms, the trapped breath. She found that the address belonged to a very large white house, rising three stories and set rather close to the sidewalk. The iron gate swung open without a squeak. The front garden, paved over, had only two plants: a pair of hard-pruned rosebushes in giant white urns on either side of the steps.

Liz practically tiptoed up the four stairs, which were free of debris and harbored no spiders. Although the neighborhood still dripped about the eaves from the recent showers, all the windows of the house shone like they had been washed that day. The brass hardware on the front door gleamed softly in the misty light. A plaque on the door, mounted slightly above eye level, read G. PONNELLE — BY APPOINTMENT ONLY.

Liz rang the doorbell and heard it shrill like an alarm clock for rather longer than she had intended. After a considerable silence, as Liz was debating ringing again, she heard the faint click of a lock being released, and the door swung open.

The woman who answered the door had eyes like dark opals. They changed in the light as she looked Liz up and down. She wore a dress of a dramatic blue that set off the pristine white of her hair. Clearly expensive. Blue and white stones glittered at her throat and on her hands. Liz wondered if they were real.

The face was as unemotional as the voice had been. "Yes?"

"Uh—I'm Liz—Elizabeth Morgan. We spoke on the phone last week?"

"We did."

Question? Statement? Liz prepared to try again in case this was not Madame Ponnelle after all. But the door swung wider.

"Come in."

She stepped inside. The woman locked the door and walked away down the narrow hall without looking back. Liz hesitated.

"Come along then, I have no time to waste," Madame Ponnelle called without turning. Liz scurried after her.

A crystal chandelier lit the entry, but the stairs were dark and the end of the hallway dim. The maroon carpet was plush under her feet; the hardwood floors gleamed with wax. The three doors that opened off the hallway were all shut tight. No pictures, not even a mirror, hung on the walls of the passageway.

Madame Ponnelle opened the last door into a large square room furnished with a gleaming grand piano, two straight chairs of dark wood and pristine velveteen, and a music stand. A full-length mirror stood in one corner. The walls were paneled in white wood below and papered with a vine pattern above. Framed black-and-white photographs—some head shots, some performance stills—lined three walls like so many small windows. Liz would have liked a closer look, but her escort demanded her attention.

"The next time you come here, Miss Morgan, you will come through the gate and round the back of the house. The entrance to the studio is there. I have a waiting room across the hall."

Liz only just kept herself from asking how she was supposed to have known this. "Fine," she said with a short nod.

"Very good. We start with the basics. Do you know how to breathe?"

"I—uh, yes." Liz laughed nervously, sure the answer was more mysterious.

"Stand up straight." To Liz's surprise, Madame Ponnelle approached her and put one hand on her belly and the other in the small of her back. "Inhale."

Liz did as she was told, aware of the pressure of the hands on her body.

"Let it all out and then in again; push against my hands."

Liz exhaled and filled her lungs with a rush.

"Hold it. Now let it out slowly, evenly. That's it." She nodded, stepping back. "Well enough. You've studied voice before?" She seemed suspicious of Liz's vocal virginity.

"Never. I was a wind player." Her left hand, deep in her pocket, felt clammy.

"What do you play?"

"I used to play flute. But not anymore."

"And now you wish to sing?"

"Well, yes."

"Why?"

"I'm doing *Mikado* with G-Triple-S-G. I'd like some help." She stopped, suddenly wary of voicing her ambition.

"I train professionals. Were you aware of that?"

"Not particularly, no. Giles Offeryn gave me your name."

"Did he?"

Suddenly Liz did not feel up to the game. "I'm sorry to waste your time. Maybe he didn't realize—"

"Miss Morgan, as you will be paying me for my time, you might just as well let me finish the interview. If Mr. Offeryn sent you to me he had his reasons."

"Yes, ma'am."

Madame Ponnelle went to the piano but did not sit down. Her wrinkled left hand, streaked with blue veins and weighed down with rings, played a five-note descending scale. Her right hand gestured to Liz as if bestowing a gift.

"Sing that. Gently. Inhale, but don't hold your breath; send it right out again and let the note ride on the air. Sing on 'ah.'"

Liz drew a deep breath, let the air float, and placed a note on its surface. A pleasing sensation hummed in her sinuses, tickling the bridge of her nose.

"Quietly," Madame Ponnelle said, and Liz repeated the phrase.

"Finish the phrase; stay strong."

She did it again. They worked up and down the range of Liz's voice, Madame Ponnelle tinkering and adjusting everything she heard. Her enigmatic gaze never left Liz's face. Disconcerted, Liz closed her eyes, not only to escape the scrutiny, but also to feel the sound buzz in her head, against her eardrums.

When they stopped, Madame Ponnelle sat down on the piano bench.

"You would practice?"

"Of course."

"You would commit to coming twice a week?"

"Whenever I can afford it."

The woman was silent again, but this time her eyes scanned the engagement calendar on top of the piano. "I teach in London on Mondays and Wednesdays. It seems I do not have any openings here in Cardiff at this time," she said, and she looked shrewdly at Liz for her reaction.

Liz was not surprised. She had been fortunate to work with Julia Bradshaw, who did not play these ego games. But she knew that it was not uncommon for the best teachers to turn down a student, only to call the next week with a "temporary opening" that eventually became permanent. Sometimes they even expected prospective students to beg. She nodded. "I won't take up any more of your time then." She pulled out her check.

Madame took the thirty pounds and pursed her lips. "You understand, I must be available for the university music department, for the serious students."

"I understand. Thanks anyway."

Madame did not call that week. Nor the next. Liz would not beg.

Chapter 13

IN SPITE OF HER INAUSPICIOUS beginning, Liz doggedly worked on the *Mikado* music in every spare moment, and she soon began to enjoy herself. In the second week of music rehearsal she lived for the newly discovered sensation of laughter rippling through her when she answered a cue and her surprised voice unwound itself from its hesitancy. But just when she began to possess the bright music, the treacherous nights of staging rehearsal started.

After Giles spent two weeks teaching the cast to sing *Mikado* as he wanted it sung, the security of hovering around the piano vanished: he turned them over to Huw, who began to stage the scenes. Huw told the actors where to stand and how to deliver their lines, and he coached them in gestures, expressions, and reactions. Blocking for the show developed inch by painful inch, with Liz crawling sluggishly behind the others as Huw gave them every step, every movement. Her body wanted to be Liz, hands in pockets and weight on her heels, not Pitti-Sing, gesturing wildly and flying around the stage on stockinged toes.

The minutely choreographed musical numbers required Liz to be alert at all times. Even when she concentrated on the capers to the exclusion of the music, she frequently found herself thinking about a move when the time for action had passed. When this happened, Caroline would calmly prepare to start yet again, but one night Diana threw up her hands.

"For God's sake, start moving when you're meant to!"

"I'm trying." Liz paced off the entrance again, whispering the lyrics to herself.

"You're throwing everyone off."

Liz whipped around, her face flushing. "I don't know it yet. Get off my back!"

Diana relaxed. "My goodness, they've tossed you in head over ears, haven't they? You'll get it." She patted Liz on the shoulder.

Liz eyed her warily as they returned to their places to start again. Caroline said nothing.

A third week sped by. Liz forgot all the subtle musical details Giles had taught them as she struggled just to be in the right place and remember all the words. A new pianist began to come to rehearsals, and Giles took up his position in the pit so they could get used to him conducting them. He mouthed every word of every song as he led them with the baton. If a singer forgot a line, they could count on him for a cue. Liz found herself relying on him often during rehearsal, though away from the theater she never forgot any of her words.

Her frustration reached a new peak the first time she, Diana, and Caroline raced through "Three Little Maids" onstage, complete with blocking and accompaniment. When Liz gasped out her first little solo line, Giles called from the pit, "Diction, Liz, I can't understand you." He kept going, but her delivery of the next line made him cut off the accompanist.

"No, no, stop. Liz, you must be clearer. Use your lips and teeth. Spit it out. Start with 'One little maid is a bride.'"

But he was not satisfied with her next attempt, either. "I didn't say louder, I said *clearer*," he said.

Liz saw Diana smirk, and behind her she sensed the impatience of each chorister who thought she should have been cast over this newcomer. Giles didn't stop again, but as Liz finished barking out her solo line, he shook his head.

She tried to make a quick escape after rehearsal, carrying her coat and not bothering to put her score in her book bag. But as she went up the stairs onto the stage to head for the stage door, Giles called to her. "Liz! A word?"

She didn't bother going back down the steps, but trudged over and looked down at him in the orchestra pit.

"Liz, you must try to put the sound way out in front of you," he said gently. "Practice just speaking it. Don't sing. Just let all the consonants explode like a percussion instrument. The sound will ride on the vowel."

"That's what I was doing," she said.

His manner cooled. "Well I need more."

Liz went home and worked on it more, spitting out consonants like darts of poison and feeling massively uncomfortable to have stripped word from song. She continued to fret about her diction the next evening as she bumbled through the second, less-well-known trio performed by the three little maids. She paid no attention when Diana repeatedly dropped out.

"It's too fast," Diana finally complained, coming to a full stop. "It may be all right for some people"—this with a disgusted look at Caroline—"but Liz and I simply can't take it so fast."

"Diana, you are a royal pain," Christopher observed from his position upstage.

"I'm trying to help. She won't admit she can't do it," Diana said.

Liz whirled on her. "I wasn't the one—"

"Let Giles do his job and mind your own business," Caroline interrupted.

"He's not doing it." The effort it took Diana to flip her long, shiny hair over her shoulder required her whole body.

Before Liz could protest Giles tossed his baton down on the stand and ran an exasperated hand through his dark hair.

"Diana, you've done this show before. What's the trouble?"

She glanced over her shoulder at Liz.

When he got no reply he turned to Liz. "Well then, Liz? Not possible?"

"I'll learn it." Anger improved her diction substantially. "I was concentrating on the blocking."

"Pass on it tonight, then. You ladies are going to have to practice. We'll do it again on Thursday. Let's not waste any more time."

They moved on to other scenes.

When rehearsal was over Diana turned to Liz as they gathered up their possessions. "He's not always right, you know."

"But I happen to agree with him," Liz said. "And it's his call. Don't do me any favors."

"You needn't suck up to him. It's not like he'll replace you," Diana replied with sudden scorn.

Liz stood for a moment, stilled by fury, before flinging on her coat and storming out of the hall.

* * *

AS HUW GAVE THE BLOCKING for each scene, Liz recorded it in the margins of her score in a bewilderment of arrows and diagrams. Long after the rest of the cast had discarded the script she carried it onstage, running scenes with it tucked under her elbow or holding it before her, a finger marking her place. She seldom referred to it, but she couldn't bring herself to abandon it.

Less than three weeks remained to opening when Liz received her final bit of blocking. In the scene, Koko enlisted the aid of Pooh-Bah and Pitti-Sing to invent details of an execution that never took place.

"I want to use the executioner's sword as a sort of baton that you pass to each other," Huw told them, holding Liz's arm absently as he thought through the scene. "You're all terrified of the Mikado. Especially because you're lying to him." He chuckled and gave her arm a little shake. "After Koko sings his verse the chorus joins in to emphasize his point. He'll come upstage to get away from the Mikado's scrutiny, and he'll catch you about here." He drew Liz to a point mid-stage, and Koko followed. "Now he'll try to force the sword on you and make you pick up the story where he left off, which is just what you *don't* want to do. So I want you to pivot around each other here, twice, and seem like you're arguing the point. You end up with the sword, sort of propelled downstage toward the Mikado against your will. You should be able to do all the business in the chorus tag and be downstage, ready to sing, when Giles cues you."

They experimented with just how much reluctance she could express in the sixteen-bar chorus part, and then Huw leaned up against the pillar of the proscenium to watch them go through the whole scene. Koko quivered through the first verse, staggering under the weight of a wooden scimitar (the "snicker-snee"). Finished, he made for Liz to abdicate the telling of the tale. When he thrust the sword at her, she revolved around him while making it seem as though she was pushing it away. As she did, the script under her arm slipped to the floor and she reached for it with her awkward left hand, blurring the gesture and making her late for her verse.

Huw leapt out of his corner. "Great heavens, Liz, you ought to be off book by this time!" He snatched her score, retreated, and dropped it on the floor at his feet with a thunderous clap. "Again," he commanded with a motion to Giles, who cued the pianist in the tense silence.

Blushing, Liz faltered through her verse, the low G she had to hit an unvoiced stream of air in her dry throat. No one spoke to her at the break.

Chapter 14

THE BRASS BELLS ON THE DOOR barely murmured when Liz entered the bookshop next morning. She shut the door carefully and turned to find Bert behind the counter, watching her with folded arms.

"Hi." She glanced around, looking for Caroline.

He pursed his lips, squinting at her. "There's a woman works here, looks just like you, has about this much energy." He held his hands wide apart. "Would you have seen her?"

She smiled a little and walked around him and into the office, where she found Caroline studying yesterday's receipts.

"Rough night?" Bert asked.

She shrugged off her coat. "Sort of."

"Look you, Caroline says you're doing quite well."

"I'm doing everything wrong," Liz countered, hanging up her coat.

"According to whom?" Bert asked.

She thought about it. "Well, me."

"And what do you know about it?"

She had to smile. "Not much."

"There you are," he said, as if this pronouncement solved her dilemma. Before she could argue with him, he left to check the work at Cygnet.

"You're doing fine. You're just not used to it." Caro calmly flipped through the first post.

"I can't put it together." Liz pressed her skull between her hands. "I was doing okay with the music, but my dialogue is hopeless."

"You're exaggerating. Everyone has that musical drop-off when we start staging. You can't think about two things at once when you're learning."

"We've only got two and a half weeks left! I can't believe that they don't regret casting me."

"Well there's one person who's plenty worried," Caroline said.

"I knew it!" Liz said, her stomach dropping. "Who is it? It's Huw, isn't it? Or is it Giles?"

Caroline leaned close to Liz with wide eyes. "It's *you*," she said deliberately—and laughed when Liz threw up her hands at her lack of sympathy.

"It's not Covent Garden. Don't take it so seriously," she called over her shoulder as she went out to help a customer.

* * *

LIZ APPROACHED CHRISTOPHER the next evening as he stood at his usual post, watching the bright stage from the dim half-light of the orchestra pit. "Hey, Christopher?"

He turned to her and smiled. "Liz?"

"Could you go through my scenes with me and tell me what I'm doing wrong? You're really good at this."

His smile broadened. She was sure he was trying not to laugh at her. "Your place or mine?"

Her face burned. "I'm serious."

He threw back his head and laughed.

"Forget it," she muttered, turning away.

"Now, now. I'll settle for supper with you some evening when this is over and we have time. Can you come an hour early tomorrow?" His face still showed amusement.

"Yes. Here?" she asked warily.

The creases around his grin deepened again. "Have you a better idea?"

* * *

THE NEXT EVENING CHRISTOPHER got the keys to the theater from the porter, and Liz met him at the stage door. He pulled open the fire door, and she followed him into the passageway that led to the stage. A single uncovered bulb lit the way. He disappeared into the wings stage right to find the light board. Liz brushed past the black curtain panels and walked out onto the dark stage. She stood near the center of the wooden floor, feeling strangely off balance.

Darkness hung above her. She could see only a few tiny lights here and there, the ones marking the catwalk over the stage. Before vertigo could overtake her, she looked out into the house. The doors showed a faint crack of light from the lobby. She heard Christopher talking to himself as he looked for the right switch. She looked up again, her eyes adjusting and making out lights and ropes and painted backdrops in the tower above her.

Help me, Mum. I can do this.

Light stabbed at her eyes as Chris found the right switch. She felt her pupils adjust to the brightness as the vast, starless firmament was pushed aside and she found herself staring into the light. A little bolt of excitement zipped through her at the sensation of being center stage in the spotlight. Rubbing her eyes, she turned to watch Chris as he flipped switches and gauged the amount of light he could produce. He put the house lights on full and with a final flourish turned on the spotlight over the conductor's stand.

"There, that should keep Giles happy."

Liz rolled her eyes but said nothing. She draped her coat over a chair and put her score on the seat. Pushing her fan into the back pocket of her jeans and rolling up her sleeves, she turned to Chris.

"This will work best if you run your lines with Caroline and I can go to the back of the house and see how it seems."

Though she seemed to make light of Liz's anxieties, Caroline had willingly agreed to join them, but she had yet to arrive.

Christopher looked at his watch. "While we're waiting for her why don't you go through that place in the first act finale, where you're teasing Katisha. I'll be Katisha." He took up a position downstage, folded his arms, and let a sour look take over his face.

Liz went through the scene, poking at him with her fan and singing, she hoped, the way Giles wanted it. When the music changed from four-four time to three-quarter time, she missed her footwork. She stopped, shaking her head. "All right. What am I doing wrong?"

"I think you—"

"You're watching your feet," Caroline said, coming onstage from behind Liz.

"You're late," Christopher said.

She ignored him, focused on Liz. "Try it again, and this time don't look at your feet when you do the grapevine step." She went over to the corner of the stage and down the steps, watching Liz over her shoulder.

Liz tried again. Chris stood with his hands on his hips, not resuming his character but instead scrutinizing her every step. To Liz's surprise, it worked. She did it again and found it easier still.

Caroline left her bag and coat in the first row of seats and came back onstage, nodding with satisfaction. "See how much better that is?"

"It really is. Thanks."

"Why don't you girls run your first scene," Christopher broke in. "I'll watch and toss in Diana's lines." He sprang down over the apron of the stage and into the orchestra pit five feet below, something they had all been admonished not to do, and strode up the aisle into the middle of the auditorium.

Liz and Caroline started their run-through. Every few lines Christopher stopped to make suggestions, most of them reminders that Liz was going to have to be seen and heard by the audience. "Bigger gestures," he bellowed from the middle of the house, waving his arm. "I can't hear you," he called more than once. "Open your eyes wider; lift your chin. Let us see your face."

And nearly every time she opened her mouth, he told her to slow down.

She was able to lose some of her self-consciousness as they continued, but when Giles and Diana arrived she stopped mid-scene and sat down on the apron of the stage.

"Good evening, ladies, Christopher," Giles said pleasantly. He put his satchel on the chair behind the conductor's stand and unbuttoned his coat.

"Since all of you are here early, let's run 'Three Little Maids' quickly. Christopher, can you help us out on the piano? I want to go up in the back of the house and see how the balance is."

"And see if he can humiliate me again," Liz muttered. Caroline shushed her.

Liz thought her apprehension was about to be proven valid when Giles stopped them only a short way into the number, but he was calling to Diana to bring out her part. His wife pouted, but he ignored her. Liz couldn't decide if she was glad or disappointed when he said nothing to her.

They finished three hours later. As Liz was struggling into her jacket, eager to get home to bed, Giles approached her. There was no avoiding him.

"Diana tells me you're having some difficulty," he said. "Can I help?"

Liz frowned. "You could stop picking on me."

He pulled back slightly. "That's not my intention."

"There hasn't been a rehearsal when you haven't made a big deal about something I'm doing wrong."

"That is my job," Giles said. "You said you had never performed before. I thought you might appreciate some help."

"I've done plenty of performing," Liz snapped. "I'm a musician."

"Perhaps we can work on a few things sometime without the rest of the cast. You have a dialogue rehearsal tomorrow, do you not? I can make a little time to go over some problem areas. If that would help." He spoke evenly, but she suspected his teeth were grinding.

"I guess so."

Diana appeared, grasping her husband's arm. "Giles, I need you to talk to Huw for me. He's blocked me behind the chorus."

"Tomorrow," he said to Liz, never looking at his wife.

* * *

WHEN LIZ ARRIVED AT REHEARSAL the following night, Giles was fiddling with the piano as usual. The ragtime piece sounded familiar, but it wasn't until he stopped abruptly and shifted into blues harmonies that she realized he was playing, or transforming, her own second act solo.

She smiled in recognition and greeting.

"Good evening. Are you in a better mood tonight?" He slid a bass chord from his left hand, added the minor transposition of the melody, and then repeated them together.

"I am. I'm sorry I snapped at you. I'm not used to being mediocre."

"You're doing fine. A little polish, and you'll be a threat to Caroline." The suggestion that she could ever aspire to Caroline's wicked comic sense and beautiful voice made Liz laugh, and Giles smiled.

Relaxing a little, Liz pulled out her score and flipped to the second act solo. Giles played it without his embellishments. After she sang it through once he began to shape it for her.

"Think through the line, right through the rests, all in one breath. Then just give the staccato notes a little pulse with the diaphragm. You won't chop it up so much that way." As he described what he meant his hands cradled his words.

Liz used her years of musicianship to translate what Giles wanted, glad to not have to think about left and right and how many steps to take downstage.

As he helped her shape the phrases and strengthen her tone, it occurred to her fleetingly that he was far and away the best musician she had ever worked with. It annoyed her that he saw her as a hapless amateur.

"Just so, I knew you'd get it," he said when she did it to his satisfaction. "It can be a bear to sing pleasantly, the way it's written, but that's lovely." He paged through the score for her next solo. "What did you mean last night, about being a musician?"

"I'm a—I was a flautist."

"Was?"

She had not had to tell the story in a long time; the ending was no longer the ending. Cautiously she began to explain, not sure she would be able to finish.

"I was a performance major at the San Francisco Conservatory."

"Did you not do well?"

She turned to him with a flicker of annoyance, but something in his face reassured her that he did not believe this. She smiled lopsidedly. "I wish I had been average. I know how that sounds, but it's the truth."

"I'd like to hear you play sometime," he ventured.

His words set off a small implosion under Liz's sternum. Memory brought aching tears to her throat, making it hard to continue.

"I don't play anymore."

He persisted. "Why not?"

She extended her left hand, flexing her fingers gingerly. The middle fingers did not move with the others. The scars were permanent tracings of white fire in the weak light.

"Last May I was in an accident with a drunk driver. My hand was badly hurt, and when they got it put back together it just didn't work well enough." She kept her voice unemotional.

He reached over and took her hand, examining it closely. At last he met her eyes without letting go. Her composure teetered.

"They did three surgeries, but there was too much nerve damage."

"How terribly sad," he said softly. "I can guess how hard it must be to lose the use of your hand."

She was sure he could, feeling his hand around hers, his fingers strong and precise. "People kept telling me how lucky I was just to be alive, but for a while I felt like it would have been better if I'd been killed." She saw a shadow in Giles's eyes as she admitted this. "It was everything; it was who I *was*." She held her breath in an attempt to keep the tears back.

The backstage fire door clanged, and Diana sauntered in. Liz tried to disengage her hand, and Giles released it with a friendly squeeze. Liz was acutely aware of how Diana slowed, watching them with narrowed eyes.

Giles stood and greeted his wife with a mild kiss, which she did not return. "Diana. You aren't called tonight."

"I thought perhaps I could help you." She settled her bag on a seat and shrugged out of her coat, arching her back in a languid stretch.

Liz glared at her.

"That's very good of you, but I need to work through a few things with Liz on her own."

"I can't see why she needs special help, anyway."

"It's still new to her." Giles smiled, picked up Diana's coat, and held it for her to put on.

Liz rippled the pages of her score a couple of times. "Can we keep going? Huw is going to want me pretty soon."

"Of course." He didn't look at her. "I'll be home shortly," he said, still holding Diana's coat. "Don't let me keep you waiting."

Diana slipped her arms into the sleeves and collected her bag slowly, watching Liz drum her fingers on her score.

"I can hardly wait to hear the improvement," she said. She gave her husband a deliberate kiss on the mouth and strolled out the way she had come.

Liz watched her leave and then turned on him. "You know, I'm getting sick of—"

"Let's start on page one-ninety, shall we?" Giles began to play without waiting for her, and she picked up the solo mid-phrase.

* * *

WHEN THEY FINISHED REHEARSING Giles continued to divert the conversation firmly away from his wife. "Have you started lessons yet?"

"No," Liz admitted. "I sang for Madame Ponnelle, but she hasn't called me, and now this seems to be taking all my free time, so I thought I'd wait till after we open."

He leaned both arms along the piano and looked at her with the intensity she'd seen in him when he was listening for tuning and balance. "Do you hope to replace the flute with your voice?"

Her desire to confide in him quivered like a drop of water at the end of a twig, but at the last second she balked. "No, this is just—an experiment."

Instantly she regretted not telling him. But the opportunity was gone, for he shrugged and began gathering his music.

Chapter 15

THERE WAS ONE SITUATION FOR which none of Liz's mentors could prepare her, and that was the arrival of the orchestra ten days before opening. When she pulled open the door to the backstage area the familiar arpeggios and experiments of the tuning ritual beckoned to her. Sharp odors of rosin and valve oil, and the softer smells of wood and musty cases, bewitched her. She drew a deep, slightly unsteady breath, and strolled out onto the stage from the wings.

A couple of dozen musicians gathered amid a crowd of chairs and music stands, community volunteers and university students. Giles stood before them, focused on the score. Occasionally he would touch a place with his finger and glance up, checking the direction in which he would send a particular cue. The cast milled expectantly; the arrival of the orchestra meant that opening night was imminent.

Liz slipped down the steps and found a seat halfway up the house, stretched her feet out in the aisle, and turtled into her sweater, glancing around. Not a single person was aware of the tensing of her gut, the shallowness of her breathing. But she felt them around her, every last unsuspecting one of them who thought of her as a singer.

The chirps and groans subsided as the orchestra came to rest. Giles gave them some preliminary suggestions, although Liz could not distinguish exactly what he said. Sitting behind the conductor disconcerted her. She wanted to leave but could not stir as Giles raised his baton. She drew in her breath as though she sat in that chair under the conductor's nose, waiting for a downbeat.

When it came, initiating a solid march punctuated by tympani, she expected the chords to rattle and the flutes to whistle through her like the wind through a bleached carcass on the desert. She waited for longing to squeeze her heart like open harmony. But her instinctive response to rhythm and harmony eased her resistance, and she relaxed, following the overture like a familiar motorway. Melodic lines wove in and out, invoking scenes with subtle hypnosis. When some of Pitti-Sing's music came laughing out of the pit she smiled in spite of herself, her toe tapping.

She was glad that she would not be hidden down in the orchestra pit this time. Gladder still that she would be onstage in that bright follow spot, inciting laughter and applause. The sound of the flute rose over the orchestra. And then her toe stopped tapping. Her smile faded. Her flute had been more than an object. Her hands missed the way the metal warmed like a living thing when it was held or played. And here she was, turning her back on it. She sighed.

The orchestra finished with a flourish, and she managed to join her applause with that of the others who had been listening. Giles kept the players poised with his raised baton and tossed a quick smile of acknowledgment over his shoulder. "Going on," he called to the cast, and gave the downbeat to continue into Act One. The unprepared men's chorus, hearing their music, materialized from all directions, scrambling onto the stage over the apron and assembling from the wings in an untidy crowd. Giles stopped the orchestra.

"Try it again. It's not too soon to know your cues, gentlemen," Huw warned them.

Liz had at least twenty minutes before her entrance. She hurried downstairs and shouldered through the swinging door to the ladies' room. Someone stood at the hand basin. She stopped with a squeak of her rubber soles.

Diana ducked abruptly away from the mirror, but not before Liz got a look at her. Fluorescent light and white tile did nothing to cool her swollen eyelids and tear-stained cheeks.

"Uh—scuse me," Liz muttered, backing toward the door.

Diana dabbed at her eyes. "I was just leaving." She glanced at Liz. "You needn't run off."

Liz pushed her hands into her pockets, shivering in the echoey room. "Listen, just for the record, I'm not interested in your husband. And it's mutual," she offered.

"That's what he says too."

"I'm sure he cares for you."

"Oh, you're just like everyone else," Diana snapped, snatching makeup off the basin and thrusting it into her huge bag. "All of you think he's so kind and so nice. He's nothing but a sanctimonious bastard. He just wants to punish me."

"Punish you for what?" Liz couldn't help but ask the question, much as she wanted to escape.

Diana whirled to face her. "Somehow he's decided that it's all *my* fault that we had to leave Paris. It's all *my* fault that he had to give up his sodding career. So now he's always trying to get back at me, isn't he? Flirting with you, giving you my role."

Liz felt the chill of the tile wall press against her shoulder blades through her turtleneck. "Jeez, he isn't flirting with me. Get that through your thick head. And Pitti-Sing, that was Huw's decision."

"Giles told me I couldn't do it," Diana insisted, new tears dragging mascara down her cheeks. Her slender fingers twisted a handkerchief. "Well, it's all his fault if I can't," she said, abruptly changing directions. "After that bloody miserable pregnancy, and being sick so long. And now he hates me, he does!" She wept, turned to the wall, her shaking hand covering her mouth.

Liz watched, paralyzed, and wished fervently for someone to interrupt them. She dared not offer even the most sincere comfort to Diana, so she stood, silent and uncertain.

This has nothing to do with me. It's about her pride.

She knew about pride. Her own ego had made her relationship with Titus a ménage à trois. Even if the accident hadn't happened, she would always have been jealous of his successes.

Giles had the power to give Diana success. And he had not done so.

Confusing and astonishing sympathy overwhelmed Liz at the memory of Titus. She reached out and touched Diana's shoulder hesitantly. "He probably meant you weren't ready right now. If you've been sick and all, maybe he thought you needed a little more time."

There was no response. The tinny room amplified Diana's grief, compelling Liz to try again. "There'll be other shows."

Diana took a few slow, shuddering breaths, her rib cage pulling hard. "I know." She wiped her eyes, not looking at Liz, blew her nose, and faced the mirror again. "And you'll be back in the States by then," she said more briskly. "Whatever he thinks he's doing by flirting with you, I'm sure you can see that you mustn't encourage him." She ignored, or missed, the astonishment on Liz's face. "And you needn't tell anyone about—" Her hands fluttered, taking in the entire scene. "All this." She slid a calculating look at Liz. "I will get Giles to want me again. And since you insist that there's nothing between you, why don't you go flirt with Christopher?" She checked her face in the mirror again. "He'll sleep with anybody."

Liz caught her breath at the swiftness and cruelty of the attack. "Nobody will hear about this from me," she agreed. "But people have already drawn their own conclusions about the two of you."

Without stopping to see what effect this had on Diana, Liz slammed out the door and stomped up the stairs, taking them two at a time when she heard the strains of music that preceded her first number. She made it with time to spare and stood a little apart from Caroline, pacing in a confined square.

Look what she got for trying to smooth things over that were none of her concern. Her job was to concentrate on *Mikado*, to focus, and to be ready. Instead she had given Diana another chance to insult her. She fumed as she waited to go on. She should leave peacemaking to someone else. It didn't mix with performance.

In a few moments Diana sailed right into the midst of the crew, daring anyone to mention her puffy face, and stood in the upstage wing calmly waiting for the entrance. Over her head Caroline shot a questioning look at Liz, who shrugged and focused on the stage.

Suddenly her mood scattered her inhibitions as if before a furious wind. She barely marked the triangles and violins playing the entrance. As she sang her first solo line she knew that her feet had propelled her to the right spot and her instinct had put the right words on her tongue, so that thinking about it was almost a danger. The stage was hers. No one could take that from her. She allowed herself to be good, insisted on it the way she had once insisted on being the best of flute players.

In the pit, Giles's gestures were contained and distracted, his cues present, his personality absent. His eyes followed his wife who, Liz had to admit, brazened it out well, although her voice had a creaky sound to it. She banished them both, drew inward for confidence, and projected Pitti-Sing beyond the pit—finally, Christopher later told her, possessing the stage.

She left the stage when her first sequence was over and sat in the house, gazing at the crooked fingers of her left hand where they were spread over her knee. Onstage, everything had come to a complete halt so Huw could repair some frayed blocking.

"The little toad!" Caroline whispered, slipping into the seat next to her. She must have heard gossip about Liz's encounter with Diana, although Liz could not imagine how. "She's jealous, that's all."

"Jealous of what?"

"You got his attention. It doesn't matter why."

"I'm not trying to break up her marriage."

"She's doing that all by herself. He isn't the kind to fool around." She cast a sly glance in Liz's direction. "But I could hardly blame him."

Liz turned on her. "Caroline!"

"Oh, I know there's nothing going on."

"I barely know him."

"But she thinks the role is a sign of his favor."

"That's crazy!"

Caroline nodded indifferently. "Yes. But that's how it is around here some-times. Do you want me to talk to him?"

"Don't you dare!"

"Someone should."

"Stay out of it," Liz insisted.

Caroline gazed at her. "I wouldn't expect you to put up with it."

"I never said I would."

But neither had she said she would confront him. Through the evening, mistakes she thought she'd conquered returned to haunt her. Her voice, for which she had developed a tolerant fondness, sounded common and unlovely to her. The charm of the madrigal vanished as she forced her harmonies. Exposed on the top line of the quintet, she heard her voice go sharp and cringed when Giles frowned, though he did not even look at her.

* * *

THE RAIN RESUMED IN TORRENTS as Liz walked home. She half expected thunderclaps and lightning bolts to charge the darkness. One moment her fury was for Pan, who had taken his flute and abandoned her; the next it was for Diana and her petty accusations.

"Liz!"

Her name shouted over the rain pulled her out of herself. She lifted the brim on the hood of her jacket to peer out from under it. A battered little Austin mini whipped over to the curb across the street, and Giles waved to her. She walked faster, head down in the driving rain.

"Elizabeth!"

She whipped around. "What do you want?"

"I'll drive you home."

"I'm almost there." She didn't budge. The rain stung her face.

"I can't have you catching cold this close to opening."

"Why do you care?"

"Damn it, Liz, get in the car!"

Subtly pleased to have rippled his patience, she crossed behind the car, through the rushing gutter, and onto the curb. She got in and wedged herself against the door, crossing her arms and feeling her socks squish coldly in her shoes.

"Up three more blocks, a right turn," she told him.

The car dragged up the hill, sounding like a large windup toy. Giles had to speak loudly to be heard.

"Caroline says that I owe you an apology."

"*You* haven't done anything," she shot back. She sensed him turning his head toward her, but she stared straight ahead.

"I will speak to my wife."

She could hardly hear him over the engine. "Why didn't you give her the damn role and save us all a lot of trouble? It's the second building," she added, pointing.

He shifted and slowed around the corner, then pulled over near her door. Before answering her he yanked the parking brake up and folded his arms across the steering wheel. "To be honest I don't think she's particularly suited to the role. But certainly not right now. She's been—unwell, and her singing is not good. It isn't as noticeable when she's in the middle of a trio, but I'm sure you've noticed that it's most awkward in the finale, when she doubles Caroline up to that high B-flat. We couldn't have her in all those exposed places. At least you sing in tune."

"Jeez, thanks for that."

He winced. "Sorry. I didn't mean it quite like that."

"Are you sorry you cast me?" she asked suddenly.

He did not answer right away. She guessed that he didn't want to tell her his regrets.

"It wasn't my decision," he finally said, looking away.

"But if it had been up to you?"

To her surprise he smiled. "You've truly impressed me. I hope we'll see you again."

"Really. And how would your wife feel about that?" she asked quietly. She put her hand on the door but kept her eyes on his face.

"Try to stay clear of her. We're having a rough go of it, but she's angry with me, not you."

The hell she is. "You better not drive me home anymore then. She might misunderstand." She shoved the door open, but Giles's voice brought her back.

"You won't quit?"

She laughed suddenly in the gloomy night. "Quit? You just try and make me. Good night, Maestro. See you in the pit." She dashed up the walk. After stabbing her key in the lock, she turned. He was there, waiting on her. She tossed him a comic salute and let herself in out of the rain.

Chapter 16

THE PRODUCTION ROSE WITH THE unwieldy sway of the Mikado's garishly decorated litter. The tech crew added a new dimension of chaos to the rehearsals. Lighting changed disconcertingly mid-scene as a bluish moonrise blossomed into an orange sunburst. Sets sprang up around the stage, obscuring what had before been perfectly obvious entrances. To her delight, Liz acquired a kimono like a satin spring sky, and a black wig with a long braid. The makeup designer showed her how to transform her eyes and cheeks. When she looked in a mirror, Pitti-Sing looked back.

On opening night she got to the theater compulsively early, donning makeup and costume before most of the cast had arrived. Then she paced, unable to settle anywhere, absorbing the fragments that would eventually materialize into a production. After an eternity, Huw gave them some final notes. Giles ran them through some of the ensembles to warm up their voices. And at last, the stage manager called for beginners. Relieved, Liz headed for the stage, her toes cold in their *tabis* on the concrete floor.

Caroline, who had been quiet and withdrawn all evening, caught her elbow as she shuffled by. "We're not on for six numbers," she reminded Liz.

"I know. I want to listen to the overture."

Her friend smiled. "Break a leg, Liz. I'm glad you stayed."

"Me too. Break a leg."

She hovered backstage, enjoying the coil of stage fright in her belly. The black-clad tech crew made a few last-minute adjustments to the set. The men's chorus milled in the low lights, unrecognizable in their complicated headdresses and severe makeup. Beyond the curtain she could hear the hum of the expectant crowd and hugged herself.

The stage manager stood at his wooden podium, ready to give all the lighting and tech cues. Giles sat beside him, on the edge of a chair, looking elegant as men do in evening clothes. His baton was balanced loosely in his fingers, and his eyes were closed.

She had avoided him for the last week, polite but reserved whenever he spoke to her, wary that any exchange might be deliberately misconstrued by his spouse. She wanted no more confidences, no more of the pain of their relationship to bleed onto her. She hesitated, watching him, and then padded over to him.

"Ready, Maestro?"

He opened his eyes immediately. "Yes, of course. This is the fun part."

She laughed out loud, and the stage manager shushed her with a gesture toward the filling auditorium. She clapped a hand over her mouth, but Giles smiled at her.

Christopher materialized out of the shadowy figures onstage, swaggering over with his hands resting on his added Pooh-Bah girth.

"Nervous?" he inquired, so close to Liz that she had to look up at him.

"A bit. But I didn't know I'd like it quite so much."

He grinned. "You must have, or why would you have kept on."

Giles stood up and moved a little away, his fingers fiddling with the baton.

"I had good teachers," Liz said, watching him go.

"He's taken, you know."

Liz peered at Chris in the shadowy light. "What?"

"Giles. Married."

She rolled her eyes.

"Set your sights on someone available," he advised her. "Someone charming, intelligent, who isn't such a—"

"You wouldn't by any chance be talking about yourself?"

His smile broadened. "Quite possibly."

At precisely seven thirty, the stage manager shooed Giles out to the orchestra. Liz listened for the familiar rise of applause as the audience spotted him, followed by expectant silence.

"You know," Christopher said softly behind her, "you quite intrigue me."

Just as she turned to him the overture began, and her pulse rate surged, her senses stimulated.

"You did promise to go to supper with me when this is all over," he reminded her.

"So I did. And so I will," she replied. She half turned away, her attention distracted by the orchestra. As the atmosphere built toward the curtain, she felt Christopher's arm go around her shoulders, and after a second she leaned into him.

Though she felt that the show was under-rehearsed (not uncommon, and not altogether undesirable, Caroline had reassured her), things seemed to go off as planned, the audience cooperating nicely as she stood in the wings watching every moment. The first act had deceptive momentum among all its silly songs and witty dialogue. The thirty-five minutes she had to wait until her first entrance flashed by. Before she knew it she was bursting onto the stage and into the brilliant light. The crowd demanded intensity, and she gave it. The other actors required energy, and she felt equal to the charge. She was unshakable, unstoppable.

Her own scenes were over before she could mark them, though her delivery brought chuckles that were not lost on her. She barely felt she had been off stage at all when the first act finale was upon them. Katisha, the contralto nemesis of all the characters, hurled threats and accusations as she entered. With every phrase she uttered, the rest of the cast pounced on her with increasingly fortissimo blasts of pseudo-Japanese curses. With each repetition of the passage, Liz felt the solidarity of the singers and orchestra that Giles had worked so hard to achieve. Not one missed cue in all the complex timing. They sang as one.

The excitement built, the voices snapping out the responses with precision. Suddenly, a split second early, one voice leapt out like a shot bird. Giles stabbed the air, the real cue sharp with annoyance. The stage erupted in the correct entrance, the explosion of sound covering the mistake instantly. But his eyes sought the culprit.

Everyone onstage knew that Diana had violated the pristine silence he had so carefully crafted. Liz could scarcely contain her shameless glee. The music changed, quickened, and drove through her, became her pulse. "*We'll hear no more ill-omened owl. To joy we soar despite your scowl, the echo of our festival shall rise triumphant over all!*"

Liz paced again at the intermission, gulping water and fluttering her fan in her hot face. She saw neither Giles nor Diana, but she exchanged excited chatter with nearly everyone else. Her mind raced ahead to the second act. It began with her solo and continued into her favorite moments onstage, her funniest lines, and her best opportunity to draw sweet laughter out of the crowd. She could hardly wait to discover how well she could play them.

The audience's appreciation made Liz bold. Her voice rang, her gestures flourished, her lines were crisp with arch calculation previously unknown to her. As Pitti-Sing she watched Koko try to convince the Mikado that he had performed the required execution. As Liz she readied herself for the spotlight ahead. Soon enough it came, and she waited for Koko to finish his verse, to thrust her in cowardly fashion at the Mikado.

But even as she inclined her body to meet him, Curtis flew right past her and cowered behind a chorister, the sword forgotten in his grasp. Awareness of a mistake electrified the stage. The chorus sang louder. Liz froze.

The blocking for the next verse, her verse, depended on having that sword in her hand.

She was holding her breath. She let it go in a rush. *Do something*, she prompted herself.

Indignation took over. She drew herself up, Pitti-Sing-the-Daring, and stalked over to Koko. She gave him a look that clearly communicated her disgust with his ineptitude. She wrenched the sword away from his surprised hand and tossed her head. The wooden prop had been replaced with the real thing in the last week of rehearsal, a weapon that threw light back from its blade like a whistle through cold air. She took the soothing weight of it with both hands, and bearing it with great respect, she padded downstage, aware of the charged silence now that the orchestra and chorus had finished. Control she'd not known she possessed forced her to walk slowly and steadily. With demure confidence she bowed low to the Mikado and flashed him her most winning smile. As she drew in her breath, Giles cued the orchestra, and they continued as if this endless silence between verses was perfectly normal.

Locked in the scene, adjusting it as she proceeded, she was only peripherally aware of anyone but Simon, the Mikado himself. She flirted madly through the verse, dodging his seeking hands with tantalizing glee instead of the apprehension Huw had wanted. Simon followed her lead, changing his own reactions to match hers. A playful, confident Pitti-Sing warbled her lies and gracefully eluded the Mikado as he lunged for her. As the verse ended she held her head high, making it clear that she had accomplished more than Koko, and casually handed the sword to a wide-eyed Christopher-Pooh-Bah.

When at last she finished the quintet and came off stage, the blood shook through her veins, and she wanted to sit down. Though she had strayed far, she was satisfied that the audience never knew. But the cast knew. "Well done," Simon whispered. Caroline squeezed her shoulder as they passed backstage.

* * *

AFTER THE SHOW, LIZ LINGERED a long time in the lobby of the theater conversing with the audience, a pleasure forgotten in the last year. As a flute soloist, she had accepted compliments with as much grace, but without the astonished gratitude she felt now. As she talked to a couple who were friends of her aunt and uncle, Huw came over to her, beaming.

He took her hands in his own cool, gnarled ones. "Liz, you nearly fooled me. Even I wasn't sure that wasn't my blocking with the sword."

She laughed. "I'm glad you thought it was okay."

"Absolutely. In fact, I'd like to keep it the way you played it. We'll work it out at the pickup rehearsal on Tuesday."

"Really?"

"You did a marvelous job," he assured her. "Like a veteran."

By the time she had shed her costume most of the chorus had gone, headed for the party. The principals loitered here and there in the dressing area, discussing the show.

She thought she had the washroom to herself, but when she lifted her dripping face from the basin of warm water, she glanced in the mirror and caught Giles's eye. He was waiting to speak to her. Resigned, she turned around, blotting with a towel. Giles spoke before she could form an insincere apology for the time she had taken.

"Nicely done."

She grinned in relief. "Thanks for not starting without me."

"I wondered how long you could milk it. You were quite composed, not to rush."

"Well, Christopher's been yelling at me for a month to take my time. I guess it sank in." She mopped with her threadbare towel at the water trickling down her neck. "You know, I can't quite believe this is the first time you've ever conducted. You're really very good."

"The first—oh, it's not the first by any means. My first G and S, yes. But I've been at it for quite a few years now." He peered at her. "Tell me, have you given any more thought to voice lessons?"

"Now that the show is open I'm going to start looking again."

"You sang for Genevieve Ponnelle. You ought to follow up with her."

His interest piqued her curiosity. "Why?"

"You have potential. And I work for her."

"I see. So you get a commission?" Liz smiled, teasing him.

"Just have a go. See what she says."

"Maybe." The woman had already summarily rejected her. And Liz still wasn't ready to beg.

Before Giles could say more, Diana appeared and twined herself around him. "Come on, you can't still be needing help." The words were teasing, but her eyes were challenging.

Liz opened her mouth to say something rude, but Giles smoothly parried. "I was suggesting that she go over and sing for Genevieve Ponnelle."

Liz bit her lip, knowing that he had given the best possible response. But Diana looked Liz up and down with an expressively raised eyebrow, a gesture that would have been brilliant if she had ever used it onstage.

"Maybe Ponnelle can help her."

It was all Liz could do not to reply, to follow Giles's peaceable lead. This time she saw him catch back a retort, but he only said, "Are you ready to leave?"

"Oh, was I holding you up?" Diana left the room with a backward glance of triumph at having had the last word. Giles hesitated, looking as if he wanted to say something to excuse his wife's behavior. The silence seemed almost humid.

Simon lumbered in to occupy the sink space next to Liz, interrupting the moment. His T-shirt clung to his rotund torso, clammy with sweat. The stark Noh makeup stopped abruptly a couple of inches down his neck, contrasting with his pink skin. He gave her a small bow.

"Well, well, a star is born—is that not what they say in California?"

Liz managed to smile up at him silently.

"Let me know what happens," Giles said, and he squeezed her elbow lightly before leaving the room.

The first layer of makeup removed, Liz started down the hall to her cubicle, walking slowly, a half smile turning up one side of her face.

"There you are!" Christopher came bounding down the hall, grabbed her by the shoulders, and kissed her. She staggered back a step, looking at him blankly.

"What a superb job! I've been taking credit for you all evening," he announced.

For a fraction of a second indignation crept up her spine, but just as quickly she recalled his help and laughed instead.

"You'll have to fight with Caroline for the honors."

"I taught her everything she knows," he said, dismissing the soprano.

Liz doubted that, but she allowed him the claim, basking in his exuberant attention.

He walked her down the hall with a possessive arm around her shoulders. "You will be here for *Pinafore* in the fall?"

She didn't bother to ask if they would have her back. "Is there a role for me?"

"I think we could make a lovely Hebe out of you."

"Then of course I'll be back."

Chapter 17

TWO WEEKS LATER, THE COMPANY bow at the closing matinee left Liz wishing for one more scene to steal. Before she was even out of her costume, the show began to fade. As she washed off her makeup, all the chatter in the dressing rooms anticipated the impending party; *Mikado* already lay behind them.

For most of the cast, this closing party was merely a continuation of the last one. Jane and Simon hosted it in their large gray stone home near Llandaff Cathedral. It was clear to Liz that most GSSSG parties were held here. In the kitchen, people set out potluck specialties and helped themselves to serving spoons. One of the choristers set up drinks on a table near the back door. David took over the stereo system, and conversations were carried on in shouts over the decidedly non–Gilbert and Sullivan music.

Liz circulated through the party, laughing and joking with her castmates, but after a while a headache began to creep into her temples. She was suddenly thoroughly exhausted. Oppressed by the noise, she retreated to the kitchen to refill her wineglass. As she took a sip she poked her head out the back door. The cool, dry silence brought instantaneous relief, and she slipped outside. When her eyes adjusted to the twilight, she realized that she was not the only one who had taken refuge there: Giles leaned on the rail of the porch, in between pots of pansies and geraniums.

Liz wandered over, her arms crossed to conceal her left hand, her wineglass in her right.

Giles's smile seemed to welcome her. His dark blue eyes had lost the wary withdrawal of the past weeks. The set of his body was far more relaxed than she had seen him recently. *Mikado* must have been an ordeal.

"They've started dancing inside." She leaned against the rail beside him.

He did not respond.

No real breeze moved the trees, but the air seemed to stir, light and unburdened. Roses mingled their scent with lavender and faint mint and clean, sharp grass. A graceful stand of some kind of white flowers seemed to glow against a dark building at the bottom of the garden. Like a subterranean tidal cave, the bass of the pop music inside rumbled. Pearly twilight dropped gently into the evening.

"Did you enjoy *Mikado*?" Giles asked, breaking the silence.

"I think I got what I was after," Liz replied carefully. "Christopher talked me into auditioning for *Pinafore* in the fall."

"Did he now?"

She looked past him. In the sky one fading red streak pointed toward the evening star. For no reason at all she remembered that tomorrow was the anniversary of her accident—that it had happened under just such a clear, still sky. The headache whirled in her brain as the upheaval of the year rushed by, the numbness of last summer superseded by the agony of the fall, then deadened by the depression of her winter. Followed by this fortunate spring.

She glanced over to find Giles watching her. She took a deep breath to steady herself.

"It was great working with you. Will you be conducting *Pinafore*?"

He acknowledged her compliment with a smile but shook his head. "No, my schedule is rather full. I'll be doing Mozart's Requiem in November for the Choral Society. You should come hear it. It's an exquisite piece of music."

"Mozart never wrote any other kind. His music makes me feel like there might be a god in heaven after all." She regretted her effusiveness immediately, remembering how Titus had scoffed at her for it.

Giles turned and leaned his elbows on the rail, gazing into the secrecy of the garden. "I know what you mean. I remember driving home from Merthyr Tydfil on the worst night of my life. So dark, like a closed fist it was." His hands clenched. "I couldn't stand to listen to myself think any longer, so I turned on the BBC3, and there was the Requiem. And I was struck that these voices clear away in London could be—well, praying my prayer for me."

"Was that when Diana miscarried?" She kept her voice low, suspecting that he had almost forgotten her presence.

He shot her an unreadable glance. Then he nodded. "That it was."

"I'm sorry."

He looked back at the garden. "With Mozart it's more than notes and words. I always feel that his music is straining to dissolve back into the cosmos." He stopped. She could hear his even breathing. "It's a generous universe, isn't it, that the middle of so much darkness offers such an exquisite light?" After a moment he turned toward her with a sheepish smile. "Tell me, then, what's your favorite work?"

They began to compare notes. She confided in him her passion for the flute music now barred to her. He met this with sympathy and encouraged her to join one of the local choral groups. "You will discover all kinds of glorious vocal music to ease your loss," he said.

"Maybe," she agreed with a shrug. She refrained from telling him that she wanted to sing solos, not choruses.

His enthusiasm for Mozart carried over to other composers. He offered her small gems that were Hayden, singing phrases quietly and shaping them with his hands. He described the Fauré Requiem so that her spine tingled. He made her long to sing the choral movement of Beethoven's Ninth Symphony.

"And of course there's Bach. Do you know the B Minor Mass?"

"I heard it once."

"Such an amazing passage there is, in the Credo. The chord progression belongs to modern jazz. There's even a walking bass line. It's a marvelous foreshadowing of music history."

"Great heavens, here you are."

Liz jumped guiltily when Bert interrupted their conversation. The twilight had faded into a cool black evening.

"We thought you might have left with someone else." He dangled his car keys from his finger.

"Sorry. I guess it is time to go." She pulled at Bert's sleeve and looked at his watch. She had been out there nearly forty-five minutes. Her headache was gone.

They went inside. Caroline looked at Giles without saying a word, and Liz wondered if Diana had been looking for him. But Diana was in the dining room, dancing with Curtis.

As she followed Bert and Caroline to the front door, Giles stopped her. "Good luck with *Pinafore*. And look you, call Madame Ponnelle. I am certain she'll be interested in you."

"Thanks. Thanks for everything."

"My pleasure. I'll see you again."

* * *

AFTER *MIKADO* LIZ'S LIFE ABRUPTLY emptied of urgency—but that sensation didn't last long, as the long-delayed opening of Cygnet, Bert's new bookshop, took place just a week later. Outside, the same black signature swan from his old shop graced the new sign, flanked by two smaller swans. Inside, the new store was airy and clean and smelled of fresh paint and glass cleaner. All week, books had come out of their shipping cartons: new paperbacks, fine sawdust clinging to the freshly cut edges; hardback books, their dust jackets shiny and without fingerprints.

After a satisfying first week, Bert had Caroline and Liz staff Cygnet. He mainly stayed at Swann's, since his first love was the old volumes and the treasure hunts.

On a Monday in the middle of June, Christopher rang Liz at Cygnet. "Where have you been hiding?"

"I've been right here."

"We were supposed to have supper."

Liz tried to keep her voice casual. "Well, it was your idea."

"Would tomorrow night suit?" He did not wait for her reply. "I'll come for you at seven."

* * *

LIZ HAD PLANNED TO WEAR her favorite green dress—a sleeveless and slim number that made her feel taller. But when she put it on she couldn't quite accept the total exposure of the scars on her left wrist and arm. Not yet. She changed to the long-sleeved black dress that had been her orchestra staple and dressed it up with a red scarf and belt. Then she bullied her hair into order, working to get softening wisps to frame her face just right.

Liz was glad she had taken so much trouble when she saw where Christopher was taking her: the French restaurant in the Angel Hotel. She couldn't think of a polite way to ask if he could afford it—and worse yet, she wondered what he would expect in return. The maître d' knew his name before Christopher offered it, and he bustled them to a table in an alcove of the dining room. The rich red carpet and the soft lights insulated the corner, making it intimate and seductive. The clatter of dishes and the murmur of voices around them were hushed.

The waitress knew Christopher too; her face was rosy and smiling as she greeted him by name. When she had gone to get their wine, Liz looked at her date over the top of the oversized, pricy menu.

"Come here often?"

"I like to impress my dates," Christopher said. "Besides, I work at the desk. I don't pay full price."

Liz was torn between relief and insult. She wouldn't cost him a fortune and let him think that she would sleep with him so soon. She would just as soon avoid that sort of awkwardness. And although his intimation that he brought dates here all the time tweaked her, she was sure he had intended that. It wasn't like she didn't already know that about him.

His very interest was flattering. He admired her dress, praised her performance again, and rewarded her disclosures with his devastating smile. Liz could not bring herself to talk about the Conservatory, but over an excellent dinner of lamb chops she found herself telling him about growing up in San Francisco, and even a bit about her childhood in Caerphilly. He proved a good listener, always offering an appropriate question or observation.

It occurred to her quite suddenly that she hadn't been so obviously courted since Titus had given her an armful of yellow chrysanthemums on her birthday nearly four years ago. The thought shifted her suddenly into a minor key.

"Something I said?"

She glanced at Christopher and realized that she had withdrawn. "Sorry, I was just someplace else."

"*With* someone else?"

She blinked, not knowing how to respond to his mind reading.

"You looked quite sad just then. Who were you thinking about?"

She looked away. "About this guy I knew in San Francisco."

"Who broke your heart?"

She gave him a wry smile. "No, nothing like that."

Christopher's eyebrows registered doubt, but he grinned. "Well, you won't break my heart."

"I wasn't worried," she replied dryly, and she changed the subject.

* * *

WHEN CHRISTOPHER TOOK LIZ back to her flat, she said truthfully that she had enjoyed the evening.

"My pleasure. We should do this again." He leaned over. His breath warmed her cheek, and she closed her eyes. As he began to kiss her his hand slipped down her left arm, seeking her hand, and suddenly she stiffened, drawing it out of his reach and curving it around his shoulder. She began to kiss him back and hoped he hadn't noticed.

To her dismay, Titus filled her mind again. It was impossible that Christopher had not sensed her withdrawal. After insisting a moment more he released her, but he kept his face close. "Perhaps very soon," he said. Something in his tone made her breath catch in a shallow pocket around her heart.

When he had gone she made herself some tea and sat at her tiny table. Absently she caressed her damaged fingers with her thumb. As much as she had wanted to pull away, Christopher's kiss had reminded her that she missed the counterpoint of Titus's undemanding presence. She had assumed that her loneliness had only to do with her flute. But Titus had warned her that she would die alone and lonely, and it didn't seem an impossibility.

At least she couldn't hurt Christopher. The idea was not displeasing. She tasted her tea—now cold—grimaced, and poured it down the sink on her way to bed.

* * *

FOR A WEEK CHRISTOPHER DID not call. When she was finally annoyed enough to call him, he wasn't home. She gave up, humiliated to be ignored that way in view of Caroline's prying eyes. Yet when Bert summoned her to the phone at the end of the month she took it eagerly.

"This is Liz," she said with forced calm.

"Miss Morgan, this is Genevieve Ponnelle. Are you still interested in studying with me?"

Chapter 18

LIZ WENT TO HER FIRST LESSON with a vague feeling of trepidation. She rang at the appropriate side entrance, and the door flew open almost immediately. Madame ushered her into the studio and turned abruptly to face her.

"Before we begin you must explain something. You told me that you have studied music. Why did you stop?"

Liz opened her mouth, waiting for words to catch up with her mind. Slowly she took her left hand out of her pocket. "I didn't have a choice. I was in an accident. I can't play anymore." She held out her hand, flexing it gingerly as far as she could, willing tears not to intrude.

Madame looked at it, looked at her. "You were good?"

"I was very good." Liz met her gaze, ready for the challenge this time.

Without another word, the teacher went to the piano. "Let's begin."

* * *

IN THAT FIRST WEEK LIZ DID not sing much. Each night she lay on the floor of her flat with a book on her belly, watching it rise and fall as she rediscovered the simple act of breathing. Each time she inhaled she felt the air sharply in her nose, stretching her chest luxuriously, strong against the diaphragm between lungs and abdomen. One night words brightened in the darkest corner of her memory: "God breathed into his nostrils the breath of life, and man became a living soul." For an instant, she lay perfectly quiet. The breath of life, *her* life, returned to her. A tiny miracle. Then she began to chuckle, and the book slipped to the floor. But when the moment passed she got to her feet, soberly wondering if anyone would understand.

Precious extra minutes of daylight swelled through the endless twilights of summer, when the waning sun slipped across the gardens and roads with the calm of a sleepwalker. As a child Liz had longed to stay out just a little longer on such nights and listen as the nightingales laughed at her from the cooling evening. She heard them again now and knew she had missed them in San Francisco, where the seasons only changed in a desultory way.

The joy in her life gradually came alive again, always associated with the simple production of sound. She discovered incredible richness in her body, which she taught to flit lightly over a scale or to sustain a single, smooth note and then round it with passion or make it grate with despair. When repeating *vocalise* endlessly to memorize the sensation of correct singing, she amused herself by imposing upon each repetition what she fondly imagined to be characteristics of various composers. Languid Debussy, enormous Wagner, ethereal Puccini. Clean, light, swift Mozart.

She missed not a day of practice all summer; discipline had never been a problem. She hurried home from the bookshop each night, eager to rendezvous with her voice again. She took possession of the parlor in the boarding house and paced about the room, imagining the air spinning up through her chest ticklishly, sound streaming after it, the sense of laughter following closely. She used her hands and arms to shape the sound, almost like a conductor. Her left arm rarely hindered her.

Walking about, gesturing and stretching, she finally threw off the last of her awkward habits. She no longer held her left side protectively. The twinges in her rib cage did not recur as she pressed down, pushed out, expanded her lungs, developed support for her voice. Her shoulder moved almost smoothly. By a couple of months into her training, only her fingers, her wrist, and her elbow bore signs of the accident. Sometimes half a day would pass before she noticed them.

* * *

AFTER A FEW WEEKS OF GENTLE scales and arpeggios, Madame gave Liz a song to learn, a charming piece from the opera *Hansel and Gretel*. Liz acquired the song easily, for melodic line was a second language to her. The process evoked memories of learning to play "Twinkle, Twinkle Little Star" on her flute, each correct note a triumph at that young age. She would never be so completely a beginner again.

The lyrics were more challenging. Madame talked her through it but clucked her tongue over the English rendering. "A good composer is aware of the singing voice," she declared. "He does not put pinched, closed sounds up high where you want the voice to be open. But not all translators pay attention to what the singer needs."

Liz shrugged. "Why don't I learn the German then?"

Madame narrowed her eyes. "Do you speak German?"

"I studied a little at the Conservatory. Couldn't I just learn it phonetically?"

"You should know what every single word means."

"I can look up what I don't know."

Her teacher fixed her with a calculating gaze. "I don't imagine you've ever taken lyric diction—phonetics and pronunciation for singers?"

Liz shook her head. "Not required for my major."

Madame pursed her lips, reconsidering the words on the page. "Well, we can try. It will work for art songs and short arias, but longer works will require some language, and some familiarity with the IPA. You must take the lyric diction course next semester at the university. I'll arrange it. Do you have a pencil?"

Liz did not miss the implication of this offer. *I train professionals*, Madame had said.

Painstakingly they went over the song word by word for the pronunciation. At the end of the lesson that day, Madame gave Liz a stapled booklet of the International Phonetic Alphabet to study, and from then on she gave her music in the original language. Liz happily took it all to the library and looked up words, or pestered her cousin Kate, who had a facility with languages.

After a couple of weeks of cautiously feeling her way through the song, it was time to add the accompaniment. Liz arrived at the white house a little early for her lesson to find Giles Offeryn sitting on the couch in Madame's waiting room, his head back and his eyes closed as if he were napping. When she came in he nodded to her and, without speaking, rose and crossed the room to gaze out the window at the clouds that had settled, ponderous with rain, over the city.

She joined him at the window.

He turned to her, his eyes circled in shadow. The gray afternoon and the dark green carpet made him look pale. "You took my suggestion."

She grinned broadly. "Yes, and I can't thank you enough." She sobered. "Christopher mentioned that Diana left you. I'm sorry."

He turned back to the window. "Told you the whole pathetic little story, did he?"

"Sorry, I didn't mean—"

"What right does he, of all people, have to be discussing my affairs with you?" He glared at her. "You don't seem terribly bothered by the ugly details."

Confused, she tried to retreat from his anger. "Aren't you better off without her? I wasn't surprised. I think she did you a favor."

"Is that what he said? He's a bigger ass than I even thought."

Before Liz could gather her wits to reply, the door to the studio opened, and they both fell silent.

"Ready?" Madame looked from one to the other. Liz pulled herself together and went into the studio, aching to reply to Giles.

For the first time her lesson was more frustration than pleasure. Only last night the song had sung itself, pouring out of the curve in the roof of her mouth and vibrating her eyeteeth as it passed. Now it refused to cooperate. She squeezed the rising line from her throat as if she were singing through a tracheotomy. She felt each thin note hover unsteadily in the air until it broke.

Giles sat silently at the piano, providing nothing more than the harmony under her voice. Madame was the go-between, badgering Liz and communicating with Giles in shorthand gestures. Finally she closed her eyes and put up a hand. The piano line faded away. The breath that Liz had taken hung in her chest, suffocating her.

Madame fixed her with her disconcertingly cold gaze. "You must concentrate, Elizabeth," she finally said.

Liz nodded meekly, feeling her face flush as she let out her breath. She could feel Giles's condemning eyes upon her but could not look at him.

When the hour was over he gathered his music and stood up.

"Thank you," Liz muttered, wishing she dared say a thousand other things. She wanted fiercely to have sung better, to have shown him what she could do. He left without comment.

Liz shrugged into her coat. "I'm sorry, Madame," she said, handing over her payment. "I can do better than that."

"Don't ever sing so that you feel you must apologize. If you can do better, just do it," Madame returned briskly.

"My mind wasn't all there," Liz admitted.

"Miss Morgan, I can teach you all about the mechanics of singing, but to really succeed, you cannot be apologetic. You must promise the audience everything, and *deliver* everything. Even in practice. Open your mouth and produce the most beautiful sound of your life *every single time.*"

"I'll try," Liz replied meekly.

"You will not try. You will do it. Now go home and work on the spots that did not come right. And do not come to a lesson so ill-prepared again."

But Liz knew she would sing them perfectly when she got home.

* * *

THE DAYS DRIFTED TOWARD FALL like the first leaves to the frosty ground. By the time *Pinafore* rehearsals began in October, Liz's voice seemed to have grown a thousand-fold. She could hardly wait to sing for an audience again. She found the small role of Hebe a disappointment after Pitti-Sing but took it as an opportunity to learn. She made herself memorize music and blocking as early as possible. She sought help not only from the principals but also from the veteran choristers, who seemed to have accepted her.

Happily, she found she was working with Curtis again. He had relaxed since *Mikado* and no longer looked down his nose at her. She loved to tease him, just to see him get huffy and then suddenly look sheepish. "Keeping me honest?" They continued to build on-stage rapport born from his fateful error with the sword, which she never quite let him forget.

Christopher ignored her at times, flirted with her at others, just enough to keep her off balance. She sometimes regretted that moment of withdrawal. He had no doubt sensed it. After all, where was the harm in a bit of fun? She appreciated the times when he praised something she did. Even when he took it upon himself to correct her, she reminded herself that she needed his help. His flirtation felt incomprehensibly more like argument than attraction. His kisses made her heart pound like fear, his lips hard, his teeth not gentle, his energy wiry and unsubtle. She knew what he wanted, why he continued to wear her down. She knew she would eventually give in to him. She knew it all during *Pinafore*, when she would lie awake after hours of being near him in rehearsal. It would come, as the resolution of a suspended chord must come.

Chapter 19

IN FEBRUARY, A YEAR AFTER SHE had returned to Wales, Liz was ready for *Pirates of Penzance*. She had fallen into a habit of life that pleased her greatly: the adventure of learning to sing coupled with the camaraderie of working with Caroline and Bert. She felt as though she had lived in Cardiff for many years.

As she gossiped with the others waiting in the lobby of Sherman Theater for the audition, she knew when Christopher arrived. She knew, too, the instant he noticed her. Although she didn't watch, she sensed him making his way over to her. With an effort, she pretended not to see him until she was good and ready to acknowledge his presence.

He enveloped her with his ebullient charm, drawing her away from the circle. "You've nothing to worry about," he assured her, kissing her hand and tucking it under his elbow possessively.

"You'll put in a good word for me?" she asked with mock earnestness.

He frowned at her.

"Thanks for the vote of confidence." She squeezed his arm in quick apology for teasing him.

He grinned his wicked grin. "Free tomorrow night?"

"How about supper on Monday before the first rehearsal?"

"You're rather sure of yourself."

"No more than you are."

"Touché. But seriously. Come with me to Swansea tomorrow night. I've got tickets for Bluehorses."

"For what?"

"Bluehorses. It's a newish band; they do Celtic rock. Really terrific."

"Celtic rock?"

"Don't tell me you're a music snob."

"Not at all. I've just never heard of it."

"Come with me then. You'll love it, I promise."

She started to tell him he was crazy. But then she realized that this was exactly what she wanted from him. She wanted a real date instead of a meal in a pub that only served as an opportunity for him to tweak her desire. "All right then, I will," she said. "It sounds like fun."

* * *

SHE AND CHRISTOPHER LEFT CARDIFF in the flap and feint of the first winds of a storm coming in off the Atlantic. He drove with a precise skill that compensated for the risks he took, weaving the MG among more timid—and, in her opinion, more sensible—drivers. Her stomach lurched every time she felt the car give way to the wind.

Seeking distraction, she rummaged through his collection of tapes, mostly Rolling Stones and Aerosmith, until she found a cassette labeled simply "Harp."

"What's this?"

He read the title and snorted. "The talented Mr. Offeryn."

She put it in the player and started it. The sound of a solo harp trickled through the car. After a moment she knew the piece to be "Greensleeves," embedded in a Celtic knotwork of theme and subtle counter-theme. "This is nice. Who did the arrangement?"

"He did. The village prodigy. He was such a clever lad he went up to university at the tender age of fourteen."

"Really? Wow."

"Oh yes, he was a regular Mozart. Writing music from his cradle. Even won a prize for it at the Eisteddfod one year."

"How long have you known him?"

"Why do you ask?"

She shrugged. "Sometimes there's this . . . friction. Almost animosity."

"Oh, he's a decent-enough chap. We grew up together in Llanberis. Our fathers were partners in the bakery. We sang in chapel together too." He grinned at a memory. "We would skip out of class early and go walking on Snowdon."

She squinted at him. She couldn't imagine Giles cutting school for any reason.

Christopher seemed to guess what she was thinking. "That was a long time ago. Once his musical genius was discovered, off he went to university."

"Jealous?" she asked before she could reconsider.

He looked sharply at her. "Not a chance. I wouldn't have his troubles for all the talent in Wales. He went up in flames when he got out into the world. And now he and Diana have split."

"So you said. I can't think that it's a bad thing."

"They never suited each other. Diana likes a bit of fun, and face it, Giles is no fun."

"Oh come on—"

Christopher raised a finger. "Enough about Giles."

She looked over at him, but his attention was back on the road. Closing her eyes, she concentrated on the ingenious weaving of the music, recognizing how he had pulled strands from the B section of the song and developed them into a haunting answer to the initial theme. It pleased her greatly. For all her performance ability, composing and arranging eluded her.

When the next number began, Christopher reached over and turned it off before Liz had time to identify the piece. "It'll put me to sleep," he said without taking his eyes off the motorway. "Talk to me."

* * *

THE CONCERT ENERGIZED LIZ; the music was strangely hard and haunting, evoking a Halloween before the Christians civilized it. Five musicians exploded among a stage bristling with equipment. Although she felt slightly deaf from the volume of the electric instruments, something about the way the current seemed to enter her body and become her pulse attracted her. The familiar Celtic rhythms seemed more primitive in spite of, or perhaps because of, the modern instruments. The voice of the lead vocalist was low and driven, but not harsh. She had a sound that seemed to pull Liz's heart straight out of her chest.

When they emerged after the concert, the cold astonished her. Patchy frost glittered under the streetlights. She wished for shoes more suited to warmth than fashion. The acid sharpness of the air stung her nostrils. She covered her face with a gloved hand to reduce the aching chill.

Christopher seemed distracted and distant. In the freezing temperatures, the MG took time to warm up. The wind nudged the car occasionally as they sat listening to the engine sort itself out. Liz glanced over at her strangely silent companion. His forearms rested on the steering wheel, and he looked thoughtfully toward the auditorium, three blocks away.

"That was pretty amazing," she said finally.

He glanced over at her and leaned back. "Stimulating."

They both sat perfectly motionless for a moment, the car and the wind isolating them. When he leaned over and began to kiss her she was pleasantly unsurprised.

After the first shock of his cold nose, his lips felt soft, gentler, and more restrained than before. He tasted of the ale he had been drinking and smelled wonderfully of a subtle cologne that evoked Mediterranean beaches and trade winds. Liz forgot her cold feet.

He murmured her name, stopped to tug off his gloves. She pulled him closer, nuzzling his jaw up to his ear. His hands quickly loosened her sweater and slipped, warm, down her shoulders under her clothes. The gooseflesh on her arms and the tightness in her nipples had nothing to do with the cold.

"Dear Liz. Lizzie, let me make love to you."

"Don't call me that." She pushed him halfheartedly.

"It suits you." He tried to salvage the moment, his breath caressing her cheek lightly.

"It's what someone else used to call me."

He took his hands away.

"Your car is far too small and it's too cold," she told him gently. The kiss lingered in her senses. She hunched her shoulders, shivering.

He shut off the engine. "Let's get a room."

"What?"

"Stay the night with me."

She stared at him. "You went to all this trouble just to get me in bed?"

The eagerness vanished. "Grow up, Liz. You've kept me waiting long enough."

Her heart fluttered and her fingers shook slightly as she buttoned her sweater.

He put his face close to hers. "It's no secret that I want you," he said in a smooth, low voice, his eyes dilated in the dark.

"Me and half the chorus," she snapped. "Just what gave you the idea that you can have any woman you want?"

He drew back. "You were ready and willing two minutes ago," he pointed out blandly. "You want to. I know you do."

She ducked her head, her heart pounding in agreement. "That's beside the point."

"Not at all. You would have done it with me here in the car, if I hadn't been fool enough to suggest a more comfortable alternative."

"No," she said—his words, as she was sure he intended, making her feel stupid—"I just don't want to be pushed around or tricked."

"Some women," he said through his teeth, "appreciate the romantic approach." He stung the car back to life and pulled away from the curb so rapidly the tires protested.

Liz held her breath as they sped through town and picked up the M4 going east. After a few minutes, speckles of rain began to splat against the windshield and race in shivering lines along the side windows. By the time they left town the rain had outstripped the windshield wipers, but Christopher did not slow down. Far from the motorway, under the storm, villages emerged and faded like fairy encampments.

Liz did not take a deep breath all the way home. Terror, and tempests of indignation and shame, paralyzed her as he spurred the car through the rain.

"Christopher?" she ventured as they neared Cardiff.

"What?" There was no sharpness in his tone. He stared out into the violent night, but the grim anger seemed to be gone.

"I know why you're angry. But you don't own me."

"Somebody else might have insisted."

She shivered. "I was being naïve."

He shifted in his seat as though the drive was beginning to wear on him.

"We do have callbacks tomorrow afternoon," Liz said. "I want to be rested. This isn't a good time to start something like this."

The wind plucked at the car as Christopher's foot relaxed a fraction on the gas pedal. He finally glanced at her. "What are you worried about? I'll see that Huw casts you."

She only just managed not to tell him to watch the road. "I don't want you to 'put in your oar.' I want to do this on my own."

"You're not serious?"

"Yes, I am."

He glanced over at her and then laughed. "My, my, we have been bitten by the bug, haven't we?"

"There's no crime in that."

"Right then, we'll have it your way. But I won't wait much longer, Liz."

* * *

When Liz got to the theater the next afternoon for callbacks, a layer of unfamiliar music settled on top of the *Pirates* music in her head. Christopher had the score to *Ruddygore* with him. As he subjected the keyboard to mild abuse, Curtis and Simon competed to see who could remember more of the lyrics.

When she approached, Christopher grinned at her as though nothing had happened the night before and scooted over on the piano bench, continuing to play.

"Here, Liz. Join us."

He proceeded to drag them through the rapid patter trio. Reading over his shoulder and following the men's lead, Liz skimmed along, perilously close to but never quite losing her place. When they'd finished, laughing and gasping, Christopher swung around on the piano bench.

"We're turning you into quite a little musician, Liz. That's not so easy to sight-read."

"Oh, I'm a fraud," she admitted, breathless with laughter and not a little pleased with herself. "I have had a few music lessons in my day."

"You're sounding lovely."

"Thank you. I'm taking voice lessons."

"Are you?" Christopher looked surprised. "Who is your teacher?"

"Genevieve Ponnelle."

"Madame Ponnelle? *Quel dommage*," he said with an exaggerated French accent. "There you go, taking yourself seriously again."

The last of the laughter slipped from Liz's shoulders. "What's wrong with that?"

"Let's not fool ourselves. G-Triple-S-G has a good reputation, but we are amateurs. Don't let your success go to your head."

"It hasn't," she said, straightening her spine.

"Ponnelle will just fill your head with self-important rubbish. If you want someone to hack through a G and S score you needn't pay her prices. Besides, you're already taking roles away from veterans," he pointed out. "What are you planning to do, make a career of it? Go on the wicked stage?"

"And what if I am?" She jumped to her feet, furious that he could be so frivolous about something that had cost her so dearly. "Is there something wrong with that?"

"It's easy to be good here. Don't get carried away."

"Don't patronize me," she roared back. She stormed up the aisle and flung herself out of the hall, brushing past Caroline without a greeting, then shoved open the door to the street, which slammed against the wall with a satisfying crash. But she slowed as she headed for the car park. Where did she think she was going? Callbacks would start in ten minutes. She paced back toward the doorway, hugging herself against the cool breezes, feeling foolish for the scene she had just made. The surface ripples were about Christopher, but she knew there was more. His words had suddenly made her wonder if she could snatch back time and return the course of her life to what it had been less than two years ago.

Just as she began to think about going back inside, the door clanged open. Christopher approached her.

"Hey, Lizzie," he said softly.

The phrase stabbed under her heart and drove tears up into her throat. Annoyingly enough, Christopher never failed, inadvertently, to remind her of Titus. She turned away, surrounded by her losses. "Don't, don't ever call me that."

He shoved his hands in his pockets, taking a step back. "Caroline told me about your flute. I didn't know."

"It's not your fault I didn't tell you." How many times in her life would she be brought up short by the truth? The thing she loved best was gone from her life, and there were still times when she wished someone would hold her and console her while she wept, purging the cold silver melancholy in her chest. She wasn't over it. Maybe she never could be. She wondered what name Dante would give this particular circle of Hell.

"I was only teasing."

She pushed a hand roughly through her hair. "I know. I'm sorry I blew up. You just hit a raw nerve."

"Clearly." He came up close behind her and began to knead the tension out of her shoulders. She stretched under his hands, pulling at her healed joint.

"How about supper tomorrow night?"

"You don't give up, do you?"

"Surely you didn't think I would."

"Not you." She turned to face him, and he slipped his hands over her shoulders and pulled her closer.

"All right, tomorrow night before we have to be at rehearsal. And then afterwards . . ."

She couldn't quite say it, but she knew he understood. He had been about to tease her about her certainty, she was sure of it. But he'd refrained.

Chapter 20

CHRISTOPHER KEPT LIZ WAITING on Monday night. She sat brooding in a dark corner of Conway's, absently watching the dart game and waiting for her shepherd's pie to cool. In spite of her elation at getting the part, her thoughts had already skipped ahead past the rehearsal.

He had not been wrong about the fact that she wanted him. She couldn't hold out against his persuasion any longer, nor did she want to. He must want her badly, to be so patient. But he could (and did, she was sure) sleep with just about anyone he chose. In spite of her resolve, she kept coming back to that point.

When he appeared with a pint of stout and a steak-and-kidney pie from the bar, she still had not made up her mind.

"There's my little star."

"Should you be drinking before rehearsal?"

"No harm in it." As if to emphasize his point he took a long pull. "Huw told me you'd been cast."

"Was there any doubt?"

"Kate's nowhere near as big a role as Pitti-Sing, but you'll learn a lot."

"Oh, but I'm doing Edith."

"You're . . ." He stopped, forgetting to close his mouth.

"What? Don't you think I can do it?"

"It's not what Huw and I talked about."

She put down her fork, sat up straight, and stared at him. "You talked to him about me?"

"I had a word with him, yes. I do have an interest in your progress." He winked.

"Who do you think you are?"

"I didn't want you to be disappointed." His tone was soothing.

Liz took a deep breath. "I don't need your help. Obviously Huw knows what I can do, or he wouldn't have let me do *Mikado*."

"*Mikado* was all right as far as it went. But your performance lacked a certain consistency." He began to devour his pie. A dart hit the board with a hollow *thock*.

"Lacked consistency?"

"No worries. You're still a beginner."

"A *beginner*?"

He didn't have the sense to stop. He leaned closer over the table. "I can teach you so many more subtle things. You've a lot to learn before you're a real actress."

"You don't need to teach me anything. I'm getting coaching."

He burst out laughing. "Oh, Lizzie, you take yourself far too seriously."

"You bastard." He surprised it out of her.

"Watch that tongue of yours, little girl." He grinned.

Her fury short-circuited her voice. Without thinking, she shot out a hand and slapped him. She caught him right on the jaw, snapping his head to one side. "Sorry I can't stay." She shoved her chair back, slopping his beer on the table, and left before he could stop her, before the palm of her hand began to sting. The sound of whistles and catcalls from the dart players followed her to the door.

As she burst out of the pub the wind threw icy rain in her face. She swore and squinted, pulling her collar tighter. With her head down and her fists stuffed in her pockets, she barreled along the wet sidewalk.

She didn't even see him until she ran headlong into him, bounced off, and landed on the pavement. The impact sent grinding pain to bones she thought had healed. The man she had collided with crouched beside her, holding an umbrella over her. She looked up and swore again.

"And good afternoon to you," Giles replied. "You aren't hurt, are you?"

"Damn it, you're all I need!" She struggled to her feet. "What is it with you Welshmen anyway? Chris is just a weasel, and you—you're so damn moody." She started to stalk away. "I wish I'd never met either of you!" she tossed over her shoulder.

"Liz!" he shouted, getting her attention.

"What?" she shouted back, rounding on him.

He backed up a step.

She waited.

"Are you hungry?" he finally asked.

"Am I . . ." She couldn't speak for a moment. Then the pressure in her chest emptied into odd, unexpected laughter. "Yes," she admitted, wiping her eyes and nose with the back of her hand. "Actually I left my supper back in the pub."

"Would you consider a quick bite before rehearsal? Or would that be pressing my luck?"

"Why should I?"

He thought about it, shrugged. "Because as long as it's awkward in Ponnelle's studio, you will never sing as well as you are able."

She hesitated.

"Humor me."

He took her to an Indian restaurant near the castle. March froze and blew, but as they came in out of the insistent winter, aromas of ginger and cinnamon and garlic warmed her delightfully and the heat of the room made her cold face tingle. Mosaics on the walls shimmered so that she felt the sun glistening in the enamel colors.

When the waiter appeared, Giles ordered without looking at the menu and asked for a couple of Indian beers. Liz refrained from comment, remembering Christopher's derision. She went off to the loo to try and dry her hair, which was trickling cold water down the back of her neck. Her hip was sore where she had landed on it, and the heel of her hand stung.

By the time she returned the beer had been served.

"Better?"

She shrugged awkwardly.

Giles loosened his tie and rolled back his cuffs. "We ought to be able to be civil to each other, wouldn't you say?"

"You started it."

"I did. And now I should like to finish it."

She took a deep breath. "Right."

He ran a long finger down the side of his glass, examining the beads of carbonation as they rose to the top. "What did Christopher do then, to stir your wrath?"

After a long moment she said, "You don't like him much, do you?"

He considered her with a slight frown. "Look you, he doesn't even draw the line at married women. Surely that bothers you."

"I can't see that it's any of your business." Then her curiosity overcame her defensiveness. "Married women?"

"You honestly don't know?"

"Are you sure?"

"Quite. You'd be better off without him."

"I don't want your advice," she snapped. "It might be foolish, but it isn't a crime to want somebody."

"It wasn't a criticism." He leaned forward, both hands flat on the table. "Liz, Christopher is the reason my marriage broke up."

When he said it she felt the revelation right between the eyes. Of course it was Christopher. No wonder Giles had been so touchy. Feeling chastened at her lack of perception, she relaxed a bit. "He and Diana—oh jeez, really?"

Until his shoulders slumped she hadn't perceived his tension. "You really didn't know, did you?"

"How could I?"

"You said Christopher had told you everything. I thought he had been enough of an ass to brag about it to you."

"Is that why you were so rude to me at the studio? You thought I knew?"

"It did seem that way. You were so patronizing."

"You really thought I would keep dating him, knowing that? That's insulting!"

He shook his head. "I'm sorry. I was not thinking clearly. And it's affecting the way we work together, so I wanted to clear the air. Of course," he added, his ears reddening, "you are perfectly at liberty to work with a different accompanist."

She let him stew for a while as the waiter brought their food. She recognized the correlation between his presence in the studio and Madame's most vociferous dissatisfaction. "Don't be so careful. Are you afraid someone will hear you?" she'd badgered Liz at her last lesson. Giles had waited, dark and still at the piano, and Liz had wanted to shout, "Yes, I'm afraid *he'll* hear me!"

For a while she savored the tender chicken, suffused with subtle spices that warmed her inside and accented with red pepper flakes that made her nose run. But she watched Giles from under her lashes. He ate slowly, focused on his meal. Finally, she relented.

"You're good," she said. "I'd just as soon work with you. And anyway, I still have to put up with you in *Pirates*." She hesitated, then asked, "Was this going on during *Mikado*?"

"It was all over by then. Christopher says it was just one night that he regrets. She says it went on for months."

"Who do you believe?"

"What difference does that make?"

"Probably none. But you must have an opinion."

He offered her a chapati, but she waved it away. He sighed. "I'm inclined to believe Christopher. Diana is not particularly truthful. And it wasn't her first affair by any means," he added.

"Why did you marry her in the first place? She's such a little witch."

"She didn't seem to be when we met."

"Childhood sweetheart?" It came out with more derision that she intended.

"Did you never make a decision you regretted?"

She shrugged, silenced by the bitterness in his tone.

He sighed. "When I was seventeen, I went up to Merthyr Tydfil to conduct the local chorus in some psalms I had set to music. Diana's father was headmaster at Cyfartha High School, and I stayed with his family. He made sure she got the soprano solos."

"What a setup."

"I was quite a fool. One thing led to another, and I thought I ought to marry her." He did not need to say that Diana was the first girl he had ever slept with. Liz read it between the lines as clear as day. She could just imagine his naïveté and Diana's exploitation. With great effort, she refrained from comment.

"We married when I was nineteen and heading to Paris to study with Pierre Varnet. I think she wanted the exciting life of a star, and I was nowhere near that yet. I thought she wouldn't mind that I had to be away a lot." He rubbed his napkin between his thumb and forefinger, his gaze gone distant. "She didn't mind, did she? That I was often away." He looked directly at Liz. "She had taken a lover before we had been married a year."

An odd tenderness ached under Liz's sternum. She had to stop herself from reaching across the table and touching him. "Why on earth did you stay with her?"

He studied the beer glass, his eyes unfocused and still. "We lived in Paris at first. When I found out about the affair, she carried on, said she was lonely. So I brought her back here." He paused, watching his fingers fold the napkin into a fan as if they were independent of his brain. "Of course, then it happened again. And she got pregnant."

Liz took a sharp breath, and he looked at her, suddenly aware of her again. "I would have raised the child, if she had settled down. I saw it as a last chance."

"And then she lost the baby. How awful."

"She made sure of it, didn't she?"

She looked at him, frowning, as she tried to take in what he was telling her.

"She got rid of it," he said, snapping off the words. "I let people think she miscarried. I still had some pride. But it was the end. And I'll never make that mistake again." He checked his watch and glanced out the window at the rain, avoiding Liz's eyes.

"How did you find out that it was Christopher?"

"You ask a great many questions."

"Sorry." She withdrew and concentrated on the last bite of her meal.

He sighed. "No, don't apologize. I should not have burdened you with the whole sordid mess. For your own sake, you ought to know what Christopher is like. But please don't involve yourself in my personal life."

"Fine," she said softly, picking up her tea with both hands and retreating into unsociable silence.

At last he pushed away his plate. "If you don't mind my asking," he said hesitantly, "what did you and he argue over?"

She thought about telling him to stay out of her personal life, but she couldn't quite bring herself to do it. "He . . . well, he laughed at me. He teased me about being too ambitious." She stopped, feeling foolish.

Giles's grave features did not change. He listened intently, not moving. "And that is extremely important to you."

She toyed with the porcelain elephant saltshaker. "He was so encouraging at the beginning. I thought he respected me."

He watched her in a way that made her squirm. "I expect you threaten him."

"Me? Threaten him?"

He suddenly seemed to be enjoying the conversation. "You refused to remain a wide-eyed acolyte."

"But I like being around someone who challenges me."

Giles failed to completely disguise his smile, but she chose to ignore it. "Trust me, you are better off without him."

Liz sighed and pushed back her chair. She was beginning to fret about seeing Christopher in half an hour. When she reached for her purse Giles shook his head, picking up the check before she could see it.

"Keep your money."

"I can pay for my dinner."

"Don't be tedious."

She subsided.

"Do you suppose anyone would notice if I didn't come to rehearsal tonight?" she asked suddenly as they shrugged on their damp coats.

"No doubt." He thought for a moment. "But if you had a touch of flu . . ."

She bit her lip.

"Shall I say that you called me to cancel due to illness?"

"I don't want you to lie for me."

"You are a little heartsick, are you not?"

The anger that had been displaced earlier by laughter tightened in her chest again. "It's more like my ego," she said sheepishly.

Giles looked at her, eyebrows raised. "Well in that case . . ."

* * *

THE REHEARSAL WAS A READ-THROUGH, and Liz sat well away from Christopher and kept to herself. To Caroline, who looked at her curiously every now and then, she muttered something about coming down with the flu. Only when she sang did she rise to the occasion and come to life.

At the break she stayed in her chair, her head down, studiously involved in her score. She glanced up only once, to find herself looking directly into Christopher's eyes across the stage. He grinned, put a hand up, and rubbed his jaw slowly. Then he winked at her.

* * *

THE RAIN STOPPED THAT NIGHT, leaving behind a brilliant sky and a freezing wind the following morning. Liz's left hand ached as she dragged herself to work, carrying her cup of tea and the burden of humiliation.

Caroline scrutinized her over her shoulder as she raised the blinds in Swann's. "You look the worse for wear. How are you feeling?"

"I don't have the flu. I had a huge fight with Christopher before rehearsal. I didn't feel like talking to anybody." Liz shuffled into the office to shed her coat and scarf and returned, sipping from her cardboard cup and feeling how the heat of it relieved her stiff fingers. She sat on the high stool behind the counter as Caroline balanced the register.

"I did warn you about him."

"I know, I know."

"What did you fight about?"

"He was teasing me about being ambitious."

"Is that all? Well, you are rather intense."

Even if Christopher apologized for his remarks to her, Liz knew she could not forgive him what she now knew about him and Diana. But she was also quite sure that Giles would not thank her for telling Caroline about it. "I guess maybe I just know him better now. I hauled off and slapped him," she admitted.

"Oh, Liz."

Under cheeks and nose still cold from her walk, Liz felt herself blush.

Then Caroline chuckled. "I'd love to have seen that. It's not often that someone calls his bluff. Believe me, he's not worth agonizing over. There'll be someone else. Lots of good fish in the sea."

"I think I'll stick to singing for a while." Liz tossed her cup in the trash and retreated into the office.

Chapter 21

AT LIZ'S NEXT VOICE LESSON, Madame sat at the piano but did not start the vocal exercises immediately. Instead she looked at Liz with her head to one side. "Have you considered what you will do when you've used up the Gilbert and Sullivan repertoire?"

"Not really. Not yet."

"You ought to be looking ahead to some real challenges. How much opera have you seen?"

"Not a lot."

Madame clucked.

"It wasn't a priority at the Conservatory," Liz said. "I went to the symphony." She did not mention the Opera Theater and her final performance.

"And now?"

Liz shrugged. "I guess I'd like it."

Madame considered her with that slight arch in her brow that always signaled a challenge. "Do you feel like you've had to settle for second best?"

These kinds of abrupt questions, requiring so much soul-searching, made Liz both hate and love her teacher. "I—I don't think they compare."

"Of course they do. You certainly have not yet reached the level of proficiency you must have had as an instrumentalist. Does that never frustrate you?"

"I guess so, sometimes. But it's better than nothing."

"Better than nothing."

Liz heard how it sounded. "I don't mean it like that. It's far more than I ever expected or hoped for after the accident. I love it, I do."

"Go to the opera," Madame said. She did not sound as annoyed as Liz expected.

* * *

WELSH NATIONAL OPERA'S CURRENT undertaking was Wagner's Ring Cycle. Liz went alone to New Theater as though to an assignation. She bought the cheapest ticket for *Das Rheingold* and climbed the precipitous spiral staircase. Her seat was at the very back of the house, a flip-up bench in the upper circle. She leaned forward, watching the people who had come to hear the opera. At last, filtering through the overlapping layers of conversation, she heard the orchestra begin to tune. In an instant the chatter dropped reverently, as if people had been reminded that they were in a church. The house lights faded, the fire curtain lifted, and the Rhine seeped into the theater from the orchestra pit.

The opera was like nothing Liz had ever seen. This was a story of gods and heroes, and it contrasted mightily with the Gilbert and Sullivan she had recently performed, and even the Mozart and Puccini with which she was familiar. The music seemed to shake the earth and make the air tremble with power. The evening flew by in no time, and she went home in a daze.

In subsequent weeks she returned to the opera greedily to witness the following three chapters in the saga. The characters seemed like elements come to possess her: Loki and his magic fire music, Brunhilde and her white horse, Siegfried and his sword. She suspected that she would never have the voice to sing this music, but nonetheless she was drawn by it.

When the waters of the Rhine swept away the last of the opera, she felt bereft. But shortly thereafter, *Die Zauberflöte* opened. Her *Magic Flute*. And her tumbled emotions were challenged yet again.

Madame brought it to her attention, and Liz dutifully wrote it on her calendar. But when the evening arrived and she stood in the ticket queue, hugging her borrowed score and gazing into the middle distance, she could not ignore the queasiness in her gut. It had been two years; she'd thought herself over this anxiety.

"Fancy meeting you here."

She jerked out of her reverie. Giles stood before her, impeccably dressed as usual.

"Madame thinks my tastes are too plebian," she admitted, gathering her composure.

"I have no one to use my other ticket. Would you like it?"

She hesitated. "I'm not really dressed up." She pulled her donkey coat closer around her scruffy sweater.

"I don't mind."

He led the way upstairs and helped her with her coat as if she were wearing her Sunday best. When they were seated he read through the program, keeping up an educational commentary. "Bronden, hmm, interesting choice for Tamino . . . Ah, Marie Angel as Queen of the Night, we are in for a treat . . . Now I wonder why Anne is doing First Lady, I would have thought it too high for her . . ." He didn't seem to notice that Liz was only half listening. Beneath the murmured comments she fed him, most of her attention was focused on soothing her nerves. His presence denied her the luxury of dark solitude should *Magic Flute* prove too traumatic.

When the house lights finally dimmed Liz settled back in her comfortable chair with relief. She felt the opening chord in the pit of her belly. The familiar music surrounded her, and she gradually relaxed. As the overture unfolded she recognized the sparkling busyness, the sweet, warm lines, the familiar harmonies. Tears rose in her eyes, and she surreptitiously dabbed them away with her knuckle, hoping that Giles wouldn't notice. But a smile wobbled around her mouth. How she had missed *Flute*.

Rather than indulge her grief, she focused on the singers. She scrutinized their acting, their diction, their breath. She dared to imagine that she could regain access to *Magic Flute*.

As the house lights came up at the first intermission, Giles inquired how she liked it.

"It's very good," she replied. His glance seemed to label her a Philistine, and she grinned. "No, it's splendid."

"This is exactly the sort of music you should be singing," he said.

At first she couldn't reply. Unless he had forgotten their conversation at the *Mikado* closing party—which she doubted—he couldn't *not* know what that meant to her.

"Thank you for that," she finally managed. "You're awfully kind."

"It wasn't kindness. I meant it."

"I know you did." His grave distance annoyed her, but she refrained from further comment.

She listened to the following acts with renewed concentration, abandoning her posture of self-effacement. Even the flute passages failed to wound. Beneath the layers of protective doubt, she tantalized herself with possibilities.

* * *

LIZ HAD NOTHING TO SAY as Giles walked her back to her flat. Isolated in her experience and her musing, she was startled when he spoke.

"You're awfully quiet. Didn't you enjoy it after all?"

"Oh, I did! I really did," she assured him. "Thank you for the ticket." She fell silent again, but this time she was acutely aware of him as she weighed her next words. The mildness of the evening hinted at summer. Directly above, the encroaching fog had not yet obscured the stars. She kept her eyes fixed on the brightest, fancying her pulse beating in the universe.

"Can I tell you something? Promise you won't laugh?"

"Not unless it's funny," he countered lightly.

She dropped her gaze to his face. "I guess I do sound melodramatic."

"What is it, then?"

She looked away again. "I'm going to sing like that." Her heart was in her throat to be telling someone this. It sounded a further temptation of the gods, and she could just imagine her cousin cautioning her against conceit.

"I know."

She stopped for a moment. When she caught up with him again she found no trace of levity on his face.

"What do you mean, you know?"

He shrugged. "I just do. You will sing like that, and better."

They walked on, Liz marveling over his certainty. It embarrassed her that he had paid enough attention to know this. It occurred to her suddenly that he and Genevieve Ponnelle had plans for her already, plans even beyond her own hesitant dreams. She wanted them to be right.

"My mother was a singer," she told him.

"Come by this genetically, do you? What is her name?"

"Margaret Morgan. No, Gwynn, onstage it was Gwynn."

"She doesn't sing now?"

"She died of meningitis when I was almost four."

"I'm sorry."

She lifted her chin in acknowledgment. "After she died I didn't say another word for two and a half years."

"At all?"

"Nothing. Until I needed to tell my stepmother that I wanted to play the flute. That's when I finally spoke."

"Not a single word for more than two years?" For Liz, her own story finally seemed remote and almost without power. But Giles, hearing it for the first time, seemed astonished.

"Not one. It drove all the adults crazy." She kept her head down, afraid to see the question in his eyes. He walked closer as she continued quietly. "This singing—it scares me. I think I could be better than I was with the flute. But I want it so badly." She shook her head. "I feel like the world will fall around my ears if I reach for it." Her heart felt twice its normal size, thumping behind her ribs.

"Too late it is, not to want it. Besides, you're obviously a musician."

"Are you saying that it's destiny?" she asked, feeling a little foolish.

Giles considered the question. "I'm saying that most people don't get two chances."

But he didn't have the smell of blood and the heart-stopping shock, the metallic scream of pain, the piercing ache still possessing her fingers though they had long since healed. It brought her up short in waking dreams.

She waited, poised in that unknowable moment of the turning tide when waters lie perfectly still, neither coming nor going.

"I can't think that you'd be happy if you didn't try," he added simply.

The swing of those words eased something within her. "No," she agreed. "I wouldn't be happy if I couldn't make music."

They reached her door, and she felt shy and torn, retreating from the unexpected intimacy.

"Thank you, Giles. *Flute* was great."

"You're wonderfully talented," he said. "Don't waste what you've been given because of a superstition."

"I'm having too much fun to give it up now anyway."

He smiled. "You could never have stayed hidden in an orchestra pit. You love the light too much."

Liz laughed. "Can I quote you, Maestro?"

Chapter 22

LIZ CRAMMED EVERYTHING URGENT in her life between nights at the theater and delayed the rest until after hell week. But as April stepped on the heels of March, she decided quite suddenly that she needed to be out in the rising spring—so, on one rare Saturday off, when the morning spread clear skies over the hills, she headed to Caerphilly, to her aunt's garden.

Midmorning found Liz on her knees, up to her elbows in dirt, preparing the flower bed at the side of her aunt's house. Once she had cleared the leaves and other debris and turned it over with a shovel, she took off her gloves in order to feel the earth. It was cold and moist against her fingers, like a compress. The breezes missed this corner of the garden, and the unassuming spring sun warmed her back and shoulders. Keeping the sound close and light, lest the birds hear and mock her, she absently sang "Das Veilchen" to herself.

As eleven o'clock chimed down the road at St. Martin's, she heard her cousin calling from the front of the house. "Hullo, Mum? Are you out here?"

Kate came around the corner and spotted Liz. She hesitated a moment and then came over.

Liz sat back on her heels. "She's back in the potting shed." She squinted up, raising an arm to block the sun.

Kate glanced that way and then looked back at Liz. She moved into the shadow of the house. "I don't know if you've heard," she began hesitantly. "I'm seeing Christopher." She watched for Liz's reaction with visible tension.

Liz caught her breath, then shook her head sharply. "No, actually, he didn't mention it." That was surprising, given how he liked to tweak her. She had heard a rumor that he was seeing someone, and that it was serious, but she had dismissed it as unlikely. Certainly Kate's name had never come up. "I'm kind of surprised you'd settle for my cast-off."

"Cast-off?"

Liz crumbled a clod of dirt with her fingers, then scooped up a handful to squeeze back into a clump. "I dumped him. Or didn't he tell you that?"

"He said that you were too ambitious for his taste."

"No wonder the two of you get on so well." She thrust the trowel into a mound of dirt, ashamed of the irritation she thought to be under control. She squinted up at her cousin again. "What on earth do you see in him?"

"Is that your business?"

"I'm just curious how he fits into any of your requirements. It's not like he's going to want to marry you and have babies."

"Jealous? Because he prefers me to you?"

"Jeez, Kate, I wouldn't have him if he were the last primate on the earth. Go sleep with him. Marry him for all I care."

Kate's fair skin turned a rare, angry scarlet. "I could shake you!"

"Well it's only the truth. I don't care."

"I know you don't. All you care about is your marvelous career."

Liz scrambled to her feet. "Why does that bother you so much?"

"Because." Kate folded her arms. "Because next to you I feel like an utter failure. I'm sick of Mum telling me how proud she is of you, and Caroline telling me how she 'discovered' you. Even Christopher talks about you."

"That's not my fault." But Liz had a queasy sensation that Kate's anger was just.

"I hate it that you're so sure of yourself. You never doubt that you'll get what you want."

"Yes I do."

"Not to hear everyone else tell it."

"I can't help what people say. Besides, there is one thing you're better at."

"What?"

"Apparently you got Christopher to stop seeing other women. He'd never do that for me."

Kate shrugged, a sharp, impatient motion.

"I mean it. At least men take you seriously. Even Titus wasn't a real boyfriend. I just don't seem to attract them the way you do."

"How hard is it? You just don't try."

Liz kicked at a mound of dirt. "Listen, I don't want to fight with you. I hope it works out with Christopher. Really. If that makes you happy." She knew Kate didn't buy her sincerity; she didn't believe it herself. But she obviously couldn't convince Kate that Christopher was not for her.

Ellen emerged from the back of the house. "Katie, I didn't know you'd come. Will you stop for a cup of tea?"

"Oh thanks, Mum, but I've got to go. I just dropped off some things in the hall for your jumble sale."

"Tell Christopher I said hi," Liz mumbled, watching her cousin depart.

Ellen went inside to make tea, and Liz scrubbed her hands with a boar bristle brush until they stung red. They sat together on the porch, sipping tea and listening to the birds whistling and cajoling in the birch trees by the gate. Ellen talked about her plans for the garden. Liz basked in the sun, her imagination running riot with evocative names like fairy foxglove, monkshood, Michaelmas daisy, and purple toadflax.

Eventually her aunt turned the conversation away from these delights. "Are you and Katie having a row?"

Liz ducked her head to take a sip of tea. "No more than usual."

Her aunt gave her a look, and Liz wondered just how much she had heard. "This guy I was seeing decided he'd rather go out with Kate."

Ellen's mouth opened. "While you were dating him?"

"Oh no, we broke up a couple of months ago. He was a—" She suddenly remembered that she was talking to Kate's mother. "We disagreed about some important stuff," she finished vaguely. The breeze stirred the air ever so slightly, sending dead leaves tripping over the walk. "Aunt Ellen, do you think Mum did the right thing, giving up her career to marry Da?"

Her aunt pinched a couple of yellow leaves off of the climbing rose that surrounded the steps. "I wish Meg were here. By now she might have known the answer."

Liz waited.

"You know your Da was a merchant marine, before he started taking his pictures?"

"I knew he'd been to sea."

"He was the sort of man to have a girl in every port. He wanted no part of marriage, no settling down for him. He always said it was the Romany in his blood." Ellen shook her head, dismissing her brother's excuse.

"Did Mum know?"

"Oh yes, your mother knew all about him. And she loved him. When you were conceived he tried to leave. Said he wasn't ready for the responsibility. But she talked him around that one. And he gave it a good go. He even married her."

Liz looked sharply at her aunt, startled to learn that her mother had been pregnant before her wedding.

"She gave up everything for him. As he did for her. And I have to admit, not once in the next five years did she ever seem to regret it. He loved her, and I think he's never gotten over losing her, but if Meg hadn't died, who's to say it would have lasted?"

Silently Liz absorbed this altered picture of her parents.

Ellen continued to strip blighted leaves from the rose. "This young man. What was it you disagreed about?"

Down by the gate, the birds shrieked a warning as one of the tabby cats sauntered past without a glance in their direction.

"Oh," Liz said slowly, "I don't think it's anything Kate needs to bother about."

Chapter 23

WHEN A YEAR HAD PASSED since her first voice lesson, Liz began to prepare a recital for the fall. She'd participated in informal studio recitals with other students over the months, but this would be her first solo program. Language and diction, art songs and arias, and practice and study consumed every moment away from Cygnet and Swann's. Once she and Madame laid down the technical foundation of a piece, Giles helped her to shape it. He seemed to know that after the vague emotional interpretation she'd gotten away with as an instrumentalist, lyrics tangled and confined her. "What's the important word?" he would ask. "Why is that phrase repeated? What are you going to do with it? What are you thinking about there?" Sometimes she wished he would just tell her what to do, as Madame did, but she never said so.

An evening came when the last customers at Swann's would not be rushed. By the time she dashed into Hopkins Centre, which housed the practice rooms for the Welsh College, her hour was nearly half gone. She burst into the claustrophobic room where Giles sat working on something at the piano.

"Sorry to keep you waiting," she said, gasping for air.

"No matter. Catch your breath," he replied easily. He watched her shrug off her donkey coat. "Do you need to warm up?"

"No, I'm ready. Caroline usually lets me sing upstairs in the flat at lunch when I work at Swann's. And Madame got me into the practice rooms at University College, so I go there after work."

"Every night?"

"Well, not on lesson days. Or when I work with you."

"When do you ever have time for fun?"

She looked at him blankly. "This is fun."

"But don't you ever see a movie, or go for a walk, or, I don't know, knit?"

She burst out laughing. "Knitting is not my idea of fun."

"Balance," he warned, waggling a finger at her sternly. "You need balance or you'll get burned out."

"But I need to catch up."

"With what?"

"Vocal repertoire. I trained as a flautist, remember?"

"Liz, it's not a race. Everyone develops at her own pace. How old are you, anyway?"

"Twenty-three."

"You have plenty of time. Don't push now. You'll regret it later."

Liz rolled her eyes.

Giles, busy pulling out the folder that contained all the music for her recital, missed the look. "Shall we sing? What are you working on?"

"Fauré. 'Les Berceaux.'"

"One of my favorites. Tell me what the words mean."

Liz's eyes narrowed. "You don't need to quiz me, you know. I do my homework."

Giles looked startled. "I don't mean it that way. It just helps me understand how you feel the piece, where you might put the emphases."

"Oh. Sorry." Flushing, she shuffled through her untidy stack of music and propped the piece on the stand. "Let's see. Along the quay the great ships lie, which the tide—uh—sways, rocks, silently. They . . . have no care?"

Giles nodded silently.

"They care not for the cradles which are . . . hmm . . . rocked by the hands of the women." Her hands gestured in the air as she shifted the order of words to make grammatical sense. "But there comes—no, *viendras*, there *will* come—a day of good-byes, when the women will cry and the men—uh, the curious men—are lured by the temptation . . . the tempting horizons. On that day the great ships will leave the port, which fades, but will feel their mass . . . held back by the distant pull of the cradles."

She looked at Giles. To her surprise he said nothing, but he started to roll the barcarole out over the air. She closed her eyes. The ships rocked at anchor, the cradles rocked near watchful parents. She began to sing quietly, drawing the tone from some primal place inside to float on the harbored sea he painted with the keyboard. The sway of her body, her shoulders, her hands, her breath, communicated to him each crescendo and ritardando, the shape of each phrase.

When she released her last, soft note she stood perfectly still. She waited until Giles lifted his foot from the sustain pedal and took his hands from the keys. Then she met his eyes, a little awed. Though they had not discussed any of it, it had held together perfectly. She knew it was a fluke, but a shiver ran down her spine.

"How was that?" he asked, his smile telling her that he understood.

"Marvelous!"

"Do you mean to push the tempo a bit at the top of page six? I thought perhaps we ought to draw it out a little."

"'*Tentent les horizons qui leurrent*'? Absolutely not. Most of it needs to be . . ." She groped for the right word. "Well, controlled, held back, *retinue*. But the energy needs to push ahead there."

"You're right." He focused intensely on her.

"I am?"

He began to laugh. "Yes, you are, and don't you dare concede! Don't let me lead you so much. Trust your instincts. You're in charge, you know."

"But what do I know? I always feel like I'm going to get it wrong."

"There is no such thing. Less effective, perhaps, or less true. But the most important thing you can do is make a song your own. From your heart a song will sound different than from any other. That's what an audience wants to hear."

"I guess," she said.

"You're doing fine. Let's go back and solidify some of what we did."

They went over the piece slowly, dissecting it line by line. Liz scribbled notes in the margins to reconstruct the perfect, if serendipitous, interpretation. Giles waited patiently through the pauses, his hands wandering over the keyboard.

"By the way," he said suddenly. Familiar chords from Mendelssohn materialized, transposed into a minor key. "Have you heard the news?"

"What news?"

"Christopher asked Kate to marry him."

Her pencil stopped moving. "You're joking."

"Told me himself, he did."

"Is she pregnant?"

Her cynicism did not seem to surprise him. He only shook his head. "I don't know. I've never known him to marry the ones he got pregnant."

"What does he see in her? She's so quiet and so . . . nice."

"And that is bad?"

She looked quickly at him, and he disguised his smile.

"She's dull, Giles. Dull. What has she got that I don't?"

"Christopher wants a pretty girl who will sleep with him and flatter him and give him undivided attention without expecting much in return. I should guess that you wouldn't settle for that."

After a moment she said, "I think I'm jealous."

He looked at her quizzically. "Of Kate?"

"Oh, I don't want to be the love of his life. But I guess I'm a singer, not a lover."

"One precludes the other?"

"All my energy is in music. And I love it, I do. But sometimes, when I see people together, I feel like I'm missing something."

"Give it time. Maybe you need to focus on music right now. I'm sure you'll be the love of someone's life."

They continued to work, but it seemed to Liz that Giles stopped her more frequently, picking at things she thought she had long ago conquered.

He stopped again. "Relax and open that high F. I've heard you do so much more with it."

She tried again, but still he didn't like it.

"Take a couple of deep breaths."

"I know how to sing," she snapped.

He did not reply.

"Sorry. You're right. Can we try again from the same place?" So they did, but neither of them was satisfied.

"Suppose we stop for tonight?" he suggested, folding up the music. "Let's go get something to eat. No more talk about the recital."

She could feel tension in her shoulders that wasn't usually there when she worked. Perhaps, she agreed reluctantly, one night off wouldn't hurt.

* * *

THE NEXT TIME LIZ WORKED with Giles, two weeks later, she went to his home in Llandaff to accommodate his schedule. He lived in the cottage behind Jane and Simon's house, where she had now come for several cast parties. The large estate house stood at the end of a cul-de-sac off the main road. The tower of the cathedral stretched into the sky above her as she followed the driveway around to the blowzy rose garden. The oxidized green of Giles's car blended into the shrubs. Beyond it she saw the little square house, built of the same gray stone as the main house. In the window boxes, lavender petunias mixed with some tiny white flowers to drape over the edge, fragrant in the twilight. A graceful oak tree shadowed the west side of the cottage, while the other side was exposed.

She tapped at the green door, and Giles opened it almost immediately. She was surprised to find him noticeably tired, his clothes wrinkled. For once he was not wearing a tie, and he hadn't shaved in a day. He had a beaker of tea in his hand, and he smiled when he saw her.

"*Croeso.* Come in."

"How was Glasgow?" Liz asked, walking past him through the door. "Did you just get back?"

"An hour ago. It was all uphill work, with only fair results by the end."

"I didn't realize how late you'd be. We could do this some other time."

"Certainly not. Looking forward to working with you saved my week. Tea? It's made."

"Please."

She looked around as he went to get her tea. The large room was shaped like an L. The kitchen was at one end, where the oak tree shadowed the building. Beyond the windows she could see a cow pasture. In the crook of the L he had placed a rocking chair and a slouching easy chair with a small table. Behind the chairs, floor-to-ceiling bookcases held hundreds of paperbacks. From one high shelf a small Buddha gazed over the house. At the other end of the L his piano, desk, and file cabinet defined his studio. A covered harp stood silent in one corner. She guessed the bedroom was behind the closed door, filling the square of the cottage.

"I love this place," she said as Giles handed her the steaming drink.

"I owe it to Jane and Simon's generosity. When they heard that I had split with Diana, they were kind enough to offer me this. It was originally an artist's studio, built in the 1920s for one of the sons of the family. I was worried that the piano would suffer, but the temperature seems to be fairly well controlled."

The windows were all propped open, and the space was filled with the sweet, light scents of the vast variety of flowers in the garden. Liz thought that her aunt would be envious. The room was lit only with lamps, adding a sense of smallness to the uncluttered space.

"You must love living here." She sipped her tea and pulled out her folder.

"It's very peaceful," he agreed. He set his tea on the worktop and sat down at the upright piano, which jutted out from the wall at an angle. "How's the recital coming?"

"I just need one more set to round it out. Something from the twentieth century." She thumbed through her music for the piece they were working on.

"Would you be interested . . ." He seemed to catch himself.

"What?" Liz asked, her eyes on his.

"I've done some composing and arranging. Perhaps you'd be interested in including a few of my pieces?"

"I'd love to!"

He raised a cautionary hand. "You ought to hear them first, see if they suit you."

"But your 'Greensleeves' was marvelous." She noticed the puzzled look he gave her. "Christopher had a tape. It's the only one of yours I've heard, but I absolutely adored it. You have more? For voice?"

"I do. You could look them over."

"Yes, please."

"You are not obligated." He seemed to be regretting the offer.

"Maestro, you know that if I don't like them I won't waste my time."

He pulled a fat file out of the bottom of the file cabinet and set aside her recital folder. He played the pieces one by one as she leaned over his shoulder to read the vocal line, cupping her warm tea in both hands. The songs were at times dark and brooding, at times light and airy. She sang through them with increasing excitement.

"These are gems," she pronounced, sitting down next to him on the piano bench and picking out a vocal line that she particularly liked.

"You honestly like them?"

"I love them." She pushed aside one piece and found something she hadn't seen. "What are these?"

He took the music from her. "This is a song cycle I did. A year on Mount Snowdon. *Yr Wydda*." He paged through it thoughtfully.

"It's in Welsh?"

He looked over at her. "I don't suppose you know Welsh?"

"No, sadly enough. My father refused to teach me. My mother used to sing to me in Welsh though."

"Did she?"

"I can't reproduce any of it, but I bet I could give these a shot. It can't be harder than German or French." She took the songs back.

He shook his head, chuckling. "I think it could, but I'm no judge."

"Run through them for me. Please?"

He played them, singing softly, almost to himself, and stretching a translation under the rests in the vocal part. Liz listened with her eyes closed, trying not to get caught up by the tangle of consonants on the page. The garden seemed to invade the cottage with damp, cool magic, the sweetness of honeysuckle twining around the songs. She grew more and more enchanted with his music. When he finished she opened her eyes, excited. "Oh, I want to do these!"

"But Liz—"

"No, really, they're the best ones. You can help me with the Welsh."

"I don't know. It would be taking on a lot."

"I thrive on hard work. These are wonderful. You should have them published."

He smiled. "*Diolch*, that easy it is."

"Would you mind if I sang them?"

"I would not." He considered her. "I rather think you would do them justice."

A moth stumbled in through one of the open windows. Liz watched as Giles turned off the lamp that it sought, coaxed it to leave, and shut the windows.

"Has anyone else performed these?" she asked when he finished his rescue.

"Not yet."

"Then we could have a world premier!" She laughed in delight. "Can I take them home for a few days?"

"Be my guest."

"Do you have copies? These are all manuscript."

"No. But I trust you." He flopped into the overstuffed chair, stretching his legs out.

She shook her head, laying them back down on the piano. "No, don't give them to me then. Make some copies. I'd feel awful if anything happened to them."

"Nothing will happen."

"You can't let them get lost."

"Do you commonly lose things?" He laced his fingers together, putting his index fingers against his lips.

"No. Lateness is my vice."

"Then take them and welcome."

"Well, if you're sure." She stacked them neatly back into the folder, squaring the corners with unusual care. An awkward gratitude, whether for his generosity in offering them in the first place or for his trust in letting her take them home, tied her tongue. As she tried to decide what to say, she glanced up and saw the clock. "Jeez, is that the time?" They had filled the whole hour and then some with his compositions.

She pulled out her checkbook, but Giles waved her off. "I won't take your money for indulging my ego. We can schedule another hour to really work later this week if you like."

"Okay." She started gathering up her books and music.

"Will I run you home, then?"

"You don't need to. You're tired."

"I am, a bit. But it's no bother."

"I can get the bus. The last one doesn't go until nine thirty-five."

He contemplated her. "You could always stay."

Something inside her quivered at his invitation, like dew in morning sun. She met his eyes, swallowed, and said without inflection, "Why Mr. Offeryn, what are you suggesting?"

For a moment he hesitated, but then he sighed. "Something terribly inappropriate, no doubt. It's just that you looked so . . . nice, sitting there in the soft light." He shook his head briskly and pushed himself out of the chair. "Never mind. But I best get you home before I fall asleep."

He went past her to the coat rack behind the door. Liz stood, frozen, straining to identify the curious sensations rolling through her. When he turned to her, pulling on his jacket and rattling his keys, she still hadn't moved.

"Liz?"

She sprang to life, snatching up her coat and book bag. "Never mind, I don't need a ride. I don't want to bother you."

"It is no—"

"I'll call you about next week. Thanks. Bye." She waved vaguely, flung open the door, and charged up the driveway toward the sidewalk.

"Make up your mind," she muttered, rounding the corner to where the bus stopped. But she wasn't sure about whom she meant.

Chapter 24

"SOMETHING WEIRD HAPPENED last night. I think Giles asked me to sleep with him."

Caroline thought that was funny. "You aren't sure?"

Liz described the conversation, feeling like she wasn't capturing the surreal context of it.

"Of course that's what he wanted. Not such a bad idea," Caroline added shrewdly.

"Caroline!"

"Both of you need some recreation."

"I'm not going to have an affair for recreation. Anyway, he'd appoint himself my conscience."

"Aha, you have thought about this."

"I work with him enough to know that he's extremely demanding." Liz shoved a stack of books aside, nearly toppling them.

"I thought that's what you like about working with him."

"It is. And it's fine when we're working. But it would be incredibly tedious to be involved with someone who was always reminding you to live up to your potential."

"When did you ever need to be reminded of that?"

"Not yet. And I never will." She bounced the eraser end of a pencil on the countertop. "I'm not even sure I can work with him anymore. It'll be too awkward."

"Don't be a goose. He just wants a little fun. It has nothing to do with work." Caroline was laughing, giving up on her crusade.

"He didn't mean it anyway," Liz snapped. Her anger simmered for another hour, and finally she called him. He was not at the college, but she found him at home.

"I can't work with you anymore," she began abruptly.

He didn't reply immediately. When he did he spoke slowly. "Of course you are upset with me. Don't decide this in haste."

"Upset? Try angry. Try furious."

"Can we at least talk? I have to teach at one. Could you manage an early lunch?"

"I don't have anything else to say."

"I'm sure you could think of something. Besides, I would like to explain."

"Fine. But I've made up my mind."

Just after eleven, Giles came to the shop. Liz glared at him, her arms crossed.

"Ready to go?"

"I guess." She didn't budge.

Caroline whisked out of the office. "Giles. How are you?"

He had a smile for her. "I've come to borrow your clerk for a bit if you don't mind."

"Of course." Caroline raised her eyebrows and smirked as she followed Liz back into the office. "A date already? You work fast." She kept her voice low.

"Would you please just shut up?" Liz hissed.

For once Caroline backed off. "Sorry. Take your time."

Liz shrugged into her coat and followed Giles out of the shop. She didn't ask where they were going.

He glanced over at her. "Still angry?"

She'd forgotten her scarf, and the day was cool. She hunkered deeper into her coat and didn't bother to answer.

Giles refrained from further comment until they were sitting at a table in Barnaby's with soup and sausage rolls.

"I owe you an apology. Again."

"Did you mean it?" She blurted it out as though a spell had been lifted from her tongue.

He hesitated. "At that moment last night, perhaps I did. But not the way . . . not truly."

She stared at him, her chin thrust out belligerently. "Do you know how insulting that is? First you ask, and now you say, 'Sorry, no, I've changed my mind.' Am I supposed to be flattered or something? The least you could do is have the courtesy to follow up if you're going to make a suggestion like that." As it came out of her mouth she realized that this was not the complaint she'd intended at all.

Giles, too, seemed confused by her protest. His brow squeezed together as if he was trying to translate her words. "And if I did? Would that change anything?" He spoke softly and evenly.

She glared at him, trying to decide if, in fact, he would have made good on his offer if she'd given him any encouragement. "It was a silly idea. I don't have time to get involved with anybody. Besides, you're the last man I would have a one-night stand with, considering that we were working together."

"So I'm damned if I do, damned if I don't."

"What do you mean?"

"If I tell you that I'm attracted to you, you'll be offended because it interferes with your Master Plan," Giles said, shrugging. "And if I tell you that I'm not attracted to you, you'll take it as an insult."

Liz considered his statement and replied with a sharp nod. "Exactly." She tore up a piece of bread just to have something to abuse. "I actually liked you. And then you went and turned out to be just like your ratty friend Chris."

Giles stiffened and pulled back as though she had slapped him. Which, she supposed—almost regretting it—she had.

"Whether or not I'm attracted to you, I'm not in love with you," Giles said. "So sleeping with you would certainly be a mistake. I do realize that."

Liz nodded in agreement, unable to look at him.

"I'm very sorry if I hurt you."

She toyed with her soupspoon, silent. "You did mean it, didn't you?"

He didn't reply, which she took as a yes.

"I was serious when I said I couldn't work with you anymore," she insisted.

"Would you reconsider if I promise never to mention it again?"

"Don't you understand? I'll always be wondering what you're thinking." Liz looked up from her spoon. "Give me one good reason why I should forgive you."

Giles sat back, defeated. Then he raised his chin. "Where will you find an accompanist as good as I am?"

She was annoyed that he knew the one argument she couldn't counter. But the fact that he had said it also made a deep impression. It was so unlike him.

"I made a mistake," he said, pressing his advantage when she remained silent. "Don't you think I know that? I was coming off a terrible week, and your enthusiasm was . . . flattering. I got carried away. But is that a reason to jeopardize our music? And our friendship? I value those too. I don't know how to make it right, but let me try."

"I'm still mad at you," Liz warned him. But the tightness in her chest began to relax.

"And so you should be. But I hope you'll get over that. When I've earned it."

She examined her unmatched hands where they lay, side by side, on the table. "All right," she said slowly. "I don't know how I'd replace you." She sighed, feeling the tingle in her fingers. "You know, nobody's even asked in a long time. Even if you didn't mean it." She glanced up quickly as she said it.

His face was unreadable, his eyes wary and watchful. "Are you ready to go back?"

* * *

AFTER THAT, ALL OF THEIR EXCHANGES were short and edgy, to the point and only that. Giles kept his promise never to refer to that night again. He was so polite and distant, in fact, that Liz began to wonder if she had imagined the whole thing.

She'd left his flat without his songs. She briefly considered not doing them, but they were too appealing. When she rang him to schedule another hour she asked for them, but he resisted.

"The Snowdon cycle? I think you should do something else. There are some Vaughn-Williams folk songs that would suit you. Or what about some Ned Rorem?"

"I want to do those."

"You don't have time to learn the Welsh."

"You said you'd teach me."

"I don't have time," he said shortly. After a moment he continued, "Anyway, it was a mistake to show them to you."

"But I really liked them," Liz pressed. "Would you just forget all that silliness?"

There was a longer pause. "Do you always get your own way?"

"Please?"

She heard him sigh. "I'll copy them. You can pick them up at the music department if you like."

"What about—"

"I'll record the Welsh. You can learn it from a tape."

"Can we—"

"I have to go. I will see you on Tuesday. At the college," he added firmly.

As if she could be in any doubt. Liz hung up, grimacing at the phone.

To her great surprise, the incident at his cottage did no harm to their ability to work together. In the swift waters of shaping a song, she forgot anything but the work at hand. For long stretches she would be so involved that she completely forgot to be on her guard. They would almost fall back into the easy rapport they had developed. But when the hour was up, the distance returned like a cold draft.

Once in a great while she wondered if it would be better if she had taken him up on his offer.

Chapter 25

ON THE LAST SUNDAY AFTERNOON IN September Liz walked out onto the little stage in Gerient Evans Hall at the college to an astonishing amount of applause. Virtually everyone she knew, at least in this part of the world, sat before her. Her aunt and uncle had come early to get good seats. Curtis and Jane and Simon, and even several choristers from the theater, sat in a formidable block near the front. Five or six patrons of the bookshops had succumbed to Bert's enthusiastic promotion. Three of Giles's colleagues, members of the music faculty at the college, exacerbated her nerves. Even Huw, who professed never to attend such events, sat unobtrusively in the last row. Forty-six people in all, if you counted Madame, who stood impassively by the double doors at the back of the hall.

Liz drew a deep breath to slow the fluttering pulse in her throat, happy to stand sheltered in the great curve of the piano. She forced her nervousness down, away from her throat and tongue where it could interfere, down into her abdomen, where it would quiver and brighten her performance like a flame under a kettle. She pictured the music on the page. The first words rose in her mind, ready at her bidding.

She turned to Giles, who sat poised at the piano. He smiled encouragingly. Silently she said *yes* and nodded. He brought his hands to the keys and gave her one more quick glance. She faced the audience.

Giles started to play. In a smooth motion Liz inhaled, opened her mouth, and began to sing.

Five songs by Handel opened the program. The clean, simple compositions constituted a private nod to the favorite flute repertoire she'd lost. Liz had first treated them as instrumental pieces, not applying words until satisfied with the melody and line. Now her Italian rippled and rolled, each phrase a treasury of marvelous sounds.

She felt Giles's presence in his playing, subtle and sublime. Their eyes met only at the beginning of a piece, but he followed her and guided her flawlessly. A note she had trouble finding sounded ever so slightly loud in the accompaniment of the following measure. Soft chords in another place reminded her to start a particular crescendo quietly, to realize the full power of contrast by the end of the phrase. In a thousand small ways, the piano grounded her.

After the first set they left the stage for a brief break. She wanted to dash back out immediately, but Giles made her slow down and sip some water.

"Take your time," he reminded her. "Don't go out until you're ready."

"Right," she agreed, barely having heard him.

They returned to the stage, and when the audience fell silent, she cued Giles once more. The program continued with five pieces by Mozart. First, three art songs threaded together by common threads of nature and love. The third of these described meeting Cupid in the woods, and led her ever so nicely to the two precious arias she had learned from *Le Nozze di Figaro*. Cherubino's lilting "Voi che sapete" lay perfectly in her voice, as did the more impassioned "Non so più cosa son." Liz even resisted her tendency to rush the last piece, controlling the headlong tumbling of the notes while still allowing the energy to ignite the lyrics.

They took a ten-minute intermission. Liz fidgeted, eager to return to the stage. She drank water and fussed with her hair. In about three minutes, she was impatient to continue. She peeked out. The hum of conversation surrounded the milling audience. Standing, the crowd seemed twice as large. Her heart thumped, surprised by tardy stage fright. She turned away from the door and began to pace the small room.

Giles stood by the window, his hands in his pockets, watching a flock of sparrows bickering in the stripped trees. She came up behind him and grabbed his elbow.

"How can you be so calm?"

"It's going well," he said. "You've nothing to be nervous about."

"There's danger in complacency."

"I take nothing for granted," he said. "But we've worked hard. It's paying off."

"Thank you," she said after a moment.

He looked down at her and shrugged. "I'm doing my job."

"But you do it incredibly well," she insisted, piqued that he continued to maintain the distance she had insisted upon.

Madame appeared with grudging encouragement. "Respectable job."

Giles acknowledged this with a nod, but Liz protested. "Respectable? It's marvelous! Did you hear how well the Mozart arias went?"

"Yes. But mind you don't lose your concentration."

The Fauré set followed. From working with these French songs Liz now clearly understood the value of lyrics. Her flute could suggest melancholy or joy. But words, the voice, provided precious richness, the intimate detail of a lover's death, the gold of autumn sunlight in the woods. Without the flute in her hands, she felt somehow closer to her audience.

She finished the program with Giles's stirring song cycle. The four songs described a year on the mountain, evoking each season in the lyrics and the harmonies. The set began with "Gwanwẙn"—"Spring"—a simple folk song ornamented with birdcalls in the piano. "Haf" ("Summer") came as a wistful ballad, sung in a melting legato over a jig-like piano arrangement. "Hẙdref" ("Autumn") marched forward inexorably with chords from a hymnal. And "Winter," "Gaeaf," followed as a fierce, warlike curse. Just at the end came an echo of the bird trills, suggesting spring again.

The music cursed, cried, caressed; Liz reveled in it. She wanted to make Giles proud of the way she handled his work, and when she finished, she knew she had.

As she and Giles took their bows, Liz anticipated the encore the audience so obviously wanted. She would sing a comic song from *La Périchole* in which the heroine enumerates all the flaws of her lover. She planned to flirt madly with Bert when she sang it, knowing it would make the song easier to deliver. She winked at him as she turned to leave the stage.

But as she passed Giles, exchanging a look of complicity with him, an idea came to her that was too good to pass up. She did know better. To change the plan without warning or rehearsal begged for mistakes. But her scheme pleased her unbearably; it would be the perfect payback for the awkwardness he had caused.

Carried away with the approval of the crowd, Liz led Giles, unsuspecting, back onstage.

As the audience settled down in what she sensed as satisfaction, she turned to Giles. He smiled, relaxed and pleased with the performance. His eyes asked, and she nodded, returning the smile. He played the introduction. She put her hand on her hip, tossed him an arch look, and began to sing.

"*You are not rich, you are no beauty, your manners cannot be admired.*" She addressed not Bert, but Giles, with obvious distaste. Though clearly startled, he did not falter.

"*You have no proper sense of duty, your wit leaves much to be desired.*" She noticed his flush and wondered too late if she had made a mistake. She was committed now.

"*As for your gifts, you are no musician,*" she jeered.

The audience chuckled while her accompanist, professional to the end, kept a straight face.

"*You've not the slightest claim to fame, nor are you burdened with ambition, there's nothing to you, but all the same,*" she warbled, easing around the piano to swoop down on him from behind.

"*I adore you, my sweet, and everything that you do, I love you and I cannot live without you.*" She draped herself over his shoulders like a mantle of whipped cream and felt him resist. "*I adore you, my sweet, I have no notion why. I shall love you, I shall love you till I die.*"

She flitted off to a safe distance for the second verse. She sensed tension in Giles's playing—the staccati were sharp, the tempo was brisk, he even made a mistake once—but he pulled it off. For the second chorus she merely leaned over the piano and batted her eyelashes, sweetly making vocal love to him. The audience loved it, and the burst of applause at the end drowned out her doubts.

Though Giles smiled, and even offered her his own applause, his eyes had the depth and chill of a winter sea. As soon as he had followed her offstage, out of sight of the audience, he caught her arm.

"*Beth y diafol?* How dare you spring that on me!"

"But you played it up perfectly! What's the big deal?"

He ignored the compliment. "It was inconsiderate and unprofessional."

"Well the audience loved it," Liz snapped back, and she pushed past him to return to the stage and the appreciative crowd. She gave him no choice but to follow. When they joined hands for a bow his fingers felt hard and unfriendly.

As the hall cleared, she and Giles did not speak to each other. It didn't help that people kept mentioning the encore. Their mutual friends teased them mercilessly. Maintaining an ebullient facade grew harder. The discord encroached, advancing Liz's normal letdown.

Caroline, Bert, Christopher, and Kate lingered after the rest of the crowd.

"Let us take the pair of you to supper," Christopher offered. "Of course you're welcome too, Madame," he added as an afterthought.

Liz, who by this time simply wanted to get home, wondered with irritation if it ever occurred to him that such a situation might be awkward.

"Thank you, no, I shall be going." Madame touched Liz lightly on the shoulder. "You should be proud of yourself. I am."

Startled, Liz could not reply before her teacher was gone, but warmth spread through her at the rare compliment.

"I think I will be going as well," Giles said, tucking his music away in his slouching leather satchel.

"Come on, boyo, don't be shy," Chris badgered him.

"It was your success as much as hers," Caroline added.

Giles reluctantly agreed. The group bickered amiably over where to go but finally ended up at Savastano's. Liz sat between Caroline and Bert, across from Christopher, who had Kate on one side and Giles on the other. Her was body relaxed now, the adrenaline rush slowing. She ached where tension had all but held her together. She wasn't hungry, only sleepy, the brightness of the afternoon worn away to a dull glow deep in her belly. She munched absently on breadsticks and observed the rest of them from what seemed a great distance.

Christopher and Caroline speculated enthusiastically about *Merry Widow*, which began rehearsal next week. Huw was presenting a one-performance-only fund-raiser for the Arts Council. Some famous names would take the main roles, and he had handpicked his chorus from the best of GSSSG. Liz had declined his invitation, but hearing their excitement, she wondered if she would be able to stand the loneliness of being left out.

Bert added an occasional opinion to the flow of conversation. Kate had little to say, but her eyes followed Christopher with singular attention. Only Liz and Giles sat silently, separate.

When the wine came, Christopher poured and raised his glass. "A toast," he said. "To Liz and Giles. The next Sutherland and Bonynge."

Liz's hand nearly knocked over her glass. As Kate, Bert, and Caroline agreed, clinking their glasses, Liz didn't dare look at Giles. The blood rose swift and hot in her face. In jabbing back at him she had exposed the whole silly mess to their friends and led them to the exact wrong conclusion. She understood precisely why he was angry.

Chapter 26

LIZ PUTTERED AIMLESSLY ABOUT Cygnet all the next day. Snippets of recital music materialized now and then, but she let them go, nearly content. By midafternoon her mind was as empty of the program as the obvious, cloudless sky. When a customer complimented her on the recital, she blinked and paused before smiling her thanks. It seemed a year ago, not a day.

In the afternoon Bert called her to the phone, and to her delight, it was Huw.

"Liz, you were charming yesterday. What a wonderful stage presence you have."

"It's so nice you called," she said, her voice softened by her smile. "If I have presence it's thanks to you, you know."

"All the more reason why I should be thoroughly ashamed to ask you this favor."

"Ask away."

"I need more good voices for *Merry Widow* at New Theater. I know you said you couldn't, but I wonder if I could persuade you to sing in the chorus, just this once. It's only one performance, and you would be so wonderful."

She started to reply, but he rattled on. "A lot of our regular choristers aren't up to it, but it might be a nice opportunity for you to work with professionals. It's not a great deal of music, and I would be very careful of your time. But it's a splendid show and we'll have the sets and costumes from English National Opera. Plus a choreographer. I'm sure you'd enjoy it."

By now Liz was chuckling to herself. "Of course I'll do it," she broke in.

"Will you? Will you really? "

"I'd love to."

"You are kind. You're sure now? I had to bribe Mr. Offeryn."

"With what?"

"I told him he could conduct *Yeomen* in the spring."

"So he's going to sing in the chorus?"

"Not for the first time."

"But he should be conducting. How is he ever going to get anywhere?"

"Ah, he's on his way, never fear. I've known the boy a long time, and I actually think this detour has been good for him. You might say his personality caught up with his intellect."

"But hasn't he burned his bridges?"

"I doubt it. Whatever damage might have been done, he has the humility and patience to negotiate his way back. And people thought very highly of him, I do know that."

"I hope you're right."

"I do confess I'm taking shameless advantage of my favorites."

She could just imagine the elfin grin squeezing the corners of Huw's eyes. She laughed. "So what will you offer me?"

"I'm afraid all I have left is my undying gratitude. That will have to do."

"That's plenty," she assured him.

* * *

LIZ HAD NOT FORGOTTEN, PERHAPS would never forget, that her teacher had said she was proud of her. But Madame did not mention that again. She put Liz back to work immediately at her lesson on Tuesday. They evaluated the minor details of the recital, the small blurs that no one but she and Madame and perhaps Giles would ever know about. Liz vowed to attend to them, blithely aware of their insignificance. But when she thought they had finished the critique, Madame brought her up short.

"What about that encore?" she said at last. "Why didn't you do it as rehearsed?"

Liz blushed. "It was spur of the moment. I thought it would be funny. He didn't like it much that I didn't warn him."

"Was that it? I thought perhaps he didn't like being twitted about his lack of ambition."

"What do you mean, 'lack of ambition'?"

"He apprenticed in Paris, you know, as a conductor. I'm told he was quite the rising star. But he lost his nerve. He gave it up rather suddenly and ended up back here."

"That doesn't sound like him. He's one of the most grounded performers I know."

"A recital hall in Cardiff is entirely different from a concert hall in Paris. You saw how making a little change affected him yesterday."

"That was my fault. He's a great accompanist and a wonderful coach. I'm in his debt."

Madame frowned. "I hope you aren't getting the wrong idea."

"What wrong idea?"

"It would be easy to misunderstand the commerce between singer and accompanist. Don't get carried away just because he's a personable young man."

"Don't be silly," Liz snapped. "I've worked with accompanists all my life. I'm not that naïve."

"Good. Because I confess, I wondered yesterday."

"I was acting," Liz said through clenched teeth.

With a sharp glance, Madame abruptly changed the subject. "Tell me what's next."

Liz hesitated. "Huw called today. He's directing *Merry Widow* with a London-based producer. It's a fund-raiser, one performance only. He asked me to be in it."

"You're not ready to sing Valencienne."

"I know." Liz took a deep breath. "I said I would do chorus."

Madame raised an eyebrow and waited for an explanation. Liz stood her ground, arms folded.

"Elizabeth, it's time you stopped merely amusing yourself."

"Huw asked me to do it as a favor to him. He's the first one who ever took a chance on me, and I want to pay him back. This is terribly important to him."

Madame swept her up and down with her gaze and came out from behind the piano with a less than gracious sigh. "Sit down."

Liz sat.

"When are you going to take this seriously?"

"I do take it seriously. I work hard."

"I don't mean that. You do work hard." She considered Liz for a moment, and Liz tried not to squirm like a guilty six-year-old.

"You've outgrown those amateurs, but you seem determined to stay there and stagnate."

Liz, silent, glanced across the room to a photograph of her teacher, her arms full of flowers on the stage at La Scala twenty-five years earlier.

"How do I make you understand? You could do this professionally."

A slow, familiar trickle of adrenaline began in her solar plexus. The half-hour chimes from nearby Llandaff Cathedral welled up in the charged atmosphere. Liz went to the dark window, her hands in her pockets. Reflected in the glass she could see the studio, and Madame watching her.

"'Amusing myself,' as you say, is the whole reason I want to sing. It makes me happy. Is there anything wrong with that?"

"It should make you happy. But done properly, singing is far more than rehearsals and cast parties. It can be a difficult life. Nothing can take precedence over your work."

Liz barely marked the warning. "My mother was a musician. I feel like I owe it to her memory to be one too."

"Do you realize that this is the third time you've talked about what you owe someone else? First Giles, then Huw, now your mother. Try this: You owe it to me. And you owe it to yourself."

In the silence it occurred to Liz that her teacher must want to shake her. She faced her. As she opened her mouth a shiver surged up her spine and over her scalp. She couldn't bear to be told she was merely average. But she was almost more afraid to hear that she was not. Her left hand, hidden away in her pocket, seemed to heat and throb. "What do you honestly think of my chances?" she asked.

The blue eyes glittered. "Do you expect me to tell your fortune, to say that you'll be a great diva?"

"Of course not, but I—"

Her teacher cut through her protest. "I will not tell you that. You must not go out expecting to be blessed. You must earn the privilege each time you sing." She turned her back, continuing so softly that Liz could barely hear her. "But if you sing every day because you cannot bear not to, then yes." She looked at Liz over her shoulder. "I do think you could be . . . great."

Her unexpected admission started a fluttering in Liz's chest that lay somewhere between fright and exhilaration. She reminded herself to breathe.

"It's easy to succeed if all you ever expect of yourself is to be better than the amateurs at the Gilbert and Sullivan Society. It is time you tested yourself."

Liz remembered what Giles had said, that most people did not get two chances. She pulled her left hand out of her pocket and inspected it. Maybe she did have an obligation.

Madame walked over to the piano. Her fingers touched but did not sound the keys.

Liz could not see her eyes. "This means a lot to me. It's my whole life."

The silence gave way to a single note, played softly and dying away slowly. The vibrations faded beyond hearing, but Liz strained to know exactly when they stopped.

"Very well." Madame looked up, taking her hand off the keyboard. "You have a lot of work to do. It's time I prepared you for a formal training program. I want you placed in one of the best: London, or Manchester. If you don't get out of the provinces, you will never rise as you should."

Liz drew a deep breath, anticipation tingling through her.

"If you must sing Gilbert and Sullivan," Madame continued, "I want you to prepare Elsie for *Yeomen of the Guard* next spring."

"But that's—"

"What?"

Caroline's role, she had been going to say. But she did not.

"The music is very fine for operetta, though it's not done as often as some of the others. Do you know the story?"

Liz shook her head.

"It's not a comedy. It takes place in sixteenth-century London. Elsie is a street singer who needs money for her sick mother. She travels with the jester Jack Point, who thinks they will be married. She ends up in a political intrigue; she's convinced to marry a prisoner named Colonel Fairfax for a payment of one hundred crowns. She expects to be a widow when he is beheaded that night, but instead he escapes." Madame scanned her shelf and pulled out the score, handing it to Liz. "I think you'll find her an interesting character. She's caught between the factions who want him dead and those who want him alive. Finally she determines that he must really be dead, and she falls in love with someone else altogether. At the very end he turns out to be the maligned Colonel Fairfax."

"Sounds messy," agreed Liz.

"Elsie is not one of these silly *comprimarios* you're used to playing. You can pull it off. I will say this for Huw Parsons: he's making an actress out of you."

* * *

COLD BUSTLED AT LIZ'S HEELS as she walked home. Beside her danced that temptation—the temptation she had resisted until now. Madame's assessment had been correct. She hadn't been taking her singing quite seriously, though not for the reasons Madame suspected.

Until two years ago, failure had never seemed a real risk. But the graphic reminder of her accident on her left hand made her always alert to the fact that some things were not in her control. Now, nothing was certain. Perils rose at every turn.

And once she failed, what then?

The risk of losing something she so loved ached in her belly like hunger, a familiar fear.

Chapter 27

MADAME HAD BEEN RIGHT IN another way. Gratitude to Huw notwith-standing, Liz had agreed to do *Widow* at least in part because she needed the camaraderie of rehearsals. She went the next night for the first read-through, happy to lock the door on her silent flat and walk to the theater to join the friendly cluster of singers. Before rehearsal began she intended to glance over her score, but it remained closed under her arm as she chatted and gossiped with the cast.

Caroline and Christopher, both handsomely tall and dark, waltzed about the stage in dramatic sweeps. Liz watched them, idly thinking about her friends and her own plans.

How odd it would feel to leave here.

In this comfortable, predictable universe, she, like Christopher and Caro-line, could remain unchallenged indefinitely. But if she longed to soar with col-oratura grace, longed for a bigger stage, a brighter light, she would have to give up her place, as they would not, and move out of the ever-tightening circle.

And she would have to go through Caroline to do it.

"Deep thoughts?" Huw inquired, interrupting her daydream. Although he was a tall man, all elbows and knees, he had a way of materializing without warning.

She glanced at him with a foolish smile. "Oh no, I was—" Over his shoul-der she suddenly spotted Giles at the piano. "Nothing important," she contin-ued with an effort.

She responded to Huw absently as he thanked her again for her partic-ipation, but she couldn't keep her eyes off of Giles. Suddenly he looked up, straight into her eyes, obviously aware of her. She quickly shifted her attention back to Huw, but the sound of the piano seemed to cover the director's voice.

A few moments later she extracted herself from the conversation. Hugging her score against her chest, she sauntered over, hesitated, and then slid onto the piano bench next to Giles, crowding him a bit. He stopped playing, but he did not move away.

"What on earth are you doing here?" He was smiling, almost as though he was glad to see her.

"I'm not singing anywhere right now. So when Huw called I said I'd do it. I owe him."

"Does Madame know?"

She hesitated. "Yes."

"She agreed to it, did she?"

"Not really. But it's my decision."

"Is it difficult, to go from being a principal to singing in the chorus?"

"You think my ego is too big to handle it?"

"Not at all. But the rewards are different."

"I have a lot of work to do on my own, but I need to be with people and work on something real, something not too demanding."

Giles said nothing, watching her until the flush rose in her cheeks.

"You think I'm being foolish, don't you?"

"Does it matter then, what I think?"

"Well you always have an opinion."

He seemed surprised for an instant. "You should do what pleases you," he said finally.

She gave up trying to get him to validate her choice. "I'm sorry about Sunday. It was rude not to warn you, but I only thought of it when we were taking our bows."

"You caught me rather off guard, that's all. It actually was quite funny." He tipped his head. "I didn't spoil your day, did I?"

She shrugged and didn't answer.

He leaned over and caught her eye. "Truce?"

She smiled. "If I haven't fired you by now, I'm not likely to, am I? Anyway, it would be far too much trouble to break in someone else."

"Good. A pleasure it is, to work with you."

She ducked the compliment. "By the way, what are *you* doing here? I would have thought you'd have lots better things to do with your time."

"You're not the only one who owes Huw a favor. I've got some big changes coming, so I'm taking a last bit of a holiday. This should be good fun."

She did not comment, preoccupied. "Can I ask you something?"

"Certainly." His hands lay in his lap instead of wandering the keyboard, as was his conversational habit.

She considered how to put her question and found it was not so much a question as a desire for reassurance. "What made you lose your nerve so badly that you gave up your career?" She felt his shoulder tighten; he drew away.

"Who told you that? Christopher?"

"Madame Ponnelle," she said uncertainly.

"She knows nothing about it. I will thank you to remember that."

"I'm sorry."

He softened. "There, it's not your fault. How could you know? But it is not for her to judge."

"How could you give it up, though? I can't believe you aren't good enough."

"I was 'good enough,' whatever that means."

"Did everyone think you had lost your mind?"

"Yes. But eventually the people who mattered understood." He seemed disinclined to continue. She almost pressed him, but something in his silence warned her against it.

His hands reached for the keyboard, began to play a steady, silver stream of sound that was the Moonlight Sonata. He watched his fingers and she watched his face.

He began to speak, softly blending into the Beethoven the way she placed a song on the currents of accompaniment.

"After university I went to Paris to study with Pierre Varnet. My father died one Saturday afternoon when I was conducting a concert in Lyon. No one could find me to tell me until the Monday when I got back to Paris. Diana would have been able to contact me, but she was away." He stopped playing and gestured as though he would say more but didn't have the words.

Liz shivered. "You were close to him?" she asked, not knowing what else to say.

He nodded slowly, as if reaffirming it to himself. "After the funeral, on the way back to Paris, I had a lot of time to think. I questioned everything: why I was in France, why I had married, even why I was a musician. I had made all those decisions when I was far too young to know what I was doing. They were not really even decisions. And then I returned to Paris to find that my wife was cheating on me." He reached out and started a slow trill between A and B-flat, gradually increasing the speed. Liz marveled at his technique and control.

"So you came back here."

He stopped the trill abruptly and put his hand in his lap. "Playing the piano was the only thing I knew how to do well, so I taught and played for studios and rehearsals to pay the bills. Huw turned me around, gave me a chance to conduct again. He's been there for me since I was eleven years old. I really owe him this." He gestured toward the stage, where the company was assembling.

It pleased Liz to have this intimate knowledge of Giles that he withheld from Madame.

"Where did you meet him?"

"He was the judge at the Eisteddfod who heard my work and convinced my parents to let me come to university down here and study music."

"Did you always plan to be a coach?"

He shook his head. "I wanted to be a conductor from the very first. Accompanying was only meant to support myself and Diana. But I find that I thoroughly enjoy it." He smiled his self-effacing smile. "Combined with the conducting, it's finally right. But it took time. I'm nowhere near as single-minded as you are."

"After the accident I really missed the attention," Liz confessed. "I can't imagine giving it up by choice."

"You and I are two very different creatures."

She glanced up at him but found no trace of condemnation.

"You are to the manner born. You'll make a success of it simply because of who you are."

"But so could you. Don't you know how good you are?"

"At the moment I'm content with my life as it is. The glory isn't so much in the individual, it's in the music. And I have that, wherever I go."

"Don't be so damn humble."

"*Mae'n ddrwg gen i?*"

"You're too good to stay here and be mediocre."

"Mediocre?" He looked as if he was trying to decide if she was serious. "You do realize that it isn't any of your business?" But his faint smile took the sting out of his words.

"It's wrong to waste what you've been given. Didn't you tell me that once?"

"But I don't think I am. If I've helped you, how can anyone call that waste?"

That silenced her for a moment. "Well, I guess it's selfish, but I'm glad you came back to Wales."

He pressed her hand, her left hand, and she did not recoil. "I am too."

Chapter 28

THE CHOREOGRAPHER, A SHORT, stout woman named Chloe, appeared at the next rehearsal, a remedial dance session. Before she allowed them onstage, she subjected them to a lecture about posture (Liz self-consciously straightened her spine) and proper shoes (Liz tucked her feet, in their flat, rubber-soled trainers, under the chair). Finally she waved them out of their seats.

"Get yourselves up onstage, then. Line up by height. No, no, women in one line, men in another," she said with a sigh, yanking people by their elbows to position them. "Why can they never give me dancers? Singers are hopeless." In spite of her stature, she moved nimbly and lightly among them, a little fireball who never hesitated to prod anyone who was not quite right.

Fourth from the bottom of the queue, Liz was not displeased to find Giles behind her. She had always thought that he moved with the conservative, compact grace of a dancer. He gave her a formal little bow.

"Right," Chloe said. "Keep the same partner. Spread out a bit." She arranged the twelve chorus couples in a circle around her.

"She means business," Liz remarked as she and Giles moved to their corner.

"No worries. I know what I'm doing."

"Basics first, then," continued the plump choreographer. "Watch me." She grabbed the closest man and bullied him into position, demonstrating the hold. "Don't be shy, gentlemen, get a good grip on her. Right, now you lot try it."

Giles put a hand on Liz's shoulder and turned her to him. They took up the pose and waited for Chloe's critique. Liz's hands were light and hesitant after the misunderstanding on Sunday, for she and Giles and even Madame had all danced around the heart of it . . . *the commerce between singer and accompanist . . .*

Giles smiled in the conspiratorial way he did before they made music together . . . *a personable young man . . .* Liz fidgeted and looked away.

The choreographer glanced at them, moved Giles's arm closer around Liz's back, pushed Liz's shoulders back and tipped her chin up, and moved on.

Liz met Giles's dark eyes and felt an implosion in her chest.

You'll be the love of someone's life.

Oh good God.

The rehearsal continued, but Liz found no grace, no poise in her whole body. Every time they tried something new she stumbled as though her feet were stuck to the stage. Chloe gave them basic steps, and between lectures on posture and balance she gradually got them waltzing to her satisfaction. Just before the break she let them practice free-form, observing, prodding, stopping, and starting.

Liz lurched into Giles one too many times and finally gave up.

"Let me lead," he suggested with a hint of a smile.

"I can't do this," she replied, throwing up her hands.

"Of course you can." He reached for her, but she backed away.

"I need to sit down," she insisted.

He seemed about to argue, but then he shrugged. "Right, then."

She sat out, miserable, and watched him cut in on Christopher. When Giles said something to Caroline as they danced she laughed in reply. He showed her the same courtesy, gave her the same smile, that he had given Liz. It meant nothing more, or less. But something between tears and anger burned in Liz's throat.

At the break the chorus members chatted excitedly with one another. Liz alone was silent.

Giles sought her out and sat down beside her. "Are you not feeling well?"

Though she had watched him closely for the last five minutes, suddenly she couldn't look at him. "I'm not a dancer."

"The first time we met you weren't a singer. Come on, let's try it again." He drew her to her feet and put his arm around her. "Ready? One-two-three, one-two-three," he counted and began. Within two measures her resistance made her run into him, and she stopped.

"Just relax. I'm not going to back you into anything." He took her in hand again. She concentrated fiercely on her feet. She knew he had no idea why she was so clumsy; he proceeded to teach her just as he did in the studio.

"One-two-three, don't look at your feet, look at me!" She raised her head and managed not to stumble.

"That's it, don't fight it."

"Not exactly graceful," she objected.

"Just keep on." He began to sing the words to one of the waltzes. Tentatively she joined in, meeting his eyes and finally succumbing to the rhythm. His left hand gave her cues; his right arm pivoted her. When he started the verse a second time, he smiled his approval and she grinned back.

She suddenly understood why, two hundred years earlier, society had condemned the waltz as scandalous. Centrifugal force bound their bodies into a single energy. The three-quarter time suggested a shared pulse. This close, Giles seemed taller, his hands bigger. She felt the warmth of his body, smelled the faint spice of his aftershave. She leaned into the comfort of his arm across her back. As she became steadier he spun her faster, laughing, challenging her to keep up. The smooth speed eliminated her growing protest, a whirlpool drawing her away from the rest of the world.

When they finished the verse, she made herself pull away.

"There, I knew you could do it," he said.

"Thanks," she said inadequately. In that moment she was tempted to quit—but she could not quite let Huw down.

The next day Liz sternly reminded herself that she needed Giles's piano, his encouragement, his wisdom. And then she went back to rehearsal and danced with him. But she never felt quite calm—never felt anything but disconcerted by desire.

* * *

OCTOBER AND NOVEMBER SWEPT over Liz in a jumble of new music and new emotions. She went to bed thinking about Rosina and woke with Despina. She memorized, forgot, swore, relearned. Common sense told her that she didn't have time for *Merry Widow*. But she was unable to give it up, especially now that it was suddenly before her that she would soon leave not only her friends but also Wales. And Giles.

He often came to the last half hour of her lesson to play one of her new arias. She watched his agile fingers scramble over the keyboard and shivered at the thought of what those long, sensitive fingers could do. At rehearsal she fantasized about putting her head on his shoulder and feeling his arms around her. But the waltz, perhaps mercifully, required a graceful formality—in fact, none of the dancing afforded any room for tenderness. She realized one night, as they sat together upstage after the vigorous folk dance, that they were breathing in unison, and even that sent a shock of pleasure through her. She had never experienced such a debilitating attraction.

But when she pictured telling him she loved him, even the thought made her face flush hot. At the studio he was silent and seemed somehow disapproving. She worried that he knew of her infatuation and wanted to keep her at a distance. Hadn't he told her he would never make such a mistake again? That he was not in love with her? So she held her tongue and shielded her feelings even from Caroline, who would have scoffed at her hesitation and bullied her into speaking.

The performance came too soon. The lush, romantic music, which said everything Liz could not say, seemed laced with sadness. In the second act she lingered in the wings, letting the music work on her. She had made her choice, and she would live with it. But for one more night she let the one-sided romance exist. Soon, nothing would be the same.

As the act played out, she waited backstage, pressed among the dusty flats, for her next entrance. Tears rose in her throat as she listened to the stunning quintet, the gem of the second act. Ten or twenty years from now she might do *Merry Widow* again, and she was sure the loss in this moment would flood back to her even then. Mesmerized, she felt a shiver overtake her that started at the nape of her neck. An instant later a voice behind her said, "Lovely, is it not?"

Liz thought she heard her own regret in Giles's voice. "Splendid," she agreed without looking at him. Suddenly the music no longer held her attention. There in the dark she felt the warmth of his body, his breath near her ear—he was so close to her. She stood quite still so that she would not be tempted to lean against him. They watched together in silence, completely separate, as the characters wound their tangled love affairs onstage.

The piece climaxed and faded. Giles put a warm hand on her thinly covered shoulder, and her heart tripped. She turned to him swiftly.

"See you onstage," he said, and then he vanished, leaving her to whisper "I love you" in the listening darkness.

She did not talk to him the rest of that night. Nor did she attend the cast party.

* * *

CHRISTMAS CAME WITH A STINGING cold wind and bright sunshine that hurt Liz's eyes and alleviated the torpor of too much food and over-warm rooms. She telephoned California late Christmas Day, when Madly would have already put in an appearance at church and her night-owl father would have surfaced for his duty visit with his wife's family. They lurched through a conversation, but her parents seemed preoccupied by the party at their backs. Liz could hear Grandpa Andrew's cough and the shrill, vodka-enhanced laughter of her stepmother's sister. Beyond them, the Mormon Tabernacle Choir repeated sounding joys from the stereo. And in Caerphilly, the sharp, cloying smell of the pudding and bursts of laughter from her relatives distracted Liz as well. She gave it up with a promise to call again soon.

After she hung up the phone she sat for a minute longer in the dim passage, listening. Behind her in the kitchen her aunt and Kate talked over the rattle and crash of dishwashing, their voices so alike that Liz couldn't tell them apart. Her uncle and great-aunts and Christopher were in the parlor, and soon she heard the piano, and her uncle's unaffected tenor singing, "*From out of darkness we have Light, which makes the angels sing this night.*"

Liz folded her arms, hugging herself. She remembered her mother singing that carol.

Kate poked her head out of the kitchen. "Don't you start without us, Da," she called.

"Then hurry along," he returned, and the piano started again.

Kate spotted her. "Come on, Liz. He won't wait. Help us finish."

Liz followed her cousin to the kitchen to earn her Christmas pudding. She picked up a tea towel and began wiping the plates while her cousin scraped the roasting pan that had held the goose. Ellen set the teakettle going and left them there to finish.

"I'd love it if you and Giles could do something for the wedding."

The casual linking of her name to his, as though any other combination would be unthinkable, was not lost on Liz.

"Sure, I guess so."

"You will come, won't you? Even if you've gone up to London?"

"Of course."

Kate sized her up. "Maybe this is beneath you?"

"Jeez, Kate!"

"Well you don't sound much like you want to."

A piercing need to have someone else know her burden made Liz incautious. "Can you keep a secret?"

Kate considered her warily. "What sort of secret?"

"Just my own stupidity. But nobody else can know about this. Especially Christopher."

"Well, what?"

"The problem is Giles. I'm really attracted to him, and it makes things awkward."

"Trust you to think that's a problem."

"But it is. He doesn't want to get involved with anyone. He said so."

"How do you know that includes you? You don't know till you ask, do you?" Kate balanced the clean roasting pan on the drain board and began to dry her hands.

For an instant Liz flashed to the time he had invited her to stay the night. But that had been put to rest, at her own insistence. "He's married," she reminded her cousin.

Kate dismissed this obstacle with a flip of the dishtowel. "Oh, now. If you gave him a reason he would get divorced, wouldn't he?"

"But if Madame sends me to London to train next year? How can I start something that I'm only going to have to leave?"

"London's not so far."

"Listen to me. I don't want him to know. It'll just complicate things."

"I was right all along. You're willing to sacrifice anything, even your own personal happiness, for this—this *fame* you're seeking."

"Don't judge me," Liz snapped. "Your idea of personal happiness is a lot different than mine. Besides, I'm trying *not* to hurt him. I'm trying *not* to sacrifice him to my ambition, as you insist on putting it."

"He's a grown man. It's his choice."

"He's made it quite clear that he's not in the least bit interested in me. He sees me as someone he works with—his protégée, maybe, and I hope a friend, but nothing more. So it's a moot point."

"Are you sure?"

"Kate!"

Her cousin shrugged. "So you won't sing at the wedding?"

Liz gritted her teeth. "Did you have something in mind?"

Chapter 29

LIZ RARELY SAW GILES IN THE early weeks of the year. He was away in January, conducting in Ireland, and after that his rehearsals for a choral concert in Bath made it hard to schedule time to work with him. She found this both a frustration and a relief. She would begin to anticipate the ebb of her attraction, only to be stung with it when he called or turned up at a lesson.

He recommended another accompanist to fill in the weeks he was away, and she continued doggedly to work on the arias for the audition in London in May. But a more immediate question haunted her every time she sang. The GSSSG audition in February would be a watershed. She wasn't sure she was ready to face the implications of her choice.

Rain was assaulting the city for the fourth day in a row when Liz came in to work ten minutes late, dripping and cold, one Monday.

Caroline looked up from her paperwork. "Kettle's hot. Dry off, no rush." She trailed Liz into the office, shuffling through the first post. "Would you be auditioning for *Yeomen* next week?"

"I'm not sure. Ponnelle is on a mission to send me to the Big City."

"It's a beautiful show. And you will be a splendid Phoebe. But it's not Huw, so I guess all bets are off."

"Huw's not directing?"

"No. He said he was taking a proper holiday for once, to Italy. It's some young chap who just got his master's at Welsh College. But Giles is conducting. That's a plus."

Liz's nervous system sprang alive at the mention of his name. It only added to her dilemma. "Yes. It is." She went back out to the main store.

"I was listening when you were upstairs yesterday. You're sounding terrific," Caroline said, following her.

Liz ducked her head. "Thanks," she answered, a smile slowly spreading from the inside out. She often spent her lunch hour upstairs in Bert and Caroline's flat, vocalizing.

"What are you working on these days? It sounded like Elsie's first act aria yesterday."

Liz had been waiting for this with trepidation. Tension drew across her shoulders like the burden of a winter coat. "It was."

Silence. Then, "Trying to impress someone?"

Liz could feel Caroline's gaze upon her, but she kept her head down.

After a time Caroline said, "This is my chance at Elsie. *Yeomen* isn't done very often."

"Maybe neither of us will get it."

"Oh right. And maybe the Queen Mum will come for tea today."

Liz could think of no defense to which Caroline would concede, so she did not reply. She wanted more than anything to talk to Giles, who would put everything into perspective. But it would be wrong to put him in that situation. And on second thought, he would be irritatingly fair and impartial.

* * *

AT LIZ'S NEXT LESSON, MADAME spent very little time on the warm-up exercises.

"How is Elsie coming?" she asked when they were done, turning away from the piano. "How do the arias feel?"

"Fine." Liz offered nothing more; she pulled her score from her book bag and waited for Madame to tell her where she wanted to start.

"Just fine?"

Liz nodded. "They'll be ready."

Madame kept looking at her until Liz could feel a blush rising over her cheeks. "You hardly sound enthusiastic," the older woman said.

Liz hugged the score to her body. "I was thinking maybe I should skip this and just concentrate on the audition in London."

"You've already spent the time to learn it. Why give it up now? Are you afraid that because your friend Huw isn't directing you won't be cast?"

"It just doesn't seem like a good idea."

"I decide what's best for you. It is true: working with Mr. Parsons's group is not what I would have you doing anymore. But it's better than allowing you to be idle."

"What do you mean?"

"Being in a show is a stimulant. It enhances the rest of your work."

"But I—"

"You needn't be defensive," Madame said, putting up a hand. "I know that you still work when you aren't in rehearsal. It just brings out your best when you are."

"No, it's Caroline," Liz managed, thrusting herself back into the conversation.

"Caroline Butler? Don't be absurd. You're afraid of competition from her?"

"It's not the competition. She's my best friend. She got me started."

"If you're going to get anywhere you'll have to get over that."

"She thinks I'm trying to take something that by rights is hers."

Madame scrutinized her. "And it's a forgone conclusion that you will prevail?"

"She seems to think so." Liz did not add that she agreed.

"If you are better than she is, you ought to get it. And you are."

"Am I?" Liz hunched her shoulders and shoved her hands in her pockets.

"Don't fish for compliments. You know you are."

"I wasn't—"

"You can't be squeamish about such things, not if you're serious. If Miss Butler has any professionalism she will know that these things are not to be taken personally. And if not, it's none of your concern." She raised an eyebrow at Liz's expression. "You think that's callous? Not in the least. I've no interest in her success. Just yours. And that is how you ought to feel."

"Why can't I do Phoebe? It's a great role."

"It's too low for you. Elsie sits nicely in your range, and you can do a lot more with the interpretation if you aren't fighting to be heard."

Liz had run out of arguments.

"Let's start with the finale of Act Two." Madame spread the score on the piano and looked at Liz. "You insisted on working with them. So make the most of it. I will not allow you to quit."

* * *

BY MID-FEBRUARY MADAME had tweaked, prodded, and perfected her Elsie, and Liz had allowed herself to fall for the role. But she knew she could do justice to the scheming, thwarted Phoebe as well. For a short time she considered not asking for a specific role and leaving it up to the fates. But she couldn't relinquish that control. On the day of the auditions, she firmly wrote *Elsie* on the form, ticked the Soprano box, and thrust the paper into Simon's hands before she could change her mind.

Giles appeared to have assumed the role of liaison between the singers, most of whom he knew, and the new director. He greeted Liz with his usual polite warmth and introduced her to the man sitting beside him. She smiled and shook hands with them both, observing in some remote part of her mind what an actress she was becoming.

Her audition was some of the best singing she had ever done. She left the stage with her heart pounding. Giles complimented her sincerely, seemed pleased and surprised at her performance. She would certainly be called back. And she would certainly face Caroline. The mixed blessing kept Liz awake far into the night, adrenaline bombarding her with excitement and regret.

* * *

THE NEXT DAY AT CYGNET, Liz and Caroline spoke to each other only when necessary. Acid churned in Liz's stomach, and her chest was tight. She didn't dare ask to leave early to prepare for the callbacks.

When they closed up, she hesitated, winding her scarf slowly around her throat. "I guess I'll see you later."

Caroline looked up, the corners of her eyes hard. "Right."

She shouldn't have said anything.

She walked home, taking deep, soothing breaths. She changed her clothes and warmed up her voice, trying to slip into a trancelike state where nothing could touch her. She remembered Giles, the pleasure in his smile after her audition, and let that warm her and bolster her confidence.

As she arrived at the theater she decided to confront the worst of her anxiety and put it behind her. She approached Caroline immediately.

"Good luck, Caro. I know you'll sing well."

Caroline gave her a brittle smile. "Mind yourself, Liz. You haven't beat me yet." She deliberately turned her back.

As Liz looked after her, Christopher sauntered over. "Well, well, the battle of the divas. This ought to be entertaining."

"Shut up," Liz snapped.

Chris merely grinned. "Make it decisive, Liz. Uncertainty is annoying." With a wink, he removed himself before she could reply.

Giles arrived with the stage director precisely at seven thirty. Liz caught his eye and smiled, but he returned the gesture with merely a nod. She had to remind herself that he was always rather distant when his mind was elsewhere. And what was she doing, seeking his attention? This was an audition, not a party.

Separated from some of the people who usually supported and encouraged her, a weight of loneliness settled over her. It began to feel like the *Mikado* audition, when she'd had nothing to lose. But when her turn came, she wrenched herself from the emotional abyss into which she was slipping and focused on her voice. She played to Giles, elated to have a reason to sing for him again, and tried to forget that Caroline was scrutinizing her every move.

She went home with the unbearable burden of knowing that she could easily have Elsie—and that she would have to spend her days trying to hide her pleasure in the role when she worked with Caroline, and her evenings trying not to give away her feeling for Giles.

With the awful sense that she was making a mistake, she accepted the role when the director called later that night.

Chapter 30

THE NEXT MORNING ANOTHER STORM howled into Cardiff. On her way to work Liz noticed tree branches scattered in the park and crippled umbrellas in trashcans. Leaves and papers blew into corners and against buildings. The awning over Swann's strained in the swelling gusts. She could smell a sweet ripening of the air that anticipated rain.

Her gut, the place of support for every note she sang, lay empty and anxious. She knew, in a deep place untainted by her ego, that she had sung brilliantly at the callbacks. But this morning she dreaded going to work. Peering through the glass, Liz opened the door, hoping to see Bert. But Caroline whisked out of the back room at the sound of the jangling bells and stopped.

"Morning." Liz unbuttoned her coat but hesitated, almost expecting to be given the sack.

Caroline tapped her pen nervously on the counter. "I guess congratulations are in order."

So she knew. "I'm really sorry." Liz shrugged off her coat and folded it over her arm, still noncommittal about starting work.

"Sorry? Why be sorry?" Caroline turned away.

"Because . . ." Liz struggled to find the words. "Because I wanted to sing like you the very first time I heard you. And because I would never intentionally hurt you."

"Don't you get it?" Caroline faced her abruptly. "You're better than I am. You're better than I'll ever be."

Liz hugged her coat to her; Caroline's praise was an indictment.

"Why don't you just go and have your career? This is no place for a professional like you." Caroline threw down her pen and retreated to the office. After a moment Liz put her coat over the back of the stool and started to count the change in the register. She wished faintly for something fizzy to settle her stomach. She could hear Caroline talking on the phone.

She had no idea if the cash drawer balanced yesterday's receipts or not. She put it back and helped a young woman select an inexpensive collection of poetry. When the bells jangled the customer out, Caroline returned wearing her coat, her purse under her arm. She would not meet Liz's eye.

"I'm going over to Cygnet today. Bert will be here by ten."

Liz rubbed at an ink spot on the counter. "Look, I'll withdraw. I can't stand this."

"How dare you patronize me?"

"I wasn't—"

"Do you think I would do it now? It's clear they want you. Do the damn role."

"I didn't mean to hurt you."

"Then why did you do it? You must have known it would end up like this."

"How could I have known that? Madame said I shouldn't be squeamish about it. That I couldn't mix up my feelings with my professionalism."

"Then she's turning you into a monster. Don't forget who got you started. You wouldn't be here if it weren't for me."

"I'm aware how much I owe you. This isn't important."

"Of course it is, you fool. It proves that you are good. It proves that you're probably wasted here. It proves that you ought to go away and have a career if you're so ready to walk all over your friends."

"You aren't going to let me off the hook, are you? I'm offering it to you. It's yours by right. I was wrong to challenge you."

"I don't want it. But you better do a damn good job. It better be worth it for them to have cast you and not me." She slammed the door, escaping before Liz could respond.

Everything inside Liz's chest sagged. After a moment she picked up the phone. She must have gotten the director's last name wrong, for there was no listing, so she called Giles's number at the college. He was not available, but she left a message for him to call her. She had to put a stop to this before it got worse.

It was closer to eleven when Bert blew in with the storm behind him. He looked around, satisfied himself that the store hadn't burned down, and proceeded to unwind his scarf and coat.

"Everything all right?"

"Oh, everything is just fine." Liz looked at him miserably.

He held up a cautionary hand as he hung his old cord jacket on the rack inside the office door. "Don't you start. I can't take sides."

Liz shook her head. "I know, and you're right. But I feel rotten."

He turned on her. "Don't you dare ever apologize for your voice."

She recoiled from his vehemence. "It's not worth losing Caroline's friendship."

He ran his hand over his untidy hair. "I hope it doesn't come to that. But sometimes"—he looked at her sympathetically—"sometimes we pay a high price for what we want."

* * *

GILES CALLED HER BACK WITHIN the hour. She had a pleasant, if half-conscious, awareness that he sounded concerned.

"Congratulations, by the way," he said after they'd exchanged initial pleasantries.

"Oh. Thanks." In her misery she had nearly forgotten that it was something praiseworthy. "Do you have a few minutes today? I need to talk to you."

"Walk over about twelve thirty and have lunch with me, then."

"I wouldn't be interrupting?"

"Not at all."

* * *

WHEN LIZ GOT TO GILES'S OFFICE at the college the door was ajar. When she tapped on it he immediately called to her to come in. The room was barely big enough for a desk, a bookcase, and an upright piano. The light from the window behind him, filtering over five African violets, helped the claustrophobia only a little.

Giles got up and gave her his chair, moving over to the piano bench. "You didn't bring lunch? Have some of mine, will you?"

Liz shook her head.

"No, I insist," he said. "I shall feel rude eating while you watch." He gave her some fragrant segments of a blood orange and half of his cheese sandwich, then cocked his head. "You sounded a bit put out this morning."

"It's about *Yeomen*."

"If you tell me you aren't ready to sing it I will laugh in your face."

She smiled reluctantly. "No, it's not that. I can do it. But Caroline's never going to speak to me again."

Giles's ease diminished, and his face went blank, giving nothing away. "Yes, I know. I had the unenviable task of telling her."

"Is that all you have to say?"

"What would you like me to say?"

She sighed. "Something wise and comforting."

"You don't ask much, do you?"

"Some of this is your fault, you know."

"Why?"

"Because you cast me! That wasn't fair to her."

"So you think these things should be decided by seniority?"

"No, I guess not. Then I'd never have gotten a role."

He finished his half of the orange and wiped the sticky juice off of each finger with his handkerchief before he spoke again. "You know, I half agree with her."

"What?"

"It was unfair for you to challenge her. She's comfortable. You'll be gone in a few months, but she will still be here, and that was her niche."

"I thought seniority wasn't a criterion."

"You have outgrown GSSSG. You have no business letting us take advantage of you for this role, and you have no business displacing her when you so clearly intend to move on."

"Then why did you cast me?"

"It isn't up to me to make those decisions for you. I'm invested in making *Yeomen* the best it can be. Why would I turn down such talent when it presents itself?"

"Madame insisted that I do this. I just have to trust that she's right."

"Caroline will recover. She has to face the fact that there are other people in the world who can do what she can do. And if you gave way to everyone who wanted what you have, you would have nothing left."

"Whose side are you on?"

"My own, I suppose," Giles said after a little pause.

Liz made a strangled noise of frustration. "I thought we were friends."

"What has that to do with it?"

"Why are you doing this to me?" She nearly shouted her frustration.

He backed away as though she had shoved him. "You were the best of the choices. For heaven's sake, you'd think I *hadn't* cast you."

"I'm no better than she is."

"You are, whether you'll admit it or not. Caroline is a good comedic actress, but you delivered something more for this role, something we were looking for. It's a serious, complex role, and you seem to understand it."

"But she can learn anything you want her to."

"Perhaps. But why go to that much trouble when we have someone else who can already do what we want?"

Liz had no answer.

"You sang splendidly. You even surprised me. I couldn't put you on Phoebe's part; it's the completely wrong tessitura. It crawls around in the least powerful part of your voice."

"I can sing it, though. It's what I wanted."

"That isn't what you asked for," he reminded her. "Was I to read your mind?"

She glared at him.

"Your voice is changing. You have to adjust. Yes, you'd do Phoebe well, but this will be better for your voice."

Liz sighed. "That's what Madame said, too. It's how she conned me into this to begin with."

"Would you like me to talk to Caroline?"

"It won't help. I think I should just quit while I'm behind."

"If you do withdraw there is no guarantee that she'll get the role," Giles pointed out.

"Be serious. Who else have you got?"

"You don't know. But to replace you we might even have to look to the college. What I'm trying to say is that the damage is done, and dropping out will not improve anything."

"Maybe it is too late." Liz shrugged into her coat. Giles stood up and tried to help her, but she moved away from him. "You know, I don't feel much like singing tonight. Maybe we should call it off and work on the Puccini another time."

He hesitated, and she thought he would pursue it but he did not. "As you wish. Do you want to reschedule?"

"No. You're awfully busy. Let's just leave it for now."

Giles's hands toyed with the keys and change in his pockets. "I am sorry. I wish it hadn't blown up like this."

"It isn't your fault, as you already pointed out." Liz picked up her bag and swept out of the office, slamming the door behind her.

Chapter 31

LIZ KNEW BERT WOULD NOT keep them apart forever; he had a business to run. After a week, Caroline came back to Swann's.

Liz came to work expecting to see Bert, and she froze in the doorway when she saw Caroline at the till.

"Morning, Liz." She just managed to smile. "Don't let in all the cold air."

Liz shut the door and came warily into the shop. "Hi."

"There's water if you want tea."

"Thanks. I do." She hung her coat and pushed up her sleeves. "It's cold out." She snapped on the kettle, which chattered and hissed, already close to the boil. Caroline came in and sat at the desk. Rather than face each other, they both watched the pot. Liz searched for the right thing to say, but Caroline broke the ice.

"I . . . I'm sorry about what I said last week."

"I don't blame you."

Caroline rocked back and forth in Bert's aged swivel chair. "I was rather mean about it, but I meant it when I said you should move on to bigger things." She looked up quickly.

Liz held her gaze. "I never wanted or expected to compete with you."

Caroline nodded. "You need to leave the amateur stuff to us amateurs."

Liz purposely overlooked the slight edge Caroline put on the word "amateur" and poured water into her mug. She moved her face out of the cloud of rising steam. "I couldn't have accomplished this if it wasn't for you. I really mean that." She prodded the tea bag under the water. "If it's any consolation," she added weakly.

Caroline worried the tape on a burst seam of the chair. In the front of the store the bells demanded attention, and she stood up. "I guess that will have to do." She went out to the counter, leaving Liz stirring her tea.

* * *

OF ALL THE GILBERT AND SULLIVAN she had done, *Yeomen of the Guard* was Liz's favorite. Her voice soared in the higher range. The role demanded good acting to keep Elsie from seeming like a shallow social climber. Liz was determined to show that Elsie was not immune to the pull between old friendship and new passion. Wasn't she herself torn just so? Compelled to forsake the comforting friendship she had with Giles—something that, if encouraged, might have turned into the love of her life—to make her way out of Cardiff, on to London, and beyond? Didn't she have firsthand knowledge of the torment of such a choice?

Rehearsals went long from the beginning. Alan Pierce, the new director, was hardly as organized as Huw, though Liz had to admit he had some interesting ideas. Only three weeks into the schedule Liz found herself there late for the third night in a row. It was close to ten o'clock, and she struggled to keep her burning eyes open. She wondered if she could safely leave, or if he would want her in the last ten minutes. Not unlikely, she decided. He'd done it before.

She sat in the first row of the audience seats, just to the right of where Giles perched on his stool, conducting the rehearsal accompanist. It didn't hurt, she mused, that she got to spend time with him, even if she would never tell him how she felt. She watched him with no objectivity whatsoever. In rehearsal he conducted with his left arm folded across his chest unless he needed it for a cue. She saw his concentration in the bend of his neck, the forward thrust of his shoulders, as he listened to the singers. It always amazed her how he could discern the tiniest thing out of the rich fabric of an orchestral score. Sometimes she could not even hear that something was amiss, yet when he caught it and corrected it, she heard the difference.

Onstage, Pierce stopped the ensemble yet again.

"Par for the chorus," she murmured to no one in particular, rolling her head back against the seat.

Giles turned with a little chuckle, eased off the stool, and came to sit next to her. "They are improving, you know."

"I know. I just want to get home." She yawned broadly.

"How are you holding up?"

She considered, aware of how he watched for her answer. When he put his full attention on her like this she felt deep regret. "Okay, I guess. I've gotten past most of that nonsense with Caroline."

"You're sounding splendid."

It was only something any musician might say to another, but she flushed with pleasure at the compliment. "I thought I would regret not doing Phoebe, but I'm liking Elsie a lot. The subtext of the character is so honest, the way sadness is always a part of joy, and how confusing it is to have to give up something you cherish to have something more."

"You've got it precisely. Perhaps that's why this is my favorite G and S." They spoke in low, intimate voices as the blocking rehearsal continued onstage.

Liz was dangerously close to her own emotions, so she briskly shunted the conversation away from herself. She glanced over to where Christopher stood, poised like a wild animal as he watched the action onstage. "I still can't believe that Christopher is actually getting married. I feel like somebody ought to warn Kate about him."

"What if he's sincere? Would you ruin his chance of straightening out his life?" Giles shot her a bemused glance. "Or are you jealous? Is that why you want to throw a spanner in the works—because you were with him once?"

She bristled. "I never slept with him, if that's what you mean."

"*Mae'n ddrwg gen i.* Forgive me." Giles pinched the bridge of his nose as if he had a headache.

She was glad she had not gotten up and left, for he looked chagrined. "We weren't lovers," she said firmly.

"You certainly fought like lovers."

She blushed. "That's just how we are."

"Passionate?"

"Argumentative. And stubborn." She sat back. "How do you tolerate him?" she asked suddenly. "Don't you hate him for what he did to you?"

"Should I hate him for giving me my freedom?"

"But he slept with your wife," she exclaimed, unable to comprehend how he could be so calm about it.

"And she slept with him. She's at least as responsible."

"Did he even apologize?"

"As a matter of fact, he did. When he told me about Kate. It might have taken me a long time to leave Diana if it hadn't hit so close to home. It was despicable, yes. But he's my oldest friend. Besides, if it hadn't been him, it would have been someone else."

"I wish I could be so generous," Liz said wistfully.

They watched Pierce run the chorus through the blocking again. Giles broke the moment of silence.

"Do you remember what you said at the first *Widow* rehearsal? That I was wasting my time?"

Liz hunched her shoulders at how it sounded. "I didn't mean it like that."

"But you were right. I've been thinking about what you said. I'm going to get my agent to take me on again. I may even move up to London." He looked over at her. "What do you think?"

She swallowed. "If I'm there too we could maybe have dinner once in a while."

"And commiserate?"

Giles did not follow up with enthusiasm—did not, as she had hoped, suggest they work together. Or share a flat. She shook her head, abruptly banishing the thought.

"I know people there, people who could help me," he continued.

"You don't want to stay here."

"Oh, I shall always return to Wales. But professionally it would make my options broader to go back to one of the capitals." He shrugged. "It's just an idea I had. It depends on what opportunities come up."

"Well, I don't know why you're asking me. Sounds like you already know what you want to do." She was too tired to hide the acid in her voice.

He looked at her quizzically. "I hoped you would think it was a good idea. You usually seem to understand what I'm thinking."

"Do I?" She did not bother to explain why that might be. She couldn't have said, at that moment, whether she was upset at the thought that they would soon go their separate ways, or at the idea that he was so much closer to real success. Perhaps both. But she didn't want to fight with him. "I'm sorry. I didn't mean to be rude." She leaned toward him earnestly. "You are better than you think you are. If you really want it, I think all the doors will be open. But that's just my humble opinion."

He acknowledged her words with no more than a grave nod. Then he sat forward, poised to stand and conduct again now that the scene was finally progressing.

Liz watched him as he watched the stage, trembling emotion rising in her chest again.

Another pause came, and Giles turned back to her. "If I said something to offend you, I am sorry. I do value your opinion. And I know you wouldn't hesitate to tell me if I was way off the mark."

"It's not you. I guess it's just that . . . everything is going to change soon. Sometimes it makes me a little testy. Don't mind me."

"Get some rest," he said, touching her shoulder lightly. Then his attention was focused on the stage again. He'd forgotten she was there.

* * *

TO REHEARSE WITHOUT CAROLINE'S gossipy friendship felt odd and incomplete. This was Liz's last show at G-Triple-S-G; Madame had made that clear. Perhaps she would never again be onstage with Caroline. If she'd needed it spelled out, here was evidence that nothing would ever be the same.

Through the weeks of rehearsal she wished daily for someone to talk to—a confidante—who could help her with affairs of the heart. The genuine friendship she'd had with Caroline, where they could be both blunt and personal with impunity, had devolved into cordial exchanges about the weather. Bert had cautioned her to give it time, but the situation saddened her. She found herself alone, where she had chosen to be, and hating it.

The familiar pattern of rehearsals moved inevitably toward its culmination. Monday night of hell week brought the orchestra and cast together to run the second act. All through the evening Liz felt the grit of sleep deprivation in her eyes. She had to work to concentrate on her performance, for her mind wanted to slip away for a little nap. She stayed on her feet the whole time, afraid that if she sat she would doze off and miss a cue.

After the first laborious run-through, the company seemed to pull itself together. The second time was better, with only a few stops for details.

After a few hours, to everyone's relief, they reached the finale for the second time. The chorus was onstage, eager to finish and go home. Liz heard her cue and began to move through the blocking of the wedding scene. The chorus sang heartily of her joy as she turned upstage with the golden-haired tenor, Colonel Fairfax. Then a hush snuffed the joy onstage. All eyes turned. Her companion from the first act, Jack Point, trudged into sight, his face woebegone.

Although the cast was in street clothes, Liz felt a shiver of reality touch the tableau. She faced the vulnerability she had built into Elsie's character, this genuine regret in her moment of greatest happiness.

Curtis reprised the haunting song that he and Liz had performed early in the show. His eyes beseeched her not to abandon him. The chorus sang it back to him in tones so sweet and soft that she felt pressure in her chest as he looked away in despair. Suddenly she was remembering *Mikado*, when Curtis's panicked eyes had thrust her into the limelight. He was one of a number of friends with whom she had worked here in Cardiff whom she would miss. Now it seemed he was begging her not to leave, and she couldn't bear the idea.

She came back to the present and stepped downstage to touch his arm.

"*I have a song to sing, O!*" she sang in clear, ringing tones.

"*Sing me your song, O!*" the chorus replied with a sound like a Bach chorale.

"*It is sung with the ring of the songs maids sing,*
Who love with a love life long, O!
It's the song of the merry maid nestling near,
Who loved her lord but who dropped a tear
For the moan of the merryman, moping mum . . ."

As Liz sang, Jack Point turned away from her, and she felt Colonel Fairfax gently draw her back. Suddenly the pressure in her chest rose and took hold of her throat, and hot tears rolled down her cheeks. Although the support in her abdomen had collapsed, she kept singing, her voice a squeaking whisper through her tears.

"*. . . Whose soul was sad and whose glance was glum*
Who sipped no sup and who craved no crumb
As he sighed for the love of a lady."

She kept mouthing the words to the end, but no sound came out. Tired and lonely, Liz understood the heartbeat of her character.

The chasm of the orchestra pit separated her from Giles, for which she was thankful.

She managed to finish, and David firmly pulled her away from Curtis's devastating Jack Point. She turned to him, working at not breaking down altogether. He held her more tightly than usual. The chorus began to sing uncertainly, edging toward their final formation with eyes darting around for a signal for how to proceed. The director came up onstage, and Giles stopped the orchestra.

"You need to be ready for that," Pierce admonished the cast. "What if that happens Saturday night?"

The chorus remained silent, embarrassed by Liz's breakdown. The principals drew a little closer to her, and David patted her on the shoulder.

"All right then, luv?" Pierce asked.

"Yes. Sorry." Liz wiped the tears with her fingers, sniffing. "It got a little too real." She snuck a quick glance at Giles. He had gotten to his feet and was watching her with folded arms and a slight frown. When he caught her eye he inclined his head and raised an eyebrow. She shook her head and nearly began to cry again.

"Right then, let's try again from '*The moan of the merryman.*'" Pierce went back out into the house.

Giles counted in his score with his baton. "That's the pickup to seventeen measures after letter I," he told the orchestra, and he raised his arms. He hummed a measure or two to help them find the place and looked up at Liz for her cue. She took a deep breath and plunged back into the scene.

* * *

AS THEY PACKED UP TO GO HOME, members of the cast stopped to reassure Liz, though they couldn't know what was so affecting her. She felt both ridiculous and appreciated.

Pierce warned her to keep a handle on her emotions. "It's lovely, very tender the way you three play it. Just right. But don't you be crying, luv. Your job is to make the *audience* feel the way you did tonight. Get some sleep," he added kindly.

It was silly to hope Giles wouldn't say anything. He hung back, giving notes to the instrumentalists and a few of the singers. When most of the cast had gotten notes from the director and gone home, he wandered over to her.

"Are you all right then, my dear?" he asked as she tucked her scarf into her coat.

She felt the trembling under her sternum again and took a deep breath. "I'm fine. Just really tired. And Curtis is so good at Point, he makes me feel sorry for him."

"You make Elsie devastatingly sympathetic. I can't think of anyone doing it better. All eyes will be on you."

She wasn't sure that was a good thing; certainly Curtis and David would not think so. But she nodded in acknowledgment. "Thanks. I'm glad I'm living up to your expectations."

"Wasn't I sure you would?" He patted her shoulder. "Rest up, then. Long week."

* * *

LIZ SURVIVED THE STRAIN, MADE it to closing night. With purposely heightened awareness she took in the moments as they passed—the faces, the other voices blending with her own. The sustenance of Giles in the orchestra pit, sending direct and personal contact to each singer. She missed Caroline's presence. She savored even the familiar pattern of the curtain calls, watching as the chorus got their well-deserved accolades, noticing the gestures and style of each principal, recognizing the swell of joy in her own breast when she burst into the light and took her bow downstage.

She and the other principals joined hands for a group bow and then turned to invite Giles and Pierce to join them. When he'd brought the orchestra to its feet, Giles moved back between Liz and Curtis for the final bow. As he took Liz's hand he kissed it, and suddenly the roar of the audience seemed to dim. She remembered herself as he tugged her forward for the last bow. It made the whole ordeal worth it.

* * *

A MELANCHOLY CLOUD HUNG over Liz's gaiety, but she did her best to shoulder it aside as the audience thanked her. Suddenly, Caroline stood there, hesitant, Bert behind her with his arm around her.

Liz felt her eyes go big. "I thought you wouldn't come."

Caroline shrugged. "I was curious."

Liz hesitated, unsure what to say.

"You were quite good. Excellent, in fact." Caroline was calm but unsmiling.

Liz swallowed. "Thank you. I . . . I don't know what to say."

Giles appeared, putting an arm around Liz. "Caroline, I'm so glad you came. Aren't you proud of her?"

Caroline flicked a glance at him. "Yes. But I think you're more responsible for this than I am."

"Will you come to the cast party?" Liz asked.

Caroline bit her lip, but then her chin went up, almost defiantly. "Of course. They're still my friends."

Chapter 32

DESPITE LIZ'S DOWNRIGHT SKEPTICISM, Christopher was to marry Kate the following Saturday. In December, Liz had agreed to sing, but now, in May, she could hardly bear to practice with Giles. Kate had chosen one of Giles's own songs, a setting of a text from the Book of Ruth. The words made Liz ache with loneliness, and she avoided rehearsing it until the very last moment. "I don't have time," she insisted, realizing that he knew perfectly well that she did.

Finally they met on the Thursday before the wedding. When Liz saw Giles waiting for her in the cramped little practice room, a sensation zipped through her like someone had run a finger lightly down her spine. She sang sotto voce, with little emotion, and when they had gone through it only twice, she pronounced it ready. "It's fine," she said brightly. "It's not hard."

"Well, if you are satisfied. But I would like to do the third page again, to be sure we agree on tempo."

"I really have to leave."

"Humor me," he said dryly.

She did—it was his work, after all. It was only fair. But she did it with little grace.

*　＊　＊*

THE WEDDING WENT OFF AS PLANNED, the vows spoken in voices that Liz hardly recognized. She sang, and Giles played, although they might have been in separate rooms, for she met his eyes only once—at the beginning, to indicate that she was ready. As he offered her his arm to escort her back to her seat he murmured, "Lovely." She acknowledged it with only a slight lift of her chin.

At the reception, Liz made an enormous effort to smile when people complimented her singing, but the song haunted her. *Whither thou goest, I will go, and where thou lodgest, I will lodge; thy people shall be my people, and thy God my*

God. Where thou diest, will I die. She had performed it with a disgraceful overtone of emotion that Madame would have deplored. Tears she had not shed at the end of *Merry Widow* shimmered dangerously close to the surface.

She tried to fulfill her duty and circulate through the crowd, awash in names she would never remember. Finally she escaped outside, where the cool of the failing day refreshed her. Leaning against the stone wall surrounding the veranda, she gazed across the grounds to the hazy horizon. For some time she was aware of nothing more than the burdens that had weighed on her for most of the spring. Occasionally, in a few giddy moments, she had nearly risen free of them, but for now, in the quiet, she was content to let them be. She felt the stone cool against her arm, the sun soft on her cheek. It would not do to cry; that could come later. She must get through the rest of this day.

"Not sure am I, that I ought to give you this," Giles said at her elbow.

She turned, not in the least surprised to find him there. He offered her a glass of wine.

"You probably shouldn't," she agreed, nonetheless taking it from him before he could change his mind.

"You looked terribly sad just now."

She focused on the sunlight that made the wine glow red in her glass. "Did I?"

"You aren't still wanting Christopher, are you?"

"Good God, no. Why do you keep saying that?"

"What is it, then?"

She shrugged, feeling foolish. "Weddings just do this to me."

"And that is all?"

She gazed at him for a long time. "No."

"Then what?"

"Don't make me tell you." But she said it quietly, dropping all pretenses.

"Tell me what?" he asked, so close that she hunched her shoulders, turtle-like, about her ears, dangling between her desire and her resistance.

He remained silent.

The thin ice of her control broke and plunged her into cold, awakening waters. She reached out and put her palm against his waistcoat, over his heart. "I'm in love with you." All the accumulated months of secrecy gave her away in an instant, and tears started.

After a moment he wiped a tear from her cheek. "Are you, then?" He took the glass out of her hand and put it, with his own, on the ledge. Then he took her in his arms, holding her so that she could smell the spicy carnation in his lapel. "*Dod yma.* Hisht, dear heart."

She fought her tears, fought his arms around her, but he rocked her. She wasn't sure who began it, whether she put her face up or he sought her out, but suddenly he was kissing her, and she held him, unable to breathe, unable to stop.

Finally, with an effort, she pulled away, wiping her eyes with her hands. "Please," she said as soon as she could speak. "Don't. I can't handle it."

"What?"

She tried to remember all the rationalizations she had conjured to protect herself over the past months. "You're my best friend. I don't want to ruin that. Besides, you told me you weren't in love with me."

He seemed to be taken by surprise. He caught his breath and seemed to consider his words before saying, "I may not have been entirely honest with you."

Liz's whole body flamed with embarrassment at the subterfuge she had practiced for the last seven months. "You—"

He only watched her in silence until she looked away.

"But there's my singing," she stumbled on. "It would only make a mess of our work."

"What makes you think that?"

"Madame."

Giles raised his hands in a gesture of impatience so rare that it surprised her. "Liz, she does not own you."

"But she wants what's best for me."

"She wants you to succeed. That is not the same thing. What about your happiness?"

She had no answer.

He leaned over and spoke so quietly it was almost a whisper. "Liz, when you sing you are potent. You are powerful. You are incredibly sensuous. I want you every time we work together."

"Jeez-us." Her heart pounded, and she couldn't meet his eyes.

He ran his fingers down her left arm to grasp her hand. The scars on her fingers seemed to grow tight under his touch, but she did not pull away.

"Come home with me tonight?" he asked.

She shook her head, smiling ruefully through the tears that were threatening again. "I'm not ready for what will happen if I do."

He waited—something he did too well.

She took a deep breath. "Giles, I'm going to London next year, and after that, who knows? I don't want to start something that's going to be hard to finish. It wouldn't be fair to either of us."

"It might be possible to be with me and to sing as well," he observed mildly.

"That's just it. I don't want to sing 'as well.' I want to sing. Full stop. I can't do both as well as either one deserves, so I have to choose just one. And I chose this a long time ago. Before I ever met you."

"Sure you are, that you're going to London?"

Her head snapped up. "What do you mean?"

"Just that. There are eighteen places and hundreds of applicants."

She stared at him. "You don't think I'm good enough."

"I did not say that."

"You meant it."

He did not deny it.

"I thought you believed in me."

"No one more." He paused. "You are going about this all wrong. Your stamina and range need at least another year. Why not wait, make the foundation solid? What is the hurry?"

"Madame thinks I should go now. *She* thinks I'm good enough."

"Listen to me. She's on the faculty, and I have no doubt that she could get you placed, but that does not mean you are ready. When it is your time, no one will be able to take it from you. But if you go now—do you honestly think you can tolerate failure?"

She turned her back on him, devastated by tears.

"Elizabeth, I cannot bear to see you disappointed. I am sorry, my timing is poor." He put gentle hands on her shoulders.

She shrugged him off roughly. "Some accompanist you are." She left him there, and left the reception without a word.

Chapter 33

WEDNESDAY MORNING SPREAD ACROSS the sky with indecent eagerness. Liz climbed from her bed with a grimace at the days' heartlessness. She ate and washed with eyes turned absently inward. She stood for a long time at the door of the wardrobe, unable to decide which of two choices she should wear for the audition. At last, pushed by the clock, she grabbed the blouse and skirt and packed them up, for the silk dress she would have preferred to wear would wrinkle impossibly before she could unpack it.

Just before she left she glanced around indecisively, as if she had forgotten something, and heard the postman downstairs. She went to collect the post, prepared to toss it on the table to wait for her return. But one envelope caught her eye, the script familiar. She leaned in the doorway, keys in hand, and ripped it open.

> *My dear Liz,*
> *I am terribly sorry for having upset you the other day. Please forgive me and accept my best wishes for your trip to London. You are gifted and intelligent, and I always find it a pleasure to work with you.*
> Gorau o ran,
> *Giles.*

She crumpled it, but as she aimed for the trash can she paused. Instead she shoved it in her pocket, slammed the door and locked it, and went to London.

* * *

LONDON LOOMED OVER LIZ. She stayed in a bed and breakfast in Bloomsbury, a clean but tired-feeling establishment run by Middle Easterners. The windows of her room faced the brick wall next door, the floor showed through the carpet in spots, and the bedclothes felt limp and over-laundered. She slept badly, stage fright plaguing her hours before it was needed. In her dreams a flute tantalized her, and through billows of smoke, a satyr with Giles's face bobbed just ahead of her. His flute gave back a gunmetal shine in the dense air. She fought to keep up, pursued by some unknown demon behind her, but she could not catch the pied piper that wove a skein of flute music to snare her.

She woke with hot eyeballs and cold hands. After a breakfast of corn flakes and cold toast and hot tea, she forced herself out the door. She took the Tube to the Guildhall, swaying on her feet beside the commuters as the train racketed through the tunnels. She scanned their bland, early-morning faces and suddenly wished she could be satisfied with a pay packet and a roof over her head. As she emerged from the station, the griminess of London choked her.

Her audition was at ten thirty, but she presented herself forty-five minutes early, for Madame had arranged for a practice room so she could warm up her voice. She paced as she encouraged her voice out into the open, stretching her body and breathing into her belly. She tried to forget where she was, tried to pretend she was in a room in the music building, waiting for Giles to play for her—

She stopped and shook her head as if a mosquito were whining in her ear. Then she set her jaw, drew herself up, and began to pour her first aria out into the claustrophobic room.

*　*　*

THE PROCTORS WERE RUNNING LATE, so Liz loitered down the corridor, within earshot, and tried to calm her racing heart. It was reasonable to be so nervous. This was the most important audition she'd ever done. Nervousness was an asset.

She stopped pacing, faced a blank wall.

I'm not ready.

She nearly bolted, but just then the student at the table down the hall called her name. A jolt of adrenaline shot through Liz. She froze. Then, somehow, she walked to the desk, smiled tightly, and allowed herself to be ushered into the hall. Her music was taken from her and delivered to the pianist. The panel of four judges sat together halfway up the house, huddled in desultory conversation, until they saw her. These were Madame's colleagues. Whatever Liz did in the next five minutes would be reported back to Cardiff before she herself could return. As she took her place onstage they settled back in their chairs.

Her heart was beating so hard she could see it shaking the gold locket that lay outside her blouse. She smoothed her hands over her skirt, felt the crinkle of Giles's letter in her pocket, and swallowed.

"My name is Elizabeth Morgan, and I will sing 'Non so più cosa son' from *Le Nozze di Figaro.*"

No one moved, and no one acknowledged that she had spoken. Her choice might be dangerous, for every mezzo called it her own, but she trusted that Mozart would not let her down. She looked at the accompanist, who began to play instantly.

Caught on the hop, Liz barely had time for a breath, for her entrance came only two bars into the swiftly moving number. She squeaked through the first phrase. As she gradually caught up to the accompanist, she tried to slow the tempo a shade, but the automaton at the piano hunched over the keyboard and punched out the arpeggios with frightening accuracy. The grit of London's air made her cough when she drew her first deep breath. The legato section rasped over the frog in her throat, and she finished weakly, although she tried to reflect strength in her stance.

The race finished, Liz waited breathlessly to know what else they would ask her to sing. After a silent conference, one of the judges asked, "May we hear the 'Batti, batti,' please?"

Of course. The last learned, recklessly approximate in her mind and muscle memory; she had gambled by putting it at the bottom of the list of pieces she was prepared to sing.

"Certainly." She smiled.

The impassive pianist gave her the note; she heaved off her anxiety with a deep breath and began to sing. She maneuvered over-cautiously through the song without suggesting a single emotion. As she began the second section her mind skipped ahead to the last page, which she knew well enough to truly enjoy. She was absently calculating an impressive finish when the Italian slipped from her memory. She could conjure nothing but nonsense for about three measures. Mercifully, she recalled the words just in time for the fluid, high turns near the end. But the dryness in her throat caused by the shock of forgetting snagged what would have otherwise been smooth passages, and she stumbled to the end.

She could feel the blush pounding in the roots of her hair, but she at least knew enough not to make matters worse by apologizing.

Predictably, they thanked her and allowed her to leave.

Chapter 34

MADAME PONNELLE EXPECTED to hear from her when she got back to Cardiff, but Liz refused to stand in the hallway on the public phone, fighting her emotions, and hear the disapproval in that voice. Besides, she realized, unlocking the door of her room and tossing her bag on a chair, Madame had no doubt already talked to London—already knew that she had failed.

She sat at the table, not drinking the cup of tea she had made, watching without interest as the light softened and relinquished its hold on the day. Occasionally a single thought drifted by, but she drove it away before it could make her cry. Distantly she heard the phone in the hallway ring and ring, but she ignored it. A little later it rang again. Another lodger answered it and came to tap at the door. Liz remained silent, and the girl went away.

The sky turned silvery rose against a few timid clouds. She sat on in the evening dimness. She could have listened to Giles. But she'd been too busy running away from him. Disappointment and loneliness sewed tight, puckered seams through her solar plexus.

The door buzzer sounded, making her jump, but she ignored it as she had the phone. When it insisted, she cursed and got up to see who dared to bother her. She peered out the window. Giles stood on the step with his back to the door, checking his watch. Something wild surged through her, and she pelted downstairs to fling open the door.

"What the hell are you doing here?"

"I came to see how it went," he replied mildly.

"Well, you were right. I choked. Are you happy?" She glared at him.

"May I come in?"

She didn't answer at first, because she couldn't make up her mind. Finally she shrugged and left the door open as she turned away. "I don't care."

He closed the door and followed her up to the bed-sit. He stood awkwardly near the table where she ate and did her work. "Liz, I did not want you to fail."

"I guess we all overestimated my ability." She paced up and down the long room, not listening to him. "Maybe I should stop all this nonsense and go back to San Francisco."

He sat down abruptly, as though he had lost his balance. "It was only one audition. You have friends here, and family, and we all support you. There is no reason to give up all of that over one audition."

"At the end of the day, all of my friends and family go home to their spouses or their kids or their lovers, and I'm alone," she flung at him. "What exactly do you think I'd be giving up?"

That silenced him for a moment. "Well, dear heart," he said finally. "I am fresh out of all three. Perhaps we can work something out."

"Oh Giles, I didn't think. I don't mean you!" She pressed her hands to her temples.

"Never mind. A diva you are. That entitles you to a few good scenes," he said lightly.

"But I'm not a diva! I can't sing!" The tears spilled down her cheeks, and she turned her head away, acutely embarrassed. He got up and gave her shoulders a little shake.

"Don't be absurd."

"But it's true!" she insisted, "You don't understand. I couldn't control it; I couldn't *fix* it when it went wrong. I haven't sung well all week. I've lost it!"

"Listen to me. You must not take this all upon yourself. Ponnelle had no business sending you there. Regardless of what happens in the future, she has done you no favors."

"It's all . . . all I had," Liz stuttered through chattering teeth. "The only thing that's . . . my own. I can't stand . . . to lose it. Not again." The blood beat fast in her head, and the sobs crowded her lungs.

Giles took her in his arms then. "Gently, *fy annwyl, ysgafn* . You must give yourself a chance. Remember, once you could not do it at all. And you learned. Patiently. And you will find it again. Patiently. It is not gone. I promise you. It will always be with you."

He rocked her until she stopped shaking, stopped weeping. A calm that had been missing for months, possibly all her life, settled over her. *Whither thou goest.* At least this time the gods had given her one person who would follow her to Hades and help bring her back.

When he drew away he made her meet his eyes. "Elizabeth, I would take you on a bad day before most people on a good day."

She tried to smile.

"Let me take you out and distract you for an hour or two."

"I'll be lousy company."

"I shall risk it."

* * *

HE TOOK HER TO THE ARMLESS DRAGON and fed her roasted lamb and sweet spring peas and crispy roasted potatoes. He insisted on treating her. "To celebrate," he told her.

"Celebrate what? My foolishness?"

"If you like."

She astonished herself by eating it all. By tacit agreement they did not refer again to London or her voice. The surreal day ebbed, until she could almost believe that her entire world had not crumbled in the last twelve hours. Sipping the last of her wine, she watched silently as Giles placated his sweet tooth with rhubarb crisp. When he caught her watching him he licked the last of the double cream off his thumb and pushed aside his bowl.

"I have a problem."

"What is it?" she asked, completely off her guard.

"What am I going to do with you?"

She flushed, her throat closing. "Don't worry about what I said about being alone. It was just melodrama. You know me."

He smiled a slow, deep smile, bringing up dimples. "That I do. Tough and independent, you are." He considered her, and all the bones in her chest cavity seemed to melt and expose her heart. "But you are also quite vulnerable. I should not like to leave you alone again."

The heat in her face was unbearable. She had no idea what to say. But she couldn't take her eyes off him.

"Liz, I will not give up and go away. My feelings have not changed. You must not go back to San Francisco."

That startled her. She barely remembered saying it. "I didn't mean that."

"Then come home with me tonight."

"Okay." She answered before he'd finished the breath of his sentence, and he paused, listening to the echo of her reply. Then he leaned over and kissed her lightly.

"Come then, *cariad*."

* * *

SHE THOUGHT AT FIRST THAT it was a bad idea. The sex was supposed to be a means to an end; she expected nothing from her body. She wanted him to hold her, to rock her, to comfort her for the failure of the day.

But he had the patience of a teacher. Her shyness he gently pushed aside a little at a time. He looked at and touched and kissed her, and when she wouldn't meet his eyes, tense with anxiety, he whispered, "Open your eyes, look at me, dear heart." And he stopped and waited until at last she looked up at him. Something weakened in her chest, and she smiled and then laughed for no real reason. He would not allow her to withdraw but kept her with him, aware, present, and made her accept what he gave. He drew a climax from her like sleight of hand—unexpected, delightful, sudden.

"You made me laugh," she said later, in wonder.

"What else can one do?"

"You didn't do this just to be kind, did you?"

"Taking you to dinner was kindness. This," he said, tracing his finger down between her breasts, "this is not mere kindness."

* * *

SHE WENT EARLY TO SWANN'S to catch Bert before opening.

"How did it go?" Caroline pounced the instant Liz came into the shop.

It took her a shocked moment to realize that Caroline was asking about London. The last twelve hours had effectively driven away the anxieties of the week past. She made a face and briefly described the debacle.

"Surely you're exaggerating?"

"I was truly awful. But there'll be other auditions." A week ago such an idea would have been an unwelcome comfort. Liz abruptly steered the conversation clear of her failure. "Is Bert here?"

"He is," Bert's voice called from the office.

Liz poked her head around the door. "Would you mind very much if I didn't work tomorrow?"

Bert looked blank for a moment, then surprised. "You've only just come back!"

"Giles wants to go away for the weekend." Liz tried to sound matter-of-fact and was annoyed to find she was blushing.

"Oh, I see," Bert said with an avuncular smile.

"So, the rumors are true." Caroline joined her in the doorway.

Liz stared at her. "What rumors?"

"About you and Giles. They were all over *Widow*."

"What are you talking about?"

"I should know. I started half of them."

"Caroline! Nothing was going on!"

"The way you were flirting?" She shook her head in amusement. "It was rather hard to tell. I bet that's why you got Elsie. Because he's sweet on you."

Liz stiffened at the mere mention of the *Yeomen* fiasco. Then what Caroline had said penetrated. "What did you say?"

"I suspect that half the reason he cast you was because he wanted to get you in bed." Her tone was offhand, but Liz felt a shriek like a teakettle build inside.

"How dare you?"

"Don't tell me you didn't guess."

"I earned that role! There was never a suggestion of anything else."

"Oh, I'm sure he was entirely circumspect. But I'm also sure it was there."

"I know you were pissed off with us, but you have no right—"

"I'm not making this up. Ask him if you don't believe me."

Liz could not gather her wits enough to reply.

Bert cleared his throat. "You go ahead, Liz. We'll make do without you tomorrow. Best be getting over to Cygnet now. I'll be along."

Chapter 35

A TEARING WIND SCRUBBED THE SKY smooth on Saturday. They drove to St. David's on the southwest tip of Wales, one of Giles's favorite places for birding. Part of the Pembrokeshire Coastal Path clung to the toothed peninsula, a circular trail that edged out over the savage Ramsey Sound and retreated to Porthclais Harbour. They picked up the trail going west, toward Ramsey Island. The blunt sun followed a shaving wind that cut across the Atlantic.

For long stretches of time they met no one. In Giles's deliberate presence, Liz found herself content to follow and acquiesce, the wind buffeting all volition and anxiety out of her. He stopped frequently to point out tiny sea pinks and ladyfingers, or to hand her his binoculars so she could follow the flight of a pair of fulmars that spiraled about the cliffs, oblivious to the wind. They spotted gray seals in the waters and watched in awe as an outcropping of rocks on the island tore the waves brutally.

As they crossed Trefeiddan Moor, Giles stopped and pointed out an unassuming weed that stood knee-high. "See this? Mallow plant. This particular one that grows in the marsh is fairly rare. It gets lovely pink flowers in late summer. People used to make sweets from it. Marshmallows."

She squinted at him. "You're making that up."

He smiled. "Not at all. Look it up for yourself."

"Where did you learn all this stuff?"

"My father," he said as they continued toward the sea.

She caught the surprise of renewed grief in his eyes and put her hand in his.

* * *

THEY STOPPED AT TWO O'CLOCK to eat their sandwiches and drink the tea Giles had brought in a thermos flask. Afterwards a stupor came over Liz. The skin on her face felt tight and warm, her body pleasantly relaxed as though she'd had a beer. Across the channel, Ramsey Island lay like a whale in the pewter water. Between coast and island, seawater shattered against the rocks, dribbling trails of foam down to the ocean. Over the island, a flock of terns with swallow wings and cricket chirps swooped and shifted, black to white, like an Escher print.

"Nap time," she said around an enormous yawn, and she settled herself with her head in his lap. The wind had dropped, leaving gaps of near silence between the thud of the waves.

He stroked her hair soothingly. "Entrancing, this music."

"Mmm." She didn't move.

"For centuries man has shaped rhythm and harmony, but never do we get this close to perfection."

"Mmm." She kept her eyes closed, but her senses were alert. The sun scalded her windburned cheeks, the noisy colonies of seabirds argued and agreed, and the waves cast themselves into the jaws of the cliffs again and again. The perfection of the balanced earth hummed around her and through her. She remembered something he had said long ago, something about Mozart that she had never forgotten: *His music is straining to get back to the cosmos.*

"But the basis of all our music is right here. Do you know why the C major chord is the most pleasing to the human ear?"

"Nnn." She wished he would be quiet.

"The ratio of the vibrations that make up a one-three-five chord in that key is identical to the ratio of the curve of the human eardrum. It's called the Golden Mean, or Fibonacci's Curve. The same pattern is all over nature, in shells and plant growth and crystals and such."

She opened one eye and put a hand over his mouth. "Hush."

He chuckled, taking her hand. "I should have missed you if you had gone away to London."

A little shred of anxiety caught her breath for an instant. "Giles, I will go someday." Instantly she wanted to take it back. "You know," she added quickly. "When I become famous and you can't stand my ego anymore."

"Yes." He kissed her hand almost absently. "And I shall be quite proud to say that I knew you when."

But she had seen his eyes.

* * *

THAT EVENING THEY SAT TOGETHER in front of the fire at the bed and breakfast, and Liz felt herself melting into Giles, her body lax and satisfied after the day's exercise. He sipped a cup of tea. She had declined, already sleepy.

A question came to her in her sloth. "You know, Caroline thinks you were biased when you cast me for Elsie."

"Not exactly an impartial observer, is she?"

"But were you? Did you give me an advantage?"

"And if I did?"

She sat up straight. "Then she was right, it wasn't fair."

He pulled her back against him. "I never said I did."

"I don't want to use people. I want to do this on my own."

"You could hardly be accused of using me if you didn't know how I felt about you. And everyone needs help sometime. There's no shame in taking it."

"You don't."

"I've had plenty of teachers and mentors. And I am grateful to them. As you should be."

At first she didn't answer. Then she shook her head, frowning. "I need to know I can do it on my own."

"Nobody, *nobody* does it alone. Trust me."

"Did you give me a preference in *Yeomen*?"

"I probably gave you more preference for *Mikado*," he answered thoughtfully.

"What do you mean?" She turned to watch his enigmatic face.

"I'm the one who suggested that Huw give you a chance."

"But you didn't know anything about me."

"I thought you had potential."

"So Diana wasn't imagining things."

He looked nonplused. "That was a professional decision."

She leaned back, bumping against him gently. "It's okay, Maestro. You never showed anything in the least bit questionable."

"You got my attention as a performer. That's all."

"And then you turned around and made me feel like I was totally incompetent."

He put an arm around her. "I probably did give you that impression. I'm sorry."

"Caroline said that you were picking on me because I was worth the effort."

"Oh, you are definitely worth the effort."

* * *

TIRED FROM THE DAY, LIZ nevertheless found herself awake at three o'clock the next morning. Giles, looking closer to eighteen than thirty, slept on with his characteristic containment. Liz got out of bed and wrapped a quilt around her shoulders, feeling oddly vulnerable. Beyond the window the night lay smooth and still, the silver moon silencing breezes and birdcalls. The tabby that had commandeered Giles's lap for over an hour earlier that evening tiptoed across the path, blending into the moonlight. The scent of jasmine at the bottom of the garden colored the night air.

Her eyes were on the landscape, but her mind was on the man in the bed behind her.

"Can I ask you something?" she had asked as they'd headed inland through the long twilight to the bed and breakfast.

He grinned. "Can I stop you?"

She rolled her eyes. "You don't have to answer."

"What is it, then?"

"I don't understand why you left Paris."

"I told you. Diana—"

"But I don't buy that."

He gave her a quizzical look. "What on earth do you mean?"

"I don't believe that you'd give up your music on her account. It's too important to you."

He looked taken aback.

"I'm right, aren't I?"

"Well . . ." He paused and sighed. "Yes, as a matter of fact, you are. How did you know?"

"I didn't know. I just suspected." She suddenly felt like she had violated his privacy, and she backed away. "You don't need to tell me about it. I just thought I knew you better than that."

"And you're satisfied?"

She grinned at him. "Well, if you want to tell me . . ."

He laughed but sobered quickly, putting an arm around her as they walked. "I've never told anyone about this. I never thought I would."

"Never mind," she assured him. "Don't tell me if you don't want to."

"No, I think I want you to know."

She said no more, giving him time to collect his thoughts.

"As far as it goes, what I told you is true. But there was more to it. Diana's lover was my mentor, Pierre Varnet."

Her heart thumped with shock. "Oh no! Seriously?"

"I would not joke about that," he said grimly, but he squeezed her shoulders gently as he said it. "This is the part where I look back and see just how young and naïve I was. I ought to have just packed up and left. But no, I had to confront him. I went to see him, all full of self-righteousness and bluster, and I told him what I thought of him."

"What did he say?"

He waited a long time before he answered, and Liz could feel her body tensing against what was coming.

Finally he said, "He told me that if I did not have the passion to keep my wife happy, I could not possibly have the passion to be a real musician."

She gasped. "How could he? Oh my God, Giles!" She stopped him on the path and put her arms around him, hugging him tightly as if he were a small boy in need of comfort. She could just imagine him, younger than his years in some ways, older in others, slapped in the face by the two people upon whom he depended most. She almost felt like she had taken a blow herself. He rested his cheek on the top of her head.

"That's just cruel," she said, drawing back to look into his face. Tears stung the back of her eyes, but he was smiling at her.

"Never mind, *fy nghariad,* he was wrong. It just took me a while to realize it."

"Good," she said fiercely, and she kissed him before they continued along the path.

She recalled the conversation now, as she watched the night comfort the earth, and she pulled her quilt closer. She almost understood what had previously seemed impossible to her: what her mother could have found that would compel her to give up her career.

From the window seat she looked back and pictured herself lying next to Giles only a few minutes earlier. She realized that she had already passed through a moment of pure contentment in her life, something likely to be rare and precious. She was even now on the other side, fretting about the future.

Someday I will look back at this as one of the happiest times of my life. Tears stung the back of her eyes.

"Liz?"

She turned, glad the faint light was behind her.

He stretched out an arm. She left the quilt on the end of the bed and crawled back into the warm nest.

"What are you thinking?" He settled her comfortably close.

"Oh, just about how lucky I am." It was no less than the truth.

* * *

SUNDAY SURROUNDED THEM IN DENSE gray drizzle. They loitered along the way home, exploring ruins and beaches as they made their unhurried way to the motorway. In the midafternoon, cold and damp, they finally had to start back to Cardiff in earnest.

The moment they joined the M4 the mist began to lift, though the cloud cover clung stubbornly to the sky. London and her failure slipped back into Liz's mind, surreal against the joy of the last three days.

She had successfully ignored it for a time, but her life lay waiting for her in Cardiff. She watched Giles, her mind wandering ahead. The protest she had made about their work together seemed absurd to her now. She could hardly wait to see what their music would become. She could no more do without him than she could remain silent all her life. She did not look forward to returning to her bed-sit to eat alone and sleep alone. She settled in her seat with a deep, satisfied sigh. Giles glanced over, smiling without asking for an explanation.

He had work to do that evening—the price of their truant weekend—so he dropped her off at her own flat as evening took over the day. The clouds at last began to move off the coast, making the twilight almost a dawning as the sun finally got its chance. She felt suddenly shy as he walked her up the steps to the front door.

He broke the silence as she fumbled for words. "Liz, even if Diana cooperates, a divorce will take at least a couple of years. I certainly understand if that bothers you." He placed each word carefully before her, and she knew that he had been thinking about it all afternoon. She opened her mouth to reassure him, but he continued. "I know I have no right to ask you this . . ." Again he hesitated.

She waited.

"Would you consider coming to live with me?"

"We've only just met," Liz said, faltering, with an uncertain smile.

"Nonsense. I have always known you."

She did not reply.

"If you were meant to learn to sing, you could easily have stayed in California. But then you and I should never have met."

Her heart pounded with the intensity of stage fright, and she could not understand it. "I'm touched, that you want me. But don't ask me to decide tonight." She hugged her elbows against the cool breeze.

"I thought I had overcome all of your objections."

She hesitated. "I don't know if I have the time or the energy for a relationship. Why start something that we both know can't do anything but end?"

"Don't ask for the moon and stars, *fy annwyl*. Just ask for the best possible here and now you can have. I'm far from interested in another commitment. I've made mistakes, and those lessons are still coming back to me. But that doesn't mean I want to be alone."

"But what happens when I get a job someplace like Europe or even New York or something? I can't only think about here and now."

His answer was breathtakingly swift, as though he had anticipated her protest. "What are you going to do, Liz? Seal off your heart until you've finished singing? What are you going to do when you're sixty years old and you have no one in your life? If you want nothing to do with me, I'll survive. But will you?" She started to protest, but he threw up a hand. "No. Listen to me." She didn't dare interrupt. "If you come to my cottage tomorrow, be prepared to stay, you. Or do not bother to come at all. Play your temperamental little games with someone else."

Shocked, she watched him return to the car, slam the door, and force his way into traffic without checking behind. As the sun sank near the horizon it seemed to push up the underside of the clouds with its final rays, tossing the storm back over its shoulder. She turned and went inside.

Chapter 36

TO HER RELIEF SHE WORKED WITH Bert at Cygnet the next day. She could not have borne Caroline's prying. Early in the afternoon business slowed, and they retreated into the office to eat cold sausage rolls washed down with tea.

Bert ate his lunch leaning against a bookcase, watching over her head in case a customer appeared. "What a day. I believe I'll have to hire another clerk, at least for the mornings. About time this place was a success."

Liz could not contain her need to talk to someone. "Bert," she said, swallowing a greasy bite with difficulty, "if you had to choose, would you rather be happy now, or happy in the future?"

He wiped his mouth with the back of his hand. "None of knows that we have a future, do we now? I'll take what I'm offered and be grateful for it." He watched her mull that over. "Why do you ask?"

"My life is just so complicated all of the sudden. A week ago I knew just how everything was going to be. And now it's all different."

"Surely you'll have other chances."

"It's not just London. It's Giles. He wants me to live with him."

"You don't want to?"

"Yes, I do. But I can't commit to anything, the way my life is. I told him that."

"And that didn't change his mind?"

"He just got mad at me. And he was right. I'm—very fond of him." Her voice shook ever so slightly over the euphemism. "I've never had to consider anyone else before; I don't know what to do."

Bert wiped his hands on his handkerchief, sorting out his answer. "The future you expect may never happen. You didn't think you would fail last week, now did you? If you're offered something so precious right now, take it. "

Though she didn't particularly like it, Bert's observation made sense that Liz would have ignored a week ago, when she had been invincible. When she left the shop that evening, she found herself crossing Llandaff Fields without realizing that she had made the decision. She couldn't remember the last time she'd stopped thinking about the guarantees of the future and succumbed to the uncertainties of the present. She only knew that when she could no longer sing (*Oh God, let that not be for many years*), she would regret losing Giles as much or more than she would losing her career.

She found his cottage in its hollow beneath the cathedral. His car was parked in front, but he was not at home. She stood for a moment in indecision and then walked back up to the corner. Each bus that passed on the main road released a flock of schoolchildren, laughing and shouting as they dispersed into the neighborhood. Cleaning ladies heading home to make supper sent each other off at familiar corners. An elderly man shuffled past, and he presently returned with a newspaper tucked under his arm. He greeted her both times with grave courtesy.

As the hour dropped past six, the steady traffic from the Cardiff Road slowed. Liz went back to Giles's house and sat down on the step in the last of the sun creeping around the building. The raptures of a mockingbird filled the evening. Just as she was beginning to feel foolish, she spotted his solitary figure coming around the corner. He carried his coat and his music case like burdens. His sleeves were rolled back, his tie loose, his cadence slow and measured.

Liz sat still, holding her breath and resisting the urge to turn and run away. When Giles looked up he stopped abruptly. She made herself stand up and face him. Then a smile—a rare, brilliant transfiguration—poured over his face. It was as though a fire glowed to life inside him, fanned by the draw of her presence. To have that effect on him shook her profoundly.

He came slowly down the driveway, set down his satchel, and draped his jacket over it. With no urgency whatsoever he wrapped his arms around her, pressing her against him in an embrace that forced away every doubt. For a long minute they stayed there in union. When he released her she staggered back a step.

"I'm so sorry that I gave you an ultimatum," he said.

The apology she had prepared while she waited evaporated. "You know," she told him, running her hands up over his shoulders, "I've always wanted to make love with Wagner's 'Liebestod' in the background."

He began to laugh, and after a second she joined him.

* * *

The next morning they walked together through the quickening spring as far as the college. She said little, filled with wonder at the oldness of their intimacy.

"What time will you be home tonight?" he asked, and the word *home* resonated through her like a high D that obliterated all else.

"Half six, a little later. I have my lesson." She sighed. "You know, for the first time in my life I'm dreading it."

"Why? London was a learning experience. You will go on."

"I think it was an even bigger deal to her than it was to me."

"You did your best. She will have to be content with that."

Liz reminded herself of Giles's words all day, but they did not assuage the anxiety that filled her when Madame opened the door of the waiting room without a greeting and led the way to the studio. Silent, her teacher turned and inspected her, arms folded. She found her tongue before Liz did.

"So. You failed."

As Liz expected, she had spoken to someone in London.

"Yes. I guess I did." She withheld the automatic "I'm sorry."

"Your excuse?"

"I think I was less ready than I needed to be."

"I prepared you."

"It wasn't enough time. I was terrified, and that's not like me. It was because the arias weren't completely in my voice yet."

"You sang '*Non so più.*' You've known that for years."

"It wasn't just the arias. It was everything. I don't see why I couldn't wait until next year. Even Giles thought it was too soon." Instantly she knew she had chosen the wrong ally for herself.

The icy blue eyes narrowed. "Is he your teacher? Or am I?"

Liz's mouth went dry, and she swallowed. "Well you are, of course. But he does know me. He knows my voice."

"That young man has overstepped his bounds. I will not have him second-guessing me."

"But he was right!"

"Elizabeth! You forget yourself." The ring in her voice reminded Liz that Madame herself had once been a singer. Her teacher paused before continuing in a more controlled fashion. "You let him sabotage you."

"I sabotaged myself," Liz insisted stubbornly. "I know how to work around stage fright, but the whole thing unnerved me. I'm not ready to compete at that level."

"Oh yes you are. You let him tell you otherwise, but you are ready. Obviously I cannot have you working with him anymore. I'll find you another accompanist."

"No." Liz felt the pulse in her throat, but she spoke firmly and calmly.

Madame stared at her. "What?"

"No. I won't work with someone else."

The silence unnerved her.

"That's enough of this foolishness," Madame finally said. "In my studio you will do as I say."

"Then maybe I shouldn't be here."

Madame moved her head sharply, as if she heard a new note in the wind.

"What has he done, seduced you?"

Liz didn't bother to answer. She knew her face gave her away.

The teacher shook her head slowly, disbelieving. "You are going to let some man take away everything we've worked for."

"You have to let me live my life. First you got me into that awful mess with Caroline, and now you don't want me to have Giles. Why must I push away the people who care about me? What harm do you think they'll do me?"

"People who don't honor the work you do will only drain you, claim your time and your energy. No one, not your friends or your lovers, will care for your voice as you must." Madame made friends and lovers sound like vermin.

"I don't believe you. I can't just give up my whole life."

"You could be a great singer, Miss Morgan. But you will never be. Because you are a fool."

"If I'm a fool to care about someone who loves me, then I'd rather be a fool than the greatest singer of the century," Liz said, her voice rising. "But you're wrong. I will succeed. And I'll do it without you!" She finished in a full-throated shout, turned, and threw open the studio door. It crashed against the wall as she fled. The outer door opposed her. She yanked at the locks with clumsy fingers. Her hands shook, her heart slammed, her temples pounded. At last the door gave way. She barreled down the steps and out the gate. Madame would not pursue her; it would be undignified. She was free.

Chapter 37

THE SHARPEST EDGE OF LIZ'S ANGER had eased by the time she reached the comfort of Giles's cottage. He was still at the college, so she found herself alone there for the first time. She wandered about like an uninvited guest, hesitant to touch anything. She peeked under the heavy cover of the triple-stringed harp, read all the diplomas on the wall, and scanned the bookcases. His tastes ran to history, philosophy, natural history—subjects about which she knew little or nothing. But she smiled to see a copy of her father's book about Wales, clearly much thumbed.

She opened a drawer of the filing cabinet and found it stuffed with teaching methods, piano music, orchestral scores and vocal music, meticulously filed by composer and date. The bottom drawer was filled with his own compositions, vocal and orchestral music for the most part. She opened a ring binder that stood on the desk. It was heavy with newspaper clippings and concert programs. The collection documented his appearances clear back to an Eisteddfod in the mid-sixties where he had won a prize at the age of twelve. The most recent entries, mostly from French newspapers, stopped three years earlier, the year of her accident. Though she couldn't make out all the details, he seemed to have made an exceptional impression on reviewers. As she turned them over, she was struck by just how far he had gone before dropping out. Out of her league, certainly.

Sighing, she drifted into the bedroom. Everything stood neat and silent, records lined up under the stereo shelf, clothes folded away or hung in the wardrobe. Her book bag gaped open on a chair, the only untidy feature of the room.

Perhaps this was a mistake.

Two photos stuck in the frame of the mirror caught her eye. One made her smile, slightly reassured. She wondered where he had gotten a picture of her in the sapphire evening gown from *Merry Widow*. She guessed immediately that the other was a photo of Giles with his father. Giles, the ten-year-old explorer, looked soberly at the camera with his arms folded. His red sweater stood out against the cloudy, gray-green landscape. His father stood behind with a hand on his son's shoulder. A black-and-white dog grinned maniacally from behind the knees of Giles's father. *Yr Wyddfa, 12 Mai '66* was written in unfamiliar script on the back of the square little picture.

To occupy herself, she rummaged through the kitchen until she assembled a meal. When Giles arrived, she was frowning at the potatoes, willing them to boil as the air thickened with a suspicion of smoke from the bangers. An hour earlier she might have fallen upon him, but now her rashness left her feeling shy and foolish.

He gave her a puzzled look. "I never intended for you to become all domesticated when I invited you here."

"I know. I just wanted to . . . I don't know, to do something for you."

He came up behind her and kissed her neck as he turned down the heat under the sausages. "Early you are. Did you not have a lesson after all?"

She faced him, the cooking fork in her fist. "I've quit."

He stood completely still. "You've what?"

"I can't work with her anymore. And what's worse, I probably got you fired."

He blinked and took the fork, which she still brandished. "Tell me."

She told him. As she talked he silently took over the cooking, slowing the meat, tossing a carton of frozen peas in a saucepan, chopping an onion. He listened almost absently. She could not see his eyes, and she found herself babbling faster and faster until she ran out of words. She waited, her right hand absently massaging her left, as he tested the potatoes.

He finally turned to her, frowning. "What if you agree to use a different accompanist?"

"That's not the point. Besides, it's too late for that. She made me so mad, pushing me around and putting me in that position. I can't go back."

"What will you do?"

"Well I hope someone else will take me."

"Anyone would be delighted to get their hands on you." He smiled faintly. "But audition the teachers carefully. You're losing her influence, you see."

"I can't quite believe what I did." She watched him push the onions around in a sauté pan. "I'm mostly sorry about you. I never even meant to bring up your name."

"Never mind. It would have been awkward now anyway."

"But what are you going to do?"

"I'm really concentrating on composing and conducting again. I will not suffer for it." He checked the potatoes again. "Thank you," he said earnestly. "For standing up to her on my account."

"Foolishness," she said, shaking her head.

He put down the fork and put his arms around her. "You put me before your career. I am humbled," he said softly against her hair.

* * *

OVER THE NEXT WEEK LIZ PACKED up her possessions and gradually moved from Rhymney Terrace to Giles's cottage. She brought very little with her beyond her clothes, her books, and her music. She took the unmatched silverware and a sharp little paring knife. She left the saucepans and ugly brown-patterned bowls and plates she had bought at the Oxfam shop for the next tenant. Knowing that she and Giles would share expenses now soothed her conscience for the job he had lost. When she admitted this to Giles, he smiled.

"You may not have realized, but I only stayed on with her to play for you."

She caught her breath in a little surprised gasp.

"Speaking of whom," he said, "have you found a new teacher?"

She shrugged, touched him lightly, and turned away. "Oh, I've been busy moving in. I've never lived with anyone; it takes getting used to." She looked at him covertly, but he seemed to accept her excuse.

Another week passed. Giles went to Oxford to conduct one of his symphonies. When he returned he asked if Liz had chosen a new teacher, and she reluctantly admitted that she had not started to look.

"Do you need some recommendations? You might try Bath or Bristol if there is no one here who suits you."

"Maybe," she replied. But she did not pursue it.

Not once, since London, had she gone to the piano to vocalize. Not once had she considered what the next audition might be. It was her guilty secret from him, this insidious depression that seemed so like the days after the accident. It was nothing she could explain. But she knew that he would eventually notice.

Three weeks after her violent departure from Madame's studio, Liz and Giles sat together at breakfast. The early sun in the oak tree dappled the kitchen table. After years of not bothering with breakfast, Liz was coming to appreciate the meals Giles so carefully prepared for her each morning. Even more, she relished the quiet moments alone with him.

He talked about the rehearsal he had conducted the night before while she held a soft-boiled egg in a napkin and scooped it out of the shell onto her toast.

"By the way," he said, "what have you decided about a new teacher?"

She said nothing, poking at the egg yolk to break it into the bread.

"What is it?"

She did not answer.

He sat back in his chair, watching her. "I cannot believe you are afraid of failing."

"I'm not afraid of anything."

"Then what is stopping you?"

She sawed off a piece of egg-soaked toast but left it on the plate. "Maybe you're the only real musician in the family."

"You know better than that."

She glared at him through narrowed eyes.

"Perhaps Ponnelle was right to worry," he said deliberately. "Perhaps all your passion for singing is drained by our relationship."

"Don't be stupid," she said.

"Then tell me what you are afraid of."

"Nothing! I'm not afraid of anything. Just leave me alone!" She stormed out of the cottage, though whether she was furious because he had called her a coward or because she *was* one she wasn't sure.

* * *

THAT DAY SHE WORKED WITH CAROLINE, who immediately made matters worse. "Trouble in paradise?" she inquired when Liz, her mood obvious, blew into Cygnet.

"Do you ever mind your own business?"

"Ooh, you are in a foul temper today. Is it Giles?"

"Just drop it."

The lightness in Caroline's manner evaporated. "Not if you can't keep a civil tongue in your head. What ever is wrong with you?"

"Well, it's not Giles."

The bells on the door jangled, and Liz retreated to the office to shrug into her smock. Caroline conversed briefly with the customer, and Liz heard the sound of the register, followed by the doorbells again. She came back into the shop, avoiding Caroline's eyes.

"I'm sorry," she conceded.

"So are you going to tell me? Or must I pry it out of you?"

Liz doodled complicated rhythms in the margin of the newspaper. She glanced at her friend. Caroline waited expectantly.

"When I came back from London I felt like I'd been exposed as a fraud." She scribbled through what she had drawn and tossed the pen on the counter. "What if I'm just average? What if I've been making a fool of myself all this time?"

Caroline stared until Liz felt ridiculous. Finally she said, "What does Ponnelle think?"

Liz shrugged. "I don't work with her anymore. We disagreed about things."

"About time."

"I haven't sung since London, but I have to find a new teacher pretty soon."

"You could sing for Ruby."

Liz frowned. "Your teacher?"

Caroline rummaged in her purse. "Let me give you her number. She might do until you find someone with more prestige."

"What do you mean, prestige?"

"Well I imagine it matters a great deal, politically, who you work with."

"I just need a good teacher."

"Well, she doesn't brag about internationally successful students. And she doesn't mind that my only ambition is to be the biggest fish in this little pond. But I think she's quite good."

"I'm sure she is; I've always enjoyed your voice."

Caroline rolled her eyes. "Don't be patronizing."

"I'm not!" Liz protested. "I'm serious; I love the way you sing. But I need someone who . . ." She faltered, realizing the trap she'd set herself. "Someone who can teach at my level," she finished, knowing how it would sound to Caroline.

"I dare you to sing for her. I'll bet you anything you like that you'll get something out of it."

"I don't know. She's probably biased against me."

"She's quite fair. And she did say you had a nice voice."

Something in the way she said it alerted Liz. "Did you bring her to *Yeomen?*"

"I really wanted to know what she thought." Caroline seemed to struggle with the next words. "She said it was understandable why you'd gotten the part."

Liz knew that this could have felt like betrayal. Instead, Caroline had conceded, reluctantly, and finally moved on. Liz began to be curious about Ruby Binns, who managed her student so adeptly.

"You're sure you wouldn't mind?"

"Go ahead. I think she'll do you some good after that witch."

Liz started to object automatically to the word "witch," and then realized she did not disagree.

Chapter 38

UPON LEARNING THAT CAROLINE HAD referred her, Ruby Binns agreed to hear her the same afternoon. Liz dutifully left the shop at four thirty and followed Caroline's directions to Rhigos Gardens, fighting down a panic like the one that had compromised her in London. She wished now that she had told Giles about her fears.

Ruby's flat was over a chip shop, and the smell of vinegar and grease lingered in the humid stairwell. Even with the curtains tied open, the windows all faced the wrong way to invite the sun. A cat slept in an orange heap on top of the telly, and a pair of rugby cleats lay in front of the sofa. The upright piano was pulled out from the wall, revealing a colony of dust mice. Liz felt like she was visiting a relative who did not feel the need to tidy up.

Ruby was a large woman in her late forties or early fifties, with coppery hair and a broad, generous smile. She greeted Liz with a firm handshake. "Pleased to meet you. I've seen you in Caroline's shows. What can I do for you?"

Liz had the feeling that Ruby's alert brown eyes were scanning, like a fortune-teller, for subtle clues. She went for ambiguity. "I'm considering a change of teacher. I should have brought my resume. I've studied voice for three years, and before that I was at the San Francisco Conservatory, studying flute."

"You took a degree?"

"No, my hand was hurt in an accident, and I had to withdraw." Liz observed, with something like relief, how objectively she was able to talk about it now. It almost seemed that she had never been anything but a singer.

Ruby accepted this without comment. "Caroline says you're ambitious."

Caroline would. "I'm going to pursue it professionally."

Ruby held up a finger. "Your voice is still forming, child. Don't load it with all that responsibility yet. The only reason to sing right now is for pleasure."

Liz opened her mouth to insist, but she suddenly realized that this was exactly what she herself had tried to tell Madame Ponnelle. She said nothing.

"Let's hear the pipes, then. Are you warmed up?"

"I'm sorry. I came straight from work. I haven't sung today." Or yesterday. Or last week.

"Of course. Let's start with some staccati arpeggios then, on 'ah.' Ready?"

Ruby drew Liz up and down the scale, inquiring into her range. Cautiously at first, and then with growing confidence, Liz tested her technique and found it blessedly whole. Her body knew how to do this even without her participation. She stood straighter, raised her chin, and assumed what Giles called her diva personality. They moved on to slow scales and continued with some Marchesi exercises. After three weeks off, she had to concentrate more than usual, but as she flourished through the coloratura she expected Ruby to be suitably impressed.

Ruby, however, withheld judgment. "Very well," she said, after twenty minutes of vocal acrobatics. "Sing me something you love. An art song, or an aria. I play piano rather badly, so I'll just do the bass line and keep out of the way."

Liz suggested "*Non so più*," hoping to erase the debacle in London. As Ruby hunted down the music, Liz thought again of Giles. She knew he would tell her that she could do it. And she damn well could. She shoved back her anxiety with a toss of her head as Ruby started the introduction.

When she began to sing, the song settled into her vocal chords like a bird returning from migration. She sang carefully, with particular attention to pronunciation and diction. Some of the doubt she had accumulated over the weeks dissolved into relief. Her mind backed away and let her body take over, tossing off the aria in autopilot, like a meditation.

After a page, Ruby stopped her. "Just a moment, Liz." She tapped a blunt forefinger against her upper lip, thinking. "Do you like your voice?" she asked finally.

The question momentarily stymied Liz. It had not occurred to her since the early days of singing. "I suppose so."

"You suppose so? My child, don't you know?"

"Well, yes, of course I do," Liz said, stiffening.

"Then for heaven's sake, let me hear that! You have excellent technique. Don't take it so seriously."

Disconcerted, Liz tried to adjust. She suddenly realized that she tightened her whole body to reach the high notes, much as she had tightened her embrasure when she played the flute. It was correct technique for playing the flute. It was contrary to everything she'd been taught as a singer. When had that started? She took a deep breath, shook her head, and started over. Now she marked every flaw and wished she had insisted on a few days' practice before auditioning.

Ruby stopped her after two lines. "Well. That's all very correct and polite." Liz's face burned.

Ruby appeared not to notice. "Liz, what's this song about?"

"It's where Cherubino is—"

"No, not the context. Give me one word that describes the whole song."

"Love," Liz replied instantly.

Ruby shook her head, smiling. "Oh dear, no. Try passion. Desire. Lust, even. Are you married?"

"No, but I'm living with someone." She couldn't help the small smile.

"Think about the first time you slept with him. Can you remember how much you wanted him? Desperately, maybe?"

It required very little effort to evoke images of their lovemaking. Liz's blood seemed to slow and expand; her belly tightened. She remembered coming up behind him, both of them naked, and pressing her breasts against the solid muscles of his back as she wrapped her arms around him. She shivered, recalling.

This Ruby noticed. She smiled. "Try again."

Passionate breathlessness came easily.

But halfway through the piece, Ruby stopped her again and leaned back, scrutinizing her. "Do you ever go to the sea?"

"Do I what?" Liz blurted, confused and frustrated.

"The sea." Ruby sat forward earnestly. "When was the last time you were there?"

"I was at St. David's Head last month."

"Excellent. Picture standing at the very edge of the cliffs out there, with the sea on three sides of you."

Liz looked at her skeptically, but she closed her eyes.

"Feel how big, how open that is? When you sing, I want you to fill that entire space, the sky and the sea, all the way to the horizon. But very, very gently. Don't push the sound."

Liz conjured up the primal music of the coast that Giles had brought to her attention. She took three deep, slow breaths, as though making room to draw the whole landscape into her lungs. Calmed, she opened her eyes and nodded. After a pause, Ruby touched off the introduction once more.

This time Liz produced a voice nearly unfamiliar, a voice that rolled and bubbled and yet was as smooth and as deep as a swift river. Her lungs and diaphragm worked with the rhythm and certainty of breakers. She forgot the metronome and the bar lines and the specks of black on the page and allowed the aria to rise on eddies of energy from whirlpools in her belly and tornadoes in her head. Words vanished. Instead, the sensation of desire and excitement poured out of her as each phrase tumbled over the next. For the first time, she felt what the song meant.

It took every ounce of control to leave the music untamed and at the same time resist running away with tempo and dynamic. This positive tension bound the aria together, raw energy striving against training. She finished the piece, wide-eyed and exhilarated with a sense of having negotiated unimaginable risk, and looked at Ruby. The teacher, who had dropped out of the accompaniment early on, watched her with undisguised pleasure.

"Brava, my dear," she said quietly. "*That* was music."

"I've never sung it like that," Liz whispered.

"You should always sing like that. Could you feel the magic?"

Liz nodded.

"Well," Ruby said, "you have a well-trained voice, there's no doubt of that. What you need is experience, and a lot more freedom and imagination. I would be delighted to work with you. Do I meet your expectations?"

For an instant Liz thought Ruby was making fun of her, but she remembered Giles's words and realized that she was being sincere.

Imagination. Freedom. Magic. Words not even in Madame Ponnelle's vocabulary. She shoved both hands deep in her pockets and sighed. "Can we try it for a while?"

"Of course."

* * *

LIZ CAME HOME TO FIND GILES hunched over the piano keyboard, one hand capturing notes on lined paper while the other chose and discarded harmonies. His head was bent forward, listening. When he looked up, a moment passed before his eyes focused on her.

"Late, you are. Bad day?" He seemed not to remember that they had been at odds that morning.

"I sang for Caroline's teacher this afternoon." She leaned against his desk, no vibration of her earlier energy apparent now.

For a moment he did not react. Then he nodded slowly. "Did you? That would be Ruby Binns. What did you think?"

She looked down and then directly at him again. "She's interesting, I'll say that."

"Her style is entirely different from what you are used to. That might not be such a good idea," he said, looking at the manuscript on the piano without seeing it.

"Don't start telling me—"

He looked up at her, and she saw that he was trying hard not to smile.

She crossed her arms. "You wanted to make me mad this morning, didn't you?"

"Guilty."

"I've never known you to be so devious." She put her arms around him.

He drew her down onto the piano bench beside him. "Impossible it is, to help you otherwise. You resist everything."

"Do you think I should work with Ruby?"

"At the risk of biasing you, yes, I think she would be good for you."

Liz sighed.

"Didn't you sing well?"

She smiled reluctantly. "Eventually." She sobered again. "As a matter of fact, I've never sung so well before. It was . . . oh, this will sound conceited." She shooed the thought away with a dismissive hand.

He shook his head. "Tell me."

"I felt like"—she ducked her head shyly—"like Jessye Norman, or Marilyn Horne. It was so big and so pure, and so exciting."

"And you liked it."

"I'm terrified of it. I practically have to start all over."

"The process is a spiral, *fy annwyl* . You don't ever really start over." He kissed her. "And remember, no teacher in the world can help unless you already have the gift."

She looked at him for a long time, hoping she could live up to this gift. But she knew better than to say that out loud.

Chapter 39

MERCIFULLY, RUBY DID NOT ASK WHY Liz had left Madame Ponnelle. Liz suspected that the strengths and flaws of her voice provided her with most of the explanation she needed—and Caroline, no doubt, filled in the details.

Over the weeks Liz nurtured, with uncharacteristic patience, the astonishing voice to which Ruby had introduced her. The feel of it resembled her desire for Giles—a sense of suppressed laughter released—and it surprised and pleased her. The tension in her shoulders and the tightness in her jaw dropped away. Inconceivable power channeled through her slight body, a power that hollowed her out, humbled her.

Ruby coached her relentlessly as she sang Marchesi exercises. "That's it, Liz, commit to the sound. *Be* a singer, don't just pretend to be one," she roared over Liz's *vocalise*. "Put yourself out there on the edge of that cliff and sing!" She pushed Liz higher and faster, until Liz felt drunk with the vibration in her head and the huge sound surrounding her.

All summer Liz felt her confidence grow with her voice. In the fall, she went to her lesson with a question for Ruby. She was sure that the answer would be to at last pursue some opera role. She was vastly unprepared for the answer she got.

"I'd like you to get some formal training."

Liz felt her spine stiffen. Her experience in London still rankled.

Ruby seemed to notice the tone of her silence. "What do you think?"

"I did audition for London Guildhall."

"And?"

"Not one of my better days." Liz shoved her hands in her pockets, rocking on her heels.

"Yes, I know. That's why you came to me, isn't it?"

Liz opened her mouth and closed it again without comment.

"Caroline did tell me. Don't you suppose that you're ready to try again? Isn't that the idea? To redeem your failure, or whatever you call it?"

Still Liz said nothing.

"You came here saying you wanted to be a professional."

"I've already spent a long time in school."

"Not learning to be a singer."

"But I've taken a lot of coaching."

"You need the community and the ensemble experience. If you're putting yourself in my hands, my recommendation is that you go back to school for a bit." Ruby was in a rare, implacable mood, and Liz could not find a way around her. "I don't think I'll send you off to London, though. You'd be better off here. Welsh College has an excellent undergrad program with an emphasis on performance. Perhaps you could start midway, seeing how you've already done a lot of course work."

Something in Liz's chest relaxed. "I could still work with you?"

Ruby laughed in her robust contralto. "Bless you, of course. I've made you my personal project. I'm not about to let you go."

Liz managed a small smile. "Okay. If you say so."

"You don't sound convinced."

"It's just that I thought by this time I'd be getting on with it, you know?"

"Don't be in such a hurry, Liz. When it's your time, nothing will keep you back."

"You think?"

"If you skip things now you'll only regret it later. Trust me."

"I do."

"Honestly?"

Liz nodded slowly. "Yes. I do."

* * *

BUT SHE REHASHED THE ARGUMENT with Giles as they ate supper, for her doubt resurfaced the moment she left Ruby's presence.

"It's backwards. I get paying jobs now."

"Yes, singing at weddings and soloing with the university chorus. I thought you had bigger goals."

"I do. But what can I get by going back to a classroom?"

"Repertoire and experience."

"So you agree with her."

Giles scrutinized her as if he wanted to read her mind first.

"Well, do you?" she insisted.

"You don't?"

"I asked first."

He still hesitated, pushing his peas into a little mound on his plate. "I want to be careful what I say, after your reaction to what I said to you about London at the wedding."

"Don't be careful. Just tell me what you think."

"If you are accepted, I expect you can't even imagine how much good it will do you."

"You do agree with her."

"Yes."

"Well, who am I to argue with the two most important people in my life?"

* * *

LIZ PLUNGED ON TOWARD ANOTHER audition, the first since London. The College of Music and Drama had agreed to allow her to audition for admission halfway through the three-year course, providing that she could prove her competency in elements of her degree that she had already finished. For a month Giles coached her on theory and history and she studied late into the night, only stopping when he came out and sleepily coaxed her to bed. She sailed through the written tests and was granted an audition on November 11, the day after her birthday.

At this audition she felt completely at home, for it was held in Evan's Recital Hall, where she had sung her very first recital. The memories the place generated warmed her, as though the resonance of her singing still lingered, to be amplified today. At a long table in the back sat two men and two women, including Ruby. When she entered the room, the older man gave her a little bobbing nod, and the other smiled. Liz recognized the second as a friend of Giles's who had been at her recital. Ruby nodded to Liz and winked.

The woman to Ruby's right greeted her soberly, standing to shake her hand. "Good morning, Miss Morgan. I'm Julia Shelton, the chair of the vocal department." She was tall, with hair pulled back in a graying braid and a pair of reading glasses suspended around her neck. Her muted plum-colored suit contrasted with Ruby's attire—rich autumnal colors in flowing fabrics and copper and gold jewelry that shone and clinked when she moved.

"I really appreciate you taking time to hear me," Liz said to the group after Dr. Shelton had introduced her colleagues.

"I've heard quite a bit about you, Miss Morgan," Dr. Shelton said.

Did she know about London? Liz clutched her music folder a little tighter.

"Yours is a highly unusual case. I confess I'm intrigued. Your record in San Francisco was outstanding. You also did well in the two courses you took at University College last year. But they were academic classes, not performance."

"I have done some performing locally," Liz pointed out, making every effort not to sound defensive.

"Yes, I see that," Dr. Shelton replied, turning over the second page of Liz's resume. "I'm quite curious to hear your voice. Professor Binns guaranteed that we would not be disappointed. And Mr. Offeryn encouraged me to consider you as well. You have quite a lobby." For the first time she relaxed into a smile.

Liz looked at Ruby, whom she had known only four months. Her teacher shrugged matter-of-factly.

"Tell me," Dr. Shelton went on, sitting down and meeting Liz's eyes. "What do you hope to gain by coming here?"

"I want," Liz said slowly, "to take control. I know a lot about theory and musicianship—"

"You tested exceptionally well," Dr. Shelton agreed.

"But my education as a singer is thin," Liz said. "I need to be more familiar with the literature and work on my performance skills. I don't want to be a singer by accident. I want to make it happen."

She kept her eyes on Dr. Shelton, but in her peripheral vision she saw Ruby nod emphatically. After a moment, so did Dr. Shelton.

"Very well," she said, "let's see what we have to work with. Carry on. Tell us when you're ready."

Liz crossed the room and went up onto the carpeted stage to give her music to the accompanist. Even he was familiar, a friend of Giles's who had often played for *Yeomen* rehearsals. Liz sidestepped Mozart this time, though not without regret. Instead she sang "Una voce poco fa" from *Barber of Seville*, which was firmly established in what she thought of as her new and improved voice.

She found great comfort in having Ruby on the audition panel. Naturally, it helped to know that she had at least one vote automatically in her favor—but the greater benefit was that Ruby's presence made her feel nearly as comfortable as she did at a lesson. She expected that at any moment her teacher would burst out with something outrageous, designed to make her laugh and let go of her inhibitions.

When Liz finished her first song, Dr. Shelton thanked her warmly. After she and the others had consulted the list Liz had prepared, she said, "This sounds interesting. May we hear this contemporary piece?"

Liz was glad she had included the American setting of Psalm 142, though she had been doubtful at first. The wringing despair in the heart of the piece resonated with her experiences. *"When my spirit was overwhelmed within me, then Thou knewest my path."* The song lay in the rich middle register of her voice, great with despair and longing and finally, hope. The lovely, intense finish, *"Attend unto my cry!"* drifted to almost nothing on a perfectly placed F-sharp. She loved to sing it.

As the last, fine note faded into the afternoon, Liz had to force herself to stand still, to not hug herself with joy at the beauty of it.

"Very nice," one of the men said. Liz looked at Ruby. Her teacher pressed her hands flat together against her lips, her eyes solemn. And then Liz knew how well she had sung.

* * *

THAT SAME NIGHT LIZ HOVERED by the piano, lingering over an aria from a Handel oratorio. When Giles came home he caught her hand briefly and squeezed it, but he went off to the kitchen without a word. They had a tacit agreement that practice could be neither deferred nor interrupted. One of the things she loved most about living with him was curling up in bed with a book and listening as he meticulously worked at his piano. She loved even more the idea that he was somewhere about, listening, when she sang. She played to him ever so slightly.

In the days when her life had borne only her own burdens and joys, it had been easy to say that she didn't need this simple contact. She had never experienced the pleasure of someone waiting at home for her, the knowledge that someone else wondered where she was or what she was doing. Now that she knew how good it felt to hear his key in the lock late at night, she wondered every so often if she would ever be able to leave.

After half an hour more, she spun through the whole aria one last time with great satisfaction, then joined Giles in the kitchen half of the room. He sat at the table with a newspaper and a cup of tea. The smell of cheese toast thickened the air, though all that was left was the plate of crumbs. He leaned back in his chair, arms folded; he'd obviously been listening. When she came over to him he got up and kissed her.

"What was that for?" She put her arms around him, hoping for more.

"When you sing like that it raises the hair on the back of my neck."

She kissed him slowly, provocatively. He could have given her no better praise.

He drew back, swaying with her. "Do you know, you have improved more in the last four months than over the whole year before? I knew I was right about you all those years ago. Huw told me that it was a gamble, but I insisted."

"But you didn't even know me then." She'd never seen him so smug.

"Imagine that. Could it be that you are talented?" He kissed her again, quickly, and released her.

She poured herself a cup of tea and sat at the table, idly browsing his newspaper, while he started supper.

"Tell me how the audition went."

She should have known he wouldn't forget. She savored the recollection for a moment. "Do you remember telling me that when you heard the Mozart Requiem it felt like someone was praying your prayer for you?"

He paused, potato in one hand, scraper in the other. "I told you about that?"

"At the *Mikado* party."

"Yes, I guess I did," he said slowly, resuming his task. "What I remember most about that night is knowing that I had to keep my hands off you."

She stared at him until he glanced over and noticed her.

He laughed. "This is not a recent phenomenon, dear heart. You brought me a great deal of solace that night, whether or not you realized it." He began to cut the potato into precise, thin slices. "You were saying?"

"Saying?" She closed her eyes, shunting away the shiver of erotic pleasure that had shot through her at his confession. "Oh, the audition." She opened her eyes. Her fingers toyed with the corner of the newspaper. "I always felt like my music justified my existence. More, even. Like I'd been blessed. My voice is finally, finally putting to rest my accident. I sang better today than I ever have in all my life, and that makes me feel like I've died and been reborn. Like a phoenix." She could feel the heat of her blush as she struggled to describe it. "It sounds silly out loud."

"Not at all, *fy nghariad*. Sometimes I think that is what nighttime is for. So that men and women can say what is in their hearts. But never," he said, looking over at her with his dark eyes, "never doubt that you are blessed."

She watched him cook, idly anticipating the eighteen months of study.

"I probably should not tell you this, but you were the talk of the voice department today," he told her.

A shiver of pleasure wriggled up her sternum. "Seriously?"

"When I was over there this afternoon, Jones cornered me to say that my protégée sang one of the best auditions he's heard in years. And Julia Shelton asked me where I'd been hiding you."

"Think that means I'll get in?"

"I would be cautiously optimistic." He paused to adjust the flame under the pot. "I do think you should reconsider and not try to work for Bert while you're at the college."

"I told you, I can't afford to do that."

"Let me help you."

She shook her head. "You can't pay for my school. There's no reason to."

"Think of it as a loan."

"Please understand, Giles. I have to do this myself. I will get a grant from the Education Authority, and I have two scholarship auditions next month. It'll only be part-time."

"But you would do better to plunge in and do it twenty-four hours a day, rather than dilute it. You work better at a high intensity."

"You're probably right, but this is the way I have to do it."

He shook his head, his mouth drawn in a tight line.

She got up and put her arms around him. "Besides, you do help me. What I need from you is your support. Not your money."

"Stubborn," he said, kissing her.

"Very," she assured him after he released her.

Chapter 40

ON AN UNUSUALLY MUGGY APRIL day in the middle of spring term, Liz decided she needed to take a domestic day to catch up with bills and laundry and other long-delayed errands. Giles was home with a terrific cold, and she nursed him through the morning with soup and tea and aspirin in between getting her own life in order. In the late afternoon he fell into a deep sleep. Hoping he would rest for a while, she stuffed clothes, towels, and sheets into bags and hauled them to the Laundromat. Fortunately, the only other people there were two university students in red Welsh Rugby Union shirts. As they argued with gruff, obscene fervor about a recent match, Liz filled three machines and set them going, then retreated to the far side of the room to try to read.

The humid, warm room made her eyes heavy. An occasional exclamation from one of the two men jerked her awake, but she knew with some annoyance that she was retaining nothing of what she read. She stood up and stretched. One of the rugby fans was stuffing his clothes in a rucksack, scooping them off the scuzzy floor when they tumbled from the dryer and adding them to the clean clothes. He and his friend continued their argument as they left.

Liz sat down again on one of the hard plastic chairs and propped her feet up on another. Before she could read a paragraph, someone else came in. She glanced up; it was Caroline, staggering under the weight of two full baskets piled on top of each other.

"Hi there. What are you doing here?" She jumped up to help, but Caroline had already dumped her load on the floor.

"The washer's broken. You know how handy Bert is for that sort of thing. And the one near the flat is just too busy."

Caroline began tossing laundry into two machines. Liz abandoned her unsuccessful studies and wandered over to her friend. "So tell me—what it's like, being a director?"

"Assistant director," Caro replied, but her face was alight with enthusiasm. "It's terrific. *Fledermaus* is so much fun anyway, and this way I get to work all of it, and not just my own part. Everyone is being really helpful, and Huw says I'm doing well."

"I'm sure he's right. I am so proud of you. You have to tell me when it opens. I'll be there, and Giles too, if he's in town."

Caroline nodded, setting the dials on the panel. "If you have time. I hardly see you anymore." She continued before Liz could protest, "How's the college? Do you like it?"

"Mostly. It's hard," Liz admitted. "These people are really good."

Caroline laughed.

"I'm not surprised," Liz said hastily, "but in G-Triple-S-G the range was pretty wide, all the way from you to—well, Diana. Now I have to be better than excellent."

"But you're driven like that anyway."

Liz shrugged. "I suppose. I'm doing pretty well. Thank God for Giles. He keeps me sane. Every time I'm about ready to quit he takes me someplace green for a day or two, and then I'm okay again. Last week during the break he took me to Hay-on-Wye, and we went walking in the Beacons. It was heaven."

"How do you like Ruby?" Caroline asked. She was examining her nails as she said it, but Liz could hear the challenge in her voice.

"For a while she drove me nuts," Liz admitted. "She's so chatty when you go for a lesson. But she just does it to kind of clear out the day and help you focus, doesn't she?"

"She is always telling me to stop making grocery lists in my head," Caroline said, nodding.

"She's amazing. My voice has just taken off. Thank you," she added hesitantly. "For recommending her. You didn't have to."

Caroline's face remained motionless.

"You didn't even say 'I told you so,'" Liz said. "And you have every right."

Caroline began to smile at that.

"She really has helped me do terrific things with my voice."

Caroline dismissed this with a laugh. "I think Giles has something to do with it too. You even sing like you're in love."

Liz blushed. "What's that supposed to mean?"

"I don't mean schmaltzy or anything. I just mean, when you sing it's so open—wild, almost. Like you're giving birth or something."

"And you think it's due to my love life?"

"Well, maybe," Caroline said with a chuckle. "Hasn't Ruby given you the speech about how all singing is emotional?"

"There is no such thing as beautiful sound for the sake of beautiful sound in singing. No matter how beautiful," Liz said in her best Ruby imitation.

"Exactly. That's what I hear now in your voice. You're happier. It's not just you against the world anymore."

"I guess I better keep this affair going then," Liz said flippantly.

* * *

WITH THE COMING OF SUMMER, Liz luxuriated in the long arc of the days, feeling like she had more to accomplish, and more time to surge ahead. In July, between terms, Ruby set her to work on the soprano solos from *Messiah*. "Practicing Handel is very healthy for the voice," she declared. "Besides, I want you to sing this year for the Choral Society competition. No reason you shouldn't walk away with it."

Bert found Liz a used *Messiah* score—much thumbed and marked, but only in the choral parts—and she set to work, but she struggled as she studied her assignment. It wasn't because of the complexity of the music—most of it actually suited her well, and after very little study it gave her great pleasure. She devoured "Rejoice Greatly," and it soon flowed with the agility of a swallow in her voice. But the aria that opened Part III developed awkwardly from the moment she began to learn it.

She first read "I Know That My Redeemer Liveth" mechanically, one page at a time, barely noticing the vague uneasiness hovering in the periphery of her mind. As she worked phrase by phrase she made notes in the margins to help with the process. The air made its statement in a cadence of serenity, without flash or agitation. She would need to make the smooth surface of the music brilliant with fervor and faith. But that would come later.

Momentarily satisfied with the first section, she turned the page and read the next line. "*And though worms destroy this body*—" Her voice faltered and died away. The moment of anguish, of knowing what she could not bear to know, washed over her. She cupped her left hand against her breast in a protective gesture. She tried again, but memories caught and held in more primitive senses than the mind mocked her. The old anxiety weighed down her chest as it had for months after the accident, smelling of iodine, tasting of acid, and rendering her voice tight and her pitch sharp. The song suffocated her with extinguished hope the way that an unexpected whiff of a hot engine could still pin her back in the seat of the Sirocco.

As she stood there, Liz's disquiet faded to a loneliness she could hardly bear. She wanted her flute—wanted to run her fingers over its familiar surface, make a delicate play of music in the air. How utterly foolish to think she was over it. She had congratulated herself for the composure with which she had recounted the accident to Ruby. She had no idea that so powerful a shadow slept shut away in her memory.

She closed the score and made herself a cup of tea. As she sipped it, she inspected her hand, remembering how raw and frightening it had looked four years earlier. She brushed the backs of her fingers gently over her lips, feeling the puckered scars and smooth skin stretched cool. For a moment she recoiled, shuddering, but slowly she relaxed and cradled one hand in the other for comfort.

"I'm all right now," she whispered to herself, to her injury, as if forgiving it.

Chapter 41

LIZ TRIED FOR TWO WEEKS TO FORGET what "I Know That My Redeemer Liveth" had done to her, turning instead to learning her scenes for the fall term. When she finally revisited *Messiah*, she was better prepared for the images that the aria triggered, but sadness crowded her breathing at times. She resisted the overpowering emotions and instead strove to make the aria technically flawless, carefully plotting dynamics and phrasing to disguise her reluctance to embrace the lyric.

Ultimately, she didn't get away with it. Ruby's casual manner camouflaged a sharp ear and an incisive diagnostic skill that made Liz feel like she had no secrets.

"No, no, child, that's the old voice," she chided. "Don't come over all stuffy on me."

Liz rubbed at the frown of concentration between her brows. With a deep breath she started over.

Ruby stopped her before she'd gone eight bars. "Nobody wants to hear you sing perfectly if you're boring. I daresay you know all the notes better than Handel did, but the human voice is made for human emotion. Let go; sing with abandon."

Liz flinched at the suggestion that she was boring and sang the passage again.

But Ruby shook her head. "Relax, Liz. Tell you what: A quid for every note you sing wrong."

"What's the point of that?" Liz asked defensively.

"I'm only teasing," Ruby said gently. She sat back and considered Liz seriously. "Why are you resisting?"

"I'm not."

"No, be honest with me. Is there something I'm not getting?"

Feeling cornered, Liz shrugged.

"Accuracy is terribly important," Ruby said. "But don't be a slave to it. The feather is not the flight. It's lovely to have a range from low G to high Q-sharp, but it's far more exciting to have a range that covers pain and rage and joy and faith. *That's* what I want to teach you."

To Liz's horror, tears rose in her eyes, which she quickly blinked back.

"What is it?" Ruby asked.

Liz sat heavily on the faded green love seat, flopping back against the firm cushion. "I don't think I can sing this."

"Whyever not?"

Liz flexed her stiff left hand as much as she was able. "I pretended for months after my accident that I would be able to play again. I was probably the only one who believed it," she admitted. "This is like finding out all over again. There is no *God* in my hands anymore." She said this with sudden, vicious sarcasm. "I feel like I'm going to burst into tears every time I sing it."

Ruby drew her breath in sharply, then let it out in a slow sigh. "But think: 'And though worms destroy this body, yet in my flesh shall I see God.'" Her voice underlined each word in the second phrase. "Surely it means something different now?"

Liz shook her head and nursed her hand. "I don't know."

Astonishingly, Ruby understood. "Of course. That moment will always be with you. But it's a moment of great power. So use it. Don't even try to put aside the despair. Believe in it, but believe in the redemption, too. It will give the music an extraordinary intensity that the most perfect reading can never give it."

"But I feel so exposed. Like, if I draw attention to myself, the gods will get me again."

"That's superstitious nonsense. The worst has already happened. It can't hurt you again. Do you remember how you sang the first time you came here? Do you know how differently you sing now than you used to?"

Liz nodded.

"When you sing with courage, you can't hold on to your fears. The rest will come."

* * *

THAT NIGHT LIZ DREAMED THAT a gypsy was prying her clenched fingers away from a golden flute, laughing with Ruby's hearty laugh. "Let go, Liz, let go!" the gypsy cried, and the flute dissolved, dripping red through her grasp. She woke, and her left hand ached as though she had clenched it in an impossible fist all night.

Ruby did not press the issue of that single aria; the oratorio contained plenty of other material to learn, and Liz's studies at the college, which would resume shortly, took precedence. But eventually Liz had to face it again. She waited until a night when Giles was out at a rehearsal. Then she approached the piano, opened the score, and skimmed through the music again.

"Believe in the despair," Ruby had told her. Liz sang the piece slowly, pausing after each phrase to call upon the specters of the past. As she reached the hardest passage, the phrases came willingly, rising through her body with unnerving immediacy. The tears she had anticipated filled her throat and weakened her support. But she made herself continue, pushing hard down into her abdomen as humid grief suffused her chest. She stopped, breathing deeply to allow it to spread through her. Then she sang the two pages again, feeling the resonance of her loss enlarge the words.

"*And though worms destroy this body,*" she sang, with a defiance she had never felt before, "*Yet in my flesh shall I see God.*" She caressed the hope with reverence and then repeated it, spontaneously changing the words, "*Yet in my voice shall I hear God!*" She sang it again, over and over, until the repetitions sounded alike and she no longer had to fight for control. Finally she sat down on the piano bench, trembling. The tears found their way down her cheeks. But they were not tears of grief.

* * *

IN AUGUST, LIZ RETURNED TO her studies at the college. The golden gift of summer passed into autumn, but she hardly paid attention to the swift passage of time except to wrap her throat in a wool scarf as the air became sharp and cold. November brought day after day of gray weather. On her birthday, as she waited for the bus and the damp mist began to solidify into rain, the pace began to catch up with her. Fragments of various ensembles spun in and out of her consciousness, weaving a surreal spell of too many characters residing in her head. Her day had started with a two-hour class, which she'd followed with two hours of singing. She had worked at Cygnet all afternoon, and now she faced more practice this evening; she must memorize the Puccini by Thursday.

She got to the cottage at six thirty. Dropping her book bag and umbrella, she wrenched on the heater, hung her coat before it, and headed for the bath. As the tub filled, she put BBC3 on the radio and pulled off her clothes. Then she sank into a few minutes of relaxation, her only concession to her birthday. The hot water reddened her skin and melted the cold, wet day from her bones.

Thirty minutes later, as anxiety about her waiting studies began to filter through some piano sonatas, she heard a sound out in the main room. Her heart flipped. She grabbed a towel, stepped out of the tub, and peered around the door to see Giles adjusting the volume of the music.

"Happy birthday." He came and folded her into his arms, towel, bathwater, and all.

"I thought you weren't coming back until tomorrow." She threw her arms around him, unbalancing him, and they collapsed against the wall as she kissed him. All thoughts of practice were driven from her mind for the moment.

"I changed my flight from Munich to get here a day early."

"I missed you dreadfully."

"Honestly? You missed me?"

"Of course I did."

"Don't be indignant." He kissed her again, gently this time. "Do you still consider this just convenient and temporary? Or have you realized it's more?"

Her throat ached, and her breath rode light and shallow in her chest. "Well of course it's convenient. It's much nicer not to have to get up and go home after we make love."

"Stop it, Liz. This isn't casual. It's a love affair, isn't it?"

"Don't push me," Liz said. "You promised you wouldn't."

His grip on her tightened, and he drew his head back, closing his eyes. Then he took a deep breath. "Right. Not until my divorce is sorted. Shall we go back to the part where you swept me off my feet and were about to have your way with me?"

She managed to smile, as he had no doubt intended. "Don't you want any supper?"

"Shall I take you out?"

"I've got lamb chops in the refrigerator. You could cook for me. Before we go to bed." She did not mention the work she also had waiting.

The tension dissipated. He took her hand and kissed the palm. "I'd like to stay home anyway." He laughed, seeing her wrinkled fingertips. "How long were you in there?"

"Long enough. The water's getting cold."

He bundled the towel around her. "Dress warmly, dear heart. Do you never turn on the heat when I am away?"

She put on a turtleneck and corduroy skirt and joined him in the kitchen, where he had already begun to cook. She shuffled through the post until she came up with a letter from Madly. Her stepmother had sent her a check for her birthday, along with gossip about people Liz knew only by name.

"Oh good. I'll be able to pay you for last month."

"I can wait."

She frowned, setting the check on top of the pile of envelopes. "I don't think I can afford you anymore."

"What do you mean?"

She rubbed her temples. "I never have enough money. It'd be more sensible if I just worked with one of the students at the college."

"You need someone more experienced."

"Not if I can't afford it." She got up abruptly and began pacing around.

"I don't mind if you don't pay me."

"You can't be giving away your livelihood."

"You are certainly the only person to whom I would extend that offer." She shot him a look.

"Right then, if you insist on paying me, how about a barter?"

"Like what?" she asked warily.

He pulled her close. "You sleep with me, and I'll play for you."

She stiffened. "I'm serious. I already take advantage of you enough as it is."

He let go of her to test the chops. "How?"

"I know there are bills I never see. And I'm sure I'm not paying half what this place costs."

He bent over the cooker, concentrating, and she knew her guess was right.

"You can't do that. I have to pay my way."

"I don't want your money."

"What happens when I leave after I've been living off you?"

He frowned. "It's not all about money. You can't do this alone, and I want to be of some help."

"I'm sorry. I'm just afraid I'll get so used to being with you that I'll forget how to be alone."

"You don't need to be alone."

"But I will be, Giles. We all are at some point. All any of us has, really, is ourselves."

"Don't make something cosmic out of it."

"But what happens if I really go away? Or if you leave me?"

"I will not leave you."

His emphasis gave her pause. "Even if you don't plan to, there are things out of your control." They ran through her mind—auto accidents, meningitis, infidelity—but she didn't enumerate them. He would only say she was being morbid.

"Yes, there are. I guess you are one of them."

Unwilling to argue the point further, she slipped her arms around his waist from behind. "I wouldn't trade this for anything in the world right now. I just don't want to forget how to be alone. I'll need that someday. "

He pulled her around, kissed her hair, and whispered, "You'll survive. You are too strong and vital not to."

"I can never repay everything you've given me."

"I don't expect you to. Besides, you aren't leaving just yet. Here and now I am content, so let it be, dear heart. Don't worry so about the future. It may not turn out the way you think."

"But I warned you this wasn't permanent."

"Oh, my dear. Nothing is. Nothing at all."

Chapter 42

THE SOUTH GLAMORGANSHIRE CHORAL Society oratorio competition came and went in November, somewhere in the flurry of midterm performances at the college. Stretched by her course load, Liz nearly decided not to compete. She said as much to Giles one night when she got home after ten o'clock, knowing she still had work to do.

He had only just come in himself, and he was making Liz's favorite comfort food, scrambled eggs with rashers of thick bacon and his homemade bread. She sat watching him, knowing she should be working out the translations for her next role but incapable of getting up to find her score and dictionary.

"I think I'm going to skip the oratorio competition," she told him, watching for his reaction. He was her touchstone of common sense.

He glanced over at her. She couldn't read his expression. "Are you sure?"

"I'm buried," she said. "I think I bit off more than I can chew."

"You've only eight months to go."

"Yes, but will I live that long?" She put her head down on her arms, resisting the urge to go to sleep.

"You may want to reconsider about *Messiah*."

"Why?" she mumbled. She was afraid he would have a good reason.

"They are going to announce the conductor next week."

When he didn't say any more she raised her head and squinted at him. "And?"

He smiled slowly.

"Is it you?"

"That it is."

She sat up, grinning. "Well then, I guess I'll have to win."

"Look you, I have nothing to do with the competition. I'm only the conductor."

"I can hardly wait."

* * *

PERHAPS BECAUSE OF HER BURST of preparation, perhaps because she willed it so, Liz did indeed win the honor of singing the *Messiah* solos under Giles's direction at the newly opened St. David's Hall. For the performance she used some of Madly's check to buy a dress the deep, secret red of the inner petals of a rose, a classical design made elegant by richly patterned damask. After years of wearing sophisticated black in poorly lit orchestra pits, she still found color a relatively new pleasure. She borrowed a garnet pendent and earrings from her aunt and polished her scuffed black pumps.

When she appeared in her finery, Giles walked slowly around her, inspecting her from every angle. She fiddled with the dangling necklace as she waited for his opinion.

"Dear heart," he said, facing her. "No one will care how you sing, looking like this."

She stuck out her tongue. "I'll make them, you watch."

He laughed. "No doubt. How is the voice?"

"Wonderful. It's such a privilege to sing these arias. They're constructed perfectly, with all the dynamics and the drama built in. You just can't sing them wrong."

"*You* can't. Proud of you, I am." He came close and ran a finger along her collarbone.

She caught his hand and kissed him.

* * *

AS LIZ PACED BACKSTAGE SHE thought she would strangle, her heart was beating so high in her throat. *I've been here before*, she chided herself. But with a lurch of fear she suddenly knew that she had not. Her flute career had been cut short of this terrifying and wonderful moment. Familiarity lay behind her.

"If you're lucky, someone may come down from one of the London papers," Ruby had said casually only the night before.

"London?" It had come out as a squeak.

"Not unheard of, child. South Glamorgan has launched a few careers in its day. David Powers, for one. And that soprano, what's her name? Anne Bingham. She was Mimi at Covent Garden this season."

"Why didn't you tell me sooner?"

"Now, don't get your knickers in a twist. It's only a chance. Maybe I shouldn't have said anything," Ruby added doubtfully.

Liz clenched all the muscles of her body and then released them. She took deep breaths until her jaw and shoulders and chest relaxed into a yawn, melting her tense determination. She paced in little circles, swinging her arms. Under her breath she coached herself: *This is my time, this is my chance. Only I can make it work. No one owns my voice but me. Not Madame, not Caroline, not Ruby. Not even Giles.*

She followed the other soloists onstage. The staccato roar of applause pelted her. The stage lights spread incandescent arcs, merging the audience into a collective organism. She bowed with the others, and stillness overtook performers and audience. Someone coughed. Giles raised his arms. Fingers found their places, rosin-tough bows bit into the strings, lips kissed hard mouthpieces. The orchestra suddenly seemed to breathe in unison. Liz closed her eyes. *Messiah* began.

She sat for nearly forty minutes before she sang a single note. Given no release, her first edge of nervousness dulled. Her heart and lungs seemed to slow to hibernation rates. Around her the other three soloists shared the oratorio with the chorus and orchestra. Liz listened, mesmerized, detached. When the soothing pastorale began she pondered how nice it was to have Giles conducting.

The instruments lingered over a familiar phrase. Her cue. Shock jolted her like electrical current. She should be up, prepared to sing. But before thought translated into action, the bass line moved on. Relieved, she realized her mistake. This was the first pass and not the *da capo* repeat.

Now her heart thundered double time. Panic stimulated her, every sense hyperalert. The pastorale plodded on, stabilizing her racked nerves. She gathered her wits and hummed a little, sotto voce, to prime her voice. The orchestra circled back on itself, and as she heard the passage return, adrenaline melted and burned in her gut.

The final note lay calmly in the air. She rose, stepped away from her chair, away from the alto soloist at her elbow. Isolated before the chorus and orchestra, she faced the nearly two thousand people blurred beyond the spots. The instruments spread out into a C major chord. She lifted her face to the light. Now it was between her and Handel.

Her voice responded kindly from the first note. The recitative flew by, words surfacing briefly—angels, glory, fear, joy, savior. She could not hear her voice, but her throat gaped as the unheard music poured forth with molten energy. Her diction burst and snapped. Vibration roared behind her eyes, across her sinuses, in her ears. She felt with every pore the lush, round sound emerging from her body. By the time she finished her narrative and the chorus chimed in with "Glory to God," certainty simmered in her gut. Tonight everything would fall easily into place.

The chorus finished, and the instruments dwindled away like a retreating band of angels. Though she could hardly wait for the continuo to grind out the downbeat and the nimble strings to follow with the delightful introduction to "Rejoice Greatly," she curbed her impatience. Every cell in her bloodstream churned and bumped through her veins in exhilaration, though to the world she presented a dignified calm.

Another moment passed, more energy dammed behind the pause. Giles's baton counted two silent measures, and the orchestra answered joyfully. *Feet on the floor*, Liz reminded herself. And then there was no more time to consider.

Her pent-up energy poured forth, the runs clean, the legato section seamless. At the center of the whirling universe, motion and sound touched her and spun away in shattering beauty. To sing the genius of *Messiah* was to link herself to undying brilliance, to herself become brilliant. It required every kind of discipline to resist momentum, to control her rising elation. *Rejoice, rejoice greatly, shout!* In the end she could not contain herself. She spiked an F to a high B-flat with the deliberateness of planned ornamentation. The laughter that threatened to well up only opened her jaw more, loosed more sound.

"If you sing it well you will have the audience eating out of your hand," Ruby had predicted. But Liz had not expected so tangible a response. The well-informed audience had not interrupted the flow of the oratorio by applauding each soloist, but when she finished, Liz felt their radiant approval in a shimmering second of silence. As she turned to take her chair again, someone shouted "Brava!" and scattered applause erupted. She tried unsuccessfully to hide her smile, resisting the desire to look up and encourage them. Giles waited with his back to the audience. Only his eyes moved to congratulate her. When the alto rose, impatient to continue, the audience subsided. But Liz understood.

Over an hour later, the audience settled itself after the "Hallelujah" chorus, and Liz waited with downcast eyes before continuing with "I Know That My Redeemer Liveth."

"Don't rush into it," she heard Ruby say. "Let them get that chorus out of their system."

So she waited a little longer. In that naked moment, disengaged from every soul in the hall, she clasped her hands, touched her scars. *Such a gift*, she thought, for the first time feeling no embarrassment, no regret, no revulsion at the damage. With the audience waiting now in expectant silence she lifted her head, rose, and cued her conductor.

Chapter 43

GILES BROUGHT LIZ AN ARMFUL OF white roses in the green room. He crushed her in a hug, squashing the flowers and pricking her with the thorns. When he released her, friends and colleagues surrounded her. She thanked and hugged and laughed her way through the crowd, still a little stunned at what she had just done.

Caroline appeared, uncharacteristically at the edge of the crowd. Liz held out her arms and pulled her close in a fierce hug. "Thank you so much for coming," she whispered, inhaling the arresting sting of Caroline's perfume.

"You belonged up there," Caroline said, squeezing her. "I could never hope to sing so well."

Bert, splendid in a three-piece suit Liz hadn't even known he owned, patted her shoulder. "Brava, Liz. Simply marvelous."

"Was that you who shouted after 'Rejoice'?"

He winked. "Don't I have better manners than that?"

Liz laughed. Over his shoulder she noticed Ruby waiting patiently, pink with pride. She squeezed Caroline's hand and struggled over to hug her teacher.

"You were terrific, child! Even I didn't know you could sing that well. And where, oh where did that B-flat come from?"

"I couldn't resist." It was exactly the kind of thing that Madame would have chastised. Her grin broadened.

"I want you to meet a friend of mine from Edinburgh. Donald Ross, my student, Elizabeth Morgan." The smiling, rotund man with Ruby wore an impeccable white tie and tails of another era.

"How do you do," Liz said, putting on her best manners and offering him her hand. "I hope you enjoyed it."

"I did, thank you. Yes, very much. You have a lovely voice. I was most impressed, most impressed. Have you done any opera?"

"Here and there. I hope to do more soon."

"Oh you must, you must. I look forward to hearing more of you. I have a bit to do with a little company up north. For young singers, you know, to give them experience. Perhaps you would be interested?"

"Yes I would. I need all the experience I can get. When do you hold auditions?"

"It's fairly informal. Let me give you my card. You can ring me in the fall. We normally run from February through the Festival in August and into December."

She took the card from him. "Thank you, I—" Two people, hesitant in the bright crowd, caught her eye. "Oh good God," Liz whispered, staring. She looked back at Ruby and Donald Ross. "I'm sorry, it was very nice to meet you," she babbled. "Please excuse me." She darted past Ruby and wriggled through the crowd. "Da! Madly!"

For a wild moment she thought it was the wrong family, for they seemed like bewildered strangers. She stopped short of throwing her arms around her father. But he put an awkward arm around her, and Liz reached across him to take her stepmother's hand. "I can't believe you're here! How did you find out?"

"Ellen rang," her father explained. "Asked, would we come for Christmas, and by the way, did I know what my daughter's up to?"

"You didn't tell us about this," Madly said.

"I guess I've been busy." Liz shrugged, suddenly shy. "So, what did you think?" Never had she dared ask either one of them this question, but the triumph of the evening insulated her.

"Well." Her father seemed to be searching for something to say. His shoulders slumped, and he watched her, shaking his head absently as if not seeing her at all.

He's thinking of Mum, she realized with a start.

"You were amazing," Madly offered in the pause. "I can't believe it."

"Me neither," Liz admitted with a smile. She clasped her hands under her chin like a praying child. "Thank you." She didn't press her father, though she wanted to. Instead she changed the subject. "There's someone I want you to meet," she told them, feeling ridiculously fluttery. She turned to look for Giles.

As though a blanket had been thrown over her head, the chatter in the room suddenly faded to a distant whisper. Madame Ponnelle stood nearby, watching her like a rook.

Liz froze when their eyes met.

Madame moved a step closer. "You haven't forgotten all that I taught you."

"I've learned a lot since then."

"The technique I gave you is the foundation." Her eyes flicked sharply up and down, scanning Liz. "But I suppose you attribute it all to Mr. Offeryn?"

"What is it to you?" She kept her voice even, but she heard her stepmother's hissed intake of breath behind her.

"Tell me, has he begun to hold you back yet? Has he asked you to give up your career to be with him? Gotten you pregnant?"

Liz's eyes narrowed. "You've got no right to judge me."

"I told you once, didn't I, that I could make your career?"

"I'm doing fine without you."

Madame barked a mirthless laugh. "You've done nothing that matters yet. But when it comes time you will need stronger allies than your lover and that gypsy who passes herself off as a teacher."

"How dare you?"

"I could see to it that you continued your training at ENO, or Manchester. Even Covent Garden, perhaps. You see, my opinion is respected in the opera world. No matter how well you sing, there are other considerations."

The bodice of the red dress felt tight. "I don't need your help, and I wouldn't take it if I did. I can do this on my own!"

Madame shook her head. "At one time I thought you would do anything for an important career. Now I see that I was wrong. You'll give it up when it becomes too difficult, or when some other superficial thing tempts you. A shame, really. You do have such a gift. But no character."

"Yes, I have a gift. And it didn't come from you. It came from my mother, and my own hard work."

"Madame Ponnelle." Giles's cool voice cut over Liz's. "Good of you to come. Excuse us." He put a possessive arm around Liz, turning her and effectively cutting off Madame. "Ready to go, dear heart?"

She was trembling. "Um, not quite. Come over here." She drew him around to face her parents. "These are my parents, David and Madeline Morgan. This is Giles Offeryn." She glanced up at him. "He's a very, very dear friend," she added softly. She felt Madame staring at her back.

Giles's face relaxed into a smile as he shook hands with her parents. "You must be so very proud of Liz."

Liz leaned against him, forcing Madame out of her mind. Her father's face remained impassive. Her stepmother looked at her, then at Giles, and back to Liz and again filled David's overlong silence. "We always knew she was talented. But this is far more than we hoped for after she had to leave the Conservatory. Listen, Liz, I'm sure you want to be with your friends. We'll see you later up at Ellen's. Both of you?"

"Okay. I'm so glad you came." She hugged Madly and kissed her father's cheek, looking after them as they departed with her aunt and uncle.

Giles pulled her back against him. "What a nice surprise. Did they enjoy it?"

She turned to him. "You know, they're a tough audience, but I think they did."

"What did Ponnelle say to you? You were shaking."

She shook her head. "Nothing. It doesn't matter."

"Of course it does."

"Never mind. Please."

He took her stiff hand between his own. "Did I tell you that you were splendid?"

She smiled. "Only four times." She kissed him lightly. "So were you."

Over his shoulder she spotted Donald Ross. He was listening intently to a woman who stood with her back to Liz. *Madame.* He nodded, mesmerized by whatever she was telling him. Nausea tightened Liz's throat. "I think I'm ready to go," she told Giles.

* * *

ALTHOUGH SHE WAS EXHAUSTED, Liz got her second wind by the time they got to Ellen's house. They were the last to arrive and immediately got separated. Liz sought out her stepmother.

Madly couldn't get over Liz's voice. "Do you remember when we met?" she asked, shaking her head in disbelief. "You wouldn't even talk."

Liz wrinkled her brow. "You must have thought I was being a beastly little kid."

"You were a hurt, confused little kid."

"It's weird, but I don't really remember it very well. What was going on in my mind? Two and a half years is a long time not to talk."

"You talked when you were ready."

"I do remember a lot of stuff swirling around me from you and Da and Ellen."

"You worried an awful lot of people," Madly said dryly.

"Including you, and you didn't even know me."

"I felt sorry for you. Especially when I realized that David just abandoned you after your mother died. I was very mad at him about that."

"Were you?" This had never occurred to Liz.

"I insisted that he send for you. I was on your side from the minute I saw you."

Liz sighed. "And you have been ever since. Even when you wanted me to go to a regular college, I know you really were looking out for me."

"At least you got where you belong in spite of me."

"Because of you. Really."

Madly dipped her head in acquiescence. "I wonder," she said, sizing Liz up. "You know, I work with the Opera Guild. I know Terry McEwan, and people at the Opera Center. What if I called them up? Perhaps I could get you an audition."

"In San Francisco?" A little stab of excitement pulsed under Liz's ribcage.

"It's one of the most prestigious houses in the world. It could give you a great start."

"It would," Liz said. "And I'm not sure that anybody around here is going to be terribly interested." She looked moodily into her glass of punch.

"The way you sang tonight?"

"It's not just about how you sing, unfortunately. Apparently it's also about who you know."

Madly smiled. "All the more reason to go where you know someone who can level some influence for you."

Liz frowned at her. "Could you really?"

"Maybe. At least let me find out."

"It must be impossible to just walk in and get hired. They don't have a repertory company."

"But the Opera Center is specifically for training young artists who are just about where you are now. The Merola workshop is ten weeks in the summer, then they go on a fall tour. After that they pick several singers to stay for a year or two on salary with the Opera. The company continues their training, holds master classes, sponsors recitals, and gives them increasingly larger roles on the main stage."

Liz took a deep breath, tempted by the dazzling prospect. "Let me think about it. I have another six months at the college, and I'm not even sure I want to go back to California. But I do appreciate the offer—really truly."

Ian hailed Madly from across the room, and Liz wandered out to the kitchen, where she found her father and Giles conversing with animation about wildlife on the Inner Hebrides. She joined them, sheltered against Giles's side, not following the conversation so much as unobtrusively watching them. The absentminded way that Giles drew her in with his arm while continuing his discussion eased the apprehension she hadn't realized she felt about these two men meeting.

After a while, her stepmother reappeared and slipped her arm through the crook of Giles's elbow. "Ellen tells me that if I ask nicely you might be persuaded to play for us."

"I would be delighted." With a wink at Liz, he let Madly escort him away. Shortly after, Liz heard the sounds of Mozart.

Her father took out his pipe and tobacco. "Nice fellow, that."

"One of the nicest."

"Not like that boy you used to go around with. What was his name? The one with the ponytail and the shifty eyes."

"You mean Titus? He didn't have shifty eyes."

"Of course he did. Never looked you straight in the eye, did he? This chap does." He concentrated on filling his pipe. "You surprised me tonight, so you did." He paused as he lit a match. "I never heard you play your flute like that." He touched the tiny burst of flame to the tobacco and coaxed the pipe.

"Did it make you think of Mum?"

His head snapped up. He watched her as he drew on the pipe stem, shaking out the match with the other hand. "It did, as a matter of fact. Very like, you are."

Liz smiled, satisfied. The sweet smoke hung in the air like humidity, familiar.

"Before the light went out of her," he said, more to himself than her.

Something like a sob caught in Liz's chest at his words.

"Have you thought of coming home?"

Liz swallowed before she could reply. "But this is home."

"Madeline has contacts at the Opera. She'd like to see you get an audition there. Maybe even a fellowship."

"She told me." Liz wandered across to the window, where the icy fog pressed against the glass. In the parlor, the piano music had predictably turned to Christmas carols. "I have lots of decisions to make soon, Da, but I'm not ready to make them quite yet. I'll talk to her about it again before you leave. It's kind of her to think of it."

Christopher poked his head in the door. "Hey, Liz, come sing. Giles wants you."

She made a face. "I've been singing all night."

"Don't talk rot. It's only carols. Or have you gone all prima donna on us?"

"Don't be ruder than you can help." She bared her teeth in a parody of a smile and looked at her father. "Coming?"

"Lead on."

* * *

ECHOES OF THE EVENING'S ENERGY kept Liz chattering and pacing long after they returned to the tight comfort of their cottage. At two in the morning, Giles finally went to bed, still listening in amusement as she wound down. She slipped out of her clothes and shrugged into his heavy robe, covering herself against the chill of the room. As she carefully hung her red dress in a garment bag, hailstones began a pizzicato assault on the window.

"Was that Donald Ross with Ruby this evening?" Giles asked suddenly.

"Yes," Liz said. "I hope he didn't think I was rude. I just ran off and left him when I saw my folks." She fiddled with the catch of the garnet pendant, finally sitting on the bed with her back to Giles so he could help. "Why? Do you know him?"

"I do. I did some work with him three or four years ago. He started a rather well-respected opera apprenticeship program in the early seventies. He produces a high-quality product. I believe they perform at the Edinburgh Festival." He kissed the nape of her neck as he handed her the jewelry.

She turned and coiled the chain of the necklace in her palm. "So he was probably here trolling for talent?"

"It would not surprise me. He never has one of those mass auditions. Apparently he's uncannily good at finding exceptional voices."

Liz felt a flutter under her sternum.

"Has Ruby never mentioned him?" he asked.

"Not that I remember."

A strong gust tossed ice against the pane.

"It is quite a prestigious program," Giles said after a moment.

"He did ask me if I had sung any opera." She got up and put away the borrowed jewelry. For an instant she wondered what it would be like to live in Edinburgh. And then San Francisco asserted itself in her mind's eye. She did not tell Giles about the other offer she had collected that night. This was not the time.

The shower outside subsided, and in the silence the clock ticked softly to itself. As Liz replaced the garnets in her ear lobes with silver posts, she caught Giles's gaze reflected in the oval mirror.

She shook off her daydreams and padded into the bath to wash off her makeup. She came back feeling pink and disheveled, all speculation banished for the night.

"What did you do with my roses?" she asked.

"On the kitchen table, in a pitcher."

She retrieved them, the petals cool and smooth against her lips and nose as she inhaled their subtle spice, then set them on the chest of drawers opposite the bed. Giles chuckled.

"What are you laughing at? I want them where I can see them." She dropped his bathrobe on the foot of the bed.

"You should always be this happy." He invited her into the warm nest under the quilt.

"I'd just get bored."

"Wise woman." He switched off the lamp, and they settled together under the weight of the downy. Liz's muscles burned with fatigue, but a kaleidoscope of images shifted through her brain. The crackling of applause, the heat of the lights, the smell of instruments and perspiration. Ruby's pride, Caroline's envy, her parents' astonishment, Madame's threat. Giles.

She turned her head, knew he was still awake. Pushing herself up on one elbow, she kissed him just below the ear, then across his jawline to his lips, feeling the tickling scratch of tomorrow's beard. His cologne smelled smoky soft, like trees in autumn, and she tasted the dry salt of his skin.

"But you are exhausted." He laughed softly, his eyes the only light in the winter dark.

In answer she moved half on top of him. His skin felt gently rough against her inner thigh. He caught her left hand against his chest like a wounded bird. They continued to kiss, playing and caressing until some unknown thing made them both laugh, and suddenly the downy was oppressive.

She shrugged it back and pulled herself over him, the comfort of his belly pressing against hers as he pushed inside her. With a shudder she stretched out on top of him, the hair on his chest grazing her nipples and sending a ripple down her spine. For a while they lay quietly, their hips nudging each other in a gentle, nursing motion.

Just when she thought she might simply go to sleep like this, his motion became sharper, and his hips began to push in a rhythm as even as a heartbeat. His hands, which had been idly caressing the crease under her buttocks, tightened and coaxed. Her habit was to hang back, to ride out his climax before giving herself over to her own. But tonight he urged her forward.

"Come on, *fy nghariad*, come on then," he whispered. "Come with me, come on." He continued to murmur to her, his body slowing to let her catch up, then racing ahead. His voice sang in her head, and she followed his lead, huddled on top of him like a refugee on a life raft. She hummed and whimpered as they gained urgency. Her tired body threw off its passivity, and she rode him until the heat became unbearable and he came, filling her with the sound of her own name. Before that could register, her own climax, the last shock of the night, swept over her. It left a cold, ticklish trail down her spine, and the impact curled her body and wrenched a cry from her.

She woke a few minutes later. She listened to the cycle of Giles's breathing under her ear. A brief hesitation at the peak, a sigh of release, a pause before his next breath. She felt no tension anywhere in his body. Against his steady breathing beat the muffled rhythm of their hearts, her own faster than his. Though most of her body felt limp, something bound her lungs with rigid bands. She knew suddenly that she couldn't bear to leave him, that she was entirely capable of lingering and procrastinating on his behalf. And that, above all, was the reason that she must leave him—must take Madly up on her offer and go to San Francisco.

One deep breath snapped the tension in her chest, and all of the sudden, shaking tears tore open her serenity and satisfaction.

Alert now, Giles tightened his arms around her. "Hisht, *cariad*. What then? What is it?"

She could only cling to him, sobbing the heat out of her chest. He held her. She didn't hear what he said, only the soothing cadence of it. When she had calmed, he got up and brought her a cool facecloth.

"Better?"

She couldn't look at him. She nodded, wondering how to explain.

But he helped her yet again. "Too much for you, all of this tonight?"

"I guess so," she agreed, attempting a crooked smile.

"Sleep is what you need. Come, lie down."

He gathered her up again, and in spite of the continued battering of wind and rain on the glass, she slept the rest of the night as though under a spell.

Chapter 44

THE NEXT MORNING, CHRISTMAS EVE, the double shrills of the phone shocked Liz out of a sound sleep. She rolled out of bed into the chill air and staggered to the kitchen, wrapping Giles's bathrobe around her as she went. She caught up the receiver on the eighth ring. "Yes? Hello?"

"Good morning, dear heart." A quiver of amusement deepened Giles's voice.

"Giles?" Then she saw the clock and swore.

"Late, you are. I rang the shop to ask if you had seen the notices, and Bert said you were not in yet."

"Why didn't you make sure I was up when you left?" She shoved her arm into a sleeve and fumbled for the belt. Then she stopped. "Notices?"

"*The Mail* and *The Independent*. I don't know about the London papers yet. Better get them on your way to work, dear heart."

"But what did—"

"I told Bert that you would be along shortly. Cheerio." He rang off, unerring in his assumption that such hints would get her up and going faster than anything else. Half an hour later she flew through the door of Swann's, two unread papers under her arm. Bert was with a customer when she burst in, but he raised a hand in greeting as she passed him, struggling out of her coat. When he was finished, he came into the office.

"Sorry sorry sorry, Bert," she apologized breathlessly.

"It's not been busy yet. The rain's keeping people indoors." He waved his morning paper in her face. "Have you read?"

"Not yet."

He handed it over. She scanned until her own name leapt out at her, half-way down the page.

Newcomer Elizabeth Morgan gave a solid performance, balancing exceptional technique with touching sincerity.

She looked up. "That's pretty damn good for a 'newcomer.'"

"Want more?" He gave her the other newspaper. She spread it open, then straightened up and blinked. The picture that she had provided the Choral Society topped the article, reproduced in soft grays.

Stellar Debut for Local Singer

Last night Cardiff was treated to a remarkable debut at the South Glamorgan Choral Society's annual presentation of Messiah. Outstanding in the quartet of soloists, local soprano Elizabeth Morgan sang with an ease that belied her apparent inexperience, bringing fresh understanding to this oft-performed work. "Rejoice" transcended the usual coloratura showcase, and "Redeemer" was the climax of the evening, delivered with awe-inspiring power and simplicity.

Liz lifted her gaze to Bert, her mouth open.

He laughed. "Well, you were that good. Didn't I say?"

"This is amazing! Better than I ever could have hoped for!"

Bert clipped the articles and taped them to the back of his cash register, proudly pointing them out to his patrons. His enthusiasm touched her even as it embarrassed her.

Though business picked up in the afternoon, Liz accomplished nothing the whole day. She would start to do something and promptly forget what it was. She gave the wrong change twice, fortunately to patient customers. She fidgeted when sitting and paced when standing. And every now and then she paused in the midst of the Christmas Eve rush and allowed herself the sweet shock of remembering the reviewer's words.

"Come back to earth yet?" Bert asked as they closed up.

She shook her head. "Not quite."

"Shall I run you home?"

"I'd love it."

She noticed the silence in the car immediately. He was almost never so quiet. "Bert?"

She never had to pry things out of him the way she did Giles. Without preamble he said, "Look you, I don't know what I shall do without you."

"But I'm not—"

"The thing is," he continued over her protest, "When it's time to move on, you have to go. I don't want you hanging about because you think we need you. After the first of the year I'm going to hire another clerk."

"Bert! I would never leave without giving you notice. I have half a year of school left."

"I know. I'm trying to make it easy for you to resign when the time comes. Of course you can stay on and work-part time as long as you like. But you're wasted as a shop clerk. Don't make me fire you, Liz."

Taillights winked ahead in the low drizzle, leading them out to Llandaff. Bert always chose convoluted shortcuts that Liz could never reproduce, and everything suddenly looked unfamiliar.

"My parents want me to come back to San Francisco," she told him slowly. "My stepmother thinks she might be able to help me get in with the opera there."

"There you are. What a break."

"I suppose so."

He glanced at her, then back to the frosty windshield. "You wouldn't be the first person to benefit from a little nepotism."

"It's not that."

"No?"

"I'm just not sure I want to go back there."

"Think of it as a triumphal return. You owe us that, Liz, all of us who have been pulling for you." He eased the car down the narrow driveway alongside the big house. The squares of light at the windows blurred in the mist. "Happy Christmas," he said as they rolled to a stop. "See you at Simon and Jane's party on Boxing Day?"

"We'll be there," Liz promised, her mind elsewhere. Then she looked right at him. "Happy Christmas, Bert."

* * *

LIZ'S PARENTS STAYED THROUGH Christmas. As soon as they went home, her restrained energy surged forward again. Every morning she reminded herself of July, the end of her degree, the beginning of her professional life. In the cold, wet winter, it became a talisman of light and warmth.

One Tuesday in early February, at the first staging rehearsal for *Fille*, the heating in Bute Theater stayed off in spite of the constant interruptions of workmen all afternoon. Liz and the baritone stood to one side as the director talked through the scene with the soprano who had the lead. All four of them wore winter coats, gloves, and scarves. Liz huddled with her arms folded across her body, wishing she had worn trousers instead of her black flannel skirt. Her old injuries ached, and her left hand felt stiffer than usual. The cold of the bare floor numbed her feet through her shoes. She dipped her face into the wool scarf at her throat and breathed into it for the momentary pleasure of the warmth against her lips and nose. But they were only clammy and colder a moment later.

As she waited she made lists in her head—of memorization to be finished that night, of what to prepare for her next lesson, of days she needed to be off from the bookshop. When the other singer turned to her with a question, she realized her mind had wandered far from the work at hand; she must be more tired than she thought. She shrugged apologetically.

The door at the back of the hall thumped, and she glanced up automatically. Giles sat down in the last row and leaned forward, his fingers laced together before him in his usual attitude of concentration. She waggled her fingers at him, and he smiled.

"All right, let's have all of you then, from the top to as far as we've come." The director, who looked like a smuggler in his watch cap and peacoat, summoned the two idle singers with a jerk of his head. Glad to be moving, Liz took her place with her colleagues. She had the music by heart. She walked through the new blocking without reference to her score, letting her body learn without the interference of her intellect. The three of them played through the scene twice, singing sotto voce, sketching gestures into their parts, beginning to relate to each other. But the cold distracted them all, and finally the director let them go half an hour early.

"Good job, people. Keep working. We'll pick up Thursday just where we left off today. I'll see about changing rehearsal to another room. Check the bulletin board before you come."

Giles rose and sauntered down toward the stage. Liz took leave of the others, slung her heavy book bag over her shoulder, and met him halfway. She succumbed to his hug and kissed him. "Just what I needed." She drew back and looked at him when she sensed that he was waiting for her attention. "What's up?"

A smile broke over his face. "I ran into Richard Armstrong after the performance on Sunday. He wants to talk to me about conducting for Welsh National Opera."

Cold and hot rushed through Liz. She assembled a smile and deliberately put her arms around him, hugging him so tightly she could feel every bone.

"I'm so happy for you. Let me take you out to dinner. My treat."

He kissed the top of her head. "Before you know it I'll be conducting you there."

She caught her breath at the accuracy with which he'd read her mind. She tried to pull away, but he held her tighter and rocked her.

"I know," he said so softly she could barely hear him. "I know." He held her for another moment and then took her book bag. "Where shall we go?"

She forced her mood up all evening, embarrassed to realize that she had not changed much since she had envied Titus his ability to perform. The wine went to her head much too quickly, for she had skipped lunch again. Her exhaustion made her hands shake and her head throb. The lights in the restaurant dashed brilliant and brittle against her eyes. But she was determined to do nothing to spoil his excitement.

He grew more and more reticent. By the time she paid the check, he had fallen completely silent. As they walked home the alcohol began to let her down, and she stopped talking, feeling suddenly absurd.

As they passed the barren rose garden, Giles squeezed her hand. "Don't force it, Liz. Of course you're frustrated. Just leave it be for now."

She leaned into him. "I'm sorry." Tears burned in her eyes. "I want to be supportive, but I—" She swallowed. "I'm so jealous," she finished in a whisper. It was just possible to admit it in the dark, intimate night.

He stopped looking for his key and put both arms around her. "You're only human."

"When am I going to deserve you?"

He did not answer.

Chapter 45

AS IT HAPPENED, HER PROFESSIONAL debut had none of the fanfare Liz imagined it would. Her success with *Messiah* caught the interest of several directors working for small companies nearby. Tempted by an offer in Bath, she went to see Ruby one February morning armed with a notebook full of plans.

Winter stung and assaulted like a curse, rain surrendering to sleet and wind. Her face was so cold it felt hot when she arrived at the administration building, and the wool of her scarf seemed to scratch her lips and nose raw. As she climbed the stairs she undid her coat and pulled off her gloves, her face tingling with the sudden change of temperature. She tapped at Ruby's door and poked her head in.

Ruby had a napkin spread over her desk, and on it were a scone and a cup of coffee. She was taking a bite out of a red pear.

"Oh sorry, I can come back."

"Never mind, sit." Ruby swallowed the bite and wiped the juice from her face. "Talk while I finish my breakfast."

Liz shut the door and dropped into the chair opposite Ruby's desk. "Okay, you're my adviser. Advise me."

Ruby chuckled. "You couldn't be more specific?"

"I've been offered a tiny little role in *Suor Angelica* at Bath Opera Workshop. It's right between spring and summer terms, and I think I could fit it in." Before Ruby could respond she added, "It even pays a little."

"Which role? Is it worth your time?"

"The Nursing Sister. It's only one page of solo, but I have to start somewhere."

"You do indeed. If you think you can manage it, I'd say go ahead." Ruby broke her scone into four pieces and offered one to Liz, who shook her head.

"Tell me something. What are your plans, when you've finished here?"

Liz laughed. "Sing and get paid for it. What else is there?"

"There are ways and ways," replied Ruby. "If you pursue smallish companies like Bath you'll get experience, and believe me, they'll be delighted to have you. But I'd like to see you go somewhere as an apprentice. You'll flounder less in the long run."

"Like where?"

Ruby stirred her coffee, pouring in an alarming amount of sugar from a small plastic container. "English National Opera takes a number of singers, and Manchester and two or three others. There's Festival Opera in Edinburgh as well. That's Donald Ross's company. I have a list." She took a sip from the cup and made a face before pulling open a large, well-stuffed file drawer and pawing through it.

"If you spend a year or two someplace where they take an interest in you, you'll meet the right people and have some references that no one can dismiss. It's not practical to hope that some important casting director will just happen to catch you when you're starring in something in the provinces. Ah, here we are." She handed Liz a couple of sheets of paper with double columns of information. "You're too good to leave it to chance. I want you right under their noses."

Liz could feel her heart beating faster in the updraft of the sudden, heady rush toward her goal. The sheet had names on it like Royal Opera, Manchester Opera, and English National Opera.

How different from Julia Bradshaw's advice, so long ago. She had advised Liz to be content to teach and vanish into an orchestra pit. Ruby was offering her the path to center stage.

She leapt up, smiling. "I'll get right on these." She snatched a piece of Ruby's scone and popped it in her mouth before Ruby could object. "Thanks. See you tomorrow."

She bounced back and forth between Cardiff and Bath, preparing for two competitions and working on her performance workshop for the college while she rehearsed *Suor Angelica*. Ruby laughed at her when she came to each lesson, energized and bumptious. But Liz thrived on the self-perpetuating momentum of her crammed schedule.

With only one page of impassioned singing to her role, Liz did not expect the audience to distinguish her from the other cast members, all of them dressed in hot black nun's habits. That did not diminish her pleasure in their applause. But the stakes were higher than the four performances of *Suor Angelica*. No one needed to tell her that directors of other companies would be there, trolling for talent. She knew her performance, brief as it was, could make an indelible impression.

On the Monday after the opera closed, Liz returned to the college for her final term. A mild wind stirred the late April skies, and spring fever raged through her as she hopped and skipped to class. She fidgeted all morning, barely taking in what was said concerning course requirements. After lunch she danced her way over to the administration building and bounded into Ruby's office.

"Guess what?" she demanded, and she didn't wait for an answer. She hugged herself. "Ian Maltman from Bristol Opera came to the performance yesterday. He needs someone to do Rosina in August. He asked me to come sing for him!"

"This August?" Ruby's face was a mix of delight and doubt, her eyes wide at her student's prospect, her mouth pursed anxiously.

"He had somebody lined up, but she withdrew. She needed surgery or something. Isn't it great?"

"Congratulations." Ruby smiled. "When do you go for the audition?"

"Thursday, if I can get Bert to give me the afternoon off."

"You're ready for the role."

"I know." Liz folded her arms and raised her chin, unable to contain the smile.

"Oh you, off with you." Ruby waved her away. "And bring the score to your lesson tomorrow. We've got work to do."

* * *

LIZ FOUND HERSELF THE SLIGHTEST bit impatient with the academic world during her final term. The lengthening twilights hung on in the garden, drawing the roses into bloom. As the weather grew warmer, she left the windows of the cottage open while she practiced, sweetening her tone with the scents of potent flowers and pungent herbs. Though she often felt like she was moving in slow motion, the ripening garden comforted her with the reminder of the passage of time. Even during her graduation ceremony, which took place on a stifling afternoon in July, her mind leaped ahead, lured by the idea that she would be starring in *Barber of Seville* in six weeks.

Rehearsals had begun in the first week of July, overlapping with the end of her term. She focused on Rosina as she focused on everything she undertook—single-minded, thorough. She went to Bristol by train four times a week, returning to eat a hasty supper and continue to work, either on her role or on other repertoire for upcoming auditions. If Giles was not at home to make her behave sensibly, she rarely got to bed before midnight anymore, but she did not mind. She was a working singer at last.

* * *

HALFWAY THROUGH AUGUST, JUST before *Barber* was to open, Liz got a fat envelope in the mail from her stepmother. It contained an application for the San Francisco Opera Merola program for the following summer. Giles was away, so she could not ask him what he thought; instead, she took the application to her lesson and showed it to her voice teacher.

"Of course you should try for it," Ruby said in answer to her hesitant question.

Liz sat on the straight chair, pulling her hair up off the back of her neck and inclining her body toward the open window of Ruby's flat. The humid day made her feel slow and stupid. "You really think I'm ready?"

"Your chances are every bit as good as your chances of going to London or Manchester." Ruby switched on the electric fan. It made a peculiar high-pitched whine that made it impossible to use when a student was singing, but without it, the room was deadly hot.

"I thought you'd say that. I'll send them an application. Do you think it's too early to ask Mr. Maltman for a recommendation?"

"Wait until *Barber* opens. He'll have more time then, and a better idea of how you are onstage. But what about Giles?"

"What about him?"

"If they want a respected professional to recommend you, he seems an obvious choice."

"I'm afraid someone might think he's biased."

Ruby chuckled. "Only if you tell them you're sleeping with him. They aren't likely to know that in California, are they?"

"I guess." Liz shrugged aside the issue and rummaged in her music case for some information she'd copied from the bulletin board in the voice department. "Tell me about this Cardiff Singer of the World thing."

"The BBC cooked that up for television. It's held every other year. They want young, talented singers without terribly long resumes." Ruby pursed her lips, thinking. "It might be a good idea for you."

"Seriously?"

Ruby seemed surprised at the question. "Yes, of course. It's time to stretch. If you win there's a nice cash prize and a concert at the Barbican in London. Not to mention that everyone who's anyone will know your name."

"When is it?"

"The auditions come up sometime in October. They select one singer from each of twenty-five countries for the finals in June." She rummaged through a stack of paper on her desk. "I'm not on the panel this year, but it's easy enough to find out. Here we are. Call them up and get an application. What have you got to lose?"

Liz grinned. "I won't have any time to practice."

Ruby fixed her with the sternest gaze she was capable of. "Don't you let me down, Miss Morgan."

"Never," Liz promised.

* * *

LIZ COULDN'T HELP FEELING, as she took her bow on closing night of *Barber of Seville*, that she was more fortunate than most to be able to earn even part of her living in this way. She stayed over that night in Bristol and went home to Cardiff the next day, still cushioned by the fog of kindness from the audience and staff at Bristol Opera.

The train rocked along the track like a cradle. Feeling sleepy, Liz shut the score she was studying and gazed out the window at the scruffy industrial landscape of Newport. Across from her sat an older couple. The woman, pink-faced and white-haired, knitted complacently in the seat by the window, occasionally glancing up as her stubby fingers continued to automatically count stitches. The man sat with his arms folded across his chest. His face was ashen gray and his features tight, as though he was in pain. He reminded Liz of her father, actively discouraging contact or conversation. He kept his eyes fixed on the tabletop before him.

The glance of the knitter flickered up, and she caught Liz watching her. She beamed. "May I ask you something?" she said familiarly.

"Sure."

"Are you the lady who sang Rosina last night? Elizabeth Morgan?"

Liz shivered as if the finger of God had reached out of the heavens and touched the crown of her head. "Yes, I am."

The woman sighed in obvious pleasure, the knitting needles momentarily stilled. "There, I was just saying to Dad that I hoped we would see you again. Didn't mean on the train, of course." She gave a small cluck at her own wit.

Liz smiled. "I'm glad you enjoyed it. I had a lot of fun."

"Will you be back?"

"Actually they've asked me to do Zerlina next January."

"Isn't that lovely? Dad, isn't that lovely?" she said to her husband, who looked at Liz for the first time.

"Oh aye," he agreed, his mouth relaxing. "A splendid voice you have, young lady."

"He tells me, last night, that he forgot all about his—"

"Mother." He growled the word, but he reached out to pat his wife's hand gently.

"Well he forgot about everything," she continued, unchastened. "Listening to you, you see."

Liz couldn't find her voice for a moment. "I'm very glad," she managed at last.

Chapter 46

THE LAST WEEK OF OCTOBER FOUND Liz back in Sherman Theater, auditioning for the Cardiff Singer of the World competition. As she and Giles stood backstage in the drafty wings, she watched him watching the singer who was currently onstage, his face solemn in concentration.

He had regained the confidence that had once carried him to the Paris Opera. That summer he'd taken her to Llanberis, where he'd grown up, and they had climbed Snowdon. He'd walked surely and steadily, but every now and then he'd turned and waited for her. Similarly, she saw that he had turned in his career—turned to wait for her. Now that she was catching up, he had resumed his progress, drawing her along in his wake. She smiled at him as they went onstage, earning a questioning look from him.

Three judges sat together at the midpoint of the house. Liz's nerves recoiled when she recognized her former teacher. Odd that they did not cross paths more often.

She drew back toward Giles, who was spreading his music on the piano.

"Ponnelle's out there," she said softly.

His head did not move, but his eyes scanned the people in the house. He looked up at her. "You can do this," he said distinctly.

"Is there a problem, Miss Morgan?" Madame's voice.

"Steady, *fy annwyl* ," Giles whispered.

"Miss Morgan? We're waiting."

Liz took a deep breath and faced the panel.

She had done all of her Gilbert and Sullivan roles there, giving her the advantage of the stage. She planted herself on the sweet spot just left of center, where her voice sounded the most resonant. She drew herself up, raised her chin, and dropped her shoulders. Every movement felt slow and exaggerated. "My name is Elizabeth Morgan. I will sing 'Una voce poco fa' from Rossini's *Il Barbieri di Siviglia*." The precision of her spoken Italian comforted her. She turned her head and met Giles's eye. For a long moment, she withheld the signal to begin so she could take in his encouraging presence. Then she nodded slightly. He smiled and, as she turned away, began the deliberate introduction. Something approaching indignation kept Liz's spine stiff and her body imprisoned for the first few bars. Feeling it confine her voice, she mentally shook herself, reminding herself to be Rosina, not Liz. The innocence and excitement of the character opened her body, and she floated to the high G-sharp.

From there all went well. Giles's strategy for the fast runs worked wonderfully. She slowed them down ever so slightly, allowing better definition of each note to make them sound even faster. The technique kept her grounded and precise. As she relaxed and put Madame out of her mind, the aria took on its own character, and Liz rode it to the triumphant end.

As she waited for the judges to determine the next request, her mind was already racing over the possibilities, second-guessing and anticipating.

"Thank you. That will be all." Madame's voice broke through.

For an instant Liz didn't realize what she had said, still expected her to ask for another aria. "I—" She managed to stop herself short of embarrassment. "Thank you."

Thank you? She managed to maintain her dignified stance until she was safely off stage. She fled through the wings, oblivious to the other competitors, and hurried to the green room.

"Oh jeez, tell me it was okay, tell me it was fine," she begged Giles when he caught up to her in the green room. She pressed her hands to her temples.

"Of course it was," he replied. She picked up her music case, but he stopped her, his hands massaging the tension in her neck. "You were terrific."

"Then why didn't they ask for something else?"

"Maybe they didn't need to." He turned her to face him. "Come, you, you've been through this dozens of times."

"I know, but not for her."

He squeezed her shoulder and picked up her coat. "Never mind. She wasn't the only judge. And she will have to justify herself."

He helped her into her coat, and they left the hall. They walked toward Queen Street, where he had promised to treat her to dinner at the Indian restaurant when it was over. She was silent.

Finally he looked over at her. "Let it go. Even without her, it is long odds."

She glared at him, but he laughed it off, putting his arm around her. "I'm not impugning your talent. Just suggesting some reality."

She punched him lightly. "Whatever would I do without you to keep me honest?" she asked, rolling her eyes.

* * *

IN HER STUDENT DAYS, WHICH WERE rapidly becoming a distant memory, noon concerts had been one of Liz's favorite pastimes, both as performer and observer. They were a place to try out new pieces and hear interesting music in a relaxed atmosphere untainted by class marks. Giles still occasionally played such concerts, testing out new compositions, and in early November he invited her to come. "I'm introducing that theater music I'm working on for *Tempest*. Remember, the commission from Chester Theater Workshop?"

"Of course," Liz said, "I'd love to. I don't have to be in Bristol until two thirty. I can grab a ham roll at the student union on my way to the train."

"Don't make yourself late, dear heart."

"I won't. But I don't get enough chances to hear your work."

The tiny Caird Studio on the third floor of the administration building had a capacity of only fifty people, and the performers sat in the house until their turn came. Liz liked singing there; the wooden floor added a resonance to her voice that she preferred to the concrete floor of Bute Theater. She sat to one side near the front of the studio as she waited to hear Giles. A flautist played an instrumental arrangement of 'Mon cœur s'ouvre à ta voix' from *Samson et Dalila*. Liz had been learning it when she left Madame's studio. Before Ruby had determined that Liz was a soprano, and not a mezzo, she had helped Liz release the aria's enormous power and longing.

She hadn't sung it in a couple of years, but the music settled over her with the satisfaction of familiarity. Only gradually did Liz, hearing the lyrics in her head, examine her true reaction—realize that, as beautiful as she found that silver sound, she missed the voice. The flute could not darken or weep; the flute could not exploit the heart of the words. She remembered how, at the climax, the back of her throat gaped, her head buzzed, her lungs and belly and heart expanded to pour out her passion. *My heart opens to your voice.* Liz knew that she could never have expressed the same desperation and desire if she had played it on the flute. She could have reproduced the technical brilliance of the high notes, the warm vibrato, and the gentle pianissimo. But she could only infuse it with full, ripe passion by using her voice.

As the Saint-Saëns ended and Giles took the stage, someone approached and stood nearby, but for a while Liz, concentrating on the pleasure of his music, took little notice. Finally, feeling her space invaded, she shifted slightly and glanced over at the person.

She caught a quick breath and started as if someone had shot a cap gun near her ear. Madame Ponnelle was there, watching her. Liz got up to leave.

"Aren't you going to stay to the end?"

Liz squared around, her chin thrust forward. "I have a rehearsal." Immediately she wished she had not felt the need to explain.

"Tell your teacher not to waste your time. She'll only ensure your failure if she pushes you where you don't belong."

"Like you did?" She stepped closer and hissed it through her teeth, mindful of the music behind her.

"I did no such thing. But you aren't ready for international competition."

Liz stiffened, clutching her folder of arias and feeling the hard edge of the plastic biting into her fingers. "You mean the Singer of the World audition."

"That was ill advised."

"Did you—"

"I did my job." Madame smiled. "Whatever has made you so arrogant that you think you are entitled to a charmed life?"

Liz tried to reply, but her throat was stopped with fury, and she didn't know what to say. "Why do you hate me so much?" she finally managed. Someone in the audience nearby shushed them.

"You ought to know better," Madame whispered with a shake of her head.

* * *

IT MEANT RISKING MISSING THE TRAIN, but Liz waited to collect Giles as he came off stage. She hustled him out to the hallway. "She was here."

"Who?"

"Ponnelle. Just now when you were doing your pieces. She all but told me that she made sure I didn't get to be a finalist."

He looked startled.

"I'm going to call the officials. They have to know about her."

"Wait a minute, calm down." He patted her shoulder.

"Don't tell me to calm down."

He raised his hands. "You can't go accusing her of fraud. Even if that's what she said, she'll deny it, and it's foolish you'll sound."

"You don't think they'll believe me?"

"She has more credibility."

"But she has this grudge against me."

"It will sound irrational if you can't explain why that should be." He put an arm around her. "Talk to Ruby. She might be able to lodge a protest. It may come to nothing, but at least it won't go unnoticed."

"Only unpunished."

"I know it's frustrating. But don't shoot yourself in the foot, dear heart. If you can't prove anything you won't be doing yourself any favors."

"Maybe I should call the other judges."

He shook his head. "Leave it to Ruby." He kissed her quickly and gave her a little push. "Go now, you'll miss your train."

She ran down the steps, dodging students. Just as she reached the bottom, a thought stopped her in her tracks. She made a hard U-turn and bounded back up the stairs. She nearly knocked him down as she hit the top.

"Hold on, what are you doing?" he said, catching her.

"Your music," she said, out of breath. "It was terrific. I wanted you to know."

Chapter 47

GILES SPENT MUCH OF THE END of October and early November in Birmingham, where he was rehearsing *Fledermaus*. He came home on the train a day or two at a time to teach and otherwise catch up. He arrived on Liz's birthday bearing tickets for *Don Giovanni* at the Royal Opera and an exquisite silk scarf with a rich red and gold pattern. But the gift that pleased her most was the extravagant pleasure of an afternoon spent in bed together. After they made love they cuddled together, talking and sipping tea, until early-evening darkness pressed at the window.

When Liz's stomach began to growl, Giles laughed and suggested they get up and eat before she fainted.

"Don't you hate this?" she asked him, reluctantly pushing aside the downey. "We're hardly ever here at the same time anymore."

"But it makes days like this that much better. I shall never be able to take you for granted," he replied, pulling her back for a quick kiss.

* * *

AFTER SUPPER LIZ WASHED THE DISHES, her mind gnawing on her future like a translation that did not make sense. Her audition dates for Merola had come in today's post. She had not told Giles about her application, but she could no longer postpone it. A month ago she had almost given up the notion of going to San Francisco as she auditioned around Britain. But in that month Genevieve Ponnelle had changed everything.

Faltering piano music filtered around the corner. Giles was studying a score he would conduct in the spring. Subconsciously she realized he was struggling, so she was not surprised when the music stopped abruptly and he wandered around the corner, his hands in his pockets.

"Feel like a walk, dear heart? I am restless."

278 | Magic Flute

She hesitated only long enough to dismiss the sensible part of her brain that reminded her she had work to do on the Mozart before rehearsal tomorrow. She wiped her hands on a tea towel. "I'd love it. I need to talk to you."

They draped themselves with scarves and hats and heavy coats and walked across to Llandaff Fields, sauntering along the path. It was dry but cold. Liz could see her silvery breath on the air. The darkness made her walk close to him. He tucked her stiff left hand protectively in his own.

"Tell me, then, what is on your mind?"

"I'm starting to worry about where I'm going to end up next year."

"It doesn't matter to me where you end up. I can base myself in London or Manchester as easily as I can here."

His willingness to follow her reminded her of something. She glanced up at him. "Why didn't you move to London that time, like you told me you might?"

He dipped his head sideways, looking at her almost apprehensively. "I thought you needed me to stay here a bit longer."

A protest rushed up through her chest cavity, but it dissolved before she could voice it. "I did," she admitted softly. They walked for a while in silence.

"Was that what was worrying you?"

"Not exactly. It's Ponnelle."

"What did Ruby say about the competition?"

"Same as you. She said she would make a formal complaint if I really wanted her to, but it might be better not to."

"I know you don't want to hear this, but there is no guarantee that it would change anything."

"Oh I know. It's not just that one competition. I feel like she was warning me. She's got influence, Giles. I think she's making it hard for me."

"Don't you think you might be reading more into this than is really there?"

"She's a vindictive old woman. She got mad because I stood up to her."

"Suppose you are right. If she blocks you from the places where you auditioned, what will you do?"

"There is one other option. When my stepmother was here at Christmas she suggested I go back to San Francisco. The opera there has a series of training programs that start in the summer. I sent them an application."

Giles stopped walking and pushed his hands deep in the pockets of his coat. "Why didn't you tell me?"

They both knew that she would usually have sought his advice for such a decision. She couldn't put into words the uneasiness that had silenced her. She said nothing, holding his gaze until she could feel the cold air against her eyeballs.

"You've begun to establish yourself here. Why go where you are completely unknown?"

"If I'm right about Ponnelle I probably won't get anywhere for a long time. Not in London, anyway."

"You must have patience."

"San Francisco has a yearlong artist-in-residence program. I'd get to do roles on the main stage and audition for important directors. It would be terrific exposure." She spoke in a rush, willing him to see the benefits of such a move.

"What about Edinburgh? I'm sure Donald Ross would listen if I called him."

She kicked a small stone in the path and began to walk again. "I'm not your 'Liza Doolittle. I can do this on my own."

"But you'll go to San Francisco and let your stepmother help you."

She flinched at his uncharacteristically sharp retort. "What's wrong with going to San Francisco? Don't you want me to have the best?"

He pulled her against him, but she deliberately walked out of sync with him, bumping against him until he stopped her and made her face him. "Did it never occur to you that I might miss you?"

She frowned at him, not willing to reveal the warmth that filled her at his words. "It wouldn't be forever."

"Yes, I know." He slowly began to walk again, looking ahead of them to the road. "I've gotten rather used to having you nearby, that's all. Of course you should go to San Francisco. If you really feel that's your best option."

"It's a power trip. She's pushing me around to show me that she can run my life."

"If you let her drive you away she'll have done just that."

"What the hell do you want me to do?"

He didn't reply to her outburst.

She tried to think what would make him feel better. "Of course I'm going to sing for Donald Ross. But it doesn't hurt to audition for Merola too. And if I don't get in I may still need your help," she conceded, slipping an arm around him under his coat. "I'll always need you." It was the most she could offer him.

* * *

LIZ WENT TO SAN FRANCISCO IN the middle of November, arriving on the day before her audition. That very afternoon she made a pilgrimage that she had anticipated ever since she had left.

No one recognized Liz as she went up the stairs in the Conservatory and along the low-ceilinged hallway. Julia still had the same office. Liz tapped at the door.

"Yes?"

Her heart did a funny little leap, like stage fright, which she supposed this was. She opened the door and peeked around it. "Hi, Julia."

Her old adviser started and looked closely at her. "Elizabeth Morgan! My goodness, where did you come from?" She sprang up to give Liz a hug.

"I've been living in Wales the last few years," Liz explained.

"Are you happy? You look happy. What brings you back?"

Liz allowed herself a small, pleased smile. "I'm auditioning for Merola tomorrow."

Julia's reaction was wholly satisfying. "You're singing now? Liz, that's great!"

Liz grinned. "I'm pretty damn good, too."

"I'll just bet you are. I always felt a little guilty, after you left. That I discouraged you." Julia stood back, shaking her head. "The last time I saw you, you moved like a cripple. Now you seem a foot taller. Merola. I'm astonished."

"Me too," agreed Liz. For suddenly it seemed like she had never been gone, that the transformation had come magically, overnight. The years of hard work melted away, as unreal as the accident now felt.

The sensation that this was merely an extension of her years at the Conservatory persisted, for the auditions the next day were held right there in Hellman Hall, a place she was vastly familiar with. She arrived well ahead of her scheduled time of eleven forty. The woman who checked her in smiled when Liz gave her name.

"You're Madeline Morgan's girl? I'm so pleased you decided to come. Good luck."

Warmed by the friendly greeting, Liz retreated to the corridor, where several other singers paced and watched each other warily. She found a corner and breathed deeply and evenly, trying to dispel some of the fear churning through her.

As her turn approached, she was called to the green room to wait. After what seemed longer than an hour, she heard "Next, please." Immediately her hands went clammy and shaky, and her mouth went dry. She filled her lungs, expanded her belly, and yawned broadly, stretching her shoulders until she felt a small pop that eased the tension there. Then one of the volunteer staff led her to the backstage area, and she stepped through the black curtain to the stage.

The piano represented safety, and she was drawn to it. The accompanist smiled encouragingly as Liz handed her the neat folder of music she'd brought with her. Liz returned the smile as best she could, hoping her dry lips wouldn't stick to her teeth, and made her weak knees take her to center stage.

Four people, three men and a woman, sat in the house in half-lights. Liz could make out their features, but not their nametags.

The man in the middle spoke to her. "Good morning—Miss Morgan, is it?"

"Yes, sir." She swallowed. "Good morning."

"I'm Andrew Meltzer." He introduced the others, but their names slipped past Liz and away. "Thank you for coming. Can we hear the 'Batti, batti' first, please?"

Suddenly her mouth was less dry. She was even now rehearsing Zerlina for Bristol Opera; she had confidently put the aria at the top of the list of her six offerings, and he had taken the bait. Pleased with herself, she turned to cue the pianist. If Meltzer wanted to hear Mozart, she would give him exceptional Mozart.

Her stage fright quickly turned into performance adrenaline, joyous and extroverted. In the aria she humbled herself to her lover, appealing to him to forgive her foolishness with Don Giovanni and make peace. She had learned to play it as vulnerable and contrite as she could, drawing approval from both Ruby and the director at Bristol. Meltzer let her get all the way through it, and she redeemed every mistake she had carried since London. The turns at the end felt exquisitely clear and precise.

She waited while they conferred, barely containing her glee at how well she'd sung.

"Thank you," Meltzer finally said. "May we have just a little of the Gounod? I'll stop you when we've had enough."

She had prepared an aria from *Roméo et Juliette* to show her French language skills, as well as for the agility it required. Full of the giddy certainty that she had nailed the first aria, Liz easily found the exuberance she needed for the waltz-time music of "Ah, je veux vivre." When Meltzer stopped her, she felt none of the wrench of wanting to go a little farther to prove more. She had shown everything she had at its very best.

"Thank you, Miss Morgan. That's fine."

"Thank you," she replied. "It was a pleasure to get to sing for you."

How fatuous that sounded, she thought as she exited the stage. She wasn't sure if he had smiled. The woman on his right had. She hoped that he knew that she meant it.

* * *

THEY ASKED LIZ BACK ON FRIDAY for the finals. The second round of the auditions was more of an occasion. She went downtown to Herbst Theater, near the Opera House. The ornate stage and the house were larger than Hellman Hall, and she felt all the diva in her rise to the occasion as she easily imagined herself onstage at the Opera House. All the finalists sat together on one side of the stage. A concert grand piano took up the center stage. There was a small scattering of people out in the audience, her stepmother among them. The house lights were at half.

Liz sang Rossini this time, and she flirted her way through "Una voce poco fa" with all the sincerity and infatuation of her critically acclaimed Bristol performances. She forgot the others on the stage, and even her judges, who sat in the front of the house. She put on a performance worthy of an audience of three thousand. This time, although she couldn't see it, she was sure she left a smile on everyone's face.

When she finished, Meltzer asked, "How's your high C, Miss Morgan?"

She heard the piano softly prompt her, dropped her jaw, steadied her support, and released a ringing, rich C.

"Good." He made a note. "Got an E-flat up your sleeve?"

He didn't believe she was a mezzo-soprano. She had listed her voice as a lyric mezzo, still more comfortable with the repertoire, though Ruby insisted she was a soprano. At this request she summoned everything in her training and delivered a lovely, round E-flat that she could have held forever.

All right, she wasn't a mezzo.

Her stage fright did not catch up with her until after that moment. As she waited for the competition to conclude she felt the shake of adrenaline begin, now that she had nowhere to focus the energy. She tried to breathe away the clammy palms, the tight chest. It occurred to her that the delayed stage fright might really be excitement that she had sung astonishingly well, beyond her hope and imagining. The outcome was far from assured—these auditions were held in several cities around the United States—but she knew quite well that she could not have sung better.

This belief was validated when she took second place in the competition.

Madly had promised a ride to an elderly patron. Liz, her nerves over-stimulated, couldn't bear having to make polite conversation, so she opted to take a cab home. She jammed herself into the corner of the taxi, unmindful of her dress. As the city passed around her, she stared without focus, the prize envelope clutched in her hand and her music case hugged close. She longed to remain frozen in this moment: not yet required to change her whole life, but aware that she was good enough to do so.

The taxi stormed up the hill, and Liz went into the house slowly, reluctant to do anything to propel the day toward reality. She changed into comfortable clothes and packed most of her things against her departure in the morning. She made a peanut butter sandwich and opened a can of soda and took them out to the deck. The breezes had a bite to them, and little whitecaps skipped over the water around the Golden Gate.

Her mind whirled uselessly over the possibilities just opened to her. Ten weeks of Merola in the summer could lead to the Western Opera Theater tour in the fall, which could lead to a year or two as an Adler Fellow with the San Francisco Opera. If she did well, she couldn't help but be noticed by the people in the business who had power. She would have the best opportunity that she could possibly hope for. She pictured herself appearing with the San Francisco Opera, her mind dancing with images suddenly not so improbable.

Call Giles.

The thought interrupted the steady flow of daydreams. She glanced at her watch. Six thirty; it would be two thirty in the morning in Wales. Far too early. She would call later tonight.

When Madly returned they went out to dinner. By ten o'clock, when Liz could have reasonably expected Giles to be awake, she was asleep.

* * *

ON THE PLANE, IMAGES OF THE previous day wound in ever-tightening circles through Liz's restless and excited brain. By the time she got to Cardiff she had exhausted the subject in her mind.

Giles picked her up at the train station. "How did it go?" He took her garment bag and kissed her on the temple.

"Really, really well," she replied, and she said no more.

Chapter 48

THOUGH SHE CONSIDERED HERSELF a working singer, Liz did not resign from the bookshops. Her music income still did not meet the expenses of the simple life she and Giles led. So she filled in whenever Bert needed her, though she was unable to maintain a regular part-time schedule, and he patiently acquiesced to her increasing number of requests to be off.

A few days after her return from California, she waltzed into Swann's on her way to Cygnet.

"Morning, Bert. I hate to ask, but I need another couple of days the first week of December."

"Come now, you don't hate to ask. You can hardly wait to be out of here and onto a stage. When is it?"

She told him, not bothering to deny what he said.

He licked his thumb and paged through the desk calendar. "Where to now?" he asked as he wrote "no Liz" on the days.

"I'm auditioning for Festival Opera in Edinburgh. I could work the Friday and Saturday before that, if you need me."

"How was Manchester?"

"I won." She grinned. "It was a £500 prize, too."

He whistled softly, then chuckled. "Better keep on winning if you're going to keep taking days off. Will you know soon, about apprenticeships?"

"Any day. I'll probably be gone for good in January."

He raised his eyebrows, and she shrugged, momentarily ambivalent about the prospect.

"There's San Francisco," she added as an afterthought. "Then I wouldn't have to leave until the end of May."

"So you've decided you wouldn't mind going back after all?"

"I would be a fool not to, if they'll take me."

* * *

THE NIGHT TRAIN FROM EUSTON station chattered through the waking suburbs and announced its arrival at Haymarket with a slamming of doors and important whistles and shouts. Several dozen dazed passengers stumbled out of the sleeping cars, flung from London to Scotland in the time travel of sleep. But this was an impatient pause, after which the engine, a diva artfully timing her grand entrance, proceeded deliberately on to Waverly Station, the heart of Edinburgh.

It was only 7:45 a.m. All Liz desired at that moment was a cup of hot tea to wrap her hands around, the sting of orange juice in the back of her jaw, and the fortification of sausages and tomatoes. She had to sing that afternoon, and she felt wretched from half-dozing all night.

At ten she checked into the hotel on Albany Street. After shaking out her dress and taking a hot shower, she managed a two-hour nap. Then she self-consciously warmed up her voice and got dressed, completing her metamorphosis into a singer. She indulged herself and called a taxi. At two o'clock she presented herself for her appointment with Donald Ross.

His office was over a storefront bakery near the university music building, two tiny warm rooms smelling of doughnuts and cluttered with informally organized books and papers. The outer room was vacant, so Liz tapped on the inner door and poked her head in.

"Mr. Ross?"

His balding round head jerked up. When he recognized her he beamed and eagerly ushered her in. "Ah, Elizabeth, welcome! Please, sit down, let me have your coat." As he hung it on a peg behind the door Liz looked around. Posters from his Festival seasons dominated the walls, triumphant celebrations of his growing success. In boxes and bookcases, opera scores and song collections crowded around his desk like choristers in *La Bohème*.

He looked at her over heavy glasses that refused to stay up on the bridge of his nose. "You had a pleasant journey, did you?"

"It was fine, thanks."

"Cup of tea? Beastly cold these days, don't you think?"

"Yes, please, I'd love some tea."

The electric kettle soon boiled. He measured the tea with fussy precision and timed the steeping with what looked like a stopwatch, chattering away as he did.

"I'm very excited about this year, very excited, I must say. First time I've ever put on *Cenerentola*. Quite thrilling. You lot will have a chance to sing with the Symphony, as well. It's a new arrangement. They seem quite eager to have us." His round face glowed with pleasure at the prospect as he poured out the tea. "Sorry, I've no milk. Do you take sugar?"

"No thank you, black is fine."

"There we are, then." He gave her the cup and settled behind his desk again. "I've arranged several other little concerts here and there besides the full-length operas, just to give you some experience. The more you sing together the better you'll be. Of course the Rossini will be the jewel in the crown, but I don't want you twiddling your thumbs."

Liz suppressed a grin.

"Would you like to sing for me?" he asked, as though it had just occurred to him. "Did you bring something?"

She set down the teacup, fumbling for her music case. "I have 'Una voce poco fa' . . ."

Before she could offer any other selections he popped to his feet. "Splendid! Come with me, I've a studio just across the hall."

He brought her to a room at the back of the building that smelled like a clean aquarium. The wallpaper was even just the right sweet green to suggest algae. Three folding chairs huddled in a circle under the high window. A mirror covered the back wall, and the dark wooden floor squeaked as Ross led her to the piano. She put her music on the brass stand, which was black with patina.

Ross sat down and smiled eagerly. "Shall we?" He played the stately chords that heralded the aria.

Liz could watch herself in the mirror, and what she saw pleased her. She looked every inch the determined, charming Rosina, and she flourished through the piece with supreme confidence. All the while she wondered how he would be able to judge her talents as he leaned nearsightedly close to the score and played it approximately on the piano.

When she finished he beamed at her. "That's just lovely. Could you sight-read something for me? I'd love to hear what you do with 'Non più mesta.'"

She read from the music he gave her with no anxiety. She had worked on the aria, although she didn't consider it ready. Once more Ross leaned close to the music, stopping every now and then to suggest something or merely to have her repeat a phrase he especially appreciated. It felt more like a coaching session than an audition, for he had shaped the whole aria before they stopped.

"Thank you," Ross said when they had finished. "You sang beautifully. Are you stopping overnight?"

Liz only had time to nod.

"Then let me invite you to hear some of our current singers," he said. "They're performing *Orfeo* tonight over at Queen's Hall. I'll leave your name at the box office. It would be a delight to have you with us, Elizabeth." He offered his hand, helped her into her coat, and shortly thereafter she found herself on the street again, breathless, but wanting to laugh. She went into the bakery to buy a doughnut. She wasn't particularly fond of sweets, but she had to satisfy the overpowering craving the aroma had given her. She went back to the hotel shaking her head at the immediate gratification.

* * *

A STORM HUNKERED OVER THE whole of Britain. From the time Liz left Waverly Station until she got off the train at Cardiff Queen Street the gray mist drizzled so low that it was like a scrim on the landscape. The gray seemed appropriate for the limbo in which she found herself. The opportunities circled in her brain like caged squirrels: Edinburgh, San Francisco, Edinburgh, San Francisco. Gazing out over the shrouded pastures of the Midlands, she let herself acknowledge the fact that London and Manchester were now out of the question. Ponnelle, with her politics, had eliminated those possibilities, just as Liz had feared she would.

She could not rule out Edinburgh. In twenty-four hours she had already taken to the city, and the performance she had attended the night before had convinced her that Ross's program was both challenging and rewarding. Still, Scotland seemed too remote, too distant from the major influences of the opera world.

But she would be closer to Giles. It was becoming clear that she could not make this decision in a vacuum. And that singing might be the least of her concerns.

The chatter, the meal trolley, the smell of weak tea and oxtail soup, the thrust of the train all faded against her disorderly ruminations. With her forehead pressed against the fogged window of the second-class carriage, the same feeling swept over her that had crushed her after *Messiah*. She knew that she was capable of sacrificing all her work for him. The thought terrified her, made her stomach queasy and her heart ache. She would have to wrench herself away from his security and go to California if it was offered. And she knew she was capable of that as well, to disregard Giles and follow her ego.

She almost wished that San Francisco would turn her down.

To her surprise, she found Giles waiting for her by the ticket office instead of out in front of the train station. He gave her an affectionate kiss as he took her bag from her. "How was it, then?"

"Actually, it was fun. But he was so casual, I'm not sure how he could tell what I'd be like onstage."

"What did he say?" He held the car door open for her.

She waited while he put her luggage in the boot and got in. "Nothing of any substance. 'Splendid, lovely.' That's about it."

"But does he want you, do you think?"

"I'm guessing he does. I don't know." She shook her head in amusement. "I went to one of their performances last night, and you would have loved it. Well produced, well performed, and it was only a concert version. When I see *Orfeo* again, I'll be comparing it to that."

"He does put out a good product."

"I met some of the singers afterwards. They all think he's great. Apparently he's a brilliant producer, even if he is a little eccentric. He gets good conductors and directors too."

"I've talked to him on and off. One of these days I may be working for him." He smiled, drawing a deep breath. "It sounds like you've found your answer, then."

"I don't know. What if Ponnelle already got to him?"

"Now, now. Why would he have agreed to hear you?"

"You saw her talking to him at *Messiah*. She's hurting my chances. Even Ruby said politics could block me. What if nobody wants me? What am I going to do?"

"Hisht, you must be patient, my dear."

"ENO and Manchester already turned me down."

His eyebrows went up, and she realized that she had not shared these recent developments with him yet. The hollowness in her chest opened up a little more. They were apart so much these days that already the fabric of their mutual life was missing threads and colors.

"Their loss," he said, touching her hand lightly. "But what is left, then?"

"Festival Opera has a lot to recommend it," she said slowly. "But I'm not ready to decide."

He looked at her when they stopped at a red light. "What else is there?"

She said nothing.

The light changed, and Giles let out the clutch too quickly, causing the car to jerk forward. "Are you serious about San Francisco?"

"Of course. It would be a great opportunity."

He digested this in silence. "That it would." He pushed his head back against the headrest. "Well. We must hope for the best, mustn't we?"

* * *

Dear Miss Morgan,

I am delighted to welcome you to Festival Opera for the upcoming season. Your audition was excellent, and I have no doubt that you will bring quality to our fine ensemble. Please let me know at your earliest convenience if you will be able to join us in February for our seventeenth exciting season.

Cordially,

Donald Ross

* * *

GILES RETURNED ON A SATURDAY for a weekend at home before dress rehearsals for *La Bohème* in Manchester consumed him. As usual, he was in bed first, reading an interview in *Opera* magazine. Liz watched him surreptitiously as she moved about the room, folding laundry and getting ready for bed. Her scrutiny finally made him look up expectantly.

"I heard from Donald Ross the other day." Though she did her best to sound casual, she suspected herself of poor acting. "He wants me." She showed the letter to Giles and watched his face as he read it, saw him smile broadly.

"Now you can stop fretting. A terrific opportunity this is."

"I know. And I'm lucky to get it. But I haven't replied yet. I have to wait for Merola."

Giles's smile faded, though his eyes were still bright. "Are you sure you shouldn't wait a year, let your voice develop more? Edinburgh would be perfect for that."

She looked at him steadily. "The last time you told me that you were right, and I should have listened to you. But this time . . . this is different. I need to go."

He closed his magazine over one finger. "I thought that if you got the job in Edinburgh you would be content," he said slowly. "That's why I rang Donald, to be sure he knew what you had to offer. I didn't realize how serious you are about moving back to San Francisco."

"You called him?" When he didn't reply she repeated, "You *called* him?"

He looked at her with a wrinkle over one brow. "I wanted to help."

"I told you I didn't want you to," she spat. "How will I ever know if I'm good enough if you pull strings?"

"Rubbish. Of course you know how good you are. But you still need people who can help you. There is a lot of competition."

"I asked you not to," she insisted.

"You did, and I am sorry. But that's no reason to turn Ross down. He does want you for *Cenerentola*."

"You had no right to interfere."

He frowned as if he wanted to disagree. "I expect I didn't. I didn't realize how important San Francisco was."

She swallowed and came close to him, touching his chest as if seeking the heat of his heart. "Do you want me to give up on San Francisco and just go to Edinburgh?"

He blinked. "It's not my decision to make."

"Don't be silly, I want to know what you think."

His eyes held the suggestion of a smile. "There is nothing more I can teach you or give you. You just want me around because it is more fun that way."

"What's wrong with that?" She clambered up on the bed and took his magazine away.

"Not a thing. Just do not let it muddle your thinking." He pushed her hair away from her face, brushing his fingers over her cheek.

"It won't." She looked at him for a moment, her lips pursed. She couldn't tell what he was thinking. "It won't hurt to wait a few weeks, until I hear from San Francisco."

"Of course not. You deserve every chance."

Chapter 49

LIZ AND GILES ESTABLISHED a tacit truce—one that did not include any discussion of the future. In the meantime, Liz's voice blossomed. Her performances earned high praise from critics. At times she felt humbled, at others vain, to be possessed of such an instrument.

Vanity had the upper hand one afternoon in mid-December when she soared through a particularly good lesson, everything falling into place effortlessly. She lingered afterwards to discuss an upcoming concert with Ruby, and she did not head home until after six. When she got off the bus near the cathedral, she walked slowly through the sharp winter evening, a cold breeze teasing her hair.

As she rounded the side of the big house and looked down the drive, she saw lights in the cottage. Giles was home. He would be at the piano, sleeves rolled up as he worked out some difficult passage. When she came in he would get up and put his arms around her. At the thought, her lungs expanded sharply, as though she was preparing to sing. The pleasures of the evening and her voice overwhelmed her, and she let loose with some Puccini that she had no business singing. "*Vincero, vincero, vin-CER-o,*" she sang, flourishing open the door.

Giles was standing by the door. "Where have you been?"

"We went past the hour. But I could have gone on forever," she said blithely.

"You forgot."

"Forgot?" Then she noticed his overcoat. "Our date, oh, Giles, I did forget. I'm so sorry!"

He received her effusive kiss reluctantly. "When did you become such a featherbrain?"

"I'll make it up to you, I promise. How about we skip dinner and go straight to bed?" She leaned against him and kissed him again, softly, slowly.

When she persisted, he relented and put his arms around her. "No, you would just wake me at three in the morning wanting cheese toast. Go along; change your clothes. It is not that late."

The dinner date had been her idea, for they sometimes went weeks without crossing each other's orbit except in bed late at night. But distressingly, the conversation jerked and lagged through supper, as devoid of emotional undercurrent as an aria newly learned.

They finally gave up, agreeing that they were both tired. He ordered dessert, and she sipped her tea, leaning back and stretching her legs out under the table. In the silence, her thoughts wandered off to her own current fantasy involving the soft gilt of San Francisco's opera house. The vast curtain drew back. The focal point of more than three thousand people, backstage and in the house, she took her place onstage and waited out the welcoming applause with poise. From the depths of the pit, the conductor cued her.

"Liz? *Liz*."

She shook off her daydream. Giles was staring at her.

"You aren't listening at all, are you?"

"I'm sorry. I was thinking about San Francisco."

"Have you thought what happens if they do not take you, in spite of your stepmother?"

When she looked at him quickly, she saw no trace of empathy. "Then I go to Scotland." She sat up straight, putting down her cup. "She only helped me get the audition, you know. My singing will get me in."

He gazed at her for a long time, then shook his head. "You know, I am beginning to feel like I have to say everything twice. Once for the Liz who seems to be standing in front of me and again for the Liz who was not there."

"You're away more than I am," she snapped.

"That is not what I mean."

She swallowed hard. "Well, I'm here now." She reached over and slipped her hand into his. "What were you saying?"

He considered her. "My divorce. It should be final by March."

When he did not continue to the obvious conclusion, she hesitated. A thousand things she ought to say vanished before she could give voice to them. "That's wonderful." She squeezed his hand, but he did not respond. "I know you'll be glad to be finished with her." She waited for him to say more, but he only withdrew his hand.

The waitress brought his trifle. For a while he pushed it about on the plate under Liz's scrutiny. Finally he sighed. "Let's go home, my dear." He set aside his half-empty dish and signaled for the check.

They wandered across Llandaff Fields as the full moon left traces of silver between long, cool shadows. Liz was as aware of Giles beside her as she was of her hands or her throat. He seemed relaxed rather than restless, though his contemplation seemed to pull him away from the present. She listened for an echo of his thoughts.

When he glanced down at her she had the impression that he'd only just remembered she was there. "I will be in Edinburgh the last week of June." He gathered her stiff left hand into his own. "After I finish with Scottish Chamber Opera I thought we might be able to have a small holiday, two or three days. Go over to Oban, or up to Inverness. Would you like that?"

She bumped up against him affectionately. "It sounds wonderful." Then she remembered. "But I might be in San Francisco by then."

After a moment he said, "Of course. You are in great demand these days."

She pulled her hand away. "What's wrong with that? You're getting on with your career. Why shouldn't I?"

They had nearly crossed the park before he responded. As the cars on the Cardiff Road came into view, he took a deep breath that seemed to give him some resolve. "Liz, what's going to happen to us? If you go?"

She looked up at him. A streetlight behind him blinded her. He'd caught her off guard, but she rallied her sense of humor. "What's wrong? Afraid I'll run off with some piano player?" When he did not respond to her teasing, her smile faded. She had forgotten that sensation of humility knowing what an impact she had on him had once given her. She had never wanted his unhappiness on her conscience.

"Well," she said, "you made me a singer. You have only yourself to blame."

"I did not make you a singer. You were born one. I only helped you a little."

"Oh, don't be so stupid. You helped me a lot! You taught me and encouraged me and believed in me," she said through sudden tears. "If it wasn't for you I never could have come this far." She held his gaze for a long, fearful moment.

He looked away. The pause grew, increasing the tightness in her gut. At last he spoke in a quiet, calm voice. "But how many times have you told me this can't be permanent? How often have you pulled away and reminded me that you always planned to leave?"

"That was before. I didn't know then that I'd want to come back," she whispered.

"But when? First it's ten weeks; then it's a couple of months; then it's two or three years for a fellowship. When will it ever be convenient to come back?"

"You know that if I say I will, I will."

"You say your work comes before everything else. Very convincing you are on that point."

"But I love you, damn it."

"Will that be enough, dear heart?" The mildness of his tone, as if they were discussing where to eat supper, caught her breath in a threat of panic.

"Come on, I just need to find my balance first. *You* know what it requires to do this kind of work. The commitment."

He nodded. "You have to be free, for instance, to choose between San Francisco and Edinburgh. Perhaps there will not be room for anyone else, as much as you may want it to be otherwise."

"That's not true."

"I would rather not end up enemies." He gave her a long, wistful look. "You hold the beat of my heart, you know." He kept walking, watching the pale silver moon as if unaware of her. Their silence lay like frost over the moon-washed park.

* * *

LIZ HEARD THE PHONE FROM outside as she fumbled with her key. It was after seven, and she was cold and hungry, having only just returned from a rehearsal for *Don Giovanni* in Bristol. She burst into the cottage and tossed her bag in the chair as she lunged for the phone.

"Yes, hello?"

"Miss Morgan, this is Andrew Meltzer."

"Oh, hi," she answered from a dry mouth. Suddenly she could not pull breath deep into her lungs.

"I'm very pleased to tell you that we've chosen you to participate in the Merola program this summer."

"Really?" she croaked. She cleared her throat. "Terrific! Thank you so much."

"We'll be sending you a contract and a tentative schedule after Christmas, but we like to notify the singers as soon as possible. I can tell you that you'll be working on Cherubino for the Merola performances and then adding Susanna for the tour in the fall. We'll have you alternate roles on the road."

"It sounds great." She had a feeling that she sounded particularly stupid, but she couldn't make her brain work except to be thankful that Giles was not at home.

"Do you have any questions for me?"

A thousand. "Not that I can think of right now."

"Feel free to call if there's anything we can do to help. I'll include information about a work visa for you. You'll need to start on that right away."

"Of course. I'm really excited about this, Mr. Meltzer."

"We're looking forward to working with you, Miss Morgan."

* * *

A WEEK LATER, ON CHRISTMAS EVE, she walked home from Cygnet through the lowering mist, her steps quick to the music running through her head. "*Danza, danza fanciulla.* Dance, dance fair maiden . . ." She had been hearing it for days, singing the Italian to herself, lost in the snapping consonants, the relentless rhythm. It drove out the debate that currently engaged her mind, for ever since the notion of returning to California had surfaced, it had hung on in her brain like an advertising jingle, appealing and annoying at the same time.

She had to tell him, and she had to do it tonight. The longer she kept it to herself the worse it became. Over the last week, she had sung Bach in Bristol and Haydn in Manchester, finishing with Mozart's *Vespers* in Llandaff Cathedral last night. Giles had been conducting Vaughn-William's *Fantasia on Christmas Carols* all week in London. Tonight they would be home together for the first time in weeks. She must tell him.

She came in, radiating the cold from the weather outside, and found Giles at the kitchen table. From a pot on the cooker a comforting smell emanated, something rich with red wine and onions. He was studying a collection of official-looking documents. His eyes were tight as if a headache pushed at them, but his face relaxed when he saw her.

"What's all this?" She kissed the top of his head and rubbed his tight shoulders while she peered at the papers on the table.

"My divorce. They've sent the decree nisi. In six weeks I can apply for the decree absolute, and it will be over." His tired face lifted a little in a smile. "Won't you feel better, knowing you're not living in sin anymore?"

She slowly unbuttoned her donkey coat and sat down opposite him. "I lose sleep over it constantly. But what makes you think that she won't try to delay it again?"

He smiled and shrugged. "My understanding is that now she's met someone else and can hardly wait to be rid of me."

Liz felt her own smile flicker at the corners of her mouth. "She's a fool. But I already knew that."

Giles looked her up and down, the fatigue she'd seen when she came in replaced with relaxed good humor. Shaking his head, he got up and stirred the stew with a wooden spoon. "I didn't realize how much I put on hold, knowing I was still legally tied to her. I want to do something about the way things are between you and me."

She hesitated. "I rather like the way things are just now."

He covered the pot, leaving the lid slightly ajar, and then came over to crouch next to her. He took her hands and looked earnestly into her face. "I finally feel like I can ask you. *Priodafi, fy nghariad*? Will you marry me?"

She had nearly forgotten that this question would come. It was the last thing she had expected tonight. She suddenly recognized that as long as he had stayed married, she had been able to postpone making her own decision. She tried to tease him a little to cover her confusion. "You want to make an honest woman of me?"

Some of the energy drained out of him, but his grip on her hands remained firm. "I'm not asking you to stay home and make my supper and have babies."

The suggestion gave her a jolt. Was that how it happened? Had her mother pictured David's child as clearly as Liz had just seen Giles's son, and given up? A gauzy layer of insulation shredded away from her soul, leaving her that much closer to her mother's choice. She shook her head sharply.

"Don't you want to marry me?"

The tenderness that rushed over Liz at this question did not seem to belong to the woman who wanted to go to San Francisco and become a diva.

She slipped down onto her knees on the lino, wrapping her arms around him fiercely. "Of course I do," she assured him.

"The light went out of her," her father had said. But her mother had been glad to shed the burden of performance. For a second, her mother's daughter had felt the temptation of that life.

He kissed her. "Let's go ahead, then. Will we set a date?"

She pulled back, looking at him and feeling tightness in her chest. "But the divorce isn't even final yet. How can we, until that's finished?"

"It will be soon, dear heart. We can at least plan."

Her breath was shallow and sharp. "I'm—I'm not ready."

He stared at her. She had clearly shocked him. "How can you not be ready?"

"I need to see what's going to happen down the road a little." Her heart hammered.

"But I thought—"

"I'm not saying no," she said. "You need to trust me."

Giles's slight hesitation did not make her feel better.

"Yes, all right. We'll wait then. There's no rush, is there?"

Chapter 50

ON THE RARE OCCASIONS WHEN LIZ and Giles made love in the depth of that winter, it was a silent, sober affair. They slept apart in the same bed, and often she fell asleep with the "Dona Nobis Pacem" movement from Mozart's Requiem swimming through her head in idle circles of grief. She wondered how it could get any worse if she did tell him, but her courage had completely left her. Every day only increased her burden, but she couldn't bring herself to add to the injury she had already done.

After the first of the year he went to York for two weeks to rehearse and conduct a choral concert. Liz was glad to leave the silent cottage to go to her lesson.

"Tell me all about it," Ruby said after congratulating Liz on her success with the Bach. As usual, they talked through the performance and Liz analyzed what had worked and what she had neglected. For once, Ruby did not seem to notice that half her mind was otherwise occupied. But when they finished, and her teacher asked what she was going to work on next, Liz shook her head.

"Can we talk today? Instead of sing?"

Ruby pulled her head back in surprise. Liz had never quite been able to tame the driven part of her that wanted to sing every moment of every lesson. "Of course, child. Come in the kitchen. I'll make tea."

She asked about the other soloists as she puttered about, and Liz leaned in the doorway, answering absently. When they sat down together at the kitchen table, Ruby stirred milk into her cup and tapped the spoon briskly on the rim. "Now then. Where are you really?"

Liz smiled sheepishly. She should have realized that Ruby would notice her preoccupation.

"I've been accepted to Merola."

If Ruby was surprised that she had not said so sooner she did not show it. "Are you unhappy about that?"

She hunched over the table. "I'm not sure I'm ready."

"Actually, you are." Ruby leaned back and watched her. "And you know you are."

Silence.

"Are you afraid you'll fail?"

"I think I'm afraid that I'll succeed."

Not a flicker of emotion from Ruby. "Would you like to explain that?"

Liz took a sip of tea, then another, arranging her words carefully. "I don't know what will happen with Giles. If I go to California."

More silence.

"Surely you're not afraid he will forget about you?"

"Well, yes." Ruby started to protest, but Liz insisted. "He wants to get married, but I'm not ready yet."

"Why not? Do you think you'll find someone else?"

"Not a chance," admitted Liz wryly. "But I could easily be seduced into being just a little less than what I could be. I don't want to get complacent, like Caroline."

"What's wrong with her life?"

Liz flushed. "Nothing. It suits her." She tried another tack. "Until I met Giles, there was never anyone or anything in my life that I thought I could choose over my music. Madame Ponnelle was even worried that I would give up my singing for him. Or at least that he would distract me from meeting my potential."

"She has never understood," Ruby said slowly, "that singers do not just sing with their vocal chords." It was the only time Liz had heard her even remotely criticize her colleague.

"But the awful thing is, she was right. He could very well derail me."

"Not intentionally."

"When I auditioned for Donald Ross, Giles called him to make sure I would get the job. It really pissed me off, at first."

Ruby sighed, shaking her head. "Oh, Liz."

"I know. But he wants me to stay in the UK. That's why he did it."

"What's wrong with that?"

"What if I don't want to stay?"

Ruby considered her. "Well, do you want to marry him?"

"Oh God, yes." Liz bit her lip, ashamed to admit the next part. "But if I marry him I might decide not to go to San Francisco. And I can't let that happen. It would be too easy. So I want to wait a bit more."

Ruby remained silent for a long time, absently picking dead leaves off the Wandering Jew that stretched along the windowsill. "Liz, this singing is an endless process. You do one role, you miss something else. You give up something good for what seemed better and find you were mistaken. All you can do is what serves you best in the moment. If you are still negotiating with Giles, then maybe Scotland would be the better choice." She smiled her enchanting smile at Liz. "You're young. I know you're impatient to sing in the big houses, but it wouldn't hurt you to work with Ross for a year."

"You don't think I'd be missing a golden opportunity?"

"If I'm any judge, it won't be the last opportunity you'll ever have."

"So you think I should go ahead and get married?"

That brought a rich, melodious laugh from Ruby. "Oh dear, Liz. You won't catch me making that decision for you. But I think at least you can be sure of him. You can't say that for a singing career." She sobered. "I think only you know what you must do."

* * *

WITH GILES OUT OF TOWN AGAIN, Liz found herself leaving early for work at the bookshops. She looked forward to the companionship of a cup of tea in the flat over Swann's. After opening night of *Don Giovanni* at Bristol Opera, she came to work rubbing sleep out of her eyes. She told Caroline and Bert about the performance while consuming a cup of Bert's strong black tea in a few swallows.

"More?" she asked, holding out her mug.

"I take it since you're still here you haven't heard about apprenticeships yet?" Bert asked as he drained the teapot into her cup.

Liz hesitated. Only Ruby knew that she had been asked to come to San Francisco. "I won't be in London or Manchester," she began slowly. "I've been accepted to Merola." She kept her eyes on Bert, but out of the corner of her eye, she saw Caroline start.

"So I guess this is my notice. I'll be gone in June."

"High time," Caroline said dryly. And she smiled a moment later.

Bert peered at Liz over the frames of his glasses. He seemed, for once, unable to think what to say. "Congratulations," he finally managed. "We shall miss you."

In an instant Liz remembered her first supper in their flat, and she wondered how many times she had sat at this table, eating fish and chips, drinking tea. Soon she would stop being family and be a visitor again. "I owe you both a lot."

Bert got up quickly with a gesture that discounted his contribution. "Well, you're not gone yet. I still have work to get out of you. I'm off to Cygnet. Have a good day, you two." He pecked Caroline on the cheek and left.

When he had gone, Liz helped clear the dishes.

"How did Giles take it?" Caroline asked as they stacked plates and cups.

"I haven't told him."

"Haven't you? Liz!"

"I can't. Once I tell him everything will change. Not that it hasn't already," she said bitterly.

"You mean to tell me that when you leave, it's over?"

"He asked me to marry him." Before Caroline could offer an opinion, she added, "I want to wait."

Caroline stared at her as the water running into the sink started to steam. "You're mad."

Liz dropped the silverware into the filling sink with a clatter. "I'd expect that from you."

"Why won't you marry him?" Caroline squeezed soap from an asthmatic plastic bottle into the water.

"Because it could hold me back."

"Oh please." Caroline started to scrub the bowls vigorously.

"I'm serious. The only thing that could keep me from going to San Francisco is Giles."

"All he wants is to be sure of you."

"He should already be sure of me."

Caro slopped water all over the drain board as she rinsed dishes. "He'd never interfere with your singing. You know better."

"He wants me to go to Scotland."

Caro looked at her. "He said that?"

Liz took the sponge and wiped the table. "He didn't have to. He called the producer to make sure I got cast."

"He's trying to help."

"I know, I know. But can't you see how hard that makes it for me? He's making me choose him or San Francisco."

"He's doing no such thing! You know, you don't avoid the issue by refusing to marry him. If you think for a minute that gets you off the hook, you're quite wrong. The relationship is still there. You still have an obligation to him."

"My promise should be good enough. It would be too easy to marry him now and compromise my work."

"If you don't learn to compromise something you'll never survive a marriage anyhow."

"I can't compromise this," Liz said desperately. "Maybe something else, but not this. I need to do this. But I don't want to lose him. Why can't he understand that?"

"He doesn't want to lose you either. Or have you forgotten that he asked you to marry him?" Caroline pulled the plug on the dishwater, and it gurgled loudly as it spun down the drain.

"This is exactly what I was afraid of. That I'd hurt him terribly."

"Then you had better tell him, Liz. And soon."

Chapter 51

CAROLINE WAS RIGHT. But Liz couldn't bring herself to tell him. When he returned from York she waited a day or two more, hoping for a better time, but she waited too long.

She knew immediately when he discovered her guilty secret. He slammed the door, dropped his music case on a chair, and threw the post and his keys on the table. Every jagged gesture snapped with anger. All the time he looked at her without speaking.

Her chest was small with anxiety.

"And when," he asked, folding his arms, "were you going to tell me?"

Liz could not pretend she didn't know what he meant. She stalled. "How did you find out?"

"From Caroline." He began to pace, never taking his eyes off her. "She's having a surprise party for you. Was the surprise on me? Were you planning to disappear some night when I was away?"

"You know better than that."

"Why did you not tell me?" he exploded, stopping and slamming his hands down on the back of a chair.

"I couldn't." Then her temper flared, thrusting aside her impulse to cry. "Besides, I don't need your permission!"

"That is not the point."

"It's my decision."

"You couldn't tell me?" He was shouting.

She shouted right back in self-defense. "You made it too hard."

"I tried to help you. I called Donald Ross, but that wasn't good enough."

"I didn't want you manipulating things. I just wanted your support."

She saw him check his spontaneous response. Instead he turned half away from her. "You've always been very clear about your priorities. You keep reminding me that your career comes first. Well I understand now, Liz. I understand completely. No wonder you wouldn't agree to marry me."

"That's not fair. I only wanted to wait."

"You had no intention of getting married. Once San Francisco came up you were gone. You never left it for a moment. There was no other choice; I saw that."

"That doesn't mean I wanted to leave you." That seemed to give him pause, so she pressed on. "It's because of you that I even bothered to audition for Festival Opera."

He backed away from her. "Oh no, you will not lay that on my doorstep. I will not be the reason you compromised your future."

She turned away as if he had slapped her. "This is exactly what I mean." She stalked into the bedroom, so angry she could hardly breathe.

He followed her. "You've turned the idea of being alone into something noble. How you suffer for your art. You've romanticized it until you believe it."

"Well, you're proving it. It's all or nothing for you. You don't trust that I value our relationship."

"If you valued our relationship you would have told me you were going away."

He had her there. She threw open the bureau and began pulling out clothes and stuffing them in her bag.

"You aren't leaving now?"

"It's what you've expected all along, isn't it?"

"Wait until morning." He tried to take the sweaters out of her hands, but she jerked away.

"No. Ponnelle was right. This is too hard. You'll always hold me back." Refusing to look at him, she pushed past him to the kitchen and picked up the phone. "Kate? It's me. I need a place to sleep tonight . . . I can't talk about it . . . Do you mind? . . . Thanks . . . Bye." She slammed down the phone, collected a few more things, and picked up her bag. Poised for flight, she said, "I'll get the rest tomorrow."

"Liz, this is absurd." He grabbed her shoulder. "I know how you feel."

"No, you don't." She shrugged him off, rounding on him. "I asked for one thing from you, just a little time to find out if I can do this. A little time so I could try not to hurt you. I think I've earned that."

With a violent wrench of his body he turned and threw up his hands. "I should have listened. That very first weekend you said you would leave someday. You have always had one foot out the door."

"I knew better than to fall in love with you. Look what a mess it's become!"

"So then, go!"

Liz flung open the door and charged up the driveway, hearing his shout.

Half afraid that he would follow, she set off at a near run toward Cardiff Road. Noise and lights crowded the twilight. She flinched at passing cars and kept her head down when she met people. By the time she reached Kate and Christopher's flat half an hour later, she felt like she was about to either faint or be sick.

Kate took her coat and bag and sat her down on the sofa without a word. Liz leaned against the blankets heaped at one end, catching her breath and steadying her nerves. Finally she sat forward, clenching her hands together, elbows tight to her body.

"You had a fight?"

"Yes." Liz spoke in a tiny voice. And then, because Kate would not stop looking at her, she said, "I've left him."

If Kate was surprised, she did not show it. She shook her head and started to speak, but Liz cut her off.

"I don't want to talk about it," she snapped.

Kate, for once, did not push. "Right. Well there's some supper left over if you want it. Have yourself a hot bath. Chris's out, so take as long as you like."

"Thanks. You don't need to play hostess."

"Let me know if you need anything." Kate went to the kitchen, where Liz could hear her chattering to her month-old son, Nicholas.

She sat for a while, afraid if she moved she would jar loose the lump of tears forming under her sternum. Eventually she got up gingerly and went into the bathroom. She opened the taps and sat on the edge of the tub.

She'd known all along. Titus had seen it. Kate knew about it. And now Giles, whom she had fooled for a long time, saw the same thing. She could not be redeemed, even by his love. She'd always suspected that she would hurt him eventually. For years now it had seemed that she might avoid it. But it had come in the end, as she had known it would. Her only loyalty, ultimately, was to her voice, she thought viciously.

At last, under the noise of the rushing water, she began to sob, rocking and hugging herself until some of the pressure eased. As she lay soaking in the hot water, silent tears slipped down her face in the humidity. By the time they stopped, her fingers and toes were swollen, her face stiff, the water cool. Shivering, she scrubbed herself dry, returned to the sofa, and bundled herself up in a cocoon of blankets.

Once Kate looked in on her, but Liz lay very still, and she went away without a word. When Christopher came home after midnight, Liz heard tense voices in the kitchen for a while, but soon all was silent except the occasional car in the street and a distant chime.

Sleep brought no relief. She slept heavily and woke feeling like she hadn't moved all night. Before she opened her eyes she remembered where she was and why. Sticky heat burned the back of her eyeballs, and nausea drew a wretched taste from belly to throat. She quietly left the flat under cover of the chaos of Nicholas's cries.

She showed up at Bert and Caroline's flat at half seven, feeling like a nomad. She offered the briefest of explanations, for which Bert offered solemn condolences. She couldn't quite meet Caroline's eyes. She ate a piece of toast and sipped at a cup of tea. Across the table, Bert and Caroline exchanged glances that she ignored.

"You look ill," he said cautiously. "Are you sure you want to work?"

"I need to stay busy." That was all it took. Her eyes blurred. She put down her cup. "Excuse me, please." She escaped to the bathroom and stood against the door with trembling hands pressed against her mouth to arrest the sobs that strafed the back of her throat. When she regained some composure, she washed her face and combed her hair, then returned to the kitchen.

Her friends stopped talking when she came in. Bert had his jacket on, his keys and thermos in hand. "You're welcome to stay here if you like," he told her.

"Thanks, but I'll go to my aunt's house tonight. I'd just be in the way."

"Suit yourself." He patted her on the back awkwardly. "I'm sure it'll come right."

After he left for Cygnet, Caroline poured Liz more tea and started cleaning up.

"I'm sorry if I caused any trouble. I didn't think you'd wait so long to tell him."

Liz looked up, ready to attack, but instead she sighed and shook her head.

"It's not your fault. I should have had the decency to tell him right away. No matter how he found out, it was too late for it to be okay." She got up and went over to the window. The pane of glass radiated cold from the fog that muffled the damp streets. "I can't believe that he thought I was just going to sneak off without saying good-bye."

"I just surprised him. You'll work it out."

"No."

"What do you mean, 'no'?"

"It's not fair for him to put conditions on me. If he doesn't know how much I love him without my having to marry him before I'm ready, then he just doesn't trust me." She got up and rinsed out her cup.

Caroline collected the shop keys and switched off the lights. "Don't give up on him. Give him time to get used to the idea. Perhaps you might even change your mind," she added dryly.

"I don't have any more time," Liz mumbled.

* * *

LIZ WENT TO HER VOICE LESSON the next day because she did not have the volition to decide otherwise.

"How are you, child?" Ruby gave her a small shake.

Telling Caroline any of her business had been poor judgment. "I'll be okay."

"Why didn't you tell him about San Francisco?"

"His idea about our life didn't include me going to San Francisco. No matter when I told him he was going to hate it."

"But why not marry him?"

"I didn't say no! I just wanted to wait. Do you think I'm wrong, too?" she snapped.

"Of course not. But you make him happy. Can you blame him for wanting to make it permanent?"

Liz sat down with a sigh. Hearing it in that context made her decision feel even more selfish. Her answer welled up slowly. "He's afraid he's going to lose me. That's the wrong reason. Unless he believes he can't lose me, it won't matter if we're married or not." She thumped the arm of the loveseat gently. "It's my own fault. I did tell him that I would leave him one day for my voice. And now he's made me choose it."

Ruby withheld comment.

Liz astonished herself by singing like the diva she was becoming. Her voice was the first comfort she'd felt in twenty-four hours, though in a way that only made it worse. Her sinuses, swollen from all the tears she'd shed, felt dull and muffled at first. She concentrated on placing the sound high, skimming it gently across the irritated tissue. Ruby patiently guided her through a humming warm-up and steadying slow scales. After a few false starts, the familiar strength suffused her body and she relaxed into it. Her grief hovered on the periphery of her consciousness like a fever barely controlled by aspirin. She focused with all her might on the aria from *Figaro*, not allowing the weakness to erode her power.

At the end of the lesson, Ruby commended Liz for pulling herself together and singing well.

Liz twisted her lips wryly. "I suppose it's good to know I can sing. Since that's what I've sacrificed everything else for."

"Dear Liz. I'm sorry this is so difficult."

Liz could feel her composure begin to disintegrate. She shook her head sharply. "He says I left him as soon as I started to plan for San Francisco. I didn't see it before, because I was so mad at him, but maybe he was right." What had Titus said? *There's no room for anyone else in your spotlight.* "I just hope it's worth the trouble."

"You knew it wouldn't be easy. But if it's too high a price, then perhaps it's time to quit."

Liz looked at her, wondering. "I can't quit. Then I'd really have nothing."

Ruby sent her on her way with a hug.

As the train rocked her the short distance to Caerphilly that night, Liz suddenly realized that there was nothing to keep her in Wales, suffering through the next several months until she was expected in San Francisco. She had been offered the Beethoven Mass in Birmingham. But she could turn it down. Everything in her life that bore promise lay to the west. It was time to go.

Chapter 52

BERT WAS AWAY AT AN ESTATE SALE the next day. After Liz closed up Cygnet that evening, she walked over to Swann's, hoping he would have returned. Though the blinds of the shop were drawn, she could see a light in the office when she peeked through the door. She let herself in, calling out a greeting. Bert and Caroline were both in the office.

Bert got up to offer her a seat, but Liz shook her head. "I won't stay. I've got to get the train. I just came by to let you know—well, I'm sorry it's such short notice, but Saturday's my last day."

Bert did a double take. "Your last day? Of work?"

"That's only four days away," Caroline protested.

"I'm leaving for California on Monday."

Caroline watched her for a moment. "Giles called last night. He wants to see you."

"I don't want to see him."

"You ought to talk to him."

"Please stay out of it." She had to resist the urge to shout.

"Why are you so stubborn?"

"If he loved me he wouldn't have put me in that position."

"You got what you deserved from him."

"Caroline!" For once Bert abandoned his neutrality.

"What do you want from me?" Liz shouted in a blaze of temper. "I've done the best I could. But now I have to do what's best for me. This is not all my fault, you know."

"For God's sake, Liz, it's no secret how ambitious you are. We all expected this day to come. I'm only sorry about Giles. He deserves better." Caroline slammed out of the office, left the shop without closing the door, and stomped up the steps to the flat.

Bert and Liz looked at each other.

"She doesn't mean it," he offered apologetically.

She hiccupped, startled into a chuckle that dissolved into tears. "Oh, I think she does. And she's partly right." She pulled out her handkerchief.

"At the risk of offending you, I'm going to give you some advice." Bert ran his hand over his unkempt hair. "Go to San Francisco. When you do come back, he'll see that you meant it. But before you go, talk to him. It will do no good to avoid him."

Bert, at least, believed her promise to return. "I tried to keep my distance. But when I couldn't resist him anymore, I gave him every proof he should ever need that I love him. Loved him," she amended hastily into the handkerchief. "Why should I have to give him another?"

"Because to Giles it's incomplete until you do. That's just how he is."

Her rage was spent, or she would have launched herself at him. She blew her nose again. "I won't be speaking to anyone by the time I leave. Maybe it's good I'm going so soon."

Bert did not smile as she had hoped he would.

She shrugged. "I've got to go now. Do you want me to come to work tomorrow?"

"Of course, if you're feeling up to it. I'll talk to Caroline. I hate to see the two of you at odds." He hesitated. "She envies you, you know."

"Yes, I do know," Liz said. "At this moment I can't think why."

* * *

BY THE NEXT MORNING, THE IDEA of having to treat Caroline with kid gloves irritated Liz. She arrived at the shop spoiling for a fight. But Caroline headed her off by apologizing immediately.

"Bert says I'm meddling. I'm sorry, Liz. I don't mean to make things worse."

Liz nodded in acknowledgment. "I wouldn't hurt Giles for the world. But it's none of your business. I just have to muddle through the best I can."

"And you'll be off to fame and fortune soon. Who am I to tell you what to do?" Caroline said it lightly, clearly intending to brush off the entire subject, but Liz turned on her.

"Is there something wrong with me getting on with my career?"

"Why should there be?" The shrug was a little too slow, the expression the same cool mask that Caroline had worn through the season Liz had been in *Yeomen*.

"You tell me. I'm sick of you jabbing at me. What's it all about?"

Caroline threw down her pen, looking like she wanted something heavier. "I'll tell you. Do you know what it's like to know that no matter how hard I work, I'll never have what you have?"

Liz had not expected her to admit it so candidly, and she was caught without a reply.

"Sometimes I'm sorry I told you to call Ruby. It just made it worse." Caroline's face was bright red.

"But you said you were happy being a big fish in a little pond."

"That's what you say when you know you'll never be anything better. You wouldn't know what that's like. But it doesn't stop me from wishing it was different."

"Well that isn't my fault."

"No, but you treat it like you're entitled to it, and you don't need to compromise for anyone."

"I do not! Maybe I used to, but not anymore. I *know* this is a second chance, and I know it isn't given to everyone." She thrust out her left hand as evidence. "But I also know that I have to own it. I can't spend my life apologizing for it."

Caroline suddenly seemed older, and her shoulders slumped. "No, of course not."

Someone tapped insistently at the shop door. It must have gone nine. Both of them ignored the summons. Caroline spread her hands out on the desk, examining the brilliant red polish on her nails. She spoke again, quietly. "I never thought I'd admit this, but part of me was glad that you broke up with him."

"How could you?" Liz whispered.

"I guess I'm more jealous than I realized." She balled up her hands in a single fist and finally looked up at Liz. "Believe me: I am sorry about you and Giles. I went too far last night."

Liz said nothing for a long time. The tapping at the door had ceased. The hum of the electric heater filled the small room. "Sometimes I wish I had what you do. You have somebody who loves you, you have a nice comfortable life, you sing when you want to. But you don't have to constantly live up to yourself.

You don't always have people making you feel like you owe it to them to fulfill your potential. You don't have to be so self-centered that there's no room in your life for anyone else."

Caroline cocked her head. "So you're telling me I'm lucky?"

Liz sighed. "No. But neither am I."

* * *

LIZ COULD HARDLY REMEMBER what it felt like when her only anxiety was her next audition. Over the remainder of the week the swimming in her head and the constant tightness in her chest eased, though she had little to say and never laughed. The only time the melancholy lifted was when she sang. Even then, it took an effort of will to put aside her emotions and sing in the present. She was darkly resigned to balancing precariously between her past and her unknown future for a final week, and she threw herself into work with ruthless fervor.

On Saturday Giles came to Swann's, but she refused to come out of the office. Caroline was obviously disgusted with her, but she held her tongue. On Sunday he rang her aunt's house, but Liz would not take the phone. All the while she fought down her own temptation to call him, though she never told Caroline that. Each time the desire rose she reminded herself that she had not changed her mind, and she would only cause both of them more pain.

Caroline abandoned the idea of a party. On Liz's last night in Wales, her aunt cooked a roast and made Yorkshire pudding. Ruby came for supper, along with Caroline and Bert. Kate and Christopher arrived later with a fractious Nicholas. It was an awkward little gathering. No one mentioned the missing guest, and everyone took leave of Liz with the cheerful assumption that of course she would be back again.

As her aunt drove her to the station the next day, Liz was acutely aware of the way things looked, remembering the late afternoon six years ago when she had come here, confused and crippled. She was leaving a singer. But she wondered if she was any more whole than when she arrived.

Exhausted by good-byes, she had Ellen drop her at the station and huddled alone in the drizzle, waiting for her train. The sooner this journey was behind her, the sooner she would be able to face Merola with the enthusiasm and excitement it deserved. She did not go inside the waiting room but stood with her back to the wall, her two bags at her feet, her hands jammed in her pockets, and her scarf loose at her throat. The mist caressed her face.

She saw him before he saw her. He walked quickly, his shoulders back and his head thrust forward as though great archangel wings rose from his back. The shock of seeing him gave her no time to evade or even react. She merely watched him, knowing he would see her, knowing he would speak to her. She pressed herself against the brick wall and clenched her right hand in her pocket.

When he saw her he stopped abruptly and then slowly, warily approached. It crossed her mind that this was Caroline's doing.

"What the hell are you doing here?" she asked breathlessly.

"I still love you," he said simply.

"I didn't want to choose between you and my voice. That was your doing."

"You made that choice long before you met me."

"Didn't you tell me that one doesn't preclude the other?"

He ducked his head. "Maybe I didn't know what I was talking about."

"Would it have killed you to let me do this at my own pace? Why couldn't you just let me figure it out? I would have come back."

"No. Oh no. I know what would have happened. You would decide against marriage, because you would be alone. I would not be there to convince you that you are strong enough, and wise enough, and loving enough."

"Why couldn't you trust me?" she insisted, shrinking from his prediction.

"When you cannot trust yourself?"

She shook her head sharply to throw off his words. "Do you have any idea why I wanted to wait?"

"Afraid, you are."

She started to deny it but found she couldn't. "Yes. All right. I was afraid. I *am* afraid. I lost everything once, and I'm terrified I could compromise it all again, after I fought so hard to get it back."

"Of course you would not." He leaned closer, making her meet his eyes. "Are you going to let Ponnelle win? She filled your head with such nonsense. Are you going to let her be right?"

Liz bit her lip, hunching her shoulders against his attack. "It's got nothing to do with her."

At last a train approached on her platform, and there was a general stir as people gathered their possessions. A discordant silence isolated the two of them.

"If you are convinced that you cannot have your career and marry me, I have no choice but to give in."

"I *never* said I wouldn't marry you. I just asked for some time. What do you think is going to happen? Do you think I'm going to go off and cheat on you? Do you think you have to tie me down so it won't happen to you again? Well it didn't work with Diana, did it?" Until now she had refrained from referring to his wife, but now she threw it in his face. She felt a momentary satisfaction that she had wounded him when he flinched.

"I've never given you a reason to doubt me. I've never looked at another man since we got together. And I have a terrible feeling it'll always be like that. But I won't let you own me."

Giles's Adam's apple moved, and he licked his lips. His voice came out almost harshly. "My life will never be the same without you in it."

"You'll get over me. You're stronger than I am; you always were." The words felt bitter on her tongue.

His eyes had a shine in them as he shook his head silently. She realized once more how great an effect she had on him, whether she wanted it or not. Her anger melted, and she had to resist the urge to reach out and touch him. "I never should have slept with you. It just complicated everything. Can't we go back to where we were before?"

"Before *Merry Widow*?"

"When we were still just partners. Your respect meant the world to me." She must not cry.

"I don't think that is possible."

She stared at him. He was supposed to agree, supposed to leave the door open. Well, that was that. She had no more to offer him. Liz roused herself from the shock and picked up her bags. It was cold out there. "Then I guess this is good-bye," she said stiffly.

"Take care of that throat," he said, fumbling with her scarf.

Even the contact of his gloved fingers upset her. She shouldered past him, swung herself up into a second-class carriage, and took a seat on the opposite side of the train from the platform so she would not be tempted to look at him. As the train gathered speed, she pressed her forehead to the cold glass in an effort not to cry.

Chapter 53

LIZ SWUNG OFF THE MUNI BUS and hurried along Van Ness. It was a little after nine on the first Thursday of June, and today the Merolini would read through *Figaro* for the first time. Typical for summer in San Francisco, the cool fog had not yet burned off. The orange bus steamed away into a world of gray street, gray buildings, gray skies. Workmen cleaned the steps of the State building with a pressurized hose, and the traffic honked and roared all around her. A panhandler wearing a Giants cap called to her, but she shook her head.

"Sorry. Maybe tomorrow."

She crossed the plaza to the stage door at the back of the War Memorial Opera House. The right to enter there, and all it implied, brought a smile of satisfaction she couldn't suppress. She glimpsed the main stage to her right as she headed for the elevator and poked her head in the doorway. The vast stage was nearly bare. Colored tape on the linoleum floor spiked the location of the various sets for the summer opera season.

She returned to the hallway and went to the elevator. On the fifth floor, music already came from some of the coaching rooms. When she'd found a place where she could shut herself away and warm up her voice, she paused to catch her breath. As she put her watch in conspicuous view on the keyboard, she tried to calm the excitement that stirred in her solar plexus. This was rehearsal, like any one of hundreds she had done. Yet it was the very beginning again.

Gently she hummed and coaxed her voice, taking time because of the early hour. More often than usual she stopped, shaking her head, and drew a few deep breaths before she continued. At last the notes began to roll easier, and she closed her eyes, filling the room with sound. After a while she began to run through one of the arias that she would sing that day. She paced around the small room, tossing out phrases, referring to the keyboard or the score with a grimace every now and again. She jingled her keys in her pocket like a percussion accompaniment. Finally she stood still, closing her eyes and gathering her wits. Then, with a wry smile, she collected her belongings and went across the hall to the chorus room.

She arrived on the last chime of ten. For a week, the singers had come and gone, sizing each other up—a reminder to Liz, as if she needed a reminder, to be nervous. This was not the nepotistic community theater where she had cut her teeth. She had worked her voice hoarse and stayed up into the night studying the scores in order to make the desired impression, not only on McEwan and Meltzer and Kuisak and Bergen, but also on her peers. This first read-through would expose everyone's talent.

The singers gravitated to the piano at the center of the long, narrow room. Coats and book bags were scattered over the rows of chairs. A couple of singers adjusted black music stands with finicky precision, while others held on to their music as they paced or chatted. A tenor complained about sore muscles from a game of pick-up basketball, and Liz wondered when on earth he had had the time. Marisa, a sexy Brazilian mezzo who had studied at Indiana and Juilliard, boasted of all the competitions she had won. A soprano with a Wagnerian build and a voice to match who went by the improbable name of Giselle confided to two colleagues that her mother had wanted her to be a dancer.

Rogelio, the baritone who was singing Figaro, separated himself from the basketball conversation when Liz came in. Over blue jeans and a T-shirt he wore a gray-green houndstooth sport coat with sagging elbows and misshapen pockets. The collar was turned up around his neck, and his dark hair curled over it. He greeted Liz with a bow of his head and an engaging smile.

"Good morning," he said in a lilting Latino accent.

"Hi." She couldn't help but return the smile.

"My friends at home warned me that it would be cold here in June, but I didn't believe them."

"Where are you from?" she asked.

"El Paso. It's probably eighty degrees there already." He folded his arms and pretended to shiver, and she chuckled. "Where is home for you?"

She opened her mouth and realized that she didn't know the answer. "I lived in Wales until recently, but I grew up here. It's kind of a long story," she said, shrugging.

"Perhaps you could tell me sometime. I love long stories."

"I . . . sure." She flushed. It hadn't occurred to her until that moment that he was flirting with her. She just didn't think in those terms. She supposed she would have to start.

She was saved from further embarrassment by the arrival of Daniel Kuisak and Carl Bergen. The gossiping and comparing of notes evaporated as people noticed them. Though he was a small man, Kuisak commanded attention. He had a round face and hair like corn silk, which seemed at odds with his wiry hands and ropy forearms. He looked around and took roll in a split second. "Good morning. Welcome. Are we ready to make some music?" He sat down at the piano, and the rehearsal began.

Liz took her assignments as a good omen. For Stern Grove and Montalvo she would sing Cherubino in *Le Nozze di Figaro*. For the next ten weeks she would also be working on Susanna for the same opera, for she would alternate roles for the Western Opera Theater tour in the fall. Apparently management wanted her to forge into soprano territory. Mozart would not let her down.

She was not in the opening scenes of the opera, so she wrapped herself around a chair and watched with calculating intensity. Sharon Kyle, a young soprano from Boston, had been cast as Susanna. She dressed like a university dean, down to the silk tie, and had the fair skin and dark hair of her Irish ancestors. She knew her music well and used this advantage to begin to connect with the other characters. Rogelio performed with the license of someone who had already done the role. His arias were crisp, though he used his score to refresh his memory for much of the recitative. Liz scrutinized the interplay between Sharon and Rogelio, aware that she would be working the same scene later, when the tour approached.

Kuisak moved directly through the score, stopping for nothing but tossing prompts or suggestions over the music. Like Giles, his perception and his knowledge of music humbled her, but unlike Giles, he did nothing to mitigate the force of his opinions. Bergen, the stage director and acting coach, listened without comment, occasionally writing notes at the podium where he stood. He was twice the size of the music director, his body easy where Kuisak's was taut, his expression bland where Kuisak's was anxious.

The critical young cast members watched each other intently, and although they withheld most reaction, Liz felt the stir of approval for Sharon's singing, the relaxed smiles at Rogelio's comic flourishes, the silent disapproval when the mezzo missed an entrance.

During the duet before her entrance, Liz quietly unwound herself from her chair and stood up, moving closer to the focal point of the room. The character of Susanna marshaled the rest of the cast in the first act, linking the scenes smoothly, and Sharon did a creditable job even in this first run-through. The piano thundered to a halt, and the soprano cued Liz with her eyes. They exchanged the seesaw of recitative, and before she could think about it, Liz flew into her breathless first aria. Mozart transformed her from a wallflower to a bright-eyed gamine. Cherubino came alive, and the music spilled out of her, soaring and fluttering. Her eyes saw footlights, and her ears heard an orchestra. She hugged her score to her chest, her whole body consumed by the production of sound. A hundred times over she redeemed her poor showing in London four long years ago.

The aria ended as abruptly as it began and was followed by a charged silence.

"Nice job," murmured Giselle, who was singing the Countess and had nothing to do until the second act. Friendly agreement rippled through the cast—not the shouted bravas of an audience, but the quiet respect of the informed. Liz felt herself flush, though she attempted to appear unaffected by the response, fumbling to open her score and be ready to continue when Kuisak moved on.

The rest of the morning flowed by like water unhindered. After that first frantic aria, Liz's pulse slowed and her anxiety melted, the tension all spilled out. Her body, loose and warm, tingled with the awe of making good music. The last of her doubts faded away, releasing their hold on her throat.

* * *

AFTER THE READ-THROUGH LIZ HEADED for the elevator in search of lunch before her two o'clock diction coaching. Rogelio, Giselle, and Marisa were there ahead of her.

"Come to lunch with us," Rogelio invited her, and she agreed as the elevator opened.

Geneva, the publicity manager, who was given to wearing colors like lime green and magenta, darted into the elevator as the doors began to close. "Liz, glad I caught you. Ruthe Stein called from the *Chronicle*. She wants to do a piece for the Datebook about one of our singers, and I gave her your name. Is there any time next week when she could interview you?"

Liz hesitated, sensing the eyes of the other singers upon her. If someone wanted to do an article about her tingling elbow and useless fingers, she would decline. But she had another idea. "Sure," she said slowly as the elevator stopped at the street level. "Do you think she'd mind talking to my stepmother too?"

In the last six months Madly had delivered more than a couple of phone calls on Liz's behalf, and she had underwritten all of Liz's financial support for the summer program. At the First Day party Liz had listened to her stepmother talk to the other sponsors with great pride sparkling in her voice.

"This is my daughter, Elizabeth," she had said repeatedly. Not "my step-daughter." Not "my husband's daughter." My daughter.

The others filed out of the elevator while the publicity manager consulted her ever-present steno pad for some clue. Rogelio lingered, waiting for Liz.

"I'm not sure," Geneva said, worry settling between her sleekly shaped eyebrows. "She really wants a singer, and she liked the angle that you were local talent, from the Conservatory and all."

"I wouldn't be here without her," Liz said firmly. "That's really the only story to be told about me."

She joined Rogelio and the others, hoping she had made it clear that she was nothing special.

Chapter 54

DAYS PASSED THAT PROMISED—always followed by one or two that threatened—to keep her honest, Liz supposed. She continued to sing well, and when she sang, she did not doubt. She worked eagerly with her new colleagues. Once each voice and talent became a known quantity, some of the edges of pretension relaxed. A part of her still felt amazed to be among these voices, but another part felt at home in a way she'd never felt at the Conservatory.

Her skills, which she had labored for years to acquire, now seemed amateurish and incomplete. But the constant bombardment of training stimulated her nerves and sent her blood rushing through her, renewing her every time she opened her mouth. She was awed by her own voice in the way she was awed by von Stade or Horne or Norman. It came as a surprise in odd moments that her long-ago dreams were being realized in an exponentially greater way than she'd imagined. She worked so hard all day and into the evening that she seldom had time to think of Giles.

But the nights were a different story.

By the middle of the summer, Liz's restless sleep was beginning to catch up with her. She half woke several times a night, barely aware that she had left her confused dreams. One morning she arrived twenty minutes late for movement class, and once there her eyes recoiled from the artificial light of the sixth-floor ballet studio. The room seemed close and humid with the presence of other bodies. She joined the other singers where they stood in a circle, rolling their heads and shoulders to loosen tensions. The teacher merely nodded to her and tapped his left shoulder, his reminder that she needed to challenge her old injuries.

She usually enjoyed this part of the day. She loved the way her voice responded when she exercised before she sang. Her blood flowed, her limbs were loose, and her lungs pulled deeply. Her body was ready to participate. Even her left elbow and wrist seemed to be improving from the half hour of stretching that preceded the dance lesson or other vigorous exercise. But today she felt like she was continuing her night of struggle.

After the stretching, the wiry instructor passed out fencing swords to all twelve singers from a long duffel bag at the side of the ballet studio. For the next hour Liz had to concentrate on moving her body, controlling the sword, and staying alert to the rapid commands of the teacher. She wished she had not missed the warm-ups, for after half an hour her thighs began to ache from travelling with her knees always flexed. In the mirrors that lined three walls she watched herself flounder with the new skill, awkward and clumsy. But by the time she headed for a quick shower, the workout had alleviated some of the mental paralysis that had hindered her all morning.

She went directly on to acting class in the chorus room. Liz looked forward to working with Carl Bergen. On the day of the *Figaro* read-through he had won her admiration by saying, "Mozart is the most generous of collaborators. Let him help you." He himself had helped her immeasurably with Cherubino, and now that she was solidifying the role of Susanna for the tour, she hoped for the same support. Some of her former readings now looked shallow and tenuous to her, but she worked eagerly on new vocal interpretation, drawing fresh ideas into her skein of subtexts.

Though she was the last of the four singers to arrive, she had no hesitation at singing first. "Let's hear the aria straight through, and then we'll play with it." Carl, built like a retired football player, meant exactly that. The word "work" did not appear in his vocabulary, and the time she spent learning from him flew by.

Fortunately, she was well prepared that day. "Deh vieni," Susanna's final aria, felt comfortable and settled in her voice. Liz was not unaware that the other singers were listening carefully. But Ruby and the Welsh College had given her confidence: her voice would not fail her. She rose above her sleep deprivation and was satisfied with her performance.

"Nice. You'd never know it was before noon," Carl said when she finished. "Now, tell me what's going on in the aria. Where are you, what are you doing, and so forth."

"I'm in the garden waiting for the Count. He wants to make love to me before I marry Figaro, but I'm planning to slip away and let the Countess take my place so she can teach him a lesson."

"Who do you sing this to?"

"The recitative is to the Countess, but I guess the rest of it is really to myself."

"Think about that." He laid a finger aside of his nose like Santa Claus. "You don't really want the Count, do you?"

"No. I don't even like him. But he's my employer."

"So you certainly wouldn't be singing this about the Count. This is a very tender love song. Who's it for? Who else is in this scene?"

Liz thought a moment. "Well, Figaro, but he's hidden. I don't interact with him."

"That's right. But you do know he's there; Marcellina told you. So let's try this: You *want* Figaro to hear this. You exaggerate a bit, tease him with it. You want him to *think* you're talking about the Count, but you're really talking about Figaro himself. All the sentiments in this aria are about him.

"When you were singing just now, you were acting, is that right?" He used his fingers to put the word "acting" in visual quotation marks. "You were Liz behaving like Susanna?"

"Yes?" She wrinkled her brow, although her lips were twisted into a smile.

He laughed. "You have to start someplace. But let me give you something else to think about." He glanced around, including all the singers. "To sing well, you have to find a place in your body that truly believes what you are singing. That takes having a genuine emotional attachment to it, or an *opinion* about it, which makes it real to you at a visceral level. Something to personalize it. If you're singing about revenge, surely you've had a moment, even a small one, where you'd like to see someone get what's coming to them. If you're singing about grief, surely you've lost something or someone important, and remember what that was like. And so on and so forth. Was it Stanislavski who said that generality is the enemy of art?"

They all nodded, though Liz wasn't sure, and suspected the others weren't either.

"Now then," Carl said, turning back to Liz, "is there someone in your life to whom you could address this exquisite little love song?"

She hesitated.

"You don't need to tell me who. Just know it yourself. Is there someone?"

She couldn't get Giles's face out of her mind. She nodded.

"Good. Now the other thing is, who among us goes around talking to themselves?" He glanced around, taking a casual poll. "Anyone? Especially in rhythm and on pitch." A smile brightened his ruddy face. "It helps to think of someone listening, even when you are alone in the scene. Just for the purposes of being genuine. It can be God, it can be your spouse, it can be your parakeet, but always have a sense of addressing someone."

He pulled a folding chair over to the end of the piano. "Giselle, come sit over here. Let Liz tell you all about her Figaro." He looked at Liz. "Let's just do the recitative. Pretend Giselle is your very best friend, and tell her about it. All you're really saying in this part is 'I'm so excited, I can't wait!' That's it. But I want it to overflow with your attitude about whomever you're picturing."

The pianist played the opening measures, and Liz earnestly tried to recreate her passion for Giles. Giselle listened with feigned interest. But Liz had never been one to wear her heart on her sleeve. The situation felt stiff and contrived.

"Better," Carl said when she'd finished. "But you're still removed. You're doing it *as though* you were talking about him. Here, sit down." He placed Liz knee to knee with Giselle. "You've just met this guy, and you're having coffee with Giselle to gush over him." He crouched next to Liz. "How long since you've seen him?" he asked in a stage whisper.

"Uh . . . a couple of months," she answered faintly. Five months, three weeks, and four days. If that mattered.

"Can't wait to get your hands on him again?"

She couldn't speak.

"She's turning red; this is good," he said cheerfully, getting to his feet. "That's what you want to do. Use material that will spark your imagination. Giselle, I want you to fire questions at her in the rests. Bombard her: Is he cute? What's he like? Whatever you come up with. Just keep feeding her lines so that she gets so excited talking about this guy she's just about to wet her pants."

He took Liz's shoulder. "I want your voice to just ooze with desire. It's exaggeration, of course it is, because you want to make Figaro jealous. Just keep *your* 'Figaro' in your mind's eye to fuel the fire." He backed away. "Ready?"

Liz put up a hand, closing her eyes and trying to bring some control to her disordered emotions. A few deep breaths brought her closer to balance. She wanted to stop, but with her colleagues watching, she felt the pressure to continue. She made herself think back to *Merry Widow*, when she'd longed for someone to confide in. She had nearly burst with her desire then; surely she could reproduce that agitation now. She opened her eyes and nodded to the apprentice coach who waited at the piano.

Over the introduction Giselle tossed off questions that Liz only half heard. "Where'd you meet?" "What's his name?" "Is he cute?"

When she replied the Italian came easily to her tongue, but her chest was filled with the memory of the moment she had first wanted Giles, her passion as softly ripe as a peach, and as fragile.

Another volley of questions came with the next four-bar interlude. "Have you gone out?" "Did he kiss you?" "Will he call you?" "Do you want him?"

Yes, oh yes, I want him, I want him so badly. Liz's mind responded to the question while the Italian tumbled from her mouth.

The last rest was shorter, and Giselle was only able to fit in two questions. "Is he good in bed?" "Did he make you come?" Everyone, including the pianist and the coach, laughed while Liz finished the recitative in a flourish of fervent longing.

"Good, very good," Carl said, still chuckling. "We heard from Liz that time, not Liz being Susanna. It was different, wasn't it?"

Rogelio, Marisa, and Giselle all nodded, and even Liz had to agree.

"Now right about here the mood begins to change. Where she says '*Oh, come par*' she takes in the beauty of the night, and she's overcome by tenderness for him. You drop the teasing and sing directly and honestly to him, though he doesn't know it."

He shooed Liz out of her chair and moved it out of range. "Thank you, Giselle. Let's try the same thing now, but, Rogelio, I want you to stand in this time. Not for the real Figaro, but the one Liz is thinking about." Giselle went back to sit with Marisa. Rogelio got up and stood with his hands on the back of the chair she had vacated. Bergen backed Liz into the opposite corner of the space they had marked off as the stage. "Talk directly to him. Don't think of him as Rogelio; don't even think of him as Figaro. Picture the guy you were bonkers in lust with a minute ago. Drop the giggling, girlish confidences. This is sincere and simple. You only have one thought: The night is beautiful, and you want him."

Liz met Rogelio's humid brown eyes. He winked with a shadow of a smile. She wondered if he thought he was the object of her imagination, and a flush warmed her cheeks. He was ever so subtly pursuing her. His courtly ways and gentleness reminded her too much of Giles, which attracted her and also made her very wary. She couldn't keep eye contact with him. She had to resort to the trick of focusing on the bridge of his nose.

She began to sing, thinking of an evening two years ago when she and Giles had walked along the banks of the river at Hay-on-Wye. It had been dusk, and the heavy scent of jasmine and the clean freshness of the running river had filled her senses. Birds had swooped out of the twilight like dark shooting stars. Swallows, he said. The warm nearness of him in the cool spring night comforted and ignited her. She began to sing, that night trembling in her voice and rising through her chest.

After two bars Carl said, "Don't sing with your shoulders."

She dropped them, felt her lungs open up, and kept going. Carl stood to one side, watching her and motioning with his hand as if to gently draw the aria out of her.

"Forehead." As she continued to sing he stood in front of her and rubbed with two fingers at the wrinkled concentration until she relaxed it. "Good. Keep going."

By now she was used to the coaches adjusting her body as she sang, and she accommodated him automatically. Carl stood back again, still observing. After another line or two he was behind her, pressing down on her shoulders with both hands. As she released the tension in her shoulders, it felt like her chest had suddenly split open, exposing her heart. All of her control was gone in a second. A great gasp, a silent sob, tore her apart.

She held her breath, pressing her hands to her face. "I can't, I'm sorry, I can't do it."

Carl put an arm around her and gave her a quick squeeze. "Okay, okay, stop. It's fine."

She took a couple of sharp, deep breaths to regain her composure. Rogelio had taken a few steps toward her. She could sense his frown without looking at him.

"All right?" Carl asked.

She nodded, closing her eyes.

"A good lesson you should all remember." He kneaded her shoulders soothingly. "Did you hear it change? Did you hear the rawness? This idea of particularizing your characters can be very useful, but you should never do it at the expense of your voice." He gave Liz a pat and drew away to address the other singers. "This seemed to be working for her; you could hear the authenticity, couldn't you? But if it's too raw, or too recent, it can take you places where you simply can't sing. That's not a good plan. So please remember, any subtext is disposable. It can do wonderful things, as you heard, or it can make your job impossible, as it did just now for Liz." He turned to her. "Need a break?"

"Five minutes?" she asked meekly. She did not look at Rogelio. He had gone to sit with the other singers.

"Go ahead. And Liz—"

She stopped.

"It was lovely and rich. You'll find another way in, that's all."

Chapter 55

LIZ AVOIDED EVERYONE AT LUNCH and struggled through a diction coaching in the afternoon. To her relief, she was not called for the *Figaro* rehearsal that evening.

Dundee, her father's marmalade cat, waited at his usual post when she got home. She let him in and went straight upstairs to her room. She sat heavily on the bed, her book bag still over her shoulder, her cotton scarf still protecting her throat.

Her life these days rang with the triumph of her hard work, her risks, and her desire. Yet the strength in her body that supported her singing was now at work fighting down the urge to cry. A few tears made it down her cheeks before she could stop them, and she pressed her hands to her temples in an effort to calm herself. Then she got up, tossed her coat on a chair, and washed her face in cold water.

"Work," she told herself fiercely. In a few more weeks she would be over this emptiness. She just had to get through nights like this. She collected her score and several stubby pencils, switched off her lamp, and went down to the living room. Madly and her father were out, so she threw open her music and began to pick at the phrases, singing sotto voce, spitting out the consonants. But soon she grew disgusted with Cherubino's preoccupation with love. She'd worked most of the day, singing, concentrating, thinking. She had earned this night off and deserved not to spend it buried under thousands of tiny notes.

She left the score sighing over the keyboard. She wanted to talk to someone, someone who did not merely know her professionally. Ruby, or Caroline, or Bert. Or even Giles. Especially Giles.

Perhaps she should call Rogelio. He had seemed concerned. But she resisted. He would not want to hear the melodrama. She merely wanted him to seduce her, to find out if it could take away the pain. Hadn't she learned anything?

She picked up the pink Datebook section from Sunday's *Chronicle*. Her picture, with Madly, topped the feature article. She cringed at what she had said to the interviewer, fatuous remarks about her opportunities and her gratitude. She passed over it to the listings for the week, looking for someplace she could go and be anonymous. Still preoccupied with her own thoughts, she almost missed it.

Friday, July 6, at 8 p.m.
Titus Zender and The Blenders
Yoshi's, 6030 Claremont Ave, Oakland

So, he was still in the area. And doing all right, apparently. That terrible name for the band had stuck, in spite of her protests.

She was unable to resist the temptation to see him, to hear him. She grabbed her coat.

* * *

YOSHI'S TURNED OUT TO BE A SUSHI bar in North Oakland that hosted a long-running series of jazz concerts. Liz got lost on the way, unfamiliar with the East Bay, and still the most timid of drivers. By the time she arrived the music had started. She found the room crowded, and after buying a glass of Chardonnay she propped herself up against a pillar and watched in fascination.

Titus was still thin and looked like he worked hard every day of his life. The smooth baby face was beginning to show angles and shadows that hadn't been there seven years ago. His hair was still caught back in the familiar ponytail. He wore a blue T-shirt with a tree on it and black jeans that made him seem even slimmer than she remembered.

She smiled at the ease with which he gathered the crowd to him when the number was over.

"Nice to be here again. Got some new stuff tonight, been working hard on a recording, so I wanna try some of it out on you, if you don't mind." He smiled as the audience gave its expected approval. He glanced past her at first, but then she saw the recognition hit him and he looked her way again. He grinned, nodding, and turned back to the band.

She stood through the forty-minute set, nursing her wine and watching him intently. He might have been at a rehearsal, his manner was so casual and offhand.

His playing filled her with nostalgia. He had improved, most of the clichés gone from his composition and replaced by soul-aching originality. She closed her eyes and tried to remember their good moments, moments of laughter and silliness. Far too few.

"I'd like to close this first set with a piece I haven't played in a while. I wrote it five or six years ago, for a friend of mine who was going through a tough time. Haven't seen her since, but I never forgot her. I call this 'Breath of Heaven.'"

With a shock, Liz realized that he was talking about her. He did not look at her but cued the band and began a slow, rippling blues melody. She stared, motionless. The ache of her loss throbbed through the piece, winding slowly to a peaceful calm that lingered in the air when the band finished. As it ended she swallowed hard and could not applaud. He acknowledged the audience with a nod and a gesture to his band. Then he pressed the bell of his trumpet onto the instrument stand and held up his hand.

"Thanks. We'll be back in fifteen. Don't go away."

Titus ducked past the amplifier and electrical cords, hopped down off the platform, and made his way directly to where Liz stood. His wide, amiable grin warmed her and drove back the tears she had been tempted to shed. With no hesitation, he hugged her hard.

"Liz, God, it's been years! How are you? Heard you moved back to England."

"Wales," she corrected him automatically. "Titus, you're so good!"

He laughed easily. "Hey, thanks. Come talk to me. You gotta meet Grace."

He edged through the crowd, replying to every compliment but never stopping until he had led her to a small corner table. Here, tucked away where the light was dim, sat Grace, young and obviously pregnant. Liz had a bad moment when she realized that she had not been mistaken about what Titus wanted. Grace was domesticated and therefore no competition whatsoever for his art. She managed to smile and offer her hand.

He crowded them around the tiny table and began sipping the mineral water that Grace had clearly kept waiting for him. Liz declined a second glass of wine.

"That was beautiful, that last one. Did you really write it for me?"

"Hey." He shrugged off the compliment. "Thought about you a lot at first. Kinda worried you'd do something dramatic."

"I was never that badly off." Discussing this ancient history in front of a stranger embarrassed her, compelling her to shrug off his concern.

"Yeah you were. Shame you couldn't play. Your music would have just been marinated in all that pain. What a sound."

"But you did it for me," she replied. "I got such a feeling from what you just played. Of struggle, and then peace. It really was a lot like what I went through."

Never a man of many words, Titus seemed to have even fewer these days. He looked at her, drumming his fingers on the table, still restless. "Felt bad, dumping you like that. That piece—guess it was sort of an apology." His fingers stopped, and the angles of his face softened as he smiled his familiar, cherubic smile. "It's on the recording."

It was a moment before she could reply. "All your stuff's that good now. It's like distilled emotion."

"You know, at the Conservatory people used to get all over me because they thought I didn't practice enough, or I didn't turn in my composition homework on time. But I was hanging around with people, living my life, and playing my horn, and that's where good music comes from, as much as all that other stuff. The people you know and the places you see and the things you hear." He looked at Grace, with her luminous eyes, as he said this. He turned suddenly to Liz. "'Member in grade school, every time kids got near a piano they'd play 'Heart and Soul'?"

The song came immediately to mind, the bouncy bass line and the melody plunked out on the high notes of the piano. It had been years before she'd realized that the song had words.

"It still gets me. You make music because something touches you. And then someone hears it and it touches them. Heart to soul."

It had been on the tip of her tongue to tell him about her singing, but suddenly she was hesitant. After her struggles that day, her own work suddenly seemed pale and unworthy, and she feared she'd sound just as arrogant as he'd ever thought her. She was embarrassed by what seemed her lack. She said nothing, and he did not ask.

As she drove home from Oakland that night Liz remembered the last conversation, the last fight she'd had with him. What had changed? *I'll never be ordinary*, she had insisted then. But what had she accomplished? The ability to sing in a vacuum? While he made music with his soul? He had succeeded, when everyone had said he would not because he lacked drive. And she, who had talent and drive, focus and determination, suddenly felt like she was perpetrating a fraud. As she rose to higher elevations, she was just becoming better at hiding her affliction, even as she had learned to hide her wounded hand.

She went home and took a bath in soft, lavender-scented water and then retreated to bed, her chosen dream burdening her into insomnia.

* * *

THE LAST FIVE WEEKS OF THE MEROLA program swept by. On the last Sunday in July the singers traveled two hours south to Saratoga for the first performance of *Figaro*. Scents of herbs, dry grasses, Mediterranean trees, and dusty vineyards enveloped Liz when she got off the bus. With its mission-style buildings and sumptuous gardens, Villa Montalvo might have been a delight. But at curtain time, seven o'clock, the temperature had only cooled off to 102 degrees. Sluggish and subdued, patrons fanned themselves with programs in the outdoor amphitheater. The makeup, wigs, and costumes were nearly unbearable for the performers.

A week later they performed at Stern Grove in San Francisco. Liz did not look forward to singing in another outdoor venue, where her voice seemed to vanish and only the sensations in her head told her she was making any sound at all. Dank fog lingered in the eucalyptus trees and never completely lifted.

At midafternoon Liz huddled near the stage, grateful for the coat and vest that came with her trouser role. Sharon and Giselle had to suffer bare throats and shoulders in the cold. Peeking through the bushes that camouflaged the backstage area, she assessed the crowd. In spite of the weather, enthusiastic fans covered the damp lawn on the hillside, bundled up and equipped with thermoses and blankets. Liz was touched by how much the city of San Francisco loved their opera students.

* * *

THE GRAND FINALS TOOK PLACE in the Opera House on a Sunday afternoon in August. Liz couldn't muster enough energy to know if she was glad or sorry that Merola was over. She focused every day on the tasks before her, looking neither ahead nor behind. It had almost come as a surprise to wake up this morning and know that the program was already over.

Madly insisted that Liz's father attend this final concert. Liz had not been able to think of a reasonable objection, realizing that her stepmother meant well. But as she stood backstage in the half-light, she remembered that he was present and had to consciously force the anxiety out of her throat. She whispered her first lines to herself, noted the scratch of blue taffeta against her shoulder, steadied her breathing, but nothing distracted the thought once she'd had it. She paced up and down, her hands folded in front of her, her eyes cast down. Why did it matter? What difference could it make?

He would compare her to her mother.

The idea flashed across her mind just as the orchestra began the *Figaro* overture, and it rode on the adrenaline that the music always brought her. She looked up into the vast network of ropes and flies and catwalks above her, and she drew a deep breath. The elation bubbled willingly through her chest again. She was intensely proud of her accomplishments. Her mother would be proud of her. Without a question.

Then again, she might have thought her daughter a soulless monster. Liz's throat began to feel dry. She shook her head to break the train of thought.

Giselle came up beside her, voluptuous in a close-fitting teal gown scattered with sequins that winked in the low light.

"Isn't this exciting?" The soprano squeezed Liz's shoulders. "Oops, your dress." She restored the shape of the crushed sleeve. "Could you hear the applause when Schwabacher announced the program? They love us!"

Her enthusiasm made Liz smile and relinquish her private musings. She hadn't really noticed the applause, but Giselle was right. This moment would only happen once. For ten weeks, Liz had survived by staying exactly in the present moment, forgetting past and future in favor of the present. She must finish in that same style.

She grinned at Giselle. "Let's give them something to remember!"

* * *

AN HOUR OR MORE LATER SHE PACED backstage again. Her solo was next, the aria that had given her so much angst in the acting class. She had worked hard to make the role of Susanna as seamless as it was when Sharon performed it. This was her first opportunity to try it out on an audience. She had come at last to an understanding of the character that did not touch places too tender in her own life. Susanna was smart, sure, and happy. Liz had been there not long ago. She recreated herself as she had been two years ago, sure of her love and her place in the cosmos. She merely left out the knowledge of what would come.

Chapter 56

LIZ LAY ON THE MOTEL BED, still dressed except for her shoes. It was after eight o'clock, and the members of the Western Opera Theater tour had just arrived in Madison, Wisconsin, for performance sixteen out of thirty-five. She had immediately retreated to her room with the *Ovation* magazine she'd picked up the day before. She had nearly cried out when she saw the picture on the last page.

The feature was titled "Keep Your Eye On." She read the single-page article repeatedly until she'd nearly memorized it, vaguely aware of hunger, or something else, twisting in her.

> *One of Cardiff's native sons will come home next month when Welsh conductor Giles Offeryn makes his highly anticipated debut at Welsh National Opera.*

He's from Llanberis, not Cardiff, Liz thought.

The interviewer asked the inevitable question about his early start.

> *"I don't care for the term 'prodigy.' To make music, you need a certain emotional maturity that I simply didn't have when I started my career, although I had technique and intellectual understanding. I'm extremely grateful to have been noticed by some key people early on who haven't forgotten me."*

She could picture him shrugging off the interviewer's next question about his failed marriage.

> *"Music remains mechanical if your heart is not engaged. What has happened in my life has actually connected my heart and my*

talent, and now I'm ready to begin to interpret some of these ter-
rific mysteries. Even the so-called warhorses have mystery to them,
because they are not music until the singer meets the aria, and then
it's a unique chemical reaction. With conducting, it's even more
intense, because you play out the whole story in the score. You must
convey the emotional truth even in a concert version."

To read his words, to hear them in his voice, eroded the careful control Liz had crafted over the months.

Giselle burst into the room. "You're not in bed already."

"Not really." Liz closed the magazine and turned her face away from the light.

"Come on, you have to eat. Up, up, get your coat."

Liz put on her shoes and slipped into her coat. "Where are we going?"

"To the most expensive restaurant I can find in this godforsaken place."

Liz started to smile. "Meltzer called you?"

"He certainly did. So you can stop being discreet. I know he called you yesterday."

They walked down the outside stair of the motel. It was chilly, and the smell of wet trees made the air heavy.

"I didn't want to rub your face in it, just in case," Liz admitted. Giselle had turned out to be a good collaborator onstage and a good companion on long bus rides, quick to laugh in her hearty, uninhibited way. Liz had found it difficult to hide the news that she had been selected as an Adler Fellow for the next year from her.

"You're too kind," Giselle drawled. "I hope you realize I could never have done the same for you."

Liz laughed. "They must know that. That's why they called me first."

"You Brits know how to keep quiet," Giselle agreed. "Now, let's find some-place that serves champagne. It's on me."

"We have a matinee tomorrow," Liz reminded her.

Giselle eyed her. "You," she pronounced, "are no fun at all."

* * *

WHEN THEY GOT TO CLOSING NIGHT in Philadelphia Liz was nothing but relieved. The suspicion of a tickle in her throat and a mild ache behind her eyes made her nervous and prompted her to gargle with salt water and pop aspirin. She must not get sick.

For November, the weather was blunt but not unbearable. She walked to the theater, goading her body into vigorous action after a day of hibernation. Inside the stage door the concrete passageway was dark with cold. But downstairs, where the dressing rooms clustered, the air felt warmer, the lights brighter. Pounding and shouting came from the stage as the crews checked lights and manipulated the sets to fit the space.

Between them the five principle women shared two spacious, if not elegant, dressing rooms. An upright piano and a costume rack crowded the larger of the two. Tired area carpets covered the floors. Electric heaters wound coils of warmth among the worn furniture.

Liz tossed her possessions on a gold, floral-patterned love seat and began the ritual of preparation. She put on her makeup smock—a man's dress shirt with French cuffs that reached to her knees when she did not roll them up—and with a towel wrapped around her neck, she collected her makeup kit and went down the cool hallway to the makeup room. Sterile light assaulted her from the glaring bulbs over the expanse of mirror and speckled white worktop.

Although she wasn't on until the second act, Giselle was already there, wearing her caftan with a peacock feather design. Her makeup, laid out precisely, took up half the counter. Her flamboyant red hair was hidden under the nylon cap that anchored her wig.

"You're early. I looked for you before I came over." Liz soaked her sponge at the sink and dropped into a chair.

"You know how compulsive I am," the soprano said, laughing. "Sorry I missed you. You were asleep when I left."

Liz opened her battered blue tackle box and pulled out what she needed.

"How are you?" Giselle continued to apply eye shadow.

"Ready." She silently denied the possibility that she was coming down with something. Tendrils of adrenaline warmed her belly, and she breathed deeply to diffuse the sensation. She caught Giselle's eye in the mirror, and they shared a conspiratorial smile.

A headband pulled Liz's hair back tight, giving her a severe look. She applied moisturizer to her face, which felt tight from weather and soap, and peered at herself in the mirror. She turned her head side to side, planning her makeup. At last she took up the damp sponge and the cake of base and methodically erased the contours and shadows.

They worked in introverted concentration. The clock in the makeup room permanently read 9:23; the passing time was marked by the faint sounds of the stage manager over the intercom, the distant tweaks of the harpsichord being tuned, occasional but always hurried footsteps in the hallway. Liz applied highlights and lowlights, skillfully blending to give her face planes and angles that didn't usually show.

Giselle, nearsightedly close to the mirror, broke the mood. "Damned if we haven't managed to survive the last couple of months."

"I guess so." Liz darkened her brows with a pencil. "I'll be glad to get back to San Francisco."

Giselle glanced over at her. "You're going to San Francisco for Christmas?"

"Where else would I go?"

"You always talk about Cardiff." Giselle took her brushes to the sink to rinse them.

Liz was nonplused to realize that she had, indeed, talked about Cardiff at length. "Yeah, well, Cardiff was home for a long time."

"I thought it was a little odd that you came over here. Why would you come all the way to California if you want to base your career in the UK?"

"I don't know that I'm going back there," Liz said shortly. "After all, my parents do live in San Francisco. You met my stepmother."

Liz felt Giselle's stillness behind her and twisted around in the chair. "Sorry. I didn't mean to snap." She tossed her pencil down on the smeared counter and leaned back. Her face in the mirror frowned back at her. "I wish I could go back. But I broke up with someone, and he's still very involved with my family and friends there. I have to stay away for a while." Satisfied with her eyebrows, she fiddled a narrow, wet brush in a cake of black.

"Why did you break up?" Giselle asked over the sound of the running water.

"He decided I didn't have room for him in my life." Liz leaned across the Formica worktop, elbows spread and planted to steady the brush in her hand. Holding her breath, she slashed perfect, quick lines above each eye. "I was far too busy becoming a diva." She leaned over and, with studied concentration, repeated the lines under her eyes, then fanned her face to set the eyeliner.

"Kevin and I used to fight about that regularly. We still do." Giselle laughed, though Liz saw nothing amusing about it. "When we were first married I was studying at Indiana. We had an agreement to call each other every Monday night, and every time it was my turn I'd forget or be late or have to rush off somewhere. Then I'd feel so guilty I'd come home for a weekend to surprise him and find out he had gone hunting with the guys. It really annoyed him. He told me to save the drama for the stage."

"What kind of work does your husband do?" Liz added just enough mascara to emphasize her dark eyes.

"He's a copy editor for the *Atlantic Monthly*. Paying his dues, he says."

"What does he think about all this? I mean, you being gone all summer, and now for two more months, and all next year?"

The soprano sat down again, shaking the water from her brushes. "Actually, he's the one who insisted that I do it. I auditioned for Merola twice before and didn't get in. I didn't want to go through it again, but he made me." She smiled. "So he can hardly complain now."

"Guess not."

"He knew what it meant to me. He had the guts to tell me that I wasn't good enough the first time, and to keep hounding me until I was. He never limited me, and he's never asked me to compromise my work." She grimaced. "Someday he'll call in all these favors, and I'm going to owe him big time."

Liz stared and then squinted into the mirror to see if the carefully applied eye makeup had the desired effect. Absently she added rosiness to her cheeks, only to buff it down again.

Giselle inserted her dry powder brushes into plastic sleeves. After a moment she looked up. "So the boyfriend didn't like all the travelling?"

"He didn't think I could be faithful to him when I was away so much."

"God, who has time for an affair? Unless you're Rogelio. What's the boyfriend do? Could he come here?"

"He's a conductor."

Giselle snorted. "Seriously?"

Liz nodded. "He didn't trust me, anyway. Even after I lived with him for three years, he still thought that I would cheat on him, just like his wife did." Something constricted in her chest as she said it. It was a grave injustice to Giles to describe it so. She stared at her artificial face in the unforgiving light for several seconds. Then she began to close her makeup pots and toss them into her tackle box.

"Ah. His wife. A pretty complication." Giselle carefully rolled her damp brushes in a stained towel.

"His ex-wife, now," Liz assured her, pulling off her headband and slapping down the lid of the box. She got up and sloshed her brushes in warm water, shaking them out and then blotting them dry on her shirttail. "It was my own fault," she admitted quietly. "Of course he didn't trust me. I told him I would leave him someday. And I hurt him terribly."

Giselle began to pack up her makeup kit neatly. "If you'd like to spend Christmas with us in New York we'd love to have you."

"Thanks, but I'm okay." Liz picked up her tackle box and caught her friend's eye upon her in the glass. "Really."

Her concentration faltering, she returned to the dressing room to try to regain it, only to be ambushed by the sight of a dozen white roses, sweet in the stale atmosphere. Her heart seemed to sweep up like a kite in a capricious gust of wind. Gingerly she parted the stems and found the card:

Giselle, break a leg! See you Sunday. With more than love, Kev.

Liz snatched the towel from around her neck and flung it across the room. It caught on the edge of a mirror and dangled limply as she sat down abruptly, her head in her hands. It was Giles's shirt that she used as a makeup smock, his gift the score that she carried everywhere, dog-eared and scribbled in, though she had not needed to refer to it for weeks. She had not wanted to think about him tonight. She could not afford to think about him. And yet some desperate part of her believed that he would somehow have turned up by now.

Even before this morning, she had begun to feel tightness in her higher register. She had called Ruby. Her teacher had listened sympathetically and talked about the soft palate and breathing. But suddenly she had interrupted herself. "Liz, what are you afraid of?"

"Afraid?"

"I only ask because the last time you had a setback like this it was because you were afraid of the music and how it made you feel. Remember learning *Messiah*? You withdrew emotionally, and your voice shut down on you."

"But why now? I love this role. It suits my voice perfectly."

"Ah, but are you doing it with your heart?"

A poignant line from one of her *Yeomen* arias flashed through her mind. *My bruiséd heart, my broken heart* . . . She swallowed. "I thought I was doing it the way I always have." But she spoke slowly, without conviction.

"Well, dear, if you're sure it's not a mechanical problem, you have to look inside. Something's not right; somehow, you've gotten off-center. But whatever you do, don't be afraid to be heard, Liz. Don't lose your courage."

Ruby had not mentioned the forbidden, for which Liz was glad and sorry. She'd almost blurted out his name herself, but she did not want to acknowledge the possibility. She must learn to sing without him. In spite of what Ruby had taught her, she must overcome her emotions.

Liz turned back into the room and took a few deep breaths, willing herself to relax. The sight of white roses had unmasked her neglected hope. She suddenly admitted to herself what she had not told Ruby, what she could not tell Giselle: it was impossible to separate Giles from this moment. She fingered the frayed collar of his discarded shirt.

She had work to do. Eight hundred people expected her best tonight, and it wasn't in her to disappoint. She must find her center, find her power, and sing without hindrance. The rest of the cast was arriving, and soon someone else would want this room. Her breath was steady now. Softly, she began to sing her first aria—testing, testing.

Chapter 57

BEFORE LIZ OPENED HER EYES, she swallowed twice. Then she rolled over, groaning. The aches and fever she had fought last night through the closing performance of *Figaro* had blossomed into a cold. She sat up, glared at the gray ice of the morning, and slumped back against the pillows, sneezing.

At least the tour was over. Last night she had been exhausted, soaked with sweat from her fever, legs trembling so much that she worried she might collapse when she took her curtain call. But the swell of applause had confirmed her success at overcoming the impending virus. She'd skipped the reception afterwards and gone straight back to her dorm room and her bed. But she felt even worse today.

Somehow she gathered her possessions and found a cab to take her to the airport. In a daze, she endured the five-hour flight with a two-hour layover in Chicago, the miseries of her cold blocking out every other concern.

She dragged herself home to an empty house via taxi, feeling limp in the sixty-eight-degree November weather. Madly and her father were in Carmel for the opening of his first gallery show in ten years. She had planned to join them, but the idea of driving for over two hours was more than she could bear between her cold and the jet lag she was feeling. So she called Madly and made her apologies, then fell into bed. Luckily, she had weeks to recover. No need to start working on her assignments.

* * *

ON MONDAY MORNING, LIZ slept until ten o'clock. She took a steamy bath to ease the pressure in her sinuses and soothe her throat and bundled up in her warmest clothes before heading down to the kitchen, where she ate more than her usual fare, drank extra orange juice, and nursed two cups of tea. By the bottom of the second cup, the aspirin she'd taken had reduced the throbbing behind her eyes to a dull pulsing.

No one expected her. No one would come looking for her. She would sleep all day, drinking tea and dosing herself with cough syrup. It was a relief, in a way. She could not worry about her voice. She had no choice but to rest.

Liz almost felt like an intruder in her parents' huge, empty house. She went back to bed, alternately snoozing and reading away the morning, while outside the day cleared to a fine, pale sky. She couldn't concentrate on *The Shell Seekers*. She gazed out the window at the bay, where sailboats eagerly exploited the mild weather. Her colleagues were all on their way to New York, or El Paso, or Toronto, or Buenos Aires, or elsewhere. Not a soul knew she was lying here in misery.

In the harsh daylight it seemed stupid to have insisted on remaining there alone instead of joining her parents in Carmel. This was what the rest of her life would be like. Once the acclaim of the audience faded, she would be alone in her silence until the next gratifying performance. Last Saturday night, as that final moment of applause had died away behind the muffling curtain, she'd felt the ecstasy begin to recede, felt the oncoming isolation, wanted to prolong the feeling another minute, another eternity.

She mentally nudged herself, realizing that restrictions on her voice made her melodramatic. She got up and put on her shoes, and as she did so she noted that the cough was sliding down into her chest. She made herself more tea with honey and lemon and wrapped herself up in a blanket in the breakfast nook with the Sunday papers. She passed over the crossword, which always made her feel illiterate, but not without remembering how Giles loved the *Times* crosswords. Today she didn't even bother to pretend that she was trying to forget him.

The afternoon turned toward evening. Needing more nourishment than tea, Liz heated up some split-pea soup and went out on the deck. She sat with her feet up on the railing and the warm bowl nestled between her breasts. The gold of the bridge faded in the soft autumn sunset. She could feel the fever in her body over the heat of the waning day. The wind toyed with her hair, and the mild evening surrounded her in comfort. It might have been June and not November.

She slowly sipped her soup and looked out over the water. *No one does this alone*, he had told her once. At the time, she thought he meant teachers, coaches, directors, and conductors who would acknowledge a rising talent and make way for it. But he had already experienced this sort of loneliness after brilliant performance. Perhaps it even explained his early marriage. It was this he meant, this kind of alone. She thought of Grace, waiting for Titus with water and love.

A definite sliver of silver moon countered a single star bright in the deepening blue of the evening sky, sharp as a picture on a Christmas card. A planet, probably, she realized.

Maybe he's looking at the very same star.

She shook her head. It was 1 a.m. in Cardiff. Long ago she had told Titus that she thought all the music in the world rose and reached the stars years later. Perhaps some of what she and Giles had played mingled up there with the great voices, the great pianists, the great composers made eternal.

A longing came over her, so strong she nearly wept. Hovering tears blurred the golden horizon. She wanted to send him a message of remorse in an arc of starlight over the clear, placid air. Giselle's curiosity about why she had come to California came back to her, and she felt stupid. Of course Giles thought she would not return. Why had she not seen that?

She pulled her sweater closer but stubbornly stayed on the deck until the twilight closed in, making the bridge and Fort Mason gray shadows. Then she got up and went inside.

If Donald Ross would consider her for the coming season, she would take that and lay it at Giles's feet. It was all she could offer him, and it would cost her to do so. But anything would be better than this separation of body and soul. The Adler Fellowship could perhaps be postponed a year. And if not, she would live with the consequences.

After making very expensive plane reservations for the next day, she called Madly in Carmel and told her what she was planning.

"What if he doesn't want to see you?" her stepmother asked.

Liz set her jaw stubbornly. "I have to go."

* * *

AS THE PLANE LANDED AT GATWICK, Liz felt less certain than she had in San Francisco. She had forgotten how intrusive British weather could be. It was unbearably windy, the air treacherously clear. The train took forever, for the unexpected storm of the previous two days had left the tracks slick with ice. She had plenty of time to reconsider as the train pushed against the new storm that was coming in hard from the Atlantic.

The cold was already in earnest for so early in the year; the Cardiff Queen Street station was gray with it, and the air hard. She leaned her hot head against the wall of the payphone, listening to the unanswered ring at Caroline's flat. She tried Swann's, but it was past closing, and no one answered. Her cold throbbed in her sinuses; she couldn't stand the thought of walking all the way to the shop to find no one there. With supreme effort she thought a moment more and called her cousin.

Not only was Kate home, she offered to come get her. Liz waited, shivering, as the rush-hour traffic surged and flowed past the train station. In less than ten minutes Kate pulled up, her young son bundled in the back in his car seat. When Liz got in Kate greeted her absently, her concentration on reentering the traffic.

When they arrived at the flat, Liz downed some aspirin and cold medicine as Kate peeled layers of outdoor clothing from Nicholas and put him in the high chair. The kitchen felt cold; the scent of mildew hung faintly in the air. In the sink a ring of soap clung to the bowls and cups in the water. Two apples, dull and shrunken, sat on the table like two little old ladies among the crumbs. There was a piece of blackened toast in the toaster.

Liz moved a pile of laundry from one of the chairs to a basket of clean towels and sat down. "Sorry for the short notice. I just need a place to go for a couple of hours to get warm."

"Never mind. I'm afraid we're rather a mess right now. I haven't got a moment to set things right. He keeps me running, don't you, boyo?" But Liz knew that Kate did not mind, seeing how she looked at the toddler.

Her cousin started a kettle boiling and pulled food out of the refrigerator. Liz loosened her jacket and scarf, her chill subsiding. "Where's Christopher?"

Kate glanced at her, almost wary. "He'll be along. He's late some nights." She turned her attention back to peeling carrots.

Something in her voice made Liz sorry for her. But then, everything seemed sad right at the moment.

When the carrots were simmering, Kate tried to feed Nicholas some cereal. She offered him the spoon, but the child pursed his lips and kept his eyes fixed on Liz, who smiled at him uncertainly.

"Why didn't you say you were coming?"

"It was just an impulse." She coughed, the heat and pain in her throat bringing tears to her eyes. "Giles is doing *L'Elisir d'Amore* at Welsh National Opera this month. I wanted to see him conduct."

Kate watched her in a curious, sidelong gaze, stirring up the baby's food. "In spite of what you think, I know I messed up with him. I need to fix it, if I can."

Kate tried the cereal again. Nicholas opened his mouth and automatically took in the food, mouthing it as he continued to watch Liz. "I still don't understand why you didn't get married."

Liz slumped, folding her hands over her chest. "I didn't think he trusted me."

"Rubbish. You were just too selfish to consider someone else in your plans."

"Jeez, if you're going to lecture me—" She got up.

"Do you know how lucky you were?" Kate punched at the cereal, the spoon making sharp clicking sounds against the chipped yellow bowl.

She knew very well. The odds were very much against her ever finding someone else with the patience and wisdom and gentleness of Giles. "I'm not lucky," she told Kate, sinking back down in her chair.

When Nicholas refused another bite, Kate picked him up, swaying with him. "No, listen. You and Giles started out standing side by side, looking together on a world that interested you both. So when you turned to look at each other, the world just closed around you and held you. With Chris and me it wasn't like that at all. We started out looking only at each other, and by the time we looked out at the rest of the world, there was nothing to hold us together." Nicholas let out a whoop and gleefully smacked his mother in the neck. She kissed him.

Liz frowned up at them through her cold. "Are you okay?"

Kate shot her another hard, wary look. "Would I tell you, then?"

"Not if you don't want to."

Kate sat down heavily, holding the baby close though he protested. "It's nothing, really. I guess it's just not what I thought it would be."

Liz struggled to sit up straight, coughing again. "Nothing ever is, I think." She got up and drank some water, the tears in the corners of her eyes subsiding as her cough stopped. She leaned against the drain board. "I used to think that the only thing that had any meaning for me was making music. Now maybe it's too late to change my mind about that."

"It's never too late until you're dead. You of all people should know that."

"Remember the fairy tale where the guy gets three wishes? He wastes the first two, and has to use the third wish to fix it all? That's how I feel. Like I asked for too much without understanding the consequences. I promised the universe anything if I could have my career back after the accident." She shrugged. "I got it back. But there sure is a price."

Chapter 58

LIZ LEFT BEFORE SUPPER WAS BARELY over, shrugging off Kate's offer of a ride. She caught the bus back into Cardiff's town center and walked to New Theater. The cold air, damp with impending rain, made her lungs hurt and her nose run. She spoke to no one except the woman at the ticket window, and even then, though she had to repeat her request in her hoarse voice, she said no more than ten words.

For perhaps the first time in her life, the music worked no magic on her soul. She gave cursory attention to the singers and the orchestra, noticing them only as they related to Giles. She could see his shoulders tense with concentration, noted the relaxed, open stance when everything fell into place. Reassuring calm offset his passion for his work. Even before they became lovers, she'd had only to glance into the orchestra pit to be steadied. When he was at the helm, the ship never foundered. When he was at the helm, the ship invariably carried precious cargo.

He was flourishing. She should just go back to San Francisco. Talking to him would only bring the whole thing to light again, when they had both presumably begun to heal. But on an impulse she couldn't control she went around to the stage door after the curtain. Rain assaulted her in bursts until she ducked inside the door. As she pushed back her hood, shaking the rain off her coat, the doorman gave her an inquiring look.

"Hi, I'm Liz Morgan. I'm meeting someone. Could I go in?"

He would not let her backstage.

"Well, can you just tell me if Giles Offeryn has left yet? The conductor?"

"No, ma'am, that he has not."

"Do you mind if I wait for him here?"

"As you like." He nodded once, gravely, and resumed his silence.

She leaned against the wall, her hands jammed deep in her pockets. Her face felt hot, and was wet from the rain.

As though Liz had conjured him out of thin air, Giles appeared, in conversation with a woman behind him. Stage fright shot through Liz, but she was rooted to the spot. She noted the way he held the door for his companion, something she'd once thought was his particular deference to her.

"We don't get many chances," he was saying to the woman, who carried a violin case. He glanced up toward the door and caught sight of Liz. She stood up straight and still.

"Beastly weather. Can I give you a lift?" the violinist asked.

He glanced at her absently. "No, thank you. I have my car. See you on Friday." He waited while she left, and then he walked slowly over to Liz, a smile rising over his features like a sunrise.

She thought he would put his arms around her, but their awkward little half-gestures blurred the opportunity, and the moment was lost.

"I am terribly glad to see you," he said.

"I couldn't have missed it." Her voice rasped and cracked.

His hand went to his own throat in a question.

She shook her head. "Just a cold. I'm okay."

He looked unconvinced. "Whatever are you doing here?"

"Homesick, maybe. I need to talk to Ruby."

He half smiled. "What I really meant was, why did you come to the opera? Why did you come round to talk to me?"

"I wanted to be forgiven." Until she said it even she had not realized it.

His face lost its shy smile, and he took a step back. "For making it perfectly clear that your career came first? Why do you need to be forgiven for speaking the truth?"

After a moment she said softly, "I guess I deserved that."

"*Mae'n ddrwg gen i.* It is not my place, is it, to blame you for being truthful."

"If not yours, then whose?"

They looked at each other warily.

"I think," he said slowly, "that we have a lot to say to each other yet. Are you hungry?"

She smiled, but he did not seem to remember that other time he had asked her the same question, years ago, and surprised her into laughter. "I'm not, really."

"A cup of tea for your throat?"

"Where would we go, this late?"

"Come home with me." When she started to protest he shook his head. "Come now, nothing will happen."

She had already lost the upper hand. She acquiesced, sure that it was a bad idea but unwilling to be cheated out of what she had come all this way for.

Giles seemed not at all disconcerted by her sudden appearance—in fact, he was downright relaxed, as if he had taken her by surprise instead of the other way round. As he drove through the rain he kept her talking about her work, and she realized all over again how much she missed his subtle encouragement.

"Caroline tells me you're doing quite well."

"I guess I am. They asked me back for an Adler Fellowship next year."

"How splendid! Isn't that what you hoped for?" He glanced quickly at her.

"I haven't decided if I'll take it." She watched his face carefully as he turned his attention back to the road.

"Don't tell me the Met has called you already?" He was teasing.

"I thought I might ring Donald Ross while I'm here."

"He's very interested in your voice."

She sensed in him not the slightest hope or desire that she return to Britain. "I'll see how it goes."

He did not pursue it, did not refer to it again. He kept up his professional patter, listening with complete attention and asking questions that touched oblique points she had not acknowledged or considered as she experienced the largeness of her commitment. It was the very reason she'd fallen for him in the first place, she realized, basking in his attention. She even found herself telling him her doubts and fears about her voice. And then she realized what she was doing and fell silent again.

When they got to his cottage, she stood awkwardly in the middle of the room where they had lived together while he shed his coat and scarf.

He reached for her jacket, smiling. "*Croeso*." He hung their coats on the wooden pegs behind the door and went to see about the tea.

She looked around, hugging herself against the cold, feeling very much a stranger in this terribly familiar place. On the piano stood the glass heron she had given him on his birthday two years ago. Spare and clean of line, it had reminded her of his grace and elegance. And it reminded them both of that first weekend, when he had pointed one out to her on the fading twilight as they crossed the marshes on their way inland. When she saw it her throat closed, crowded with tears she could not afford to shed. She had given this up.

She wandered over to the cooker, where he waited with folded arms for the water in the teakettle to boil. He watched her without speaking. She could not read his expression.

"You must be so pleased to be at WNO," she said, seizing the conversation when she could bear the silence no longer.

His face relaxed, and he smiled in that open, nearly astonished way he had when something tickled him, obviously pleased with his accomplishment. Or was he pleased because she knew and had returned? Liz pressed on before the conversation disintegrated into shoptalk.

"I'm glad I could come. But you were right, you know. I do have to try to explain. If it matters anymore."

His face went sober again, his eyes guarded. "Just tell me one thing, if you can," he said. "Why were you so adamant about not getting married?"

The resignation in his voice stopped up her throat for a moment. Finally she swallowed. "My mother—"

"She wanted you back in San Francisco?"

"Not Madly. My mum. I told you, she was a singer."

"Yes, that's right. Sorry."

"She had a really great voice."

"That she did. After you told me about her I looked up her *Magic Flute* recording. It's still considered one of the definitive readings, did you know?"

"You listened to it?"

"I did." He glanced at her, his eyes soft. "I think your voice will surpass hers."

Another time his words would have comforted her, but now they only squeezed at the ache that had developed around her heart. "She left the stage right after that. Got married and had me."

"And you feel . . . an obligation?"

"More like fear. That I was too weak to leave you. And too selfish not to."

"You are hard on yourself."

When she didn't answer he said, "Liz, you don't have to live out your mother's life. She could have continued her career. She made a conscious choice not to. You can do otherwise."

"When my father came for *Messiah* he said that I was like my mother before the light went out of her. I don't want that to happen," she all but whispered. She could read nothing on his impassive face.

"If I had married you right then," she tried again, "I would probably have given up Merola and gone to Scotland. I know I would have let it hold me back." Her voice squeaked and rasped like an old hinge.

"Have I ever done anything but lift you up?" Giles spoke with an abruptness that told her how angry he still was.

"I didn't understand that I might really lose you altogether." A cough caught her, and she had to stop.

He looked away. "Shouldn't you be saving your voice?"

She shook her head, putting a hand up to her throat.

The kettle whistled. He shut off the heat and poured steaming water into the teapot. The window nearby was silver with condensation against the black night sky. She continued to talk slowly, almost to herself, watching the window and scarcely aware of his eyes upon her.

"People mostly see me as a singer now, not a person. But you fed me oranges and ginger snaps, and took me to the coast, and reminded me to laugh." She floundered. "No one had ever given that to me before."

Giles did not reply. He wrapped the brown teapot in a red towel and carried it out to the main room, returned for cups and spoons and the jam jar of sugar. Liz followed him and sat on the edge of the rocking chair, watching him move aside a stack of music to make way for the hospitality. He stood with his back to the inadequate heater, which clinked and rattled.

"I didn't understand until a couple of days ago how this must seem to you. I never intended to shift my career to the US. I always meant Cardiff to be home. Not because I lived here. Because you were here."

When he still said nothing she pressed on, anxiety pushing up under her heart. She had left it too long. "What if I told you that I'm going to work in Edinburgh next year? That I'm going to give up San Francisco?"

His eyes narrowed, measuring. "That would be unforgivable. And unnecessary."

"But the point is, I was never going to leave and not come back."

"All I wanted you to understand is that it can't go on and on. I won't let you come back every now and then for a little sex and a good meal because you're lonely. I'm not interested in a casual affair when you happen to have the time and inclination."

"I wouldn't ask it of you," she snapped. "I wouldn't want to inconvenience you."

"That isn't what I mean and you know it."

"You're right, it's not. It's that you didn't trust me."

"Ah, but I do. More than you trust yourself."

He fell silent again, watching her. Her headache seemed to pulse in dazzling clouds through her vision; the cough that hung in her chest threatened to suffocate her. Her throat felt tight and hot.

After a minute, he sat down at the piano. He thought for a moment, his hands at rest in his lap. Then he began to play a rolling bass line, left hand traveling, right hand finishing the arpeggios. Liz recognized it immediately as the Fauré art song that she loved so well. She realized that his hands spoke for him, said what he could not find words for. Was he thinking of the lyrics? *And on this day, the great vessels, leaving the diminishing port behind, sense their bulk held back by the rocking of the cradles.*

Or was he remembering the first time she had sung it with him? The music had surrounded them that day, every note and every nuance rising not from intellect but from instinct. A rare and unbearably perfect reading.

His soft touch and intrinsically steady rhythm encompassed the longing and serenity in the span of the bass line. Her body knew just where to prepare, just where to sing. She turned away, ashamed of the tears spilling down her cheekbones and catching in the corners of her mouth.

The piano stopped, and before it was silent he was behind her, turning her to face him, holding her. "Hisht, dear heart, hisht." He rocked her. "You are right. All I could think was that if you left, I would lose you."

She suddenly realized that this conversation was no longer about the past but about the future. She struggled to put some distance between them. "Why do you still love me, the way I've treated you? What have I ever done for you?"

"It is no small thing, what you did for me. You brought me back to music, you did."

"What on earth do you mean?"

"When you came here my marriage was falling apart. I only stayed with Diana because I wanted to prove Varnet wrong. But I didn't understand that it had nothing to do with my music. So I left a career that was the only choice for me. I couldn't remember why I wanted to be a conductor. The magic went out of the music."

"No, that can't be." She shook her head, incredulous.

"The only thing that gave me any solace was accompanying. And then I met you. You insisted on having music, in spite of what had happened to you. Insisted, mind you, not just hoped. It made me ashamed at what I'd taken for granted. You were so excited and—well, courageous."

Liz wrinkled her brow and shook her head. Her memories were vastly different.

He only laughed at her. "I began to love my calling again, because I saw it as you must see it. A gift. And then, dear heart, you did insist on working with me, no matter how often I offended you."

"But you're such a *musician*," Liz said. "I'm a really good technician, but you—you have the soul of a composer."

He shook his head. "You underestimate yourself, my dear."

"I always looked up to you. You've been way ahead of me since we met."

"Liz, I'm getting work now that I never even dreamed of. And that is because seven years ago *you* reminded me that music is sacred and human and marvelous."

"Maybe we're even, then." She ran her hand up around the back of his neck as she said it, smiling in spite of herself.

"I understand that singing comes first for you."

She started to protest, but something in his face stopped her from the automatic response. "Not every day. And not forever. But yes, it has to be a priority, for now, anyway. Can you live with that?"

He smiled a little wryly. "I haven't a choice, now, do I?"

"You could walk away."

"I will not. I'll take what I can get."

"You shouldn't settle for less than what you want."

"I want you. I'm not settling for anything. You would be incomplete without your work, and I much prefer you whole. Besides, do you think I'll be hanging around the cottage, pining away for you?"

"But it's not fair to you. It takes too much of me to sing."

He shook her, but gently. "Elizabeth Morgan, you are the most exasperating woman! What will your art come to if you have no love, no richness in your life to draw from?"

She paused, overcome. She could not deny her commitment to her music. But she could no longer pass up the joy of loving him. "I don't know if I can do this."

"Of course you don't. Neither do I," he replied unhelpfully. "All we can do is start again each day and do our best. With any luck, and a lot of work, we'll still be doing our best in fifty years." He took her cold hands in his own. "Think again, dear heart. Please. Marry me." The very white of his shirt made him look tired and worn. But his dark eyes, dilated in the dim room, were alive and dancing with laughter.

"But we would never be together," she argued feebly.

He looked down at her, amusement animating the angles of his face. "I told you this once before, *fy nghariad*: Don't ask for the moon and stars. Just ask for the best possible here and now you can hope for. It's all you'll ever have control over."

She held her breath, knowing what she was about to say, knowing it would change everything forever.

He waited, watching, but suddenly he turned away, put his hands in his pockets, and moved across the room before turning to look at her again. "As a matter of fact, I'm glad you turned up. I had a professional question for you."

She blinked. The moment dissolved into the mundane.

"I'm talking to Hyperion about making a recording of some of my songs. They asked if I had anyone in mind to sing them."

She looked at him, her eyes round, her head so thick with her cold that she wondered if she'd heard right. "What did you tell them?" she croaked.

He came very close, all but touching her. "That I'd heard of a terrific soprano doing *Figaro* in America who'll be snapped up in a minute. I thought if I wanted her I better ask now, before she gets booked."

She stared at him, mesmerized, and then she started to smile.

He caught her hands, kissed the injured one, kissed the whole one, and drew her to him. "Who says we will not be together?"

Epilogue

May 1995

LIZ CAME UP OUT OF THE COVENT Garden Tube station, feeling her bag heavy on her shoulder. She resisted the urge to hurry as she walked through the gathering fog toward the Royal Opera House. She wove around the edge of the crowd of tourists outside the Apple Market who were watching a busker sing "Hey Jude." Curtain wasn't for an hour and a half. She wasn't on for another forty minutes after that. She paused a moment outside the stage entrance, the battered fire door she had been in and out of for weeks. With a good heave she flung it open and crossed the threshold, unable to repress her smile of pure delight.

Walking slowly down the corridor, lost in thought, she came around a corner and nearly walked into Sir David Jenkins, her conductor tonight. She startled him out of a deep conversation with someone.

He steadied her by the shoulder, smiling. "Hullo, Liz. Sounding better every day."

"Hi, Sir David."

His companion turned, her face a blank mask. Liz felt the air go out of her lungs.

"Have you met Genevieve Ponnelle?"

"A long time ago," Liz replied, not taking her eyes off the older woman.

"You've come a long way since then." Madame's voice was as smooth and expressionless as it had been at their first meeting. Jenkins might as well not have been there.

"Yes, I have."

The conductor put a hand on each of their shoulders. "I'll leave you to it, ladies, I'm late. See you tonight, Liz. Gen, give me a call."

He departed briskly, and they were left alone together in the corridor of the opera house.

"So. You finally got here. In spite of me."

Wary, Liz nodded. After thinking, she said, "In a way, because of you."

Madame started back as though she had been insulted.

"You did give me my foundation. You taught me that technique matters. I've met an astonishing number of people with terrible habits. You never let me develop them."

Nodding in the direction in which the conductor had departed, Madame said, "He asked me what I thought of your voice when he was considering you for this role."

Even now, safe and about to make her London debut, the notion closed cold around Liz's heart. "What did you tell him?" She attempted to ask casually, as though it did not matter.

Madame turned her back and walked a couple of steps away. "I told him that you had a magnificent instrument, and apparently a deep intelligence to go with it."

Liz was silent, stunned.

"You do, you know." Madame turned, almost angrily.

"Why did you treat me the way you did?" Liz would have caught it back if she could. It meant nothing now. But her curiosity remained unsatisfied.

"I have taught singers, many of them well known, for thirty years. I had yet to meet another one who was so capable of greatness, and who was so ready to waste it."

Although she flushed under the compliment, which felt almost like an attack, Liz pursued the argument. "But what did that matter? It's my life. If I decided not to pursue it, it wasn't up to you to change that."

"It would have been a criminal waste."

"But still my choice."

"Someone with a voice like yours has an obligation to use it."

Liz conceded the point, though she did not agree. Another, more nebulous idea nagged her. "Why did you take it so personally?"

Madame seemed to consider whether she wanted to tell Liz more, but finally she sighed. For the first time Liz saw her more than sixty years weighing heavy on her shoulders and face. The teacher gestured toward the stage. "My debut here was in 1959 in *Zauberflöte*."

"Your debut?"

"As First Lady."

"Then you knew my mother. She was—"

"Pamina. Yes, I did."

"But on the recording—"

"I was Jenny Pont in those days."

"You never told me."

"You are very like her. Especially your voice."

"What was she like? Onstage, I mean."

Madame thought about it, choosing her words judiciously. "Brilliant and tender. I never knew anyone so peaceful and so powerful at the same time." She considered Liz, obviously measuring her against her mother. "Last summer at Glyndebourne I saw the same qualities in you. Something great communicated itself to the audience. They knew it. They felt like they had been allowed to touch your soul. It's rare in one so young."

Liz could feel the blush rise up her neck and her face. "But why—"

"The only time she ever seemed arrogant to me was when she had an affair with a newspaper photographer, and got pregnant."

"You mean my father," Liz interrupted her, slapping her hand to her chest. "She was pregnant with me."

Madame did not apologize, endured Liz's outburst with cool composure. "Yes, I know. She was so much better than I could ever dream of being, and she walked away from it. I never understood that, and I was always terribly jealous of her talent. And yet what I really hated her for was taking David away from me."

Liz stared at Ponnelle. She tried to picture her sad, reclusive father with this haughty, cold woman. Instead her father had been drawn to the warm light of her mother's flame. Perhaps Jenny Pont could not compare, onstage or off.

"In five years she was dead of meningitis. When you came to me, I hadn't thought about her in years. But it didn't take me very long to figure out who you were. I decided that perhaps Margaret had not completely wasted her talent, for you have her voice and more. I swore I would make you more than she had ever been, and I would get some of what she gave up. And then you seemed to be ready to throw it away for some man. I couldn't bear to see you do what she had done."

"Why wouldn't you trust me?"

"You took a great risk with your career, letting him influence you. He was taking you over. You were not listening to me anymore."

"He taught me how to be a human being, not just a singer," Liz retorted. "If I had remained in the emotional vacuum you wanted, my music wouldn't reach anybody. I need to love and hate and nurture and hurt and hope and fear just like everybody else. Otherwise I rob the audience. Not to mention myself."

Her outburst did not appear to touch Madame. The older woman's glance flicked up and down, scanning Liz for the weak spot. "So. He will be here tonight?"

"Well, no. He's conducting at La Scala this month." Though she said it with a lift of her chin, challenging Madame to see his success, Liz felt the inadequacy of her response.

"I see. So tell me, what do you have to show for your rebellion? All this support he was supposed to provide, where is it?"

Liz knew Madame was mocking her, but she didn't care. She pressed her hand over her heart as she did during curtain calls. "It's here."

Madame's expression did not change.

"Will you be out in the house tonight?" Liz finally asked.

"This is a performance I would not miss."

* * *

THE CORRIDORS TEEMED WITH production staff and musicians, all of them ready to start the run of *Die Zauberflöte*. Liz made her way through the chaos to her dressing room, greeting people absently as she passed. Madame's innuendoes slipped past her primary focus, plucking the brilliance from Mozart. Liz had not admitted to the layovers in gray airports, the loneliness she could hardly endure. But still the price was not too high.

Her dressing room was spacious and unadorned except for the necessities of piano, chairs, mirrors, and costume rack. She set her shoulder bag on the counter and immediately noticed the white roses on top of the piano. Smiling, she looked for a card but found none. They could be from her father, who had promised to try to come, but whom she was sure had not. They were probably from her husband. She would talk to him in—she checked her watch—six hours and twelve minutes.

She laughed at herself and set about her usual ritual of stretching and relaxing her body. She had sung in her voice earlier. In fifteen minutes her dresser would arrive. Then the makeup artist would want her, and the rest of the evening would fly by. These few moments were hers.

When she heard the tap at the door she sighed. So much for her own time. "Come in," she called, expecting her dresser, Denise.

The door opened. She glanced up into the mirror to see who it was and then whirled around. She opened her mouth, but no sound came out. She threw herself at Giles, and he caught her up, right off her feet, for a moment. They held each other, and she began to kiss him, small ecstatic kisses all over his face, asking breathless questions that did not require answers.

"What are you doing here? Why didn't you call me? When did you get here? How did you get in?" She stopped, looking over her shoulder. "Are those yours?" she asked, pointing at the roses.

Giles smiled.

"If you're going to send flowers you can damn well put a card on them."

"Is that any way to talk to me when I shall only be here for one night?"

"Probably not," she agreed, looping her arms around his neck. "You probably shouldn't be here," she said reluctantly, not letting go of him.

He was not inclined to release her. He kissed her and said, "I know all the right people."

"Why aren't you in Italy?"

"Because I do get nights off occasionally. And in the late twentieth century we do have the luxury of air travel. Hisht," he said, putting a finger over her lips when she started to protest. "Never mind what it cost."

"You're going to be so proud of me."

"Always. Can you stand another surprise? Or will it wreck your concentration?"

She glowered at him. "*Not* knowing will wreck my concentration. You don't want to be responsible for that."

"Certainly not." He stepped away to look at her. "WNO is commissioning a new opera for the opening of the Millennium Hall down in Cardiff Bay. I've been asked to submit a proposal."

She launched herself at him. "A commission at WNO? Really?"

"Yes, really. They want a contemporary Welsh composer to write an opera to open the inaugural season."

"You make sure you put a role in it for me."

He laughed. "That should not pose a problem."

"Oh, congratulations!" She hugged him in great glee but caught sight of the clock. "Damn. I have to kick you out." She kissed him again and made herself push him gently away. "Go away," she said, shooing him halfheartedly. "I have work to do."

He took her hand and kissed her forehead. "Sing pretty."

* * *

FOR THE NEXT HOUR LIZ LISTENED to the enchantment of *Magic Flute* unfold as she was transformed into Pamina. The backstage was filled with it, an intercom in every area, and the music followed her from place to place. With a rush of fondness she followed the flute's dance without a single regret.

At last she was ready. Perhaps because of her conversation with Madame, Liz could not shake the image of her mother thirty-five years ago, in this very place, on this very stage, in this very role, two months pregnant with Liz herself and about to give it up entirely.

She made her way to the wings long before her cue, still musing about the circle. Television monitors flickered gray, the ghost shapes of stagehands moved about, other singers waited. The quintet onstage parted. The concrete and hardware of the backstage area struck a stark contrast with the soft colors of the sets as she hovered between reality and fantasy. The scene onstage concluded. Applause rose and fell, while behind the curtain the crew transformed the stage into Sarastro's palace. Now Liz's nerves began to simmer, sending hot little surges through her belly. She swallowed, her mouth suddenly dry. Her heart beat lightly and quickly. Normal.

She stepped out into the light.

Acknowledgments

MANY THANKS TO RICK HARRELL, former Director of the San Francisco Opera Center, for taking the time to answer my questions. The ideas in Chapter 54 come from a coaching session he held for the Merola Program in the summer of 1999.

Thanks to Caroline Tess at Welsh National Opera for providing background information.

About the Author

PATRICIA MINGER GREW UP in Oakland, California. She earned her BA in English from UC Berkeley, and spent her junior year abroad in Stirling, Scotland. Her articles have appeared in national periodicals in the pharmacy industry and in local dog club newsletters. Minger spent over 25 years singing with the Lamplighters Music Theater of San Francisco and other Bay Area musical groups. She currently lives in Northern California with two cats and one dog, and is working on her second novel, about a small town at the foot of a big mountain.

Author photo by Suszi Lurie McFadden

Welsh Glossary

Beth y diafol?	What the devil?
cariad	love/lover
croeso	welcome
diolch	thanks
dod yma	come here
fy annwyl	my dear
fy nghariad	my love
Fy nghariad a dorrws 'y nghalon i bron	My love has nearly broken my heart
go dda	well done
gorau o ran	Best regards
Mae'n ddrwg gen i	I beg your pardon
Mai	May
prioda fi	marry me
Yr Wyddfa	Snowdon
ysgafn	gently

Selected Titles from She Writes Press

She Writes Press is an independent publishing company founded to serve women writers everywhere. Visit us at www.shewritespress.com.

The Geometry of Love by Jessica Levine. $16.95, 978-1-938314-62-9. Torn between her need for stability and her desire for independence, an aspiring poet grapples with questions of artistic inspiration, erotic love, and infidelity.

Bittersweet Manor by Tory McCagg. $16.95, 978-1-938314-56-8. A chronicle of three generations of love, manipulation, entitlement, and disappointed expectations in an upper-middle-class New England family.

The Rooms Are Filled by Jessica Null Vealitzek. $16.95, 978-1-938314-58-2. The coming-of-age story of two outcasts—a nine-year-old boy who just lost his father, and a closeted young woman—brought together by circumstance.

Beautiful Garbage by Jill DiDonato. $16.95, 978-1-938314-01-8. Talented but troubled young artist Jodi Plum leaves suburbia for the excitement of the city—and is soon swept up in the sexual politics and downtown art scene of 1980s New York.

Cleans Up Nicely by Linda Dahl. $16.95, 978-1-938314-38-4. The story of one gifted young woman's path from self-destruction to self-knowledge, set in mid-1970s Manhattan.

Faint Promise of Rain by Anjali Mitter Duva. $16.95, 978-1-938314-97-1. Adhira, a young girl born to a family of Hindu temple dancers, is raised to be dutiful—but ultimately, as the world around her changes, it is her own bold choice that will determine the fate of her family and of their tradition.